Praise for Lexi Blak

"I can always trust ... Blake's Dominants to leave me breathless...and in love. If you want sensual, exciting BDSM wrapped in an awesome love story, then look for a Lexi Blake book."

~Cherise Sinclair USA Today Bestselling author

"Lexi Blake's MASTERS AND MERCENARIES series is beautifully written and deliciously hot. She's got a real way with both action and sex. I also love the way Blake writes her gorgeous Dom heroes--they make me want to do bad, bad things. Her heroines are intelligent and gutsy ladies whose taste for submission definitely does not make them dish rags. Can't wait for the next book!"

~Angela Knight, New York Times bestselling author

"A Dom is Forever is action packed, both in the bedroom and out. Expect agents, spies, guns, killing and lots of kink as Liam goes after the mysterious Mr. Black and finds his past and his future… The action and espionage keep this story moving along quickly while the sex and kink provides a totally different type of interest. Everything is very well balanced and flows together wonderfully."

~A Night Owl "Top Pick", Terri, Night Owl Erotica

"A Dom Is Forever is everything that is good in erotic romance. The story was fast-paced and suspenseful, the characters were flawed but made me root for them every step of the way, and the hotness factor was off the charts mostly due to a bad boy Dom with a penchant for dirty talk."

~Rho, The Romance Reviews

"A good read that kept me on my toes, guessing until the big reveal, and thinking survival skills should be a must for all men."

~Chris, Night Owl Reviews

"I can't get enough of the Masters and Mercenaries Series! Love and Let Die is Lexi Blake at her best! She writes erotic romantic suspense like no other, and I am always extremely excited when she has something new for us! Intense, heart pounding, and erotically fulfilling, I could not put this book down."
~ Shayna Renee, Shayna Renee's Spicy Reads

"Certain authors and series are on my auto-buy list. Lexi Blake and her Masters & Mercenaries series is at the top of that list... this book offered everything I love about a Masters & Mercenaries book – alpha men, hot sex and sweet loving... As long as Ms. Blake continues to offer such high quality books, I'll be right there, ready to read."
~ Robin, Sizzling Hot Books

"I have absolutely fallen in love with this series. Spies, espionage, and intrigue all packaged up in a hot dominant male package. All the men at McKay-Taggart are smoking hot and the women are amazingly strong sexy submissives."
~Kelley, Smut Book Junkie Book Reviews

From Sanctum with Love

Other Books by Lexi Blake

ROMANTIC SUSPENSE

Masters and Mercenaries
The Dom Who Loved Me
The Men With The Golden Cuffs
A Dom is Forever
On Her Master's Secret Service
Sanctum: A Masters and Mercenaries Novella
Love and Let Die
Unconditional: A Masters and Mercenaries Novella
Dungeon Royale
Dungeon Games: A Masters and Mercenaries Novella
A View to a Thrill
Cherished: A Masters and Mercenaries Novella
You Only Love Twice
Luscious: Masters and Mercenaries~Topped
Adored: A Masters and Mercenaries Novella
Master No
Just One Taste: Masters and Mercenaries~Topped 2
From Sanctum with Love
Devoted: A Masters and Mercenaries Novella
Dominance Never Dies
Submission is Not Enough
Master Bits and Mercenary Bites~The Secret Recipes of Topped
Perfectly Paired: Masters and Mercenaries~Topped 3
For His Eyes Only
Arranged: A Masters and Mercenaries Novella
Love Another Day
At Your Service: Masters and Mercenaries~Topped 4
Master Bits and Mercenary Bites~Girls Night
Nobody Does It Better
Close Cover
Protected: A Masters and Mercenaries Novella
Enchanted: A Masters and Mercenaries Novella
Charmed: A Masters and Mercenaries Novella
Treasured: A Masters and Mercenaries Novella, Coming June 29, 2021

Masters and Mercenaries: The Forgotten
Lost Hearts (Memento Mori)

Lost and Found
Lost in You
Long Lost
No Love Lost

Masters and Mercenaries: Reloaded
Submission Impossible, Coming February 16, 2021

Butterfly Bayou
Butterfly Bayou
Bayou Baby
Bayou Dreaming
Bayou Beauty, Coming July 27, 2021

Lawless
Ruthless
Satisfaction
Revenge

Courting Justice
Order of Protection
Evidence of Desire

Masters Of Ménage (by Shayla Black and Lexi Blake)
Their Virgin Captive
Their Virgin's Secret
Their Virgin Concubine
Their Virgin Princess
Their Virgin Hostage
Their Virgin Secretary
Their Virgin Mistress

The Perfect Gentlemen (by Shayla Black and Lexi Blake)
Scandal Never Sleeps
Seduction in Session
Big Easy Temptation
Smoke and Sin
At the Pleasure of the President

URBAN FANTASY

Thieves
Steal the Light
Steal the Day
Steal the Moon
Steal the Sun
Steal the Night
Ripper
Addict
Sleeper
Outcast
Stealing Summer

LEXI BLAKE WRITING AS SOPHIE OAK

Texas Sirens
Small Town Siren
Siren in the City
Siren Enslaved
Siren Beloved
Siren in Waiting
Siren in Bloom
Siren Unleashed
Siren Reborn

Nights in Bliss, Colorado
Three to Ride
Two to Love
One to Keep
Lost in Bliss
Found in Bliss
Pure Bliss
Chasing Bliss
Once Upon a Time in Bliss
Back in Bliss
Sirens in Bliss
Happily Ever After in Bliss
Far From Bliss, Coming 2021

A Faery Story
Bound
Beast
Beauty

Standalone
Away From Me
Snowed In

From Sanctum with Love

Masters and Mercenaries, Book 10

Lexi Blake

From Sanctum with Love
Masters and Mercenaries, Book 10
Lexi Blake

Published by DLZ Entertainment LLC

Copyright 2016 DLZ Entertainment LLC
Edited by Chloe Vale
ISBN: 978-1-937608-50-7

McKay-Taggart logo design by Charity Hendry

All rights reserved. No part of this book may be reproduced, scanned, or distributed in any printed or electronic form without permission. Please do not participate in or encourage piracy of copyrighted materials in violation of the author's rights.

This is a work of fiction. Names, places, characters and incidents are the product of the author's imagination and are fictitious. Any resemblance to actual persons, living or dead, events or establishments is solely coincidental.

Sign up for Lexi Blake's newsletter
and be entered to win a $25 gift certificate
to the bookseller of your choice.

Join us for news, fun, and exclusive content
including free short stories.

There's a new contest every month!

Go to www.LexiBlake.net/newsletter to subscribe.

Acknowledgments

First of all I want to thank all of you readers who are still here and with me. This is the tenth main story line book in the Masters and Mercenaries series. I'm astounded by that because I'd only planned five. Thanks for sticking it out with me and I hope you'll be there for all the stories to come.

As always thanks to my crew: Richard Blake, Chloe Vale, Riane Holt, Liz Berry, Stormy Pate, and the best formatter in the business who also happened to emerge from my womb – Dylan.

I would also like to thank OSK (one sexy kitten) for making the sadisticks that inspired a scene in this book.

The genesis of this book happened a few years ago in Seattle when I met two crazy women and became friends with them. They were in the lifestyle, but it was their love of life and their friendship with each other that truly inspired me. So this book is dedicated to Kori Smith and Sara Buell. May you both find your happily and kinkily ever afters, my friends.

Prologue

Seattle, WA
12 years before

Kai Ferguson looked at the rundown house and felt an odd longing sink into his bones. He hadn't expected this, hadn't thought for a second that he would look at that shitty two bedroom and feel a sense of nostalgia. After all, most of the bad things in his life had happened there, but suddenly all he could see was his mom. She was all over that damn house. Though it was in a bad part of town, the yard was still neat, the front beds still had petunias blooming. Even from the driveway he could see the wreath she'd always kept.

Just because it isn't Christmas, doesn't mean we shouldn't celebrate.

She'd kept a wreath for every season. She would make them with crap she'd bought at the craft store—whatever happened to be on sale. Cheap pieces of junk that she somehow turned into something lovely. The same with the flowers in the front beds. She bought the cheapest she could find, the ones that looked half dead at the nursery, and brought them back to life.

That was his mom. God, he missed her.

Though now he supposed the flowers were being kept up by whatever chick his brother was sleeping with. His younger brother had recently turned nineteen and dreamed of Hollywood stardom, though mostly what he'd managed was to look ridiculously good in a series of ads for the local gym he spent way too much time at. He was two years younger than Kai, but Kai was fairly certain his brother had started romancing women at the tender age of five when he'd charmed a kindergarten teacher into not holding him back a grade. Jared had started young and never gone long without a woman in his bed.

It had been almost a year since Kai had made love to his fiancée.

His gut clenched at the thought of seeing her. He had to though. He had to figure out if there was anything at all to come home to when it came to Hannah.

Thanks to a stray piece of shrapnel, he'd gotten unexpected leave. One week. He had one week before he had to report to Fort Bragg, and then he'd be on his way back to the Middle East. He had another year of enlistment and then he could come home and finish up what was left of his degree. Jared had made it through high school. He'd made it plain that he wasn't going to college. Kai had done his duty to his baby brother. He'd put off his own dreams in order to keep Jared in school. Kai had put off his last two years of college and his wedding in order to go into the Army after their mother had lost her battle with breast cancer. He'd fulfilled his mother's dying request and now it was almost time to come home.

Whether he had a fiancée when he came back was definitely in question. He couldn't stop thinking about how angry she'd been when he'd left. She'd begged him not to go back and when he'd explained he couldn't leave his unit, couldn't just walk away from the damn Army, she'd sworn he'd never loved her and that she would have her revenge.

Two days later she'd called and begged his forgiveness. She'd explained it was only nerves about him being so far away, but Kai had started to think that asking her to marry him had been a mistake.

Maybe everyone was right and they were too young.

He parked his rental in the driveway behind Jared's beat-up old

Jeep and a late model Ford. Likely that belonged to whoever Jared was sleeping with. Jared never mentioned women in his letters. Mostly he'd talked about his audition for some local TV show about physical fitness or asked questions about how to do simple things like pay the water bill.

Kai groaned. His little brother's letters had taken on a tone of desperation. The kid was nineteen. He should be able to write a damn check. Kai sent him all the money he had. Their aunt had lived with Jared until he'd turned eighteen. She'd certainly taught him how to run the house, but his brother rarely listened. No. He expected the rest of the world to take care of him because he was so damn beautiful.

Kai hopped out of the car, eager to get inside, get cleaned up, and go over to Hannah's. He might be able to avoid Jared for a while. It was still morning and his brother liked to sleep in.

He stepped onto the porch and found his keys in his pocket. Hannah. What the hell was he going to do? They'd met in college, about six months before he'd gone into the Army. They'd been at a frat party together.

God, that felt like a hundred years ago. Now the thought of partying at Sigma House made him sick to his stomach. He'd seen so much, knew what the real world was like now. This whole place seemed like a dream.

He wanted to see her, hold her. Maybe once they were together in the same place, Iraq would be the dream. Nightmare. Although he'd also met some of the best people he'd ever known. It was what he couldn't get her to understand.

He sighed as he stood outside the door to the house he'd grown up in. Once he'd seen her again, everything would fall into place and all these horrible cravings he had would go away. He would see Hannah and remember how much he loved her.

God, he hoped that was what would happen.

What the hell was he going to do if it didn't?

With a long sigh, he opened the door. A weariness set in. Maybe he'd grab some sleep first. He'd been traveling for almost two days. He didn't sleep well on a plane. Or in a damn airport for that matter. His leg was aching. He was a fucking mess.

Yeah, a couple of hours of sleep and he would be ready to face her.

"I made you some coffee," a feminine voice said. He could barely hear her.

"Look, I'm not trying to be mean." That was his brother. It sounded like they were in the kitchen. "What happened between us was a horrible mistake and I need you to leave. It's not going to happen again."

There was a familiar husky laugh. "Oh, I think it will."

Was that? No. She wouldn't. He wouldn't.

Kai moved toward the hall that led to the small kitchen and family room. There was a tiny table where he'd sat and helped his brother with homework. He'd been the one who had to watch his brother while their mom had worked two jobs. He'd had to figure out how to cook dinner and get his brother to bed and try to help around the house because she would be so tired when she came in at midnight.

"It won't. I was drunk that night. I…I want the keys back. You shouldn't have them. You need to leave."

"Don't be ridiculous, Jared. If you think I'm giving you up after that night, you're crazy. We were good together."

Kai pushed through the swinging door because he had to see it with his own two eyes. He had to face it and understand what was happening. Perhaps his ears were faulty. Maybe the chick only sounded like Hannah.

Nope. There she was. She was standing in his kitchen looking smoking hot in tight jeans and a tank top that showed off her breasts. Well, he and Jared always had the same taste in women. Curvy, gorgeous women. And like all women, apparently Hannah preferred his younger brother.

"Kai." Jared was wearing a pair of pajama bottoms and nothing else, as though he'd rolled out of bed for this confrontation. "What are you doing here?"

Hannah laughed. "He's on leave. He got his ass shot up." She turned cold eyes his way. "One of your teammate people called me. They thought I should know you were wounded. I believe I told you what would happen if you went back."

"Yes, you did. So the make-up call was an act?"

She shrugged. "Well, I'd already decided what I really wanted.

Jared is going places. He's got an audition for a TV show. He's going to be a movie star one day."

"Kai, I am so sorry." Jared had gone a nice shade of pale. "She came over and offered to help with some stuff. I didn't know how to get into the old bank accounts."

Kai shook his head. "Yes, poor Jared can't figure out the world on his own so he finds a woman to do it for him. My fiancée. You slept with my fiancée."

"Aunt Glenna changed the passwords and wouldn't give them to me. I didn't know what to do and you didn't have time. She took all the money, Kai. I didn't want to worry you, but it's been rough here. Hannah offered to help me and then one night…"

Hannah moved to Jared's side. "Nature took its course. He's more of a man than you, Kai. He knows how to take care of a woman. And I sent you a letter breaking up with you. It's not my fault you didn't get it."

He turned. There was nothing else to do. His brother was still a shit. He was still the kid who took everything and gave nothing back.

"Kai, please." Jared moved behind him.

Kai didn't stop. "You can have her. I wish you both the best of luck."

"Kai, this isn't what it looks like. Please, I need you."

He made it to his car and shoved his pack back inside, his gut rolling with anger. Betrayal. It bubbled up and made him want to put his fist through something, but he was in control. He would turn around and head to Iraq and not look back.

His brother didn't need him. Maybe he never had.

Jared stood outside, a lost look on his face, but Kai wasn't buying it anymore.

* * * *

Los Angeles, California
Five years before

Kori Williamson strode through the elegant doors that led to her Master's office. She didn't come here often, tried not to use the connection she had to him in order to further her own career. She might be submissive, might need the connection, the pain and pleasure that came from D/s, but in the real world she wanted to stand on her own two feet. That's what she told herself anyway. With every day that went by, she wanted it more than ever. To be more independent than she'd been the last couple of years, to have work that was hers and hers alone.

Now it looked like that would be difficult since she'd just taken a knife to her back.

Lydia looked up from her laptop, her perfect platinum hair in a bun. The thirty-two-year-old was California perfection from her hair to her already Botoxed face, to those perfectly done breasts the Master had paid for.

No matter how hard Kori dieted, she would never match Lydia's perfection. Damn it, she wanted a fucking ice cream. A big old sundae from Farrell's, but she hadn't been there in years because she was trying to fit in with the crowd. She wasn't a sad sack, look-at-me, look-at-me actress. Why was she desperate to be so thin? She was a writer with a vision. A vision her Master couldn't possibly have stolen. It was all a mistake. Her mentor wouldn't do that to her.

Of course, she'd also told herself that her Master couldn't take a whole harem of women either. She'd definitely told herself that she wouldn't put up with that shit, but here she was four years later making excuses.

"He's in a meeting," Lydia said with a frown. "And I happen to know he told you he would talk to you when he got home. You're going to get in trouble." She leaned forward. "You're going to get all of us in trouble."

Lydia was the Master's latest project. How long was she going to turn a blind eye to this shit? She'd been the one to help him with the screenplay that made his career. He'd been a hack B-movie director before she'd taken one of his shitty scripts and turned the horror genre on its head.

He'd given her a screenwriting credit and the best four hours of her life. The night they'd debuted and he'd been called the new king of horror, they'd spent hours playing. They'd gone to the club and he'd shown her off, and they'd even talked about getting married.

From Sanctum with Love

She'd found the pure beauty of sinking into complete submission. It had been a real high and she kept trying to get back there. It had worked for a while, but lately she couldn't do it. There was no subspace for her anymore and she was worried it was because she'd lost all faith in the man she'd once cared for.

"I need to talk to him and I'm not waiting until he comes home." Half the time he no longer came home. Not until the wee hours of the morning. He hadn't brought any of his new submissives home. Not yet. He kept it to the club, but she couldn't help but wonder at what point in time he was going to expect her to fall in line and accept other women in their house.

When had the lifestyle become a noose waiting to tighten around her neck?

"He should be done in a few minutes. He's been in there for a while. He's meeting with one of the actors who's up for the *Dart* role."

"I told him he should go with the kid from Seattle." It was so obvious. Jared something. He'd had a few roles on cable shows, and he was both gorgeous and charismatic enough to take on the role of a comic book hero. She'd taken the preliminary meetings with him. He'd been funny and charming and he'd flirted the precise right amount. The boy knew who was in charge. He'd ignored the other women, including the assistant who'd made it plain she would spend some time in a broom closet with him. No. He'd smiled and then turned all that sexy charm on Kori. "He's the only one for the role."

Lydia shrugged. "The Master does what he wants. You know, you should think about how much he's done for you over the years. You act like such a brat to him."

Kori gave in to her bratty side and shot the woman her happy middle finger before turning away and pacing the lobby. Lydia only knew what the Master told her. She had no clue about the years Kori had spent propping him up and giving him ideas.

She stopped and looked at herself in the mirror. Years had passed and she could see the fine lines around her eyes.

Let me hook you up with the guy who did Lydia's tits. You're looking a little droopy there, Kori. I don't like my slaves to droop.

Her hands twisted into fists and she was done. Years she'd

wasted.

She turned and the door came open. She didn't even look at the two men walking out. No, she only had eyes for the man in the suit.

Morgan King. Her first friend in LA. Her Master. Her lover. The man who had betrayed her utterly if the news was to be believed.

"Welcome to team *Dart*, Jared. I think this is going to be a wonderful show," Morgan said, his producer smile on his face. Yes, she'd convinced him to do that, too. She'd been the one to convince him of how much money there was in producing. She'd come up with the business idea. "We'll talk soon."

Jared stopped in front of her, holding out his hand. "Hey, Kori. Good to see you. I look forward to working with you." He squeezed her hand enough to let her feel how strong he was. "I hope we can work very closely together."

Any other time and she might have wondered what he meant by that for more than a couple of seconds. Not today. Today, she simply pressed through, getting inside before Morgan could shut her out. When the door closed, she turned on him. "Tell me you didn't take my fucking script and put your name on it."

There was no smile on his face now. "You wouldn't know what to do with it anyway, Kori. I don't understand what the issue is. You'll get your proper payment."

She shook her head. "I didn't agree to this. That is my script. It's my fucking life, Morgan. This isn't something we cooked up together. This is mine. I gave it to you to look at, not to steal."

"And I'll make sure it wins an Oscar. Like I said, I'll give you story credit, but if you read the script now, you'll find there are not many of your words left. I let Claudia have a look at it and she's made it shine." He moved toward her, his eyes not leaving her once. "We're a team. All of us. You're being quite selfish, pet. Is this more of your jealousy?"

God, she was so glad she'd stopped sleeping with him. Over the course of the last year, as he'd taken new subs, she'd moved into a separate bedroom and while they played together, she'd held back on being intimate. They'd become coworkers. Not even friends. She'd stayed because it was easier than leaving and because she'd put so damn much of herself into what she'd thought was their business. Now she could see it was really all his. He'd given her crumbs and not much else.

"I want my script back."

He started to reach out for her. This was what he always did. At one point in time she'd craved his touch because he'd been the first man to show her how good sex could be, what she truly needed. He'd been the first to spank her, to push her boundaries.

She'd found one. She wouldn't let him walk on her like this. Kori stepped back.

For a moment there was a hurt look on his face, as though he hadn't expected her to reject him. Then he sighed and moved to his desk. "No. This is the script I've been looking for. It's going to take me out of horror and science fiction and put me on the map as a true artist. You can take the story credit and be happy I involve you at all."

"Or I can sue you." How had she gotten here? She'd let him lead her to this point because she'd believed in him in the beginning. She'd believed his whole line about building something together.

He didn't bother to look up. "You can try, but if you make so much as a move to discredit me, I'll release the video I have of your sister. I know you don't adore the bitch, but you do love your mother."

"What are you talking about?"

Now he looked up and the smile he gave her seemed vaguely reptilian. "I'm afraid Shawna fell in with the wrong crowd a few years back. I recently purchased three films she…starred in. They cost me over a million, but I'm fairly certain I have every copy. I could release them. She's got that movie role coming up. I don't think the production company would be very happy to know their ingénue starred in porn. Do you?"

Her stomach dropped. Her sister was horrible, but it would kill her mom if something like that got out. And she didn't doubt he had the film. Morgan never lied or bluffed. If he said he would cut her, she would expect to bleed.

"It doesn't have to be like this, pet," Morgan said, his voice turning silky. "Why do you think I bought those films in the first place? I did it for you. I did it because we're a team. I know you're jealous of the other women, but that's how D/s works. I'm the Master. I make the decisions. This is what's right for us. You'll see."

She was caught, but she didn't have to stay in the cage.

A sudden vision of her life slammed into her. If she stayed here in LA, she would always be tempted to give in. She would go to the club because she needed it, and one night he would be there and she would wonder if she could handle it, handle him.

"Kori, you know I love you. You were my first submissive," he said, standing and starting toward her. "You will always be special, always my pet. You don't handle change well."

"I don't handle douchebags who steal my shit well." Damn but that felt good.

His hand found her hair and he pulled it back with a vicious twist. It was something she would never mind during a scene. "Watch your language around me, sub."

She minded now. With a twist she managed to rear back and punch the fucker right in the nose. He didn't get to touch her. Not ever again. He cursed, falling back and cradling his face. She was fairly certain he was walking a red carpet tonight. Let him explain a broken nose to the paparazzi.

"I will walk out of here and pack my bags," she explained to him. "You will give me every single copy of those films you have and I won't sue you or make a fuss about the fact that you stole my screenplay, but I swear to god if one of them slips through the cracks, I'll go on every morning show and talk about our relationship. I've got photos and I won't hesitate to use them. You remember that. Mutually assured destruction, Morgan. Don't ever call me again."

She heard him shouting something about how she'd be back or some shit, but he'd never known her at all if he believed that.

As the elevator took her down she knew one thing. It was time to leave. There was no happily ever after for her. Not in LA.

Maybe nowhere.

Chapter One

Present day
Dallas, TX

Kai stared at his patient and wondered if she was planning on spending the entire hour trying to win the quiet game. He had to give it to her. Erin Argent was damn good. She was good at deflecting, great at ignoring, positively magnificent at pretending.

But she couldn't deflect, ignore, or pretend any longer.

"Erin, you came to me. I have to assume you didn't come here to sit in silence."

The woman sitting across from him looked gaunt, far too thin for what was happening to her body, but then she wasn't concerned about herself physically. That was the problem. Erin had lost the man she loved in a mission a few months ago. Though she claimed she was "fine," there was no way to mistake her for anything but a woman in pain.

"I came here because Case is an asshole who sticks his nose in everyone else's business," Erin said with a shake of her head. "I didn't feel like eating. Since when was that a crime?"

"Case cares about you." Kai felt the need to remind her. Again and again. Erin was the type of woman who needed to hear it until she believed it. It was how Theo Taggart had gotten through to her. When they'd left on assignment all those months before, Theo had been chasing her. They'd come back from Africa as a couple trying to find their way through, and Kai thought they could have made it work if Theo had lived. It was hard to believe that had only been a short time before. Sometimes it felt like forever. Case Taggart had lost his twin, Ian and Sean the brother they'd only recently known existed. Kai wasn't even sure where his own brother was at the moment. How was Jared doing? He hadn't talked to his brother in years, but that would change very soon. "We all care about you, Erin. And we're all still hurting. The grieving process takes a long time."

"I'm not grieving. I'm pissed. I want to get back to work and no one will let me." She turned in her chair, staring out the window. "I'm starting to think McKay-Taggart isn't the right place for me anymore. Maybe I should pack it up and start over again somewhere else."

This wasn't the first time he'd heard her say that in session. "Where would you go? Home?"

She shivered as though the idea was distasteful. "No. I wouldn't go back there. I don't know. Maybe I should get in my car and drive. There's nothing left for me here."

"Nothing except a whole family of people who love you. Ian doesn't have you on desk duty because he's punishing you. That's not his point at all."

"He thinks I can't handle it anymore." She turned around, warming to her subject. "And you know what? He's gotten soft himself. He's the one who can't hack it. If he doesn't want to handle business anymore, he shouldn't put that on me. Li and I should be the ones out in LA dealing with the Bachman case. That's our client. Ian sent Jesse and Simon. And I'm royally pissed that Big Tag decided to let Li go on that op alone two weeks ago. He wouldn't have been in the position he'd been in if I'd been with him. He gave me some bullshit about how I wasn't ready to go back to Africa. What? Does he think I'm going to cry because that was where Theo kissed me for the first time? Who the fuck does he think I am? He almost got Li killed and now my partner's taken off on a vacation when we should be in LA. "

That was overstating the situation. Way overstating what had been a minor hiccup on a short operation. Yes, she was determined to deflect. He couldn't allow her to now. They were out of time. "Erin, why didn't you eat the sandwich today?"

Apparently this particular session had been brought on by Erin refusing to eat. Case had ordered lunch for her. She'd taken one look at the pulled pork sandwich that had once been her favorite and walked right out of the conference room.

"I wasn't hungry." Her arms crossed stubbornly over her chest.

"Eve heard you throwing up in the bathroom."

Erin's eyes slid away. "Eve's got a big mouth."

He sat forward because this whole subject was so touchy. Though unlike Big Tag, he didn't think she would run. Erin came across as brash and cold, but she wasn't inside. The walls were there because she'd been hurt so terribly before. She might try to build them higher this time, might never open herself up again, but she wouldn't leave Dallas. She would stay in the house Theo had bought for her. She would quietly mourn him to her dying day.

She didn't have to do it alone.

This part had been left up to Kai's discretion. He'd allowed her to avoid it the last few weeks because she needed time, but her family was starting to get nervous and with good reason. It was time to get the situation out in the open. Kai leaned in.

"Erin, we can't not talk about what's happening."

Her face went mulish, lips flattening out. "Nothing's happening. That's the problem. I need to work and Big Tag seems to think that I should be chained to a desk like a good girl. Fuck him. Fuck all of you if you can't see that I need to get out in the field and kick some ass."

"And what about the baby, Erin?"

The room seemed to still as though everything had stopped with his words. Erin herself became motionless, her eyes widening. She shook her head. "I'm not. I've just been sick."

Shit. How could she not know? Of all the scenarios, they hadn't come up with this one. "Have you taken a pregnancy test?"

"I don't have to because I'm not pregnant." She stood up and squared her shoulders. "You can all go to hell."

She strode out of the office, slamming the door on her way out.

Shit. He'd fucked that up royally.

The door opened again and he turned, grateful she'd come back, except it wasn't Erin standing in the doorway. It was his office manager. Kori Williamson stood there, a frown on her pretty face. She was wearing a skirt, V-necked blouse, and some Boho sandals, her normally wild hair pulled back in a messy bun. She wasn't neat and professionally perfect like some of the women he'd known, but the minute she walked in a room his dick noticed.

"What did you do?" Her husky voice sent a wave through him. He wasn't sure if it was pleasure or irritation. All he knew was the woman made him feel, and that was enough for him.

Unfortunately, she was his employee and he'd learned long ago not to play where he worked. Not that she seemed interested in him at all. In fact, he was almost certain he scared her a little. He put down his notebook and took off his glasses. He was getting a headache. "You know I can't talk about what happens in session."

"Erin took off and she looked ready to kill someone."

"I'm sure she would tell you that's just her face." What the hell was he going to tell Ian? Ian Taggart ran McKay-Taggart Security Services along with his best friend, Alex McKay. They were a tight-knit family. Kai had fallen in with them after he'd met Ian, and the big guy had offered Kai a place to set up his practice.

The fact that it was attached to one of the most exclusive BDSM clubs in the country didn't hurt one bit. And now, thanks to an anonymous donor—yeah, like he wasn't fairly certain that was the Taggart brothers, too—he had enough money in the bank to continue his work helping soldiers returning from war cope with PTSD for a while. He charged his patients what they could afford, which was often nothing.

But at least he could pay Kori well now. She deserved it. He wouldn't be here without her.

"Look, I know the woman has resting bitch face, and trust me I've seen her active bitch face as well," Kori shot back. "That was not anger. She was afraid."

He would love to talk to her about it, but there was the little problem of patient therapist confidentiality. He took it seriously. "I can't talk about it."

Kori's eyes went wide. "Shit. You told her about the baby, didn't you? Damn it. I knew she didn't know. What is wrong with you?"

"Hey, that is supposed to be confidential information."

Those pretty blue eyes rolled in a way that made him ache to spank her round ass. "Nothing is confidential around here. Not about the club crew. The subs have been talking about it for the last couple of weeks. We overheard Eve talking to Charlotte about the fact that Erin's been throwing up every day around ten. She tries to hide it, but that sound is distinctive. Also, she was complaining in the locker room the other day that her boobs were sore. She said she thought her period was coming, but with the throwing up and stuff it doesn't take Sherlock Holmes to figure out that girl is four kinds of knocked up."

"How can she not know she's pregnant?" He was going to have to have a long talk with Big Tag and his wife, Charlotte, about the club submissives running amuck. They'd recently brought in a new training class and apparently they were being taught to gossip.

Kori stepped back, glancing out the door. "I'm sure she does know on some level, but there's no question she's in denial. Did you treat her like she's a delicate flower who might wilt at the news?"

"I treated her like a woman who recently lost her lover."

She shook her head. "That's where you went wrong, boss. I'll go talk to her. She headed straight for the bathroom. You have a four o'clock with someone named Squirrel. Are we taking in the furries now?"

That made him groan. His brother's best friend from high school was now a member of his entourage. The fact that the kid was at least thirty and still called himself Squirrel did not bode well. "He's one of the guys from the film crew. I had to promise to show him around Sanctum."

"Film crew?" Her eyes widened.

Had he not told her? It had only been a few days since Alex had explained what the FBI needed from him, but that was going to have to wait. He had other problems. "Can you go and see if you can coax her back in here? I would go myself, but..."

"You're scared of the women's bathroom," Kori surmised.

"You know it's actually very nice in there. I made sure of it. The guys' bathroom is a pit of despair."

"It's clean." He wasn't sure why women needed the place where they answered nature's call to be some soothing spa, but Kori had insisted on it. "It's got a toilet and a place to pee and a place to wash your hands. It doesn't need anything else."

"Then why do all the guys who know about it use mine?" She'd insisted on a budget to redo the ladies' lounge, as she called it. Kori shook her head and strode out. "Hey, McKay. Boss, Alex is here."

It seemed to be his day for fucking up. Damn it. He hoped Kori knew what she was doing with Erin because another problem strode into his office with the confidence of a man who knew his place in the world.

"Have you ever been in the ladies'? That is one tricked out bathroom." Alex glanced back. "I saw Erin running for it as I came in. Is everything all right?"

Kai sighed and slid his glasses on before moving back to his desk. McKay wasn't here for a therapy session. Kai would be the one who needed the couch if anything. No. He needed the sturdy feel of his desk under his hands to get through this conversation. And the beer he'd bought and put in the fridge upstairs to get through the next few weeks. "Apparently she didn't know she was pregnant. I can't say she believes it."

Alex nodded as though his suspicions had been confirmed. "Eve was worried about that."

Kai didn't understand. "If I had lady bits I would track that shit. I would know the minute I missed a visit from Mother Nature."

Alex grinned as he sank his big body into the chair opposite Kai's desk. "I can imagine. But then Erin's not likely to live the life of a manwhore."

"Yeah, I'm living it up," Kai complained. "Don't take every rumor you hear as truth, Alex. I haven't actually had a girlfriend since I came to Dallas and I'll be honest, sleeping with my play partners has gotten boring."

He wanted something more. He wanted the connection that came when a Dom and a sub truly fit together, when their needs dovetailed and they could give to each other.

"I thought you were humping Kori's sister."

Not for all the money in the world. Shawna was a hot mess with a tendency to addiction and a severe narcissistic bent. How they were even siblings he had no idea. "She's a patient. I don't fuck patients."

Or employees. Even when he really, really wanted to. He had to wonder if Kori wasn't the real reason he'd lost interest in Sanctum's pretty subs.

The ones who weren't scared of him anyway. He was known for being a bit more hardcore in his play than the other Doms. Hell, some of the subs called him Dexter—the undercover sadist.

He wasn't undercover, damn it. He put that shit right out there. It was probably why he didn't date much. *Hello, my name is Kai and I would really like to hurt you. But only if you enjoy getting hurt. How about some coffee? We could talk about the proper use of exotic anal plugs.*

Yeah, that sent the ladies running and not into his arms.

"Is Erin all right?" Alex asked, his tone turning serious.

"She's fucked up in numerous ways." And ways he couldn't talk about with Alex because no matter what or who paid the bills, she was his patient and he took that seriously. He wouldn't tell Alex that Erin's issues hadn't started with Theo. No. Theo's death was merely the latest in a long line of deep disappointments and scarring episodes that made up Erin's life.

How was she going to handle being a mother?

"You don't think she's a danger to herself?"

Kai shook his head. "No. And now that the pregnancy issue can be dealt with, I actually think she'll be careful. The question is going to be what happens once the child is born. I don't honestly know that Erin will feel like she deserves a child."

"Deserves?" Alex sounded horrified, but then Alex hadn't grown up the way Erin had. Kai happened to know that Alex had been his parents' darling child, beloved and sheltered. Not that a sheltered existence couldn't lead to heartache, as Alex and Eve discovered, but how a person grew up, the love and support they got from their parents, could make the difference in how they handled tragedy.

"This is something I'll try to work through with Erin." To say any more would be to break Erin's trust, and he refused to be one more man to do that. "Since you're here, I suppose the mission is still on."

"Don't sound so excited," Alex said with a shake of his head. "Yes, I talked to my FBI contacts this morning and the op is a go. The advance production team flew in last night. They'll be scouting locations in the area including Sanctum and the McKay-Taggart building."

"Is Ian sure he wants to do this? I don't think he understands the kind of disruption something like filming a movie can bring." A production company was filming the adaptation of a book titled *Love After Death*. It happened to be a book written by a woman named Serena Dean-Miles, a close friend of Kai's. Her husbands—yeah, she was a traditional kind of girl—Jake and Adam, worked for McKay-Taggart. As far as Kai could tell, the romantic series *Soldiers and Doms* that Serena wrote under the pen name Amber Rose was pretty much fictional retellings of the lives of McKay-Taggart operatives.

He was totally hoping Ian figured out *Love After Death* was all about him.

"Ian is working with the feds on more than one op right now," Alex admitted. "Let's just say he's in a quid pro quo situation with them."

He was scratching their backs so they would scratch his. "What does Big Tag need the feds for?"

Alex sat back, his expression going stony. "You have your secrets and we have ours. I need to know if you're ready. If you don't think you can handle this, I'll try to convince them to let me run point on this op."

The production team was coming to Sanctum for more than realism. They were coming because the star of *Love After Death* needed a mentor. The lead actor had requested a Dom to mentor him through the role of the crop-wielding ex-spy whose dead wife returned from the grave.

Him. The actor had requested Kai. Jared Johns had been plain in his contract. He wanted Kai to be the expert on this film. Baby brother was putting him in a corner, but then his dipshit actor brother likely also had no idea the FBI was following him because they suspected he was a serial killer.

His brother wasn't smart enough to be a serial killer.

"I told you I'll do it and I will." It was actually good to get to focus on the professional stuff for a bit. "I've got a meeting set up with his…I don't know what the hell he is. From what I can tell, my brother has an entourage around him at all times. I'm meeting with one of them in a bit."

"Good. Do you think you can come in this evening and brief the rest of the team?"

"I thought we were keeping the real motives quiet."

"We are, but Ian and I both think it would be good to have a few people around you," Alex explained. "Case is going to stay close. You'll be mentoring him as you mentor Jared. Case will also be helping Jared with the military aspects of the role."

"Ah, so his cover is a baby Dom." It wasn't a bad play. It meant that Kai had backup, which was good because while he'd served his country, it had been a long time since he'd actively fought. It would also give Case something to concentrate on.

"Yes," Alex agreed. "Case is going to be involved, and Charlotte and Eve will be watching over the subs. No one else knows about this being an investigation. If Erin wasn't pregnant, I would send her in, but I can't expose her to a serial."

"She's not this particular serial killer's type, but I understand." He'd spent the last couple of days pouring over everything the feds knew. "I'll brief you all this evening and then we'll hit the club tonight. I don't suppose there's any way I could force my brother to take the training class. There's one going on right now. Actually, he missed the Dom pre-training. I think he should have to take that."

The first class for all Doms and Dommes centered around understanding what it was like for their subs. They couldn't be okayed to use any equipment they hadn't tried out. He would love to force his brother to take a spanking from Mistress Jackie. She wouldn't go easy on him no matter how good he looked. And she enjoyed a good plugging.

Alex stood and chuckled. "I think he's going to require more personal attention, but feel free to put him through anything you think will be helpful. Thank you for doing this, Kai. You can't know how much this helps."

He was beginning to suspect there was something going on at

McKay-Taggart he didn't fully understand, but he wasn't a stupid man. "The feds are going to help you find Hope McDonald, aren't they?"

Hope McDonald had managed to flee after Theo's death. She'd been involved in her father's business and that had led straight to the deaths of two McKay-Taggart operatives. There was no way Big Tag simply allowed her to get away.

Alex's face became a polite mask. "Something like that. They've got resources we can use. That's all I can say."

Why wouldn't he talk about it? There was something about the way Alex looked away that told Kai he was withholding some serious information. It wasn't his place to pry. "I'll make sure things run smoothly, but I don't like the fact that we're basically opening up Sanctum to a potential killer."

"We'll talk about it at the meeting. Be at the office at seven tonight. If anyone asks, you're there on a routine briefing," Alex said. He made it to the door before turning around. "And Kai?"

"Yes?"

"I know how hard this is for you. Thank you. We need this. We need the feds."

Kai nodded. "I can handle it."

The door closed and Kai hoped Kori was able to persuade Erin to come back in. He thought about going into the ladies' room, but eased back. Women could be a mystery. If Kori thought she could get through to Erin, then he would give her a shot.

Losing Theo Taggart had left a hole in everyone. It had even made him think about his own brother. Years had passed. Was he ready to deal with Jared again? The anger was still there, but was it doing anything for him at this point?

Why had his brother insisted on coming here? There was really only one reason. Jared wanted to confront him and there was no way he could walk away from this.

There was a knock on his door. Ah, yes. He got to deal with that idiot Squirrel.

Before he could make it to the door, it opened.

"Hey, brother." Jared stood there, blocking the way out.

Like it or not his past had caught up with him.

* * * *

Kori pushed through the door and into the bathroom. When they'd taken over this building, she'd made certain there was one feminine space. Kai liked the whole Asian, super-sleek tranquility look. Everything was in natural colors with very soothing sounds.

Sometimes a girl needed some pink, a bit of bling.

Which was why Erin was currently sitting in the lounge section of the bathroom looking perfectly incongruous on the hot pink velvet settee.

"Hey, you done puking?" She held up a frosty green can she'd found in the fridge. "Because I thought you might need one of these."

Erin looked up and her lips curled the tiniest bit. "I would kiss you but I really did puke so that wouldn't be such a great payment." She held out a hand and Kori pressed the drink in her palm. Erin immediately sat back and ran the cold can over her forehead. "Thanks. It got a little real in there. Your boss is an asshole."

He wasn't really. Kai was kind of the nicest man in the world, but if calling him an ass made Erin feel better, she would go with it. "He's a dude, but he means well. He doesn't get that you're knocked up, not dying."

Erin stopped for a moment, her body going still, and Kori wondered if she was about to deny it. "Yeah, they definitely don't get that."

"So how far along do you think you are?" The key with a chick like Erin was to ask direct questions. Erin didn't need to be treated like an invalid. She did, however, need to talk.

"I don't know. I think it probably happened after we got back from Africa. Sometime before Theo got shot to shit." Erin looked straight ahead. "It's his. That's all I was trying to say. Do you think everyone knows?"

"That it's Theo's? Yeah. I don't think anyone believes you've been trolling, E."

Erin groaned, but her lips had curled up slightly. "I wasn't talking about that. I was talking about the pregnancy. I really…I guess I didn't want to think about it. I knew deep down. I haven't been drinking or anything. I did right after I got home from the

Caymans." She turned quickly, her face white. "Oh, god. Do you think that hurt the baby?"

And there it was. There was the instinct. It might get buried again. Erin might shove it under a mile of pain and bravado, but her first impulse was to protect her child. Kori reached out and put a hand over Erin's shaking one. Of all the women she'd met since she's started playing at Sanctum and working for Kai, Erin was the one she understood the best. There was a soft heart under all that tough skin. "The baby's fine."

"It was only two beers but it helped me sleep, and then the next night I threw them out because I wanted them. I wanted them so fucking bad, but I didn't dream. They made me not dream and that's where I saw him." She seemed to realize she was on the edge emotionally and pulled back. "This is so stupid."

"It's not," Kori replied. "Nothing you feel now is stupid and two beers won't hurt the baby, but not seeing an obstetrician might."

"You sound like Kai."

"Don't tell him I said this but Kai is very often right." It wouldn't do to make the man more self-confident. He was already gorgeous and smart and sexy as sin. And a sadist. She was not going there again. Not for anything. "And he's right about this. You can't hide from it. You have a decision to make."

She shook her head. "Seems like the decision's been made for me. I guess I can't quit now. I need the health insurance."

Like she was going to quit in the first place. Kori happened to know that Erin loved McKay-Taggart. She'd found a home here. A lot like Kori had. She'd ended up in Texas because it had seemed about as different from LA as possible. A producer friend of hers, Sullivan Roarke, had called his old buddy Ian Taggart and gotten her a job at Sanctum, which had led to taking the job as Kai's assistant.

It was far from Hollywood, but she'd made a real place for herself.

"I can make an appointment for you," she offered. "I've heard Charlotte's OB is very lifestyle friendly."

Erin took a deep breath. "Yeah, I don't think I'll need her understanding about the bumps and bruises that come from playing.

I won't be doing that, but if you don't mind making the call."

"I'll make the call and I'll go with you."

Erin shook her head. "Nah. It's cool. I can handle it. It's only a baby. I suppose it's going to get worse around the office now. No one will treat me like they used to. No one jokes with me or fucks around."

"You want to be normal. I get it."

Erin flipped the top of the soda open and took a sip. "Yeah, well, I doubt that."

She wanted to throw down a "my pain is greater than your pain"? Kori could play that game. "My father had a heart attack in front of me when I was twelve. I was in the car with him. One minute he was talking and the next we were driving off a bridge. You're not the first person in the world to lose someone and you won't be the last. I won't treat you any differently than I did before because I remember so vividly the one thing I craved. Normalcy. I couldn't have it. Not really. He was there one minute and not the next. He was a constant in my life and then he was gone, so the world couldn't truly be normal again, but I wanted them to stop looking at me like I was a victim."

"A widow." Erin stared straight ahead. "They look at me like I'm a widow, but we weren't married. It wasn't that serious. Now I've got a decision to make."

This was where Kai would gently ask her leading questions. He would use that soft voice of his and ease her into a discussion. Kori wasn't that girl. "Are you high? You were in love with him. Now you're pregnant. What decision is there to make?"

"I didn't have a mother," she said quietly. "She took off and my dad was a shit. I don't think I'm ready to be someone's mother."

"No one is. The good news is you've got like seven months or so to start to deal with it."

"I'm so mad at him."

"I would be, too."

Erin turned slightly, giving Kori a disbelieving stare. "You would be pissed off at the angel of McKay-Taggart?"

"That's what death will do. We take all the annoying things about a person and forget them immediately. And yes, I would be pissed. He died. He wasn't supposed to do that. He wasn't supposed to leave you alone and aching, and now he left you to deal with a baby."

Erin stood, pacing. "Yes, exactly. He's the reason I'm here. I didn't want any of this. I didn't want to buy what he was selling. He was too young for me. What the fuck was I thinking? And it was his big dick that broke the fucking condom." Erin stopped and laughed. "He had a really big dick." Tears started to leak from her eyes. "I miss him. I don't want to miss him so much."

This was what Kai couldn't do with Erin. He couldn't push her until she broke. Kori stood and walked to her, wrapping her arms around Erin. "I know you do. I'm so sorry, but I'm also here for you."

This was what she'd missed those last few years in LA. She'd missed real people. Somehow her whole world at that point had become about the "business," with everyone concerned about themselves and their careers. It wasn't all of LA that was bad, but she'd found herself stuck in a group of overly ambitious, greedy people.

She'd been surprised by how much she'd felt when she'd gotten to Dallas. Within a few weeks, she'd started to feel empathy and compassion, and not only for characters she wrote. Somehow, she'd lost her way, and being in this place and with these people helped her get it back.

Just not all the way back. She still didn't write a damn word.

"Maybe it would be good if you did go with me," Erin said, moving back. She turned and faced the mirror, grimacing slightly at the way her mascara had run. "Stupid makeup. Why do I bother?"

Kori could handle that. "There's a box of makeup removing wipes and some little samplers in the drawer."

Erin chuckled as she found them. "You're very prepared, K."

"I'm lost on this place. Most of the patients are men," Kori admitted. "Some of them still sneak in here. I think they heard I keep a stash of granola bars and snacks in the other drawer. Not to mention the fact that some of those dudes believe in a skin care regime, and I say good for them. I go to department stores and ask for samples. Most of the time I get turned away, but every now and then someone will stock a sister up. Especially when they hear what we do."

Erin opened the second drawer and pulled out a protein bar. "Thank god. I'm starving. How can I throw up one minute and want to eat my own arm the next?"

"I think that's the fun part of pregnancy," Kori admitted.

"What's the shitty part?"

"When you have to push a baby head through your lady bits. I've heard that sucks."

Erin laughed and ran one of the towelettes over her face. "Yeah, it sounds that way. You know you're the only one who treats me like I'm still Erin."

"You are and you aren't. You're never going to be the same. I should know." It was time to impart a little truth since Erin had opened up. "I wasn't after what happened with my dad. I started living in this fantasy world in my head and I didn't come out of it for a very long time."

Erin turned, leaning on the vanity. "Fantasy world?"

She'd never told anyone with the singular exception of her best friend, Sarah. Sarah was the only person who knew who Kori had been. "I wrote a lot. I wrote in a journal, but I would make up stories. I didn't write down feelings, but they came out anyway. I had my first play produced when I was sixteen. It was about teen suicide."

"Wow. I bet that got your mom nervous."

"Oh, yes. She had to figure out that writing that dumb play was my way of not killing myself. It felt good. It's still used in a couple of school systems as an educational tool to prevent suicide. From there I wrote some plays and screenplays and some seriously kinky *Doctor Who* fan fiction. I think it was a lot easier to live in the world in my head than it was to face the fact that my dad was gone."

"Why did you stop? Writing, I mean." Erin frowned when she didn't answer. "Don't hold out on me, K. You're the one who initiated this session. Or did Kai send you in here for vagina talk?"

"Of course he sent me in here and I won't tell him shit if you don't want me to. Also, I wanted to come and talk to you. I know Faith is your bestie and all, but she's not here right now so you can count on me. As to why I stopped writing. Ugh, I don't even like talking about it."

"Well, I live to talk about Theo's murder and my pop-up pregnancy."

The woman had a point. If she was going to dish it out, she better be able to take it. "Okay. Sanctum wasn't my first club."

Erin snorted a little. "No shit. Sorry, but if you were trying to play the newbie sub, you shouldn't jump into suspension every time there's a training session. Most newbs are afraid of being suspended ten feet off the ground and having their nipples tortured."

She liked what she liked. She actually forced herself to pull back from most of what she truly craved. Submission, she'd found, was like her drug. She tended to make poor choices when she fully invested in it. And yet she couldn't completely stay away. "I got into the lifestyle young. My boyfriend became my Master and then he turned into a total prick who stole my every idea, turned it into his own, and shut me out. He took other subs and I stayed. He cheated on me and I told myself it was all right. He gave my best screenplay to another woman, who ripped it apart and turned it into dreck, and that was when I finally left."

"Wow. Should I kill him? Because that might actually make me feel better. Don't worry about the baby. I can totally snipe him from afar. No danger to the fetus."

Kori had to smile because Erin might not be joking. "It was years ago. I'm good. I made my choices and I walked away. All I'm trying to tell you is that you might never be normal again, but you find a new normal. You find a...what should I call it? Peace. I'm at peace."

"What am I going to do?" Erin asked, her voice so quiet.

It didn't matter. Kori could still hear her. "The best you can. It's all you can do."

It was all any of them could do in the end.

Ten minutes later, she promised Erin she would send her all the information on Dr. Melinda Bates, including her first appointment time. She gave Erin a hug and turned to go into Kai's office. She wasn't going to tell him what Erin had said, merely that Erin was going to the doctor and she had everything well in hand.

A vision of Kai smiling and telling her she deserved a treat for a well-done job floated across her brain. He would thrust his hands in her hair and force her to her knees. He would offer her a choice.

The cane or the whip. She loved the way the man held a whip. Once he'd warmed her up, ensured she would feel those stripes he would leave on her ass for days, then he would lay her out on his desk and shove his face in her…

Damn it. She couldn't think of him that way. She couldn't. He was her boss, and he was a fucking gloriously beautiful sadist.

Not again. Never again. She wasn't going back into that particular part of the D/s world. No more serious sadists for her. She'd promised herself.

So why was it getting harder and harder to not think about Kai? To watch him with other subs?

She hated the thought, but it might be time to move on. He was too tempting. Maybe she was hormonal or something. She couldn't leave now. Erin needed her.

She was about to walk into Kai's office when she saw the door was open. Kai was talking to someone.

Her heart nearly stopped as she recognized Jared Johns. Flipping Jared Johns was standing in Kai's office. He was older than she remembered, but time had done nothing to dilute that man's hotness. He was roughly six three and had the body of a tank that had been designed by Michelangelo. When she'd met him he'd been a kid starting out in the television world. He'd been working on some Canadian soap when she'd told Morgan he would be perfect for *Dart*.

She might have sworn off going back into that world, but apparently she couldn't stop it from invading.

Kai looked up. "Hey, Kori. Come on in. I'd like you to meet my brother."

Brother? Jared Johns was her boss's brother? She turned and walked away as fast as she could.

Chapter Two

"I was expecting Squirrel." Kai moved back behind his desk, putting some much needed distance between himself and his brother. Kori was apparently still in the lounge with Erin or she might have announced that they had a guest. He kind of hoped she stayed there for a while. Maybe if she stayed in the ladies' room long enough, he could avoid introducing her. "Actually, I was surprised to hear his name. Wasn't he your friend in high school? He's still hanging around?"

Jared looked good. It was obvious he took his training very seriously. There wasn't an ounce of fat left on his baby brother. Kai had been through the military, but Jared looked like a warrior with his close-cropped sandy hair and rigid jawline. It was easy to see why he was considered by millions of women to be the hottest man on the planet.

"I'm still friends with most of the guys I hung out with in high school, but Squirrel travels with me. He helps out around the set and does some stuff my personal assistant can't do." He was wearing a dark T-shirt and jeans, his shirt tucked in. Aviator sunglasses hung from the pocket of his T. Naturally it was V-neck. Wouldn't want to hide skin when he could show it off. "Would you have been here if you'd known it was me coming?"

"Of course." This wasn't family therapy. It was business and baby brother needed to know that now. "I agreed to the terms of the contract. For the time it takes to produce this film, I'll meet with you whenever you need."

Jared shook his head, an entirely unamused chuckle coming out of his mouth. "Contract. You like contracts. Don't you, Kai?"

Were they going there? "I do indeed. Contracts lay out expectations and everyone knows how to behave. Speaking of contracts, have you looked over the one Wade Rycroft sent you? He's the…"

Jared reached into the small crossbody bag he'd set down beside him when he'd walked in. He pulled out a stack of papers. He placed it on Kai's desk and then took the seat previously occupied by Alex McKay. "Manager of Sanctum. I believe he also might be called one of the Doms in Residence. He was hired on a few months ago when the old manager left. From what I understand he's in charge, though Ian Taggart calls the shots. Here's the Sanctum contract and yes, I read it."

The years had given Jared some confidence. He sounded more polished than he had before, stronger, and it was obvious he'd done his homework. "Excellent. Then we can start tomorrow. I'll expect you at the club at four p.m."

"Why wait? The club is open tonight. I'll be in the dungeon. According to that contract and the rather hefty fee I paid for a membership, I'm allowed in during club hours." He crossed his left leg over his right, sitting back as though ready for a nice long chat.

"Don't you mean the production company? They paid the fee to get you a temporary pass."

Jared's head cocked to the left and his lips ticked up in an arrogant grin. "No, I paid the membership fee and it's not temporary. I understand that I still have to pass all of Taggart's tests in order to have Masters rights, but I can come and go as I please for the next year."

Shit. He'd been absolutely certain this was a six-week thing. Why the hell did Jared need an actual membership? "Won't you have another movie to film after this? Why would you sink so much money into something you won't need a few months down the line?"

Jared sighed. "You still have the sanctimonious big brother thing down. First, I'm not filming a movie. I'm filming the new season of *Dart*. Crescent City won't save itself."

"Yes, it needs a superhero who runs around killing bad guys with freaking darts. Guns aren't good enough for you?"

Jared smiled, the expression lighting up his face. "I'm sure the producer would say it's a metaphor or something. It looks cool. Who doesn't want to be a billionaire who was kidnapped by aliens and sent back to his home planet with dart throwing abilities to save the world from criminals? Come on, Kai. You read the comic books, too. It's fun."

"I didn't read them like you did. I had too much to take care of." Including his younger brother.

Jared sobered, sitting back. "I know you did. And as for the membership, I will very likely need it. There are a bunch of books in this series and Pierce Craig is featured heavily in all of them. Given the strength of the box office from *Fifty Shades of Grey*, there's no reason this can't become a big franchise."

Jesus, Ian was going to kill Serena at some point. "I don't even know what to say to that."

There was a negligent shrug from Jared. "I think it's important to get into character. I'll be hanging around Sanctum and McKay-Taggart a lot."

He was curious about a few things. Since he intended for all their interactions to be professional from now on, it was best to get curiosity out of the way up front. "How exactly did you figure out I could be your mentor? I don't advertise my status. There's no social media page proclaiming my sexual proclivities."

"Because you hid them so well when we were kids? Yeah, not so much. I knew you were always interested in this kind of stuff. You kept bondage magazines under your bed. I never told Mom by the way. Was it Ms. Hanford who got you into it?"

He felt himself flush. Only his brother could do this to him. If anyone else had asked, he would have explained quite calmly that his first sexual experiences had been with the woman who lived next door. He'd been seventeen and Alicia Hanford had been twenty-one and fresh out of college. She'd rented the two-bedroom next door. Their mother had insisted they call her Ms. Hanford. It was only polite and she was an adult. Kai had called her hot. She'd been a stunning redhead and yes, she'd been the one to introduce him to D/s. She'd taken him to his first club and shown him that all those cravings he had could be put to proper use in the right setting. She and the rest of the lifestylers had made him feel like he wasn't some freak for wanting what he'd wanted.

Still wanted.

Only his brother had the power to make him feel like a pervert. "Yes. She was a lovely young lady, but our interests diverged."

"She was a top, too," Jared surmised. "She's still in the scene in Seattle. She's married to her sub. They seem very happy. She speaks fondly of you."

"Why the fuck would you talk to her about me?"

"I do it for the same reason I've kept up with you all along. Because you're my brother. Well, after I had the money to do it, I kept up with you. You might not give a shit what happens to me, but I needed to know you were all right."

"How can I not know what happens to you? I go to any grocery store and there you are on the cover of every magazine."

Jared's face lit up and for a second he was the same kid who'd begged and prayed for a bike at Christmas and cried when he'd gotten one.

Because Kai had told his mother to spend what she would have spent on him on Jared. Because he'd sacrificed for his brother.

"I know. Isn't it cool?" Jared said with that sunny smile of his. "Not the tabloid crap. That's all bullshit by the way. I did not almost break up Brad and Angelina in Cannes. I barely spoke to them. But the cover of *Men's Fitness* was awesome. I had to do some serious work on my deltoids to make that happen."

Kai nearly rolled his eyes. He somehow managed to maintain a bit of professionalism. "So did you hire a PI to track me?"

The smile faded. "I have someone give me an update on you from time to time. I think the work you're doing here is amazing. I talked to Frank Cross and he says it helped him."

"How the hell do you know Frank?" Frank was an Iraq war vet who had suffered from terrible PTSD and depression after he'd lost an arm to an IED. He'd been in Kai's program for over a year and then moved back to his family in California.

"He works on the *Dart* set now. He's a consultant."

"That's a big coincidence."

"Not really. I offered him the job. I interviewed him because he knew you and then I offered him the job because he was a good man and he deserved good work. He's consulting on weapons but he's also learning how to film. We got him a camera set that doesn't require two hands. You're not the only one who can help."

"Apparently." What was his brother doing? He tried to look at the problem from an intellectual standpoint. It was time to take off his anger hat and remember what he did for a living. "You do understand why you're doing this."

"What? The film? Because they are paying me a mega shit ton of money, the script is good, and I've honestly been looking for a part that shows off my glutes. I've worked hard on them. I'm naked like half this film."

Yep, his brother was an exhibitionist. "No, I meant stalking me."

It was Jared's turn to roll his eyes. "I'm not stalking you. I'm very reasonably checking in on my unreasonable asshole of a brother."

"Yes, I'm the asshole. Of course. Look, this stems back to your childhood. You always got everything you wanted. I've walked away. I don't give in to your demands. Naturally you want to control the one thing you couldn't. Me. It was also why you slept with my fiancée."

"Are you serious? I got everything I wanted? Do you think I wanted to get the shit kicked out of me on a daily basis in high school? Do you think I wanted to be orphaned at the age of sixteen?"

This was what his brother did. He tried to one up everyone in terms of who had it worse or could do it better. His competitive streak had been obvious from childhood. "Of course. You had it worse than anyone."

Jared stood, running a frustrated hand through his hair. "I didn't. I know that but you won't acknowledge that I have feelings at…I did not come here to fight with you. I thought it would be best if we sat down and talked so there's not any awkwardness."

Awkward didn't begin to cover it. Still, he put on what he hoped was a placid smile. "There won't be. Like I said, I signed the contract. I'll be your mentor in all things BDSM. If you have any questions, ask me. I'm an open book."

Jared's green eyes narrowed. "All right. That's an offer I won't refuse. How about this one? Do you ever feel bad that you walked out on your younger brother because of a girl?"

And he was done. "I said I would answer your questions about BDSM."

"Damn it, Kai. I want to talk. It's been twelve years. Do you honestly intend to go the rest of your life without talking to me?"

"I can't because I signed a contract. I can't because once again, you shoved your way in and won't leave until you get your way."

"Still a hardass, huh?"

"Only if you're still a dumbass."

Jared growled and turned away, facing the door. Thank god. Maybe he would get the point that this wasn't going to go his way. He'd picked up his bag and was almost to the door when he turned around.

"No, you know what, you're not calling the shots this time. All my fucking life, you've been the one to set the rules, but I have some power now and I'm going to use it."

"You already have. You've forced me into this position. You've got me as your mentor for this movie. I won't be doing more."

"Of course not. I don't know why I expected this would be different. You don't take my calls. You don't answer my e-mails. I'm nothing to you. You know for a therapist you hold a mean grudge. Shouldn't you be all about forgiveness?"

His brother had never really understood him at all. "I'm all about what makes a person happy and whole. I can be perfectly happy and whole and still carry a grudge against the man who fucked my fiancée."

Jared nodded. "Yes, I did, and I've regretted it ever since. Kai, I'm so sorry it happened, but what you saw that morning wasn't the truth of the situation."

"Did you or did you not sleep with the woman I had asked to be my wife?"

"I didn't intend to."

This was precisely why he'd never had the conversation. He could play it out in his head word for word. "Did you fall into her vagina? That would be odd since you're not known for being terribly uncoordinated."

"I was drunk," Jared ground out. "Something bad had just happened and she showed up and gave me a ride home. She didn't leave."

"Is that when you fell into her vagina?"

"Damn it, Kai. Why won't you listen to me?"

"Because you're not talking about the job." Sitting here with Jared made him antsy. It reminded him of so many things he didn't want to think about. All those nights he'd sat up watching over Jared, trying to be an adult when he was only a child. He'd loved his mother, but his childhood had been so chaotic. He preferred the peace and calm of his present, and he couldn't help the resentment that bubbled up when he thought of how Jared was about to disturb it. "I will discuss anything you like about BDSM, but the rest of my life is off limits. If you thought you would get some kind of public reunion for a magazine story, you're out of luck."

"I wasn't looking for press, Kai. If all I can get out of you is mentoring, then I suppose that's what I'll do. Who's the pretty girl?"

Kai stood, looking through the open door. Kori hugged Erin before waving her out the door. At least it looked like one thing had gone right today.

Kori turned and stopped, staring at his brother. Damn it. She was probably like every other woman in the world. He would be lucky if she didn't drool. The thought of Kori drooling over his perfect brother made him want to punch something.

"Hey, Kori," he said because he couldn't pretend like Jared wasn't standing there. She would find out about their relationship soon enough. "Come on in. I'd like you to meet my brother."

At least she could defuse the situation between them. Maybe once Jared realized he still had work to do he would go and find a reporter to show his ass off to.

Kori's mouth dropped open and then she turned and walked

right out of the room.

"Kori?" It wasn't like her to walk away. Kori plunged right in.

Jared stared after her. "Kori? That girl's name is Kori?"

"She's a woman and yes, that's her name. She's also my office manager." Kai did not like the way his brother was staring after Kori. Surely now that Jared was a Hollywood star, he was all about the actresses. The ass was surrounded by beautiful women twenty-four seven. From what Kai had seen on magazine covers, Jared was dating a gorgeous, way-too-thin actress who was up for an Oscar.

"Kori Williamson. Wow. Now, see, that is a brilliant coincidence."

"How do you know her last name?" It wasn't like Kori had a nameplate on her desk. "Or is this more of your creepy stalking shit? Don't play it with her. She's off limits. She's a very nice lady who happens to care about the people around her, and I'm not going to let you play games with her."

"With Kori? I wouldn't dream of it. I owe that woman," Jared said with a grin. "It seems like I owe her a lot. I always wondered where she went."

"Went?"

Jared turned around, settling his bag over his big chest. "You do know her story, right? I know that woman. Five years has not made her any less luscious."

Kai shook his head. "How do you know her? From LA? She was a secretary out there before she made the move to Dallas."

His stomach twisted at the thought of Kori in his brother's arms. Was that why she'd walked away? Had she been one of Jared's conquests?

"She was not a secretary and I never slept with her. Though I had plans to because again with the hotness." Jared had his Cheshire cat grin on his face. "Looks like I know something you don't know. Maybe we will talk about something besides BDSM. I'll see you at the club tonight. Unless you're planning on coming home before you head to Sanctum."

"Why would that matter to you?"

He walked to the door. "Because I'm staying upstairs at your place. I already set myself up in the spare bedroom. I snuck in after that big guy in the suit. Needs a decorator, by the way. You know it all kind of looks like this. You need a little color in your life, brother."

"You are not staying with me."

"Sure I am. I always bunk with my mentor. It's how I work. Maybe you should have read that contract better. My friends will be staying at the Anatole, but I'm with you. And don't worry about a key. I did this film last year where I played a cat burglar. Like I said, I'm already in. And when you're ready to talk, I'll tell you all about your office manager. I think you'll find it fascinating." He stopped and looked back. "And Kai? It really is good to see you."

He stood and watched Jared walk out.

Fuck a duck.

* * * *

Kori had to stop and take a deep breath. Her hands were shaking. What had happened? Why the hell had Jared Johns been standing in her boss's office?

She should go to her car and get inside and drive away. Maybe Florida would be nice this time of year. Anything was better than having to confront her past.

Anything was better than explaining to Kai that she'd lied to him.

She stopped at the front of the building. From the doors she could see Sanctum. It wasn't dark yet so the lights hadn't come on. Sanctum was now surrounded by a privacy fence since it had been reconstructed after some asshole had blown it up.

With Kai inside.

That had been one of the worst days of her life. She'd gotten the call from Eve, who wanted to know if Kori had copies of Kai's health insurance cards since the originals had been blown up.

Kai was fine, but she'd known that day that she was the idiot who fell in love with her boss. By the time she'd gotten to the hospital, Kai had been ready to be released. He'd been joking around and cursing a blue streak at the loss of the building where he'd lived. She'd been crying. He'd stopped and stared and for a second she'd thought he would walk right up to her and take her in his arms.

Nothing. She'd gotten nothing more than him clearing his throat and asking if she was all right.

So she'd known then and there that whatever she felt for him wasn't reciprocated. It was fine and good and they'd never mentioned it again, but god she hated feeling humiliated.

She opened the doors and stepped out. Their building wasn't protected by a fence. Big Tag had offered to include their three-story building, but Kai hadn't wanted his patients to feel like they were walking into a guard tower. Getting through security apparently didn't go with Kai's peaceful vibe.

When she saw the limo parked in the front drive, she kind of wished Kai had changed his mind about that.

The limo door opened and a young brunette in a sheath dress stepped out. She was wearing ridiculously high heels and sunglasses that had enough bling to outshine the sun. "Are you the person who runs this…place?"

"Nope."

She started for her car, which was parked in the back. It was a piece of shit sedan, but it still worked and she didn't have to make payments on it. Her phone vibrated in her bag but she was ignoring that for the time.

"Hey, I was talking to you."

Kori could hear the sound of designer shoes hitting the pavement. *"No hablo inglés."*

"Yeah, like I'm buying that with the pasty white skin."

Kori turned. It seemed to catch Designer Shoes off guard. She stopped suddenly and wobbled for a moment. "If you're looking for Jared, he's upstairs. You should go find him."

"I'm well aware of where Jared is at all times, thank you very much. I'm his personal assistant and…well, we're very close."

Sure they were. "Good for you both. I hope you're very happy together."

Kori turned and started looking through her bag for her keys. One of these days she was going to downsize. Smaller bag, less shit. Why did she need all that crap?

"Look, I need to talk to you about what Jared requires in his living space."

The one thing she didn't have? A Taser. She could use a Taser.

She would bet Skinny Bitch wouldn't even need much voltage. "Why the hell would I care about that?"

"Because you're Kai Ferguson's assistant and Jared will be living with him for the duration of the filming. Also, I'll need to see the space reserved for him at the club."

She could almost feel her jaw hitting the ground. Kai didn't live with anyone because he was a prissy, control freak who had a touch of OCD complex he couldn't seem to admit to. She didn't blame him or anything. He was a germaphobe, too. It was all part of the unique crazy that made up her boss. He didn't share well. Oh, she was sure he would be totally horrified by that statement. He was all about the love and peace and sereneness that came from self-awareness, and he could totally lead others to that place. But he wasn't exactly there himself. "Kai didn't mention anything about us having guests."

"I don't know about what Mr. Ferguson did or didn't say to his employees. I only know that I take care of Jared and that means for the next few weeks, you'll have to take care of him, too. He's going to need his favorite protein bars, coconut water, a juicer—that has to have a 900-megahertz chopping engine—the crappy ones won't do. He'll need a set of kettle balls and a space for his training. He has to keep his body fit." She gave Kori a onceover. "I don't think that you'll fully comprehend the needs of an athlete so you should probably make up a guest room for me as well. I can stay close to Jared and ensure he has everything he needs."

What the hell was going on? "Sleep on the couch. I don't care. There's only Kai's room and a tiny guest room. The rest of the building is for Kai's practice."

"That's not acceptable. We might need to bring in a designer to make the place comfortable for him. I don't understand why he thinks staying here is a good idea."

"Apparently he wants to spend time with his brother." It was still sinking in that Kai had an international superstar brother that he never talked about. They'd had a thousand conversations. She'd spent late nights talking about everything from politics to TV shows to restaurants. Never—not even once—had he said oh, and hey, my brother happens to be that dude on TV every woman pants after. Ever heard of him?

From Sanctum with Love

Then again, it wasn't like she'd said "hey, guess what? I used to write screenplays and I've had a bunch of movies made and developed some awesome TV shows that I didn't get paid for because I was way too invested in my Master."

Yeah, she'd definitely not talked about that.

How much had they kept from each other? She'd thought she was the only one who was hiding something, holding back. It looked like Kai had held out as well.

"If this guy was a good brother, I would have met him by now. I've been around Jared for three years now and this Kai person has never called or come to visit him."

Which made her wonder what the hell had happened between them. Kai had worked hard to build a new family. Kai was a man who was desperate to have people depend on him. It was why he'd started in the D/s lifestyle in the first place. He'd needed the responsibility.

And he needed to go seriously hard core on a woman who could handle it. Like she could handle it. Like she craved it.

It was precisely why she'd stayed away from him. She'd stayed away from all of them. She'd played the lightweight sub who needed the occasional spanking and service role to feel complete. God, she hadn't had an orgasm in years. Not a real one. Not a screaming, eyes rolling to the back of her head, wail his name orgasm.

"Look, I don't know what's going on, but it seems like it's none of my business." If Kai hadn't talked to her about his brother, he didn't want her to know. Despite the fact that she was dying to know, it seemed too personal. If she got involved in this, she would be stepping over a line she'd decided a long time ago she wouldn't step over. She'd decided it about three minutes after meeting Kai because she'd immediately known that this was a man who could dominate her, who could give her what she needed and she would hand over all of herself.

"It's everyone's business." The skinny chick wouldn't let up. Her foot tapped against the concrete. "Jared is important. He's going to be here for at least eight weeks. Two weeks prep. Six weeks principal filming in this hellhole. Then we get to go back to LA and civilization, so I need to know everything I can about making our time here survivable. Jared is a saint so he's staying here while the rest of us get to be in what passes for a luxury hotel in this part of the world. So you'll give me a list of the restaurants that are worth eating at, the stores I won't barf at shopping in, and clubs that he won't mind being seen in."

"Or you could fuck yourself hard." Skinny Bitch was getting on her last nerve. Lately she'd begun to miss a few things about LA. She missed West Hollywood and the dog park across from her house. She missed going out to Santa Monica and walking along the beach, going to the pier and people watching. She did not miss star personal assistants with over-inflated egos. Yeah, she'd dealt with more than one of those.

"Kori?" a deep voice said.

Fuck. She should have run.

Skinny Bitch turned on those designer heels of hers, her whole demeanor changing in a minute. The nasty look on her face turned to a sunny smile and her voice went up about two octaves. "Jared, I was talking to this secretary, trying to make sure you're comfortable here."

Jared didn't look at his PA. His eyes were steady on Kori. "Lena, I told you not to worry about that. I can handle myself. Go back to the limo and wait with Squirrel and the rest of the crew. We'll go and get a late lunch before we go to the club tonight."

Lena nodded and fiddled with her phone. "All right. Just to remind you, tomorrow is Jessica's birthday." She glanced Kori's way. "Jessica is his girlfriend. She's going to win an Oscar this year."

Good for freaking Jessica. Jessica Hamilton. Kori had never met her, but she'd read articles about the dramatic actress's relationship with Jared. "I'm going to leave now. Bye."

Jared moved in, turning his back and leaning on her car, obviously blocking her way. "Stop hiding, pretty girl. I found you."

She could feel herself flush. "It wasn't like I was hiding. I was going home."

"You know this woman?" Lena asked as though shocked to her core.

Jared's head turned and though she couldn't see his eyes through the mirrored aviators he wore, Kori could have sworn that was a Dom look. It was definitely an alpha male stare as Lena started to back off.

"I'll be in the limo." She practically ran back to the waiting car.

Jared turned to Kori. "Sorry. She tries too hard sometimes. And while Jessica is my girlfriend in a professional sense, it's not real. Like everything else in Hollywood, it's all for show. We're not actually involved in anything but a mutually beneficial friendship."

Yeah, she did kind of miss the gossip. There was always Sanctum gossip, but it was innocuous stuff, unlike the juicy scandals from LA. "You two look so cozy in pictures."

"You follow me?" His lips quirked up in a crazy sexy smile. There was a reason there were entire YouTube channels devoted to this man's workout routines. He was smoking hot.

"It's hard to miss you, buddy. You're kind of everywhere." Despite his hotness, she wasn't getting pulled into any of that. Somehow he was still a boy compared to his brother.

"That's what happens when you have an awesome publicist. He's the one who introduced me to Jessica. The truth of the matter is I'm not her type and she's not mine. It helps. No drama. Maximum exposure."

"Hey, whatever works." She didn't want to get sucked back in. Her first impulse was to ask about a million questions because there was a story there. Jared Johns was pretty much everyone's type. Straight girls. Gay guys. Anyone interested in penis would be all over that man. She kept her mouth shut though because that wasn't her world anymore. Over time she'd started to watch some TV again but she hadn't been to the movies in years.

Maybe she *had* been hiding.

"I always wondered where you went." Jared's voice went low, a bit softer than the command of before. "I kind of thought you would end up being a producer on the show."

Humiliation was one thing, but damn it she hated to pretend. It wasn't hurtful to simply refuse to talk about it, but she wasn't going to lie. Jared was standing there looking good enough to eat and she probably had mascara issues. Next time, she would run over Lena and not care because she wouldn't be here, looking utterly ridiculous. "I left because the executive producer of your show was an asshole who cheated on me, used me, and stole my script."

Jared simply smiled. "Then it's good you got out. How did you end up here, working with my brother? Was it Sully? I ask because he's the guy who keeps up with Kai for me. Didn't you work on a movie with him?"

She nodded. It wasn't so surprising they both knew Sully. It was a shockingly small world. "He helped me get out, helped set me up with a job out here. He's a good guy."

"That he is. And you are looking beautiful."

Sure she was. "Try selling that to someone who's buying, Johns. This is awkward. Kai doesn't know what I used to do."

"And he never told you I was his brother."

"Not a mention. I didn't know he had one." Which begged the question. "What did you do to him?"

Kai wouldn't cut a family member out of his life without cause. He wasn't that guy.

Jared was silent for a moment, looking away from her for the first time. "I slept with his fiancée."

Without even thinking about it, she reached out and slapped at his arm. "Asshole."

Of course it wasn't like Kai had mentioned a fiancée either. There was some chick out there who he'd loved enough to ask her to marry him. Kai had gotten on one knee and pledged his devotion and that would mean something to a guy like Kai. He would have been faithful and loving and dominant, and he likely would have slapped that girl's ass silly every night she wanted it. She could have walked around all her damn life with his mark on her and she'd chosen to sleep with the pretty boy?

Shit. Maybe she wasn't as self-aware as she thought either since she was now flaming mad at some woman for fucking over her boss. Or was she heart broken because Kai had loved someone? Likely someone thin and pretty whose hair didn't curl fifteen different ways. Someone who didn't piss everyone off the minute she opened her mouth.

"Ow and yes, I was an asshole." If Jared was seriously offended by her assault, he didn't show it.

"Hey, do you need help?" A big guy stepped out of the limo, his massive body barely contained in a tight T-shirt.

Jared sighed. "No, I don't need help taking a punch from a

girl." He looked down at her. "I call you a girl in this case because I know some women who can take me. Once you've had your ass handed to you by a female stunt double, you won't ever discount women again." His smile turned distinctly sensual and he leaned in. "Of course, if you want to move from girl to woman, I could help you out there. I have a lot of training in that area."

"We're about to see how he handles taking a girl's knee to his dick, Mr. Muscle," she warned the bodyguard.

Jared held up both hands as the bodyguard started to advance. "Get back in the limo, Bolt. She was pissed off because I explained to her why my brother hates me. I slept with his fiancée."

Bolt frowned. "You suck, Johns. Give him hell, girl. You need to follow through on your punches. I'll teach you."

"Bolt?" Kori asked as the big guy slid back behind the wheel.

"It was his pro wrestling name. I hired him because he told me that *Dart* was a stupid fucking show and I needed a serious trainer instead of a pansy ass Hollywood boy. I spar with him at least once a week. What can I say? I like honesty. I don't get much of it in my real life. It was one of the reasons I always liked you. Why haven't you told Kai what you used to do? Is it because he can be a judgmental prick?"

She liked honesty, too, and the truth was Kai could be a little prissy sometimes. He had his hang-ups. "I don't know why. At first I was embarrassed because I'd basically run out of LA with my tail between my legs. Then I guess I thought he wouldn't like the fact that I'd lied to him. Also, he doesn't think much of movies or TV. He's more of a reader. Although now that I think about it, that's probably your fault."

Jared shook his head. "Nah, he was always a snob. He was reading psychology textbooks in high school. Although at one point in time he read comic books to me. It was why I was so interested in *Dart*."

"I thought it was because you were an actor and you'd do anything to keep working." It was pretty much the same way all over the entertainment business. You worked so you could continue working, a never-ending cycle of love and hate and joy. She did miss that part.

"Maybe. But some of it was because I knew you were involved

with the project and I greatly admired your work. Hey, do you want to grab some dinner? I'm going to this club thing later on tonight. I could tell you about it over a burger or something."

"You eat burgers?" She was so not going to any club Jared was likely to attend. It would be some superhot dance club where he and his entourage would sit in a roped off VIP section and let the little people oohh and ahh over the celebrity in their midst. Yeah, she would be at Sanctum hopefully getting her ass beat on by some baby Dom. She desperately needed to find some subspace after the day she'd had.

He slapped his very likely rock hard abs. "I work out three hours a day. You better believe I eat a burger from time to time. Or some pasta. We could go and get some Italian. Maybe after we could have some cheesecake. I fucking love cheesecake."

So did she. And pasta. Her roommate had been on a total cleanse for the last week. Sarah was the one who did most of the cooking and lately she'd been all about salads. Kori's tummy rumbled. Maybe she should talk to him. Find out what he was really here for. Who was she to turn down a decadent and very likely free meal?

"Kori!"

She looked over and Kai was stomping out of the building, a frown on his handsome face. He seemed laser focused on one thing. Her.

"Oh no. Caught by big brother. Well, that answers one question I had. I haven't seen him that jealous since…well, I probably shouldn't get into that." Jared held both hands up as he backed away. "I wasn't touching, Kai. I was only talking to the girl. It was a perfectly polite thing to do."

She breathed a sigh of relief. Jared wasn't saying anything for the time being. "What did you need? I was about to head home. I dealt with the Erin situation. Tell Big Tag she's got an appointment with Dr. Bates in the morning."

Kai kept on coming. He managed to maneuver himself between her and Jared. "It's not even three. I have some notes I need you to type up."

"I can do that at home," she started. "E-mail them to me."

"No. I need you here with me." His hand closed around her arm in a surprisingly possessive manner.

She'd never seen Kai so off-center. He was always centered. Well, except for that time she'd left the window open and the bird had flown in and he'd screamed like a girl when it landed on his head. Apparently birds were nothing but disease infused rats with wings.

He was upset. Kai was the person who talked people down from being on the edge, and yet here he was.

Who talked Kai down? Who helped him and stood by him? So often the man seemed like an island. Lovely for everyone to visit but no one lived there. No one took care of the place.

She moved her hand down, lacing her fingers with his. For a moment she was worried he would reject the affection, but his fingers squeezed around hers and he moved his body closer. Like a big old caveman who didn't want the newer, younger caveman to take his cavewoman away.

What the hell was she supposed to do with that? Two years she'd been working for the man and he never gave her a second glance. Now Hottie McAction Star walked in and Kai was all over her.

She should have been offended. She should have thrown him her happy middle finger and driven home.

Instead, she nodded Jared's way. "I'll head on back to work now. You have a nice afternoon, Mr. Johns."

As Kai led her back in the building, she could have sworn she felt eyes on her. It was so odd, but someone was watching her. She glanced back and Jared was moving toward the limo.

Her imagination must be coming back online.

She shivered and followed Kai inside.

Chapter Three

Kai sat in the conference room and wondered where the hell he'd gone wrong. It was probably because he'd come back to the States. That was it. He'd made his mistake years before when he'd left the Army. He should have set up a practice in a more exotic locale. Somewhere no one could find him. Bora Bora, maybe. The wilds of Siberia would have been a perfect venue. Not a lot of veterans who needed therapy there but maybe he could counsel the bears or some shit.

And then his brother would get a fucking movie role that required him to star as a therapist to the bears and he would show up at Kai's cave and force his way in. Jared would show up and loom over his admin like some creepy fucking stalker guy and Kori would smile up at him like she was a teen at a boy band concert.

He would be damn lucky if she didn't quit on him since he'd behaved like an idiot.

She'd simply looked up at him as he tried to physically drag her away from Jared and suddenly her hand had been in his, gentling him and making him feel like so much less of a schmuck. She'd tangled their fingers together and walked back in the office with him, and when she'd tried to talk to him he'd run and slammed the door to his office and told her he'd see her tonight at Sanctum.

He was such an idiot.

"You look like a man who could use a drink," a feminine voice said as the chair next to him pivoted. Eve McKay set a cup in front of him as she slid into the chair beside him. The beautiful blonde smiled. "I got you a green tea while I was getting mine downstairs."

"Too bad it's not a bourbon." But that would be irresponsible, and everyone knew Kai Ferguson was the responsible one, the one who always was the voice of reason.

Eve's eyes widened slightly. "You never drink before going to Sanctum. Actually, you don't drink much at all. I think the most I've ever seen you drink is a beer."

Because he was the sober and serious one. He was also the one who didn't make Kori smile the way she had at Jared. She'd been frowning when he'd closed the door between them. "I was joking. It's been a long day and it's not over yet. Thank you so much for the tea. I can use it."

"I'm very interested in this case. Alex sent me the file earlier this afternoon. Now I understand why he's been so secretive about it," Eve said. It was no surprise to Kai that she'd been brought in. Eve McKay had been an FBI profiler for years before joining the private sector. Kai was interested in her take on the case and the potential killer. She had more experience in criminal psychology and profiling than he did.

"Why did he wait so long to bring you in? He's known about this case for a few weeks."

Eve sat back. "I think Alex is trying to do it all himself right now. He's been trying to take things off Ian's plate so Ian can focus on his family. I also think he was doing it out of respect for you. It's why we're bringing so few people into this. Alex wants to give you the chance to decide if you want to make the relationship public or not. I have to think there's a reason you never talk about your brother."

He could come up with a million. Unfortunately, he wasn't the only one who could out them as related. "My relationship with Jared is complicated, but I doubt I'll get out of this operation without it coming out in the open. I might keep my mouth shut, but

Jared won't. He's got some kind of agenda."

There was always drama with Jared. Whether it was his career or the collection of women who were always willing to fight over him, or himbos at the gym arguing over who had the best biceps, drama followed his brother wherever he went.

"What if his agenda is to have a closer relationship with you?" Eve asked, her voice soft.

He didn't even want to head into that territory. "How many other people know about Jared at this point?"

"Nice deflection," Eve murmured before continuing on. "Pretty much everyone at the club should know about our guest by now. Big Tag sent out an e-mail earlier today asking that everyone treat Jared like a regular club member and that the first person to drool, scream, or ask for an autograph will be shot. I'm hoping that was sarcasm. I can't tell these days. The film crew is going to shoot in Sanctum during times that the club is closed, but they're looking for extras. That particular e-mail went out about an hour ago. It didn't talk about Jared's relationship with you. I don't even think Charlotte knows about it yet."

So that explained how Kori hadn't known about the film crew. He was still mulling it over. She'd been shocked to see Jared standing there. Horrified actually was a better word.

Jared knew why and he wasn't talking unless he got what he wanted.

The door opened and the team selected for this op started to filter in. Big Tag held the door open as his wife, Charlotte, walked through, followed by FBI Special Agent Rush, Alex McKay, and Big Tag's brother Case Taggart. With the exception of the FBI agent who had contacted McKay a few weeks back, this particular op was a family affair.

Case was the only one of Big Tag's biological brothers still working with him. Ian had started McKay-Taggart with his brother Sean at his side. A few years later, younger half brothers Case and Theo had joined him after Sean had left to pursue the only slightly safer job of chef. With Theo gone, Case was Tag's last brother in the business. It wasn't so surprising he kept his baby brother close.

Case dropped into the chair across from Kai. "What can I do for Kori? Anything. I swear that girl needs a handy man, I'm her guy. She likes flowers, I'll fill her house up."

Ian chuckled as he took the seat at the head of the table. "He's happy Erin's going to the doctor. And he doesn't even have to go with her. He was willing to do that. You should have seen Erin's face when he offered to be her coach. You made her throw up again, dude."

"I think that was the baby. Any baby of Theo's is going to be trouble." Case's lips curled up and then he sobered as if remembering his brother was gone all over again. "Anyway, I'm grateful Kori's helping out. With Faith and Ten back in Africa for a couple of months, Erin needs a friend."

"Kori seems to know how to handle her." She'd definitely known how to handle him. By the time they'd gotten into the elevator, he'd been calmer. Her thumb had moved over his skin as she'd held his hand, soothing him and easing him back to normal.

It had been right there in his mind to ask her to pull up her skirt, pull down her panties, and bend over his desk. He'd needed to blow off some steam and reddening her sweet ass would have worked magic on his nerves. He would have started with his hand, slapping her cheeks until they were pink, and then he would get nasty. He kept a ruler in his desk, not because he normally needed to draw a straight line or answer some third grade measurement question. No. He kept one in his desk because he loved the way it sounded when it smacked against a sub's skin.

Instead, he'd locked the door between them and tried to find his calm through meditation. He'd sat in the middle of his office, trying to find that place of peace, and all he could see was Kori bound and gagged and ready for his pleasure.

In the war between peace and perversion, his freaky side had almost won this afternoon. He'd breathed a sigh of relief when she'd knocked on his door and told him she was going home.

"Well, I'm glad the pregnancy is out in the open," Charlotte said. "We can start making plans for how to support her through this."

"Or we can all huddle down and pray we survive Hurricane Erin," Big Tag shot back.

Charlotte shook her reddish blonde head. "You never know. Pregnancy could calm Erin. Sometimes it chills a woman out. Like it did for me."

He'd never actually seen Big Tag's jaw drop. "I don't even know what to say to that. Yeah, pregnancy made you so chill. Erin will probably turn into a happy fairy when she's got a baby bouncing on her bladder. I've found that makes all women happy. It's why I hid the guns during your last trimester. Enough baby talk. Let's introduce the new guy, for those of you who haven't met him. This is Special Agent Ethan Rush."

Rush was a big man in his mid-thirties. With dark hair and blue eyes, he looked like a businessman in his three-piece suit and expensive loafers, but according to Alex, the former football star took his job very seriously. He'd shown up on McKay-Taggart's doorstep with the working theory that Kai's brother was a serial killer. Which was utterly ridiculous. Jared was an asshole, but other than dipping his dick where it didn't belong, his brother wasn't dangerous.

Or had the years changed Jared? Should he really take a look at his brother? If he sat back and tried to think about the situation professionally, would he change his mind?

Fuck, no. Jared wasn't a killer. He wasn't capable of it. No way. No how.

"Thank you all for allowing me the access you have. I assure you the FBI is going to share any information we can on Hope McDonald," Rush said, passing out folders to the group. "We're working with Langley and a couple of foreign agencies to try to find her. She managed to get away with enough money that she can hide for a while, but I'm certain we'll find her. According to our profile, she has a deep need for credit, and I think that will eventually lead to her downfall."

That answered one question. Big Tag wouldn't put his club in danger if he wasn't desperate to find the woman he blamed for Theo's death. Hope McDonald hadn't pulled the trigger, but she'd been there and she'd backed her father. Finding Hope McDonald would likely lead to new information on the shadowy group known as The Collective. Big Tag would get his revenge. The feds would get information.

Quid pro quo.

Wasn't that what Jared was offering him? Information on Kori in exchange for Kai listening to him whine about how hard it was to be an international movie star?

Had Kori lied to him? How did she know Jared? She'd pretended she didn't know him at all, but Jared had known her name. Naturally Kai knew she'd lived in LA for years. Had she been one in a long line of women to grace his brother's bed? She was his type. It was a shame that he and Jared had always been attracted to the same women. They both liked them curvy and pretty and feminine and healthy.

Rather like this serial killer.

He forced himself to focus. This was serious business. "Have you filled in the rest of the group?"

"Mr. Taggart and Mr. McKay understand the situation, but I was asked to explain it to the rest of the group," Rush said, nodding toward Eve, Charlotte, and Case. "Approximately six months ago, an analyst came to me with a theory about a cluster of murders occurring over a three-year period of time."

"A serial working over long periods of time isn't unusual," Eve said. "I take it this killer is a drifter or someone who travels. Obviously, since this has something to do with the movie that's about to start filming here in Dallas, I would suspect you think the killer is involved in the film industry. They move around a lot if they're working on location."

Charlotte frowned, her eyes narrowing on her husband. "You didn't say anything about this to me. I thought you were allowing the film crew in because Serena asked you to."

Big Tag sat back. "I didn't tell you because you would have talked to Serena. I need you to understand that this has to look good. I know the club runs on gossip, but I can't have anyone talking about this. I love Serena like a sister, but she can't keep her mouth shut. You can. You kept it shut for five years when you could have called me and said, 'hey, I'm alive, baby.' I'm calling that in here and now and you know why."

Charlotte softened, her hand moving to cover his. "I do and I won't breathe a word. I promise. You know I want this to work as much as you do."

Kai looked over and saw Case's jaw tighten. There was an underlying current he didn't quite understand. Every line and expression on Case's face told Kai that he wanted to say something, but couldn't.

The question was why.

Charlotte looked back to Special Agent Rush. "All right, so you've been tracking a serial killer. What exactly makes you think he's involved with this particular film crew?"

It was Kai's turn to lean in. "He doesn't actually think it's a film crew member. If you'll look in the information folders, you'll see that there's only one true pattern. The murders have taken place over the course of three years. We have victims in Vancouver, Los Angeles, New Mexico, Australia, London, Croatia, and New York. Every single killing coincides with a film crew being in the city. More specifically, they coincide with a movie or television show starring Jared Johns being filmed in the area."

"The first victim we know of is a woman named Carrie Reynolds," Rush explained, his voice altogether too academic. He pressed a button that lowered the lights and started the slide presentation. A brown-haired woman was smiling on the screen. "She was a production assistant on the set of the TV series *Polly's Practice*. It filmed in and around LA."

Kai couldn't help but groan. It had been Jared's first big television role. He'd played a secondary character, an EMT who had a relationship with the much older psychologist, Polly. Kai had not watched that show. Nope. Even reading a single synopsis had made him want to pull his hair out. He would never watch a show where all the doctors slept together and with their patients and with the pizza delivery people and probably their dogs. Definitely not one where the lead slept with his brother. Though sometimes he caught Jared's various commercials for whatever he happened to be hawking that week.

"Is there confirmation that Johns knew her?" Charlotte asked. She looked up from the photos in the folder. "You know, Kai, this guy looks a lot like you. A little younger, more muscular version of you. And look at those dimples."

Naturally Charlotte picked up on that. "Not that much older, and I would have those muscles if I spent all my time in a gym and had a personal trainer on me twenty-four seven. Forgive me for having actual work to do."

Alex nodded Charlotte's way. "The actor in question's legal name is Jared John Ferguson. He's Kai's younger brother."

"Whoa," Charlotte said, leaning back. "I did not see that coming. I've watched that show religiously and I didn't see the resemblance until I was looking at a photo of him and sitting in the same room with you. Wow. You have a ridiculously attractive brother."

"So I've been told and yes, there's proof that Jared knew Carrie, though according to all reports, they were only coworkers." It was time to bring this back to the discussion at hand. "There's nothing that states he had a relationship with her that went past the set."

"Well, there were rumors afterward," Rush said. "I didn't put them in the packets because they can't be confirmed, but there was talk that she'd been seen coming out of Jared Johns's trailer late one night. However, she was the production assistant. They tend to do things like fetch and carry for the stars. We couldn't find any of her friends who would say she'd had a relationship with him. They did say she'd spent a lot of time on set and was seeing someone, but she wouldn't give them a name. She was a quiet girl and she seemed to keep mostly to herself. She was found in her apartment with multiple stab wounds. No sign of forced entry and no prints to be found."

"Did my brother have an alibi for the night of her murder?" He had to. It was ridiculous to think that Jared would stab someone.

"From what we can tell, he was out all night. He spent the night at a party at a friend's house. We've very quietly investigated this. The people at the party that night were wasted. They remember someone giving Carrie a ride home, but no one can remember who."

That was unhelpful, but then it reminded him of what Jared's life had always been like—a never-ending wave of parties he could barely remember and girls whose names he forgot. "Let's move on to the second victim. She was in London where Jared was filming some science fiction movie."

"Yeah, something about an alien princess and her warrior," Rush agreed. "Her name was Veronica Kath. She was not working on the actual production. She was a local who worked at a bakery. She delivered to the set every day for the course of the filming. She was found dead in her apartment two days after filming wrapped. Six stab wounds. Unfortunately, we didn't put her in as a victim until a few weeks ago. The police in London had an open case file, but it was marked as a homicide committed during a robbery. There was a rash of robberies in that part of London that spring."

"So we're not certain she was a victim of the killer we're pursuing," Eve said.

Rush shook his head. "The MO is the same and I think the killer is using the same knife. Our best guess is it's a jackknife. Not the best blade in the world, but when you're close enough it'll do the trick. The same types of wounds on each victim. Again, no fingerprints were left but there was a lot of chaos at this scene, which is what threw the police off. There was a struggle."

"Anything on CCTV?"

"It's a crowded part of London and there's no direct camera on her building, but we have a couple of males going past the building at the time who match Johns's height and general build. I do have confirmation that he stayed in England a week after filming ended. There's zero indication that he sent flowers, attended the service, or gave any indication that he knows the woman is dead. Or any of them."

"Do we have anything that links him to the victim?" Charlotte pointed to a picture of Jared in his *Dart* costume. "Because it's not a bunch of muffins. This man does not eat carbs."

Yep, there was a reason he didn't talk about his brother. "There's a picture of him talking to her. It was put on the film's social media site. They did outtakes every day and one of them was a shot of Jared leaning over and talking to a pretty brunette who turns out to be the victim."

"In each case, it's the same," Rush said with a frustrated sigh. "There are no firm links to Johns. There's rumors and innuendo, and most of the time the victim died and wasn't acknowledged at all by the crew because they were in the process of moving to the next set." He clicked through a series of photos, all of them smiling girls. "We have stories that Johns met Mila Maric at a Croatian nightclub he frequented while he was filming there. She was found in a back alley. Leslie Paul was a New York based actress who was an extra on Johns's last film. Her body was discovered in her apartment. I can go through them all but the information is included in your packets along with our profile of Johns."

Kai felt his jaw tighten at the mention of that profile. "Yes, I read it. Your profiler claims Jared could be killing in an attempt to punish his mother. She couldn't be more wrong. Jared loved our mother."

Rush's eyes came up, locking with his. "You're too close to the situation."

"I am a fully trained psychologist and I'm perfectly capable of divorcing myself from the situation long enough to seek out the truth. Jared is many things, but he's also the kid who brought home every stray he could—animals, people. He collected them."

"And the violence in his background?" Rush challenged.

"He was arrested twice for fighting when he was in high school. Both times the charges were dropped because it was self-defense. He hasn't been in legal trouble since."

Rush shrugged. "Perhaps because he has people around him who take care of the situation. Look, Ferguson, if I could have left you off this case I would have. I don't like bringing in family to situations like this, but it was the only way to get close to this guy."

"There's another way," Kai shot back. "You man up and bring him in for questioning. We can do it right now. I'll call him in and we can settle this without all the spy shit."

"But the spy shit is so much fun," Big Tag drawled. "And have you thought about what would happen to Jared's career if the feds brought him in for questioning? The tabloids would be all over him. His endorsement deals would dry up. He could be proven innocent, but that taint never goes away."

"Mr. Taggart is correct." Rush began shuffling through papers, straightening and organizing. "If we brought the suspect in for questioning, the press would be all over him and us. The last thing the FBI needs is bad press, so we're working this quietly. I like Johns for the killings, but he wasn't the only one at each site. He has an entourage and they go with him everywhere. Our in-house analyst has offered profiles of each of them. We'll be watching Johns and the rest of the team very carefully."

Charlotte whistled as she looked through the reports. "Wow. This could fill a book of bad behavior. The publicist has a drug problem. His agent's ex-wife accused him of assault and battery. Nice one. Why would anyone go by Squirrel?"

"He's like a puppy, always chasing after something new and shiny," Kai explained. He hated the fact that his life was spread out on a piece of paper like some fiction for everyone to read. It was Jared's file, but Kai had lived it, too. "Or at least he was as a kid. He struggled in school. The nickname stuck."

"He's got a nasty background," Eve murmured. "His father went to jail for beating his mother and he was left behind. It says here he spent some time in your home."

"He was one of the strays Jared brought home. He lived at our place for a while. I wouldn't be surprised if he's still living close to Jared."

"The trainer's been accused of selling steroids," Big Tag pointed out. "There's not a single one of these guys with clean hands. And I can tell from this picture that the assistant has crazy eyes. We should look into her. It's always the chick with the crazy eyes."

"Unfortunately, he's often right." Charlotte closed the file. "I'll very quietly look into these guys. I don't buy that it's Kai's brother for several reasons. He's too hot to be a killer."

"Yes, because a man's ability to do pull-ups while wearing three pounds of makeup means he couldn't possibly be a murderer," Big Tag shot back.

Charlotte's eyes sparkled in the low light of the conference room as she obviously baited her husband. "He's the real deal, Ian. He was on that Ninja warrior show as a celebrity guest and he got all the way through the course."

Watching Ian and Charlotte mix it up sometimes made Kai long for a partner he could spar with. Like he and Kori sometimes did. That woman didn't bother to temper herself around him any more than Ian did around his wife.

"Those aren't ninjas, baby," Ian replied. "Those are dudes who spend a lot of time in the gym. When they can do all that shit while someone's shooting at them, I'll call them special. When they can do all that shit while someone's shooting and be invisible and stab someone at the end, then I'll call them ninjas. Jared Johns is a meathead who trains fourteen hours a day so he can look pretty on a salmon ladder. I have no idea how he got cast as Pierce Craig. I finally sat down and read that book."

Everyone with the exception of Special Agent Rush seemed to go still.

Alex seemed to stifle a laugh. "And what did you think of Serena's hero?"

"You know what? I have no idea why the guys are so hard on her. Serena is a damn fine writer. This character has the douchiest name and sometimes he's a big old pussy, but he's got a good head on his shoulders. Everyone gets all over him, but the dude is doing what's best for his team. I read the whole series and I don't get why it took so long for readers to warm up to this guy. He's obviously the hero. Some of the books were better than others, but every time this guy steps on the page, the book lights up. I think she's got something with this character."

"Did he seem familiar at all?" Kai couldn't help but poke a little. "I'm only asking because you have so much in common. Pierce Craig runs a security agency. You run one."

Big Tag waved it off. "That's Serena writing what she knows. I get that. And there are a few similarities, although Pierce Craig was in Delta Force and I was a Green Beret. My only issue is he's practically a saint, but all the people around him are assholes. He's a very misunderstood guy."

"And not very self-aware," Charlotte concluded with a gleeful smile. "I think we should leave it at that. Like I said, I'll get someone looking into the entourage."

Rush shook his head. "Don't worry about that. We've got our best people on it."

"Your best people don't include my sister, and you have to follow all those inconvenient rules. We don't have to do that." Charlotte pushed her chair back. "I'll share whatever we find. I'm going to go and get ready since it looks like I'll be having a long talk with the subs tonight. While I have you here, Kai, did you spend any time with our mystery sub?"

Ah, this was one McKay-Taggart subplot he did know about. Roughly three weeks before, a woman named Mia Danvers had applied for a slot in the training class. She'd come highly recommended from an Austin club and had the money to pay for a full membership. The timing had been perfect as Big Tag was trying to find unattached subs and Doms. She also seemed to have the money and connections to forge her identification. Mia might not know it, but she'd been made the minute someone put her file in Adam Miles's capable hands. Someone had done a decent job of putting together her cover, but Adam, like Charlotte's sister, Chelsea, was phenomenal when it came to hacking personal data. He'd had a full write-up on the lovely blonde within two hours of getting her file.

"She's a reporter. Why is she still here? Is there a reason we haven't given her the boot?" Case asked. "Hell, I'd like to know why she was allowed into the class in the first place."

"Because I'm curious," Big Tag said. "She's a freelance reporter. What's she reporting on? According to Adam, she hasn't sent anything to an editor except a few opinion pieces that are unrelated to anything having to do with Sanctum. She doesn't typically write undercover pieces. For the last couple of years, she's mostly written about Austin business. Now she shows up in Dallas? She's asked a bunch of questions about McKay-Taggart."

"Not to mention the fact that Danvers isn't her birth name," Kai threw in. He'd figured this out a while back. He'd gone to Ian about Mia Danvers. It was precisely how her file had ended up with Adam. Nothing in her evaluations made him think she was violent, but he'd suspected she was hiding something. "Lawless. It's her brother who interests me. Apparently they've tried to hide their family ties. At least on paper. There are four siblings, but only one still uses the family name."

Rush was suddenly sitting up. "Lawless? Are you talking about Andrew Lawless? As in 4L Software?"

Ian nodded. "Yes, she's the sister of DrewLawless. Her other brothers are legally known as Riley and Brandon Lang. This family has done a lot to hide their connection and stay private. Adam said it took him a very long time to unravel all the paperwork and link them together. Riley and Brandon work for 4L, but as far as we can tell not even the employees there understand they're related to the boss. It's very suspicious. I want to know why a billionaire's sister is snooping around my club asking questions about my business."

"Because she's working for The Collective," Case shot back.

"It wouldn't be the first time that group sent in a reporter to gather information and cause chaos, or do you forget the London op from a few years back? Which is precisely why we should shove her out on her pretty ass."

Charlotte put a hand on her brother-in-law's shoulder. "Or we keep her close and watch her. She's here for a reason. Let's figure out what it is. If we toss her out, they'll likely send in someone else and then we'll have to start all over again."

"If she's Collective, I doubt she understands what she's involved in." Kai had spent time with Mia. While she was hiding her identity, he didn't buy that she was working to bring down McKay-Taggart. She was a woman he would bet would try to do the right things. "Read my profile on her, Case. She's the kind of woman who could be reckless if she thought it was for a good cause. I think she's actually in need of some protection herself."

Case shoved back and stood. "She's not getting it from me. She wants to come in here and try to take my family down? She has no idea. She can get her ass back to Austin. Her brother's billions mean nothing here."

Case stormed out, the door slamming behind him.

So that seemed like a firm "no" on reading Mia's file and giving her a fair shake. "Her story's more complex than he thinks."

Ian closed his file as well, standing and indicating that this particular meeting was over. "That whole family is fucked up, but it doesn't mean that her brother's not involved in The Collective. I go through what he did and maybe I'm not so picky about my business contacts either. Anyway, I'll talk to Case. I think he's our best bet when it comes to figuring out why she's here. She's shown zero interest in her training Dom. I think she wants a Taggart, and Case is the only one whose penis isn't tethered to a female. And Kai, I know this isn't easy for you. I appreciate everything you're doing."

"Enough to let me in on the secret? I'm not stupid. Something's happening here that you're not telling the rest of us." He could feel it. It was there in the way Ian's face went blank at certain moments, in how he and McKay whispered and shut up when anyone else walked in the room. It was something to do with this operation and why it was so important.

"Like I said. I'm grateful." Big Tag nodded and walked out.

And that was all he was going to get.

Rush and the rest of the team filed out, leaving Kai behind with Eve.

"I'm here if you want to talk, you know," she said as she gathered her things.

"I might take you up on that. Rush might be right and I'm too close to this to see it properly," Kai admitted. "I'm having a very difficult time believing my brother has anything to do with this. What I want to do is sit his ass down and ask him what the hell he's thinking traveling around the damn world with a serial killer. Women are falling down dead all around him and he's probably been too involved in some Xbox game to notice. That I can believe."

Eve straightened her suit. "Maybe that's what you do then. Look, no one knows your brother the way you do. In serials there are almost always signs from youth. I find it difficult to believe that you wouldn't have seen them. And kindness to strays—both animal and human—isn't usually a part of the serial killer makeup. Your brother's in trouble, Kai. It might be time to look at that relationship because if you don't do everything you can to help him, you'll regret it for the rest of your life."

This was what had kept him from finding any peace at all this afternoon. "It's easy for me to see that in an intellectual fashion, but I can't look at this academically."

"Which is why my door is open if you need to talk."

What he needed was a long night at Sanctum focused on a submissive. He could practically feel the pressure building.

What he was going to get was his brother in his face all night. He was going to be grumpy for freaking weeks.

He stepped out into the surprisingly quiet office. Grace wasn't at her desk. Normally someone was milling about even this late in the evening, but tonight the halls of McKay-Taggart seemed quiet.

He stepped toward the lobby doors when he heard Big Tag's voice. He was quiet, but Kai could hear him. From where the voice was coming from, it appeared that Ian was in the hallway that led back to the daycare. His girls would still be here, likely the last kids left along with Eve and Alex's son.

"I don't care what you have to do, Rush. I did not put my club and my people at risk on a whim." Ian's voice came out in a harsh grind. "My intel is solid, but I need your people."

Yes, this was the point when he should stride right out the door because he was a good man and good men didn't eavesdrop.

They could slow down though. Make sure they had everything. Had he left his cell phone in the conference room? He patted his pockets.

"I get that, Mr. Taggart. We're doing everything we possibly can, but you could be wrong about this," Rush replied.

No. He had his cell. He started to make his way toward the door.

"I'm not wrong. Find my brother."

Kai stopped, his hand on the door as he saw Ian stride down the hallway toward the daycare. Rush disappeared into one of the empty offices, likely the one he'd been given while he was working in Dallas.

Find my brother.

Kai walked to the elevator, his mind on Ian's words. Kai knew where his brother was, knew he was in trouble.

Find my brother.

The elevator doors opened and he walked inside. Eve was right. He had to at least try to figure out how deep Jared was involved in this mess. He pressed the button that would take him to the lobby.

It was only then that he realized what Ian hadn't said. He hadn't mentioned a body. He hadn't asked the special agent to help him in recovering his brother's body. The last time he'd talked to Ian about it, Ian had been certain Theo's body had been dumped in the Caribbean.

Find my brother.

That wasn't some verbal error on Ian's part. If he'd meant body, he would have said body. He hadn't and that meant something. It was what had been bothering Kai about this operation all along. Ian was private by nature, cautious by design when it came to his life, his friends and family. Big Tag wouldn't put his family at risk in order to find a body. He wouldn't open his club to a killer in some attempt to find closure.

There was only one reason Big Tag would risk everything. Kai thought about going upstairs and demanding answers, forcing his way into the inner circle.

Instead he walked to his car. If Ian wasn't saying anything he had his reasons and Kai needed to honor them. That man had done more for the people around him than they would ever know. Ian didn't need him to storm in. What he needed was for Kai to deal with his brother so Ian could find his own.

Theo was alive and that meant Kai couldn't fail.

Chapter Four

(MT)

"Oh. My. God. Is it true? Do you think it's actually true?" Sarah was practically vibrating as she stood in front of Kori's locker, folding the scrubs she'd been wearing. She'd worked the day shift at the hospital and driven straight from work. Normally they would have driven in together, but today Kori had been grateful for the privacy.

Kori had gone home after sitting at her desk for an hour. It had been nice to have the place to herself for a portion of the evening so she could sort through what had happened before coming here to Sanctum and throwing herself into the maelstrom again. She would likely have to watch Kai scene.

"What are you talking about?" She must have missed something because everyone was whispering and there was a definite vibe of excitement running through the room.

"The e-mail." Sarah's big eyes went wide. "Right before five, an e-mail from Big Tag came through about the fact that a movie is going to be shooting right here in Sanctum and Jared Johns is starring and he's going to be here tonight. Jared—the hottest guy in the world—Johns is going to be here in Sanctum tonight. Do you think that's real or is Big Tag fucking around with us?"

She wouldn't put it past Big Tag, but she happened to know this information was true. So Jared hadn't been talking about some dance club earlier in the day. Well, he was likely going to be surprised to see her here tonight. "I saw him earlier today. He was visiting Kai, who in a surprise twist turns out to be his brother."

Not that they were close. There was some serious tension between those two. She'd thought about it all afternoon, their relationship running through her mind like a script she was trying to write. There was the quiet, stalwart brother. Intelligent and serious. He was the hero of the story, but constantly eclipsed by his younger, flashier brother. Yes, she could work with those two. As they fought whatever the story would throw at them, they would also fight each other, trying to sort through a myriad of issues that would lead to their eventual reconciliation.

Sarah stood there staring at her. "Are you freaking kidding me? You work with Jared Johns's brother and it never crossed your mind to mention that tidbit to your bestie?"

She'd met Sarah at Sanctum and they'd become fast friends. When Sarah had needed a place to stay after her divorce, Kori had offered her a room in her cozy ranch house. Sarah was exactly what she needed in her life. Fun and energetic, she pulled Kori out into the world.

Kori gently closed her locker door. "I didn't have any idea. I thought Kai was an only child. He's mentioned his mother a couple of times, but never a brother, and it's not like he's got a bunch of pictures in his office. Even when I used to go in and water his plants at his old place, there weren't any mementos or photographs. I was shocked when I walked into his office and there was Jared Johns standing there talking to him. As for the rest of it, I don't know much except what I looked up on the Internet after finding out about Kai's Hollywood connections. Apparently a major studio is doubling down on the *Fifty Shades* trend and they're filming Serena's book *Love After Death*. Jared Johns is starring. He's going to be training here for a few weeks and then there's six weeks principal photography in and around Dallas. So you'll be able to drool all over him for a while."

She'd pulled up some of the more accurate entertainment sites and gotten the info on the production company while Kai sat in his office doing yoga or some shit. It was obvious to her that he'd been totally thrown off his game by the appearance of his brother and that meant either meditating—which seemed like complete BS to Kori—or he was doing the downward pug or something. It was all part of the super serene Kai method of dealing with stress.

Now it was time to get some stress relief of her own. If she could find a Dom to play with.

What would Kai be doing tonight? Who would Kai be doing tonight?

Damn that was starting to hurt.

Sarah leaned in. "Hey, are you all right? Does this film thing bring back bad memories or something?"

Sarah was the only one who knew what she'd done before coming to Dallas. Well, Big Tag likely knew because of Sully, but she was certain no one else did.

"It's all right. I looked into the production company. It's fairly new. I don't know any of the power players and that's a good thing." She hadn't mentioned that she'd met Jared a couple of times. It was so long ago and they hadn't truly been friends, so she didn't feel bad about it. She wasn't sure why Jared even remembered her name. "My main issue is Kai getting his panties all up in a wad. He and his brother don't get along."

"What did Jared do?" Sarah had gotten to know Kai.

Kori hid a smile. It was good to know her boss was well thought of. "Apparently he slept with Kai's fiancée."

"Bastard." Sarah leaned against the locker. "Damn it. Now I can't like him and that sucks because I was totally planning on sleeping with him."

Kori had to give it to her friend. She was an optimist.

"Are we talking about Jared Johns?" Mia Danvers came around the block of lockers, a sparkle in her blue eyes. "Because I've heard they've put a salmon ladder and a whole bunch of free weights in a new scene space so he can work out before he films."

Kori had taken to the blonde. Despite her penchant for smiling way too much, Mia was kind of awesome. She seemed to tackle even the most mundane tasks with an enthusiasm most people reserved for going to Disney World. Mia always seemed to have a smile on her face, a helpful attitude. In the couple of weeks she'd been training at Sanctum, she'd become an integral part of the club.

Sarah sighed. "I will watch that but now I'm going to watch it under protest. His abs didn't cheat, did they? I'm choosing to believe his abs are pure of heart. And those notchy hip things that make women lose their minds. They're definitely innocent."

"You go for it." Kori stepped out and glanced at herself in the mirror. She'd accepted long ago that she wasn't the sleek and graceful type. Still, she looked pretty good in her corset and leather boy shorts.

"Charlotte Taggart is supposedly coming in here to give us a lecture on how to behave around the Hollywood types," Mia said, joining her at the mirror. "Do you think he's one of those actors who doesn't want people to look him in the eye or talk to him?"

Sarah smoothed her dark hair down. She was looking lovely in a red corset and a mini. "Who looks at his eyes? I can't get past that man's chest."

"He's cool." She seriously doubted he would walk in and make crazy demands. "If anyone tells you how to behave around him, it's probably coming from his creepy assistant chick. Apparently he's got an entourage, and one of them weighs five pounds and looks like she craps sadness. You won't be able to miss her. Well, unless she turns to the side and then you might be able to. But Jared himself seems cool."

"I can't believe that he's brothers with Kai," Mia said, leaning against the counter.

All around them the other ladies were getting ready for an evening at Sanctum. Dommes and subs chatted while they primped. There were a couple of distinct groups. There was the McKay-Taggart cluster. Those were the female employees or the wives of the male operatives. They tended to stick together, but they were always friendly, if a bit mysterious. There was the hardcore Sanctum group that consisted of the Paxon sisters, who had helped run the club for a few years. Jill's husband had been the Dom in residence before his company had taken off. They were joined by what seemed like a never-ending stream of Will Daley's sisters. They all were fun and sweet and came with L names that Kori got confused. And then there was her little group. She and Sarah and

Vince and now Mia.

Sometimes Kai joined them afterward. After they'd all finished playing, they would go out to an open-all-night diner and get waffles and try to come down from subspace. Except Kai, who had to come down from his superhot sadistic topspace. She'd had a fantasy about him taking her to the bathroom and twisting her nipples until her eyes teared up. He would dominate her fully. When they went to join the others, only the two of them would know that she could still feel the ache he'd given her.

Why was she fucking everything up? Kai wasn't into her and it wasn't going to happen, so why had it felt so damn good to hold his hand? Why had she sat outside his office door like a fucking golden retriever waiting for her Master?

"Can I hang with you guys tonight?" Mia asked. "My training Dom won't be here until midnight which means if I want to be out in the club, I have to be with a member who won't let me do stupid shit. Seriously, it's written into the contract."

"But doing stupid shit is so much fun," Sarah complained.

"Yes. Everyone knows I don't do stupid shit. You can hang with me." Sometimes Kori had to step up and be the mom of the group. Like the time Vince thought it would be fun to let the new Domme put a nail through his ball sac. Yeah, she'd gotten in trouble over that one, but that particular Domme also got kicked out since she was using rusty nails. A masochist had to be sensible.

Kai would be careful. He would always take care of his sub, always ensure that whatever pain he gave her was safe and completely consensual. A masochist could let go with a man like Kai.

And lose herself all over again to a man who didn't really want her.

"I'll go grab us some seats for the talk," Mia promised with a wink.

"Hey, are you all right?" Sarah asked, her voice going low.

"I'm fine. Why?"

"Because your shoulders aren't usually located around your ear lobes. So either that corset is way too tight or you are stressed out. Is it Kai?"

Sarah saw way too much. "We had a moment today. That's

all."

"You two have a lot of moments. You're practically an old married couple, complete with never having sex. You're both too stubborn to see it."

Just because they knew each other's habits didn't make them an old married couple. "We work together. We can't play together."

Sarah's dark eyes rolled. "Why?"

"Because we're professionals."

"No one is more professional than nurses and doctors and we fuck like bunnies when we think no one is watching because life is way too short. Well, I don't fuck like a bunny because none of the doctors do it for me, but everyone else is doing it like they're on *Grey's Anatomy*. The girl who created that show must have worked in a hospital because she knows what's going on."

"Kai and I are different." Mostly because she was way too scared to jump into the deep end of the pool again and Kai wasn't attracted to her. But they were also way more professional. Kai would never fuck like a bunny. He would be in control. Always.

Had he fucked his fiancée like a bunny? Had he loved her so much he couldn't wait to have her?

"How are you different? With the exception of the fact that you're both lonely. You both come into this club week after week and neither one of you has connected with anyone."

That was patently untrue. "I play all the time."

"And you've had sex with how many of the Doms you play with?" Sarah asked.

"One and it was awful and I'm not interested." She'd had a brief involvement with a lawyer and the whole time she'd thought about Kai, so now everyone she played with knew they wouldn't be getting any at the end of the night from her. She'd been surprised at how many of the Doms seemed relieved that she was so upfront. Some of them simply wanted to play, too.

"Everyone is interested in sex. We're biologically wired that way, so I think if you're not having fun and playing the field it's because you're hung up on a guy. Since you spend all your time with Kai and Vince, and Vince is a lovely nut job, I have to think it's Kai." Sarah's eyes narrowed. "Unless you really like nut jobs."

Vince was a sweetie, but she could never be with another sub.

That boy needed a firm hand in and out of the bedroom. "I don't and you know it. Look, things got all messy today, and you know how I hate messy. Let's go out and play and forget about all this crap. We can watch Jared from afar. I'm sure he'll have twelve subs on him the minute he walks onto the dungeon floor."

They would be all over Kai, too, because she was certain Jared would try to hang with his brother. Groupies. They would be everywhere and Kai would likely have his pick. They would put their hands all over him and rub up against him.

"That's your murder face." Sarah nodded at her in the mirror.

"I do not have a murder face." Although she did look fairly unhappy. When had she gotten that crease between her brows? She tried to rub it away. Relax. She needed to relax.

"You totally have a murder face and that's it, but I'm letting it go for now. I reserve the right to come back to this topic of conversation later. I will do as you ask because I don't want that murder face to be the last thing some innocent person sees before they die. I'll be waiting with Mia." Sarah turned and flounced away. "By the way, orgasms make people less violent."

Kori stared in the mirror. She didn't look all murdery. Maybe a little unhappy, but not psycho killer. And it wasn't like she hadn't had an orgasm. She had a very nice battery operated boyfriend who required nothing from her but the occasional new double As. They certainly didn't require her submission and her trust and her flipping soul the way a good Dom would. Not that she'd known a good Dom. She knew them, of course. Sanctum was full of them, but she didn't *know* them in a biblical sense. Of course the only one she wanted in a biblical sense was Kai, and she didn't really want him that way. She was programmed to want him. They fit. Sadist meet Masochist. He was chocolate and she was peanut butter. They could be perfectly fine on their own but together they made something magical.

And produced unnecessary calories and cavities.

That was what she would remember when she looked across the crowded dungeon and caught a glimpse of him with his superhot brother and whatever gorgeous things they attracted. She would remember that she was peanut butter and didn't require chocolate to be awesome.

"Hey, Charlotte's got me rounding everyone up. She's giving them all the 'don't drool on the Hollywood star because it makes the other Doms feel bad' lecture." Serena Dean-Miles was not dressed for play. She was in a pair of yoga pants and a T-shirt, her brownish blonde hair swept back in a ponytail. "I wanted to catch you first. How is Kai? You have to know I didn't have any idea they were related. I also didn't have a lot to do with the casting."

She needed Serena to understand something. "The absolute smartest thing you can do is to take whatever money they're offering you and run. Don't look back. Films tend to wreck books for the most part. The smart author giggles all the way to the bank and leaves the agony for the screenwriter."

Serena went pale. "I am the screenwriter."

Oh, that poor girl. Kori nodded. "Then forget everything I said and know that you are the best person for this job and it's going to be so much fun. No one knows your characters better than you do." Or was as close to them and reluctant to cut out the parts that needed to be cut because no film could do a four hundred and forty-nine page book in an hour and a half. "You're going to be great."

Tears shone in Serena's eyes. "It's horrible. It's so awful. I thought I would come down here and maybe sitting in the locker room would bring on some inspiration, but I have no idea what I'm doing. We're supposed to start filming in a couple of weeks and I've got a bloated script and the director hates it, and if I don't fix it he's going to bring in a screenwriter whose last project was something about cars turning into aliens that eat the planet."

Yeah, that sounded like a lot of Hollywood types. For some producers, screenwriters were easily replaceable. They wouldn't think past their bottom line on a production. Oh, there were some great producers out there who understood the need to find the right screenwriter for every story, but many had their pet writers and didn't care that the man was likely some twenty-something who knew nothing about the lifestyle and cared very little about the nuances of romance. It was why Kori preferred her romances in novel form. The impulse to help Serena nearly overwhelmed her. She'd always wanted to try a romance. She'd mostly written horror and supernatural thrillers with strong female leads, but she loved Serena's books. She could do them justice on the screen. She could find that delicate balance between the story and the characters that was required for a film.

"I could read it for you." She couldn't come out and tell Serena the truth. Too many questions. She could help though.

Serena took a long breath. "I would love that. I'll e-mail you a copy. You've been in the lifestyle for a long time. I would love your opinion. I think I'm trying to explain the lifestyle too much."

And that was a mistake. "The lifestyle is in the story. Worry about that and not making sure the viewer understands every bit of protocol. I'll let you know what I think, but I'm sure it's fabulous. And Kai is all right. Well, he's grumpy but it's kind of cute on him."

"Hopefully it's not too much of an imposition." Serena put a smile on her face, but it was easy to see she was frustrated. "Watch out for him. I know sometimes family can be difficult, to say the least. I'm glad Adam and his brother are in a good place. I wish I could say the same for Jake. I don't think he'll ever be close to his biological family again. I think in the end we make our own families."

And Kai was like her brother. Yeah. Her non-blood between them, really wished he would slap her ass hard brother. There wasn't anything weird about that. She gave Serena a big hug. That was one of the gifts Sarah had given her. She'd never been a hugger. When she'd come to Sanctum, there had been a bitch of a sub who loved to screw with everyone. Sarah had joined and Maia had told her Kori loved to be hugged.

She hadn't been quite able to shove the girl away, and over the years she'd not only gotten used to random acts of affection from her friends, she'd come to crave them.

Another gift from Sanctum.

"It's going to be awesome, Serena. You're going to be awesome."

Serena squeezed her tight. "Thank you. I needed that."

And that was a gift from Kai. She'd watched him help people for years and one of the things she'd learned was sometimes people needed to hear that they could do a thing before they believed it themselves. It was all good and great to be able to look in the mirror and be confident without outside voices, but sometimes it was also good to hear that people were behind you.

Withholding that affection had been the norm where she'd come from. It felt so good to let it flow now.

Like that moment when she'd wrapped her fingers around Kai's hand and she'd felt him sigh in relief. He'd needed her and that had been a revelation.

She watched Serena walk away, likely back to the lounge section of the locker room where she and Avery O'Donnell kept a couple of comfy chairs. Serena would sit with her computer in her lap and type away.

And she would watch Kai with his brother and wish for that moment when he needed her again.

She quietly joined the others as Charlotte Taggart began her talk.

Twenty minutes later, she stepped out of the locker room to the sound of thudding industrial music. The sound soothed her, familiar and comforting. She looked around but Sanctum was still Sanctum. There might be a few extra people in the club, but it looked exactly the same otherwise. Somehow she'd worried she would step out and find the dungeon had changed.

"Did Lady Taggart give you the speech on respecting famous people because they sometimes have small penises and that means they want to be left alone?" Vince hurried up to where she and Sarah and Mia stood. A broad grin was on his face. "Because that was pretty much how Lord Taggart put it. He also said something about the first sub who screamed or fainted at the sight of some douchebag actor in a pair of leathers would spend the next month lighting the hamster wheel up. And the awesome part was Jared Johns was actually in the locker room when he said it. I love Master Ian. I think I would go gay for him if he had a vagina."

"If he had a vagina you wouldn't be gay," Sarah pointed out. "And Charlotte talked a whole bunch about how men can be sexually harassed, too, but I was mostly thinking about how hot his character on *Dart* is. Do you think he can really kill two men with one dart?"

"I don't understand why he doesn't pick up a gun," Mia said

with a shake of her head as she looked out over the dungeon. "That would be way easier than darts."

"It's a metaphor," Kori muttered. Everyone was a critic. "And it was also a comic book at one point. Those fan boys and girls can get vicious when they think the source material isn't being respected. Who's here tonight?"

She needed a single Dom, or one of the marrieds whose wife didn't mind celibate play.

"A bunch of the MT group is out of town. Simon and Jesse are in California and Liam O'Donnell is on vacation in the Caribbean somewhere," Vince explained.

"Doesn't that strike you as weird?" Mia asked. "I would think it would be too soon."

"Too soon after what?" Sarah asked.

"Too soon after they lost a teammate in that part of the world," Mia whispered. "It seems odd that Theo Taggart died there and now Liam O'Donnell is taking his wife and kid for a vacay."

"The Caribbean is a big place," Sarah replied. "I'm sure it's not the same island."

"And I heard they weren't in the Caribbean." She'd overheard Liam talking to Kai about the upcoming trip. "I think they're going to South America. Argentina, maybe. They probably changed plans at the last minute because it's definitely too soon."

Everyone missed Theo. His absence was a giant hole that no one was going to be able to fill. Theo's death had led to Erin's absence at the club and many of the MT group taking time off.

She missed them. Even when they were here now it was easy to see they were still grieving.

"I was looking for you, pretty girl. Might I say you're looking lovely tonight," a deep voice said.

She turned and there was Jared. Someone had Dommed that boy up. He was wearing a pair of leathers that somehow sat perfectly on his hips so they showed off those honed notches. And his six-pack was really more of an eight-pack. A black leather vest framed his torso, showing off cut biceps and broad shoulders. He had the most gorgeous scruff.

The man was stunning and he still had nothing on Kai. Kai didn't have a trainer with him twenty-four seven and no one followed around after him making sure his scruff didn't turn into a beard and his hair was always the perfect length. Kai's hair often got too long. He would get involved with his patients and writing academic papers and he would forget things like grooming, and Kori had to make sure he got to the barber. Sometimes she cut it herself because he didn't want to take the time.

"Hey, when you mentioned you were going to a club, I kind of thought it would be a nightclub." He could have been clearer on that.

He shrugged, a boyish mischief lighting his eyes. "I wanted to surprise you. I will admit that I knew you were a member. I also know you don't have a Dom. I guess I was hoping you would show me around."

Sarah leaned over, whispering in her ear. "I am fairly certain my ovaries just spit out an egg."

Kori sighed. "Jared, this is my friend Sarah, and this is Mia and Vince. Guys, this is Jared, who is a regular human being who likely doesn't want to be drooled on."

His high-voltage smile ticked up a notch as he held out a hand to Sarah. "Hey, I never say never. Hello, Sarah."

He shook hands with them each in turn, but Kori was almost certain he'd held Sarah's the tiniest bit longer than the rest. When he was done, he nodded to the men standing behind him. Yeah, she hadn't noticed them. Two were dressed in casual clothes and the other, a shorter, thinner man, looked a little uncomfortable in his leathers. "These are my friends, Squirrel, Tad and Brad."

Dear god, it was the cast of *Entourage*. They'd gotten that show right. "Let me guess, Squirrel is the childhood friend who now keeps you company. Tad has that publicist vibe about him and Brad is the decathlete turned trainer to the stars."

Brad frowned. "Triathlete. I did the Ironman in eight twenty."

Vince's eyes went wide. "He did Ironman? I kind of thought that dude was straight."

Jared laughed, his whole face lighting up. "He's talking about a triathlon, not Robert Downey Jr. And Kori is spot on. Tad is my PR guy and Squirrel and I have been best friends since third grade. He travels with me. Keeps me grounded."

"And out of trouble," the soft-spoken Squirrel said. "He needs

From Sanctum with Love

someone to play Xbox with or he tends to get grumpy."

"No Lena today?" She and Bolt seemed to be the only two missing.

"I asked her to stay at the hotel. I'm afraid this is not her scene." Jared looked out over the dungeon floor in a way that made Kori think it *was* his scene.

He seemed awfully comfy in those leathers.

"She threw a hissy fit about all of this being abusive and how Jared needs to focus on real films," Squirrel replied. "I swear she can hit a tone with her voice that makes my brain bleed."

"Don't listen to that crazy bitch," Tad said. "This movie's going to make millions. Women go for this shit."

Jared's eyes turned stony. "How about we don't call it shit? Why don't you and Brad go hang out in the bar? Or if you're uncomfortable, feel free to head back to the hotel. I'm going to be spending a lot of time here and I don't need anyone getting in the way of connecting with this character."

"I'll hang out." Brad glanced around. "It looks interesting."

"And I need to think about how we can spin this." Tad pulled out his phone and started scrolling through as he walked toward the bar.

Squirrel sighed. "I'll go make sure they don't horrifically embarrass us."

Jared put a hand on Squirrel's shoulder. "Thank you, buddy. Explain to him if he takes any video or pictures in this place, that former military men will likely visit him in the middle of the night and it won't be to party." He looked back at the group as his friends walked away. "Do you mind if I steal Kori for a minute?"

"As long as you bring her back eventually," Sarah said with a laugh. "Soon."

Mia was watching Jared, her eyes serious. "We know where she is and who she's with. That's important, you know. You have to know that you have people looking out for you."

"Yeah, that is good to know. I'll catch up to you guys, and seriously, don't let Mia do stupid things." When the hell had Mia gotten all serious and mother henny? She stepped away and found herself walking beside Jared. "What can I do for you?"

"I can think of a whole lot you could do, but I'm trying to make

89

things right with my brother so I'll go with show me around." He held out an arm as though offering to escort her like she was a lady at a ball.

It would be rude, she supposed, to tell him she was perfectly capable of walking on her own. She'd been told by Charlotte that all subs were to be polite. Damn it. She glanced around. Where the hell was Kai? "I suspect you've already been here. Are you trying to tell me this is the first time you've been inside Sanctum?"

"You've got me there." He stopped in front of the steps that led up to the main level. "I did a walk-through with the guy who runs the place, but he was very academic about everything. I want to see it all through the eyes of someone who loves it here. How long have you been a member?"

"Shouldn't you be doing all of this with Kai?"

"He kind of ditched me," Jared admitted. "I got held up in the locker room and he was gone when I came out. Not sure where. I think he thinks if I can't find him he doesn't have to talk to me, but I can be patient. This is one of the nicest clubs I've ever been to. I like it here."

She had to stop and stare at him for a moment. "Are you trying to tell me you've been to a BDSM club before?"

"Many. I've found the owners and members of BDSM clubs are way more into protecting my privacy than any other place I could relax. Also, most other places I would relax at frown on me spanking the girl of my choice. Sometimes the boy. I don't discriminate."

"You're bi?"

"No, I'm a Dom and if a male sub asks for discipline, I'll hand it out. I make it very easy. I don't have sex with anyone I'm topping in a club. That's not to say I don't have sex. I'm over the idea of casual sex, that's all."

"I thought you had a girlfriend. I know you said it was a professional relationship, but I thought it involved sex."

"Not at all. Jessica is one of the most beautiful women in the world, and her sexual habits would get her in trouble. I hesitate to involve any woman I'm really attracted to in my insane life, so it works out and keeps the press off our backs. We do red carpets together and a couple of times a year, we go to Mexico and let the paparazzi photograph us holding hands, and then we go back to the hotel and watch movies and drink beer. Every now and then she'll break down and have a cheeseburger and we have to deal with pregnancy rumors, but otherwise, we handle things." He frowned as though realizing he'd said too much. "I shouldn't have told you that. Kori…"

She held a hand up. "I would never tell. I know how hard that life can be. You don't have to worry about me gossiping. I never worked with her, but I hear she's a nice lady."

"Thank you. I forget when I'm in a situation like this. A place like this. It can feel safe. I have to remind myself that I'm not here to play. I'm here to work and that means putting the mask on. Shall we?" He nodded at the stairs.

"Of course." She let him lead her up to the second level of the club. "How did you get involved in the lifestyle?"

"I wanted to feel close to my brother. That sounds pathetic, but it's true. I've spent my whole life following Kai around and trying desperately to get his attention. Thirty something years in and nothing has changed. He's still the man I want to be proud of me. Anyway, he was into this lifestyle so I looked into it. I enjoyed it on a physical level for a long time. It wasn't until I hit the big time that I realized what a sanctuary it could be for me. Your turn."

She hesitated. Talking about how she'd gotten into the lifestyle meant dredging up all those old memories.

"Hey, sorry," Jared said with a grimace. "It's got something to do with why you left the business, doesn't it?"

She nodded.

"Then tell me about Sanctum. Tell me how it's different."

He was oddly easy to talk to, but then he reminded her more of Kai now. She could see it in the way they both smiled, in the set of their shoulders. But mostly it was in the way he put her at ease. "I guess if I had to break it down it would be the people. Don't get me wrong. This is absolutely the swankiest club I've ever been in. Most of them are industrial spaces or renovated homes. After the first Sanctum blew up, Big Tag went all out on this one."

Jared stopped. "It blew up? I hadn't heard that. Was it a gas leak?"

"Oh, no. It was a brainwashed asshole. Kai was pissed because he was living over the club at the time. I like our new building. We've got a lot more room."

Jared shook his head. "I thought he was expanding when he bought that building. I didn't realize it was because his office had blown up. Thank god he wasn't there at the time."

"Oh, he was there. He ended up getting nearly buried with Big Tag and this CIA agent, and he was pissy for days about his back being sore. I finally managed to get him to go see a massage therapist because when that man is grumpy he takes it all out on me." She was warming up to her subject. "I think it's because of the whole therapist thing. He can't exactly take it out on his patients. He has to look all calm and stuff and like he knows what he's doing at all times. It makes him cranky, and who does he turn to? Naturally it's me."

Jared had stopped, his expression turning blank.

"He's all right. It wasn't that big a deal." It had been a huge deal, but it was over.

"He didn't call me. He almost died and he didn't fucking call me. Would anyone have called me?"

"I've got a package set up with Ian in case I die or am incapacitated," a familiar voice said. "Your number is there. He would have called you."

She turned and Kai was standing there. She would never get over how different he looked. By day Kai was the deliciously attractive academic in his slacks and button-down, his golden hair tied back and his glasses on his face. He put in contacts for the dungeon and let his hair down. It flowed around his shoulders. It should have made him more feminine, but somehow all that gorgeous hair turned him into a decadent, dominant creature. The leathers showcased the lean body he hid behind khakis and Oxfords. He turned primal and so male.

Yeah, she'd probably spit out an egg, too. There was a lot of that going around tonight.

"And it wasn't a big deal. Like Kori said. The place went boom and then Big Tag started complaining about potential dust on his freaking lemon pie. I barely had a scratch on me." Kai moved over, standing beside her. "I did lose several plants I'd been nurturing and some very good textbooks. I still think if I'd been Ace's therapist, we could have worked through the issues that turned him into a brainwashed asshole, as my assistant explained. You'll have to forgive Kori. She's very technical when it comes to the work we do."

Jared relaxed slightly. "I thought you ditched me."

"You said you were interested in watching an impact play scene or a ropes one. I was busy setting it up. I think I can handle both in one scene," Kai explained.

He'd been busy finding a sub. She wondered who he'd found. There were some truly gorgeous women running around Sanctum wearing very little clothing. Maybe he'd chosen Lisa Daley. She was lovely and slender and not in the Lena, I-trade-food-for-nicotine way. Lisa was naturally thin, her body lovely and graceful. She would be beautiful wrapped in Kai's ropes.

"That sounds like fun. I've got to start getting comfortable with this kind of stuff if I'm going to play Pierce Craig." Jared moved to her other side. "I'm sure I'll have a million questions."

So he obviously didn't want his brother to know he'd been in the lifestyle for a while. Why tell her? Was he testing her? She decided to give him the benefit of the doubt. Kai didn't seem interested in spending time with Jared except to teach him about the role he was supposed to play. If he didn't need to teach Jared, he likely wouldn't talk to him. For all that glorious masculine himbo vibe he gave off, Jared knew how to get to his big brother. Kai was always serious about teaching. "Well, the good news is Kai loves to talk. He's a fount of knowledge."

How soon could she get away? She felt ungainly standing between these two gorgeous, ridiculously tall men. Did they have to be so freaking tall? She barely came up to Kai's chin. She would fit neatly against him, her head easily resting on his broad shoulder. She barely made it to Jared's collarbone. Maybe she should rethink wearing stilettos. Of course, then she would do that horrible ankle rolling walk chicks who never wore heels inevitably ended up doing when they finally put a pair on.

"I set up the scene in the back of the dungeon," Kai was explaining. "I thought we'd try to be discreet. I know Big Tag gave everyone the speech, but I'm sure there will still be gawkers. We should go ahead and start moving that way. You can watch and then

I'll walk you through a scene yourself."

Jared smiled down at her. "What do you say, pretty girl? You want to watch the scene with me? Maybe after Kai's done, you can be my test subject."

She tried not to watch Kai scene. In the beginning she had, and she would watch utterly fascinated with how hot the man was when he got his freak flag flying high, but lately it made her want to be the woman he was lavishing all that pain and pleasure on.

Lately she'd started dreaming about being the woman he tied up.

It would be easy to ask him. She doubted if she was open with what she needed that he would turn her down. In that case, he was a lot like his brother. If someone came to Kai and explained that they needed a scene in order to cry or relax, he would give the sub what he or she needed. The trouble was she wasn't sure she could hold back with Kai. The minute he put his hands on her, she was worried she would dissolve and go back to her old habits, needs she hadn't fed for years. It was easy to shove them down normally, but Kai moved her.

She was about to tell Jared that she needed to go find her friends when she felt a firm hand on her elbow, pulling her close.

"She can't watch the scene. She's in the scene," Kai said. "You'll have to find your own sub, Jared. This one is mine."

Kori felt her jaw drop. Yes, it was going to be an interesting evening.

* * * *

What the hell had he done? It wasn't like he'd planned for that to happen. No, he'd planned something else entirely. He'd set up his scene and walked off to find a sub and he'd found Jared and Kori instead. He'd just walked up to his brother and heard the sorrow in his voice and it had thrown him off.

Jared was a better actor than Kai had given him credit for.

Or he'd been really upset to find out Kai had nearly died and no one had contacted him. Kai felt like a total dick. He hadn't even thought about calling his brother. The first person he'd wanted to talk to was Kori. She was always the first person he called.

Then Jared had moved in on Kori like he had a right to touch her and Kai had lost his damn mind.

"What are you doing?" Kori asked the minute Jared stepped away.

Yes, that was the question of the hour. He shrugged, trying to make it look like this was no big deal. "I need a sub. Do you have a play partner for the evening?"

He'd been intending to ask Charlotte to find him a sub. He didn't even want to make the decision. He'd known going into tonight that this was an academic exercise. He wasn't going to get what he needed tonight. Another issue he could lay at his brother's doorstep. He certainly wasn't going to relax knowing his brother was watching him. Judging him. So he simply needed a sub who wouldn't mind taking a spanking and answering some questions about it.

Maybe one of the training subs.

That wouldn't work now because he'd seen the way baby brother looked at Kori, like he could eat her up, and his inner caveman had started grunting and dragging his knuckles on the floor.

"I don't have a partner," she replied, her blue eyes wide. "I haven't had time to find a partner because the minute I walked out into the club your brother found me."

"Well, then you're free to bottom for me." Found her? Yeah, Kai bet Jared had run from the locker room looking for Kori. She was exactly Jared's type. Curvy, pretty, round breasts and an ass he could grab and hold on to.

He turned to the prep table. He didn't need to look it over. He'd prepped it himself. He'd used the time to psych himself up to not murder his brother's friends. It was so obvious to him that they were hanging on Jared like parasites, and his brother didn't see it. He never saw things like that and when Kai tried to point it out to him he got called out for being pessimistic or dragging everyone down.

He'd show Jared dragging someone down. Little asshole didn't know what the phrase meant.

"Kai, I don't think this is a good idea."

He was definitely losing his mind because Kori's soft words made him angry. It was irrational. He knew it even as the questions floated through his head. Did she think it wasn't a good idea because she wanted Jared? Had she gotten a good look at the man she'd known at some point and realized she wanted him? Had she already had him and now Jared was back and she wouldn't even look at another man?

Irrational. Emotional. Out of control. He hated it.

"Hey." A soft hand moved over his bicep. "I was only saying that because we've never played before. We've always kept a certain distance between us."

Had they? Maybe a physical distance, but now that he thought about it she was the person in the world he talked to the most, relied on more than any other. He fixed breakfast for her because she would eat crap if he didn't. She would show up before work and they would sit together and have a nice breakfast and coffee and talk about what they would do for the day.

He missed her on the weekends. He would sit alone and wonder what she was doing, who was taking care of her.

Why hadn't he played with her? He could tell himself all day long that it was about being a professional, but it was wrong. He knew the truth now.

He was afraid of losing her.

What if she was afraid of him? What if she couldn't handle what he needed? What if they played and she hated it?

He knew she played with other Doms and he also knew she didn't have sex with them. He knew she'd asked some of her Doms to go easy on her.

He went hard.

"I won't hurt you." He would hold back. He wouldn't give her a reason to fear him more than she did. "It's for Jared's education. I'll go easy and we'll use the stoplight system."

Green meant keep going. Yellow meant the sub needed the Dom to slow down, and red put a stop to the play.

He didn't intend to get her to say red. He could control himself.

Her hand moved over him, stroking him. Somehow he could feel her warmth seeping from her skin to his. "Are you all right? Do you think he's here to hurt you again? He told me he slept with your fiancée. Kai, I'm not going to sleep with Jared. I'm not going to walk away from my job to be some Hollywood type's girl on call for a few weeks. That's the furthest thing from my mind, so if you want me to go and find a sub for you, I will. Mia's in the lounge. She's in the training program so this would be like extra credit for her."

She was giving him an out. An easy out at that. She'd seen right through him, gotten to the heart of the issue, and was now allowing him a free pass. He could go firmly into teaching mode and that would help defuse the situation and nothing would change between them.

"I would rather use you unless you're afraid of me." The words were out of his mouth before he could think to keep the damn thing shut. His inner caveman was super talkative and made bad choices. Well, maybe not bad exactly but certainly not the most expedient decisions.

He waited for her to explain all the ways he frightened her. Since she'd come to Sanctum, she'd played around in what Kai liked to call the shallow end of the pool. She stuck to Doms with a light touch, the friendly ones who winked and never brought their subs to tears. She seemed drawn to suspension play and loved rope bondage, but any impact play he'd seen her participate in had been restrained, light. So she would tell him to go pound sand and they would go back to their nice, safe, comfortable relationship.

Kori's eyes flared. "Afraid? Of you? Do you honestly believe that?"

Maybe she didn't understand what he was talking about. "Scared of my sadistic side. I can be rough on a sub. I would keep this scene very restrained. I would respect your limits and try very hard not to hurt you. This isn't about my needs. It's about teaching Jared, so you're safe."

Her arms crossed over those round breasts of hers. In her corset they were shoved up and on display, as though she was presenting them to him. He knew it wasn't true, but it looked like if she took a deep breath her nipples might pop out. They would be right there begging him to twist them and turn them a pretty red color before he would soothe them with his lips and tongue.

"You think I'm a wimp. You think I can't handle a spanking."

Something about the way she was standing, the tone of her voice, brought out the Dom in him, and he found himself moving into her space. "I am attempting to respect your limits."

"You have no idea what my limits are, Sir." Though she put that polite "Sir" at the end, there was no way to mistake the challenge in her voice.

That challenge got his dick humming. He towered over her, meeting her eyes. There was something happening between them, something that hadn't happened before. Electricity seemed to crackle in the air and he couldn't find the will to step away. "Why don't you explain them to me, Kori? Do you think I'm such a novice Dom that I can't read your body language? I think I can tell when you're enjoying the play or when you've had enough. If I can't you've always got the power of speech."

"Unless you gag me. Then I'd be totally helpless and at your mercy, Mr. Sadist." She inched closer to him, her chest almost brushing his. "You don't have to go easy on me, Kai. I can handle anything you can dish out."

"You've splashed around in the kiddie pool." His voice had gone deep and low, his inner caveman utterly squashed by his Dom. She was challenging him in a space where that wasn't acceptable. At the office she could run his life all she liked. He welcomed it, needed it, and honored her for it. But here. Oh, here, she did not get to be in charge. "You've waded in to your ankles with your water wings on, little girl. If you scene with me you better know how to swim."

How had they gone from polite to damn near sexual intercourse in point three seconds. Oh, yeah. It was because she'd leaned in, lowered her voice, and opened all sorts of doors that should have remained closed.

"I'm a freaking Olympic gold medalist when it comes to this particular pool, Sir. And I'm a woman, not a little girl, as you're about to find out. Where do you want me?"

Where did he want her? On her knees. Bent over the couch in his office. Bound to his bed, her legs spread and waiting for his penetration. "On the spanking bench eventually, but first I think you should show Jared how a proper submissive greets her Master and prepares for a scene. Does your gold medal cover that?"

He needed a minute. He needed to get himself under control because she was pushing all his buttons in exactly the right way to get him hot and bothered. The need to sink his hand into all that hair and force her down to her knees in front of him was almost overwhelming.

She stepped back, her eyes on him as she moved more fully into the scene space.

"Does Sanctum set the protocol?"

Jared had asked the question. He'd nearly forgotten Jared was there. Damn it. Kori sank gracefully to her knees in front of him and he had a difficult time concentrating. Teaching. He was supposed to be teaching, and that meant answering questions and not worrying about the fact that he had a boner to end all boners and likely everyone could tell.

"There are certain protocols set up in Sanctum contracts. As you'll see when we go over how a training class would work, submissives and Dominant members have roles and duties they owe to everyone in the club. Discretion is first and foremost. We don't talk about what happens in the club with outsiders."

"So no gossip," Jared said.

"Oh, the club runs on gossip. If we put that terminology in Big Tag would get kicked out of his own club." Fuck, but she looked sweet kneeling on the middle of the stage. When had she perfected that pose? As far as he knew she didn't practice protocol with most of the Doms she played with and yet her spine was perfectly straight, her knees splayed so that if she weren't wearing the boy shorts, he would have a lovely view of her pussy. Her hands were palms up on her thighs and her head bowed submissively. He could almost believe she loved this. No one could look that perfect and at ease without loving it. "We talk very freely amongst ourselves, but discretion is urged outside the confines of the membership."

Jared stepped up, coming to stand at Kai's side. His brother looked down at Kori, his eyes watching her, taking in the lines of her form, the swell of her breasts. "And this protocol?"

"Doms and subs form their own protocols based on their needs, but this is generally accepted here as a proper way to greet a Dominant partner and begin a scene." He placed his hand on her head, the connection nearly making him sigh. What the fuck was he doing? The question kept running through his head, but it was drowned out by louder voices that told him to go with it. She'd agreed to the scene. They hadn't done all the normal bargaining he would have with another sub, but then there hadn't been a lot of time. They'd gone from casual talk to him nearly bending her over and fucking her right there. He was worried if she turned that saucy mouth on him again, he might do just that.

"So this is what you would do with a submissive who doesn't know your habits?" Jared was the one who sounded academic now.

He needed to get his shit together. This wasn't a pleasure tour. This was about the contract he'd signed to train his brother. It was also about showing his assistant that he could control himself. She was pushing him. For what reason he had no idea.

Because she wants what you can give her. Because she's always wanted it and she's hidden it from you because she's fucking afraid.

Yeah, he wasn't listening to inner caveman or inner Dom anymore. "Yes. By bowing her head she shows me she's ready to submit. I accept her gift with a touch of my hand. Let me help you up." He held out his hand and she stared at it as though trying to decide if she was going to rise on her own. "Don't push me further than you already have, Kori. I'll need an explanation of why you disrespect me in that fashion."

Her hand came up, sliding into his as she allowed him to ease her up. "I'm not used to being helped up."

"I suspect you tend to move before your Dominant partner is ready," he surmised.

She was looking up at him, her hand still in his, though she was steady on her feet. She never wore heels. He liked the fact that she was shorter than him, small compared to him. "Probably. It never seems serious. No one ever punished me for it."

"Because you keep everything light. Because you never select a Dom who wants more out of you than a little fun. I need more tonight." He needed everything. "Jared can't learn if he doesn't see something real."

She was silent for a moment and that electricity was still there between them, though it had quieted to a low simmer. "All right. For Jared's sake." Her eyes held his for a second too long before turning to his brother. "There are a million different ways to play. There are as many ways to practice BDSM as there are people who practice it. I wouldn't be this serious with a Dom usually. My play is typically more about fun than pushing boundaries."

"Why do you do it?" Jared asked.

The real value in this impromptu scene hit him and rather forcefully. Jared would ask the questions, but Kai could hear her answers. He'd never talked to her about this, not about the lifestyle because it seemed far too intimate. She hadn't wanted to play with him so he'd dodged the topic. They talked about everything else—well with the singular exception of his brother it seemed—but in this she was a mystery to him.

"I need you to treat him as you would any other Dom in this club," Kai ordered when she didn't answer.

Her lips curled up in an impish grin. "Are you sure about that?"

She was the beloved brat of the club. "How about I amend that to asking you to be on your best behavior?"

"I do it because a long time ago I found out I enjoyed it. There's no deep childhood trauma, no horrible incident from my past. I like the feel of a paddle against my ass. I enjoy not knowing what will come next, but trusting that my partner won't hurt me. I like the rules and regulations of the lifestyle. It brings me peace and comfort and I never feel more alive than when I submit to a good Dom."

Every word that came from her mouth sent a shock of recognition through him. He could have said the very same things. He wasn't sure why he needed this, the control yes, that was obvious. He'd spent much of his childhood having to be the man of the house when he wasn't ready for it. It created a chaotic childhood. But the pain? The sadism that ran through him? It was hard to explain since he didn't feel it in his regular, everyday life. He spent his career trying to pull people from their pain.

Somehow inflicting the right pain did it for him. He had zero desire to randomly harm people, but with the right sub, one who needed what he had to give them, oh, that was like finding heaven.

"So you're saying the idea that everyone in the lifestyle is damaged and in need of therapy is wrong," Jared stated succinctly.

He wasn't sure his brother could understand but at least he wasn't turning his nose up. "Everyone's damaged, Jared. You don't live life and not have scars. Occasionally I turn down people for memberships based on psychological evaluations. Either the Dom or Domme is more interested in hurting a sub than they are in helping them, or a sub is looking for someone to hurt her or him to the exclusion of all other aid. Submission can be a form of therapy, as can Dominance, but the person has to be open to healing. I would never allow someone a membership if they weren't here for the right reasons."

"Except me, of course," Jared said, his voice going flat.

"I didn't say that." He likely should have softened his tone, but Jared needed to understand that he wasn't here to make friends. He was here for a very specific purpose. "If you were to apply for membership through regular channels, you would have to go through a psychological evaluation."

Kori looked up at Jared. "Not through him, though. He's not allowed to evaluate his own family members. You would go through Eve McKay. She's smart and fair at the same time."

He drew his hand back and smacked her ass hard without even thinking about it.

He expected her to frown his way and complain. Instead her eyes closed briefly and when she looked back at him, her pupils were slightly dilated.

"I apologize, Sir. Though I could have been making a simple statement."

"Were you?" He knew the answer to that.

She shook her head. "Oh, no, I was being a brat."

"Brats get punished."

"So you say. I'll be over there on the bench."

She wanted to push him? Oh, he would push back. "Not like that you won't. I think Jared should see how I operate. I prefer my subs to offer themselves to me. Their trust, their submission, and most definitely their beauty."

That seemed to stop her in her tracks. "Are you telling me to get naked?"

He felt the deep satisfaction that came with shocking her. He also knew instinctively that she wouldn't back off. There wasn't a lot of difference between submissive Kori and the Kori he knew outside the club. She could be stubborn, brutally so. She wouldn't back down from a challenge, which meant he would need to watch her carefully in order to assure that he didn't take things too far. "Yes. I'm telling you that for this scene, I require you to wear nothing but your lovely skin. How can Jared see what a perfectly reddened ass looks like if it's covered up with all that leather?"

She snorted as though reminding him there wasn't that much fabric on her body, but she turned anyway. "I'm going to need help out of this thing. I didn't lace myself into it. Sarah did that. And if you think you're going to pull a knife and cut it off the way I've seen some Doms do here, think again, Sir. Cutting my clothes off me is a hard limit. I work for a very tight-fisted boss. Corsets aren't cheap."

He frowned. "I am not tight fisted. I'm very reasonable. Come here. I'll get you out of it. And you should be careful how you talk about your boss or he might implement disciplinary actions at the office."

"Promises, promises," she whispered.

He worked the laces of her corset with a practiced hand. "And it's considered very sexy by some women to cut them out of their corsets."

"I consider frugality sexy," she shot back.

"Is it going to bother you to be naked, Kori?" Jared asked.

"Not at all. I've got a heavy streak of exhibitionism in me. Another thing I learned from the lifestyle," she explained quietly. "There's something freeing about it when you know you won't be judged. All healthy body types are considered lovely here, though I will admit most of the men are ridiculously hot. Any good club will welcome people of all sizes."

"Some of the sexiest women I've ever known have been curvier," Jared admitted.

"I would think being around the Hollywood types, your preferences might have changed." Kai loosened her laces, his fingertips brushing over soft skin. She had lovely skin. Even her freckles were pretty.

"Not at all. I still like what I like." Jared was watching as Kai finished loosening the corset.

"Arms up," he commanded. He wasn't about to take the time to pull the laces out. When she complied, he gently pulled the corset over her head. "Oh, now that's pretty."

She'd had the thing on so tight he could see where it had bitten into her skin, leaving lovely lines and indentions. He traced one with his finger. It started right below her shoulder blade and ran down the skin of her back to right above the curve of her ass. Now that she was without the corset, the swell of her cheeks were punctuated by the black leather boy shorts she wore. There wasn't much there. The waistband dipped low on her hips and the legs weren't legs at all. They were strips of fabric that revealed the under curve of what had to be the juiciest backside he'd ever seen.

He was about to spank it. In an academic fashion.

Yeah, that was likely going to go bad. "Now the rest of it, exhibitionist."

He'd seen her wrapped in another Dom's ropes before, her breasts thrust out and on display. He'd turned away because he hadn't wanted to. He'd wanted to stand there and stare. It had been an act of discipline to walk away. Since that first time he'd seen her, he'd tried to avoid her during play. It wasn't so odd. There were several siblings who played at Sanctum and they informed each other of what parts of the club they would be in that evening so as to avoid awkward situations.

This wasn't awkward. This was heavenly.

She pushed the shorts off and over her hips, her ass coming into full view.

"I don't think your tastes have changed either, brother," Jared said with a smirk.

His dick needed to calm the fuck down. Yeah, he understood why the siblings at Sanctum avoided each other at all costs. That shit was embarrassing. "Now you may greet me again. Jared, watch the way she holds herself. It's obvious she's done this a thousand times, likely practiced so she would show her Dom as much respect as possible."

"Or I just like looking good." Kori slid into her position with effortless ease.

"If you keep up the smart remarks, this could go from a training exercise to serious punishment," he warned.

Her head dropped forward, but not before he'd seen the heat in her eyes.

What if she wanted it? What if she simply hadn't met the Dom who could bring out this side of her yet and he was the one?

What if everything he wanted had been sitting not twenty feet away from him and he'd been too stupid to see her?

What would he do?

He wasn't sure, but he was about to find out.

"Take your place so we can begin." He held a hand out to help her.

Kori settled her hand in his and rose. She moved to the bench, settling her body down. Her ass was presented to him. She was ready to be tied down.

And he was ready to find out exactly how compatible they were.

Chapter Five

Kori settled herself on the spanking bench. Like all things in Sanctum, it was built for a sub's comfort. Padded and with comfy resting spots for her arms and legs, the spanking bench was quite nice. Oh, she supposed not everything was made for the sub's comfort since she'd been on the hamster wheel, and while the lights were twelve kinds of pretty, it still required her to freaking run to power it. When a sub didn't work his or her hardest, the spankings got a little nasty. Little. It was a word she put with spanking often since she hadn't had a real spanking in years.

So many years.

All that time had gone by and she hadn't gotten what she needed. She hadn't felt that horrible burn that sank into her bones and warmed every inch of her flesh.

Kai could give it to her. It was precisely why she'd stayed away from him until tonight.

So why did this feel so right? She didn't even want to run away. Her very bones relaxed at the thought of Kai touching her again. When he'd run his fingers over her skin, it had taken all she had not to shiver and sigh. So good. It felt so good to be touched by him, and it wasn't about being skin to skin. It was all about him.

When he'd gently told her he would respect her limits, she'd damn near lost it. Yes, she was acting like a brat but she couldn't seem to help it. When he'd questioned what she could take, something had welled inside her and she found herself playing super brat—the girl who wanted to get her ass spanked. Hard.

If you keep up the smart remarks, this could go from a training exercise to serious punishment.

She was so tempted to push him. If she said or did the exact wrong things, he wouldn't be able to stop himself. He would follow his instincts and then she would get what she wanted. They would both get what they wanted.

And she would have stolen something from Kai. His control. He needed it, craved it.

Kori took a deep breath and relaxed. The brattery had to stop. This was a training exercise and that was all it was. This wasn't even for her benefit.

"Do you usually draw a crowd?" Jared's voice drew her out of her thoughts.

They were at the back of the dungeon in a scene space known for how small it was. She turned her head to the side and sure enough, there was a crowd waiting in the background for the scene to start. She couldn't blame them. If Kai wanted privacy, he would have used one of the closed rooms. He'd likely selected this space because it was an easy entry into normal club scenes. The shallow end of the pool, so to speak.

You've splashed around in the kiddie pool. You've waded in to your ankles with your water wings on, little girl. If you scene with me you better know how to swim.

Those words from Kai had sent her right over the edge. They'd called to her inner alpha bitch, the one who submitted to none but the strongest, most worthy of Doms.

She had to bring this scene back to where it needed to be. Calm. Patient. A little boring.

"I suspect they're here to see you," Kori explained, giving Jared a smile. He was staring at her ass. Hottie McHollywood was standing there staring at her big old naked ass.

"We're here to see the hardest bottom at Sanctum go up against the nastiest sadist," a deep voice said.

She looked back at the crowd and recognized one of the Doms she'd played with before. Several of them were standing around along with Big Tag and his wife, Jake Dean, Case Taggart, and Alex and Eve McKay. Her friends had found their way here, too. Sarah, Vince, and Mia stood to the side with Jared's friend, Squirrel.

"Hard bottom?" Kai asked.

Shit. She'd worked hard to keep that from him. She could take a lot of pain. Her threshold was legendary, but she didn't do the types of scenes required to make her cry. She stayed in control. Hence the nickname Hard Bottom Girl.

"I can spank her for hours and she doesn't even blink," a Dom named Remy said. He was a bodyguard at McKay-Taggart and a very sweet man. He was easy to play with because he never got attached to any of the subs.

"I used a cane on her once and I stopped the scene because she was going to be too sore the next day," Mistress Jackie said, her hand on Vince's shoulder.

The Domme was also a fun partner. She never made it sexual in public, and Kori didn't play in private so Mistress Jackie was a safe way to find the endorphin rush she got from scenes.

Or sometimes she and Sarah took turns playing with the equipment. That was when Big Tag shook his head and complained about the "free-range subs."

Kai was suddenly beside her, dropping down on one knee. All that golden hair flowed around him, making him look like a gorgeous lion about to bare his teeth and take a chunk out of her. "Is this true? Because I was under the impression that you took things very lightly. I believe you've told me on several occasions that you never get serious in a scene."

This was one of the many reasons she'd avoided him. Lying to him here meant something to her. It was one thing to omit a few truths but another to outright lie to a Dom. She had to be honest with him. "Those scenes weren't serious to me."

"What would your partners call them?"

"Kai, it's not a big deal. I have a high tolerance for pain. That's all. It takes more for me to find subspace."

Maybe he would leave it at that.

"We're going to have a long talk about this later. If I find out that you've had issues with not properly using your safe word...well, I suspect I'm about to find out myself. Don't use that safe word unless you need it. I'll know from your body language."

"Are you threatening me? Are you telling me you'll kick me out if I don't behave the way you think I should?" Anger welled up and she was ready to get off the bench and walk the hell away from him.

Sanctum was her safe place. It was all she had some days. All she had except for him, and if he kicked her out, she wouldn't have either. Kai couldn't be the one who shoved her out and yet that was his job. He was the gatekeeper. He decided who belonged here and who wasn't ready for it.

She wasn't sure what she would do if Kai determined her unworthy. It would be worse than before. Worse than losing her script and her career. Worse than leaving California.

His hand found her back, gently holding her down. He leaned in and she could feel the warmth of his breath on her skin. "I would never kick you out. Never, Kori. I couldn't do that to you. But I have to make sure you're safe. I have to make sure you're not doing this for the wrong reasons. Tell me you get pleasure out of this."

She was getting pleasure simply from being close to him. If she turned her head the right way, their mouths might meet and she would know what it felt like to kiss him. "I get some peace out of it."

"So no one knows how to take care of you? Do you let them?"

He was making her emotional. She hated that, but she couldn't hold back. Not with him. "No. I'm just looking for a little subspace, Sir. That's all I need."

"I doubt that very much." His hand eased over her. "Remember what I said about the safe word. I want you to use it if you need to. If I give you too much, pull me back. I can be intense. I think I'll be quite intense with you."

A shiver went through her. "I'll be fine. You'll understand that I'm not here to hurt myself."

"And you'll understand what it can be like when you get what you need."

She had to take a deep breath because that had sounded like a promise to her. Or a challenge. All she knew was she couldn't fake her way through this. Now that Kai had questions, he would seek answers, and if he wasn't satisfied, she would find herself on someone's damn therapist couch revealing all her secrets.

Or she could give him this one.

She forced herself to remain still though her heart thudded in her chest.

"I'll teach you the knots later," Kai said. "Watch me now. It's important to get them tight but not too tight. You want to make sure her circulation isn't cut off. You also want to make sure that she feels bound, that she understands there's nowhere to go. Tell him what you like about ropes."

Kai used the word "him" referring to Jared, but she knew that man. He was asking the question for himself. Now that he had her here, he couldn't help but poke and prod and try to figure out what made her tick. It was part of Kai's nature. "I like the feel of them. I like the fact that they hold me here. Sometimes, when the play is good enough, I feel like I could float away, give myself up. The ropes hold me. Metaphorically, of course. I think in a lot of ways, they keep me in the moment. When I'm bound and trussed up, I'm not thinking about how crappy my day was or what I should worry about. I'm only thinking about how the rope feels against my skin, how it holds me in like arms hugging me close."

Even as she spoke, Kai slid the length of jute over her skin, winding it around her wrist and binding her to the bench. He was a master at this. Kai didn't do things by half measure. He mastered them as an art form or he didn't practice it at all. He taught a Kinbaku class here at Sanctum so she was bound quickly, the tension perfect. She sighed, her body relaxing as he tied her other wrist and moved on to her ankles.

"May I touch the ropes?" Jared asked.

There was a slight hesitation before Kai answered. "Yes, but if Kori feels uncomfortable, she'll tell you to stop."

Jared dropped to one knee, his gorgeous face coming into view. He reached out and touched the knots Kai had tied. His fingertips played along the curve of the rope, but he seemed careful not to touch her skin. "He's jealous."

The words had been whispered and it seemed Kai hadn't heard. Jared stood up again and stepped away.

Kai wasn't jealous. Certainly not in the way Jared intimated.

"I'm going to start with a crop."

With Kai's words, she braced herself for what was to come. Would he turn out to be all talk and no pain? Sometimes Doms thought they were badass when they were actually softies. It all depended on the sub. So much was subjective. Sarah thought some Doms were too rough when Kori found them to be easy on a girl. She never told them. It would be rude to tear a man or woman down that way.

Kai could be like that. He could call himself a sadist, but pain was in the eye of the beholder. Or rather in the flesh of their ass.

He flicked the crop. The sound cracked through the air, but the pain flashed and then was gone.

Damn it. He was soft.

Another three flicks. She loved the sound of the smack and then the sting that came, but he was using the flat of the crop, the leather part. It made a nice sound, but the sting was fairly ho-hum. She was sure it made other subs cry and quake in fear of his awesome cropping abilities, but she would likely take a nice nap.

He continued, laying out a pattern across her backside and thighs. He did all the right things—avoided her spine and kidneys, stuck to the fleshy parts of her body.

He was like the others. He called himself a sadist, but there was no real torture to this. There was a level of comfort in that. Kai wasn't really her dream Dom, and that was good news because she so loved having him as a friend. She could take a deep breath and know that they weren't truly compatible. He wasn't the man who could drag her into the life she'd sworn never to go back to.

He continued to warm her backside as she went over all the ways finding out Kai was fooling himself about his predilections worked in her favor. She wouldn't be so tempted by him now. She could truly find a pure, platonic friendship with her boss. After this, she wouldn't have to avoid him and hey, if it made him feel better, she would play with him from time to time. Because this was no big deal at all.

She tried to cover her yawn and heard the whispers going on a few feet away.

Maybe she should try to eek out a couple of tears to preserve his reputation. She didn't like the thought of all those other Doms talking about him. He wouldn't like it either.

"So this is a nice warm-up," Kai said behind her. "I like to use this crop because it's not particularly stingy. When I say that what I mean is I would have to use a great deal of force to provoke a pain response."

"I thought you were trying to provoke a pain response," Jared replied.

Like two professors. She had to stay awake. He would be humiliated if he was the Dom who put her to sleep. Not that it hadn't happened before. Sometimes the rhythm and the sound of flogging had been known to send her right into nappy time. It was like rain on a tin roof, the sound soothing to her soul. Not doing as much for her libido, but hey, that was okay, too.

"It is the object, but with a sub I've never played with before, I have to gauge her reactions. Some subs have a very low tolerance for pain. Some a very high one. If I use this crop and this force and I get a reaction, I know a little more about the submissive's limits. Do you see how her skin is already getting pink?" Kai's hand ran over her ass.

That felt nice, but she had to admit some of his power over her was gone. His hand felt warm on her skin, but there wasn't the edge that had been there before, the tiny hint that any moment that hand could slap at her, come down on her flesh with power.

"Yes, but she didn't have a reaction to it," Jared replied. "I don't think she found it painful at all."

"No, I suspect she found it very frustrating. Or boring. Did you find my crop boring, Kori?" He asked the question in that oh-so-deep voice he used when he was playing or someone had seriously pissed him off.

"It was very nice, Sir." She didn't want to piss him off. Politeness was the way to go.

A horrible crack split the air and she had to bite back a groan because that hadn't been a boring, sedate crop. He'd brought his hand down and smacked the shit out of her bottom. It stung and then burned, sinking into her and speeding up her blood.

"I'm going to ask you again and you should note that I have eyes and saw you yawn. Did you find my crop boring?" He enunciated each word, biting them off.

"Yes." She wasn't afraid of him hitting her again. There were other punishments she wouldn't enjoy and he damn well knew it. He could untie her and make her sit for the night, watching what went on around her and forced to be silent. He could put her on the damn hamster wheel and make her run all night. There were plenty of punishments even a masochist could hate.

He smacked her again, right in the same spot, the pain shooting through her like a drug. "Yes, what?"

"Sir," she replied, breathless. "It was boring, Master Kai."

"Better." His hand left her. "So now we understand that what we have is an obnoxious brat who's lied to me in the past and very likely to all of the Doms she's played with."

"Hey, that's not true." She didn't mean to lie. She meant to spare their feelings. Wasn't that a good thing? Even as she thought the words she realized she might be in serious trouble because the Doms of Sanctum wouldn't view it that way. They would view her lying as a punishable offense because by lying she'd kept them from doing their jobs, from giving her what she needed.

That was a grave offense indeed.

"She totally lied to me," a masculine voice with a thick Cajun accent replied. "I thought she was helping me learn. Guess I was the fool there."

Shit. Remy was a friend. She hadn't meant to make him feel bad. She'd simply wanted to hide for a bit longer. She couldn't have what she needed. If she found that again, everything she'd worked so hard for would be threatened. Her independence. Her self-worth. She could fall right back into those old patterns of giving in simply to keep the peace. "I didn't mean to lie."

She felt a hand sink into her hair but it wasn't soothing. He twisted his fingers and she felt the burn along her scalp. She hissed at the pain and felt her whole body respond to him. This was how she was wired. She knew some people would think she was a pervert, a complete freak, but god, this did it for her.

"You didn't mean to lie? Tell me what you were trying to do." All she could see of him were the tops of his boots. They were black and leather and worn. If boots could be pissed off, they were.

"I didn't want to hurt their feelings. I swear that's the truth, Sir."

"Master Remy, would it have hurt your feelings if she'd told you the force you applied during scenes wasn't enough for her?" Kai held her head off the bench, just enough to make her uncomfortable but not enough to hurt her.

The man knew exactly what he was doing. He knew the difference between a sore bottom and a hurt neck. One was treasured in her world and the other simply sucked and required a trip to the chiropractor. But Kai was holding her so she felt the bite in her scalp, knew he had all the power, and yet she was also supported.

"No, Master Kai. I would not have been offended. I would have attempted to give her what she wanted," Remy replied. "I am rather offended that she refused to allow me to try. She obviously wasn't afraid of me so I have to wonder why."

"She doesn't let anyone give her what she needs," Mistress Jackie replied.

"In her defense, she plays a lot and always talks about how much fun she has with you guys." Finally a friendly voice.

"Sarah, would you enjoy an evening spent scrubbing toilets while wearing an anal plug lubricated with ginger lube?" Yeah, Big Tag was a giver. "Because I can make that happen."

"She sucks. She should be more honest with the Doms," Sarah said quickly.

So much for solidarity.

"You will apologize to every Dom you've played with and lied to." Kai gently eased her head back down. "And if I catch you lying again, you'll be the one with the burning asshole. Jared, this is what we do with brats at Sanctum."

She heard some movement and then felt the whoosh of air caress her skin right before something thin and hard thwacked against her flesh. A gasp made her chest pulse as pure fire licked over her backside.

"This is a cane," Kai explained. "It's bamboo, nice and not too flexible. It leaves a mark if you apply enough force." He brought it down on her again, this time on her thighs. Again, she struggled for breath. "Are you bored now, Kori?"

"No, Sir." She barely managed to get the words out of her mouth.

"Excellent, then we're making headway." The cane came down again and again. "Where are we on the stoplight?"

"Green." She didn't even hesitate. The pain was doing its job, heating her up and making her soft. Each strike of the cane lit her up and then brought her back down, sinking deeper and deeper into that soft, fuzzy place of submission.

"Now we're getting some truth." He kept up his punishing pace. "She didn't take her time trying to find a way out of what she didn't want to say."

"Why would she lie?" Jared asked.

"That's a good question." The blows continued, making her ache as Kai spoke. "I suspect she didn't want anyone here to know that she's a naughty masochist who can't get off without a little bite of pain. Or a big one. She hasn't accepted her nature. Or she has and expects that no one else will."

"I accepted my nature a long time ago," she managed to say.

The caning stopped and suddenly Kai's boots were in view again. He dropped to one knee, that hard hand in her hair again. "Then tell me why."

She couldn't tell him. It was too much. "I'm yellow now, Kai. Don't make me safe word out over an explanation I'm not ready to give."

"Fine." His hand moved from her hair down, skimming over her skin until his fingertips found her breast. Kai Ferguson was touching her breast. God, he was cupping her and she couldn't breathe. "How about I put a scenario forth and you think about it for a few days. I think the reason you didn't mention your utterly beautiful and sexy inclinations is me. You didn't want me to know because you were perfectly aware that I'm the only one here who can possibly give you what you need. You knew that once I found out, I wouldn't be able to help myself because you're the only one who can do the same for me, baby. Do you know how fucking good I feel right now? How good this makes me feel?"

He rolled her nipple between his thumb and forefinger and twisted with a vicious bite that left her panting.

She squeezed her eyes closed because she couldn't look at him, couldn't see how beautiful he was. "It won't work, Kai."

Another nasty twist got her squirming. "It's working right fucking now. Darling girl, your ass is up in the air and that means I can see how wet your pussy is. Tell me some other Dom here got you wet and ready."

"You know I can't." She tugged at her restraints, but they didn't move. The rope rubbed across her skin, keeping her here with him. She couldn't run, and she had to admit she didn't want to. She wanted this moment with him. Her pride might make her get up and stride away but every other part of her begged for what she'd denied herself for so long. He was the only man here who could give her what she needed. It wasn't about who hit the hardest. Any of those other Doms could have adequately provided her with pain. She needed more. She needed connection, the ebb and flow of pain and pleasure coming from a man who was there with her.

Her dark shadow lover. Kai.

"I'm not the exhibitionist you are," Kai admitted. "And that's the only reason I'm not fucking you right now, but we're going to have a long discussion in the morning about the way this needs to go. For tonight, I'm going to start the process that will allow you to remain friends with all those people you lied to. So you are going to give me everything I want. You're going to cry for me. You're going to let go and show them that you'll cry for me."

She shook her head. "You're asking too much."

"It's cry or come, baby. One or the other, unless you want to find yourself in Big Tag's office. Let me show him I can handle you."

"I can't. I haven't done either in a very long time." She hadn't cried since leaving LA. She couldn't. Wouldn't. She hadn't come either. Not a man-given orgasm. Her mind worked overtime. He wasn't joking about getting called into Big Tag's office. Whatever punishment Kai could come up with—nothing would touch Big Tag's disapproval. They were all mad at her. It was enough to make her want to run away again.

Except it wasn't that they wanted to see her humiliated. This punishment wasn't about hurting her. It was about this group of people knowing that someone among them could take care of her.

When she looked at it like that, it didn't seem like punishment at all. It was about the Dominants giving a shit.

Morgan hadn't cared when she'd lied to him. All he'd wanted was the next bit of work from her. After a while, he hadn't cared about her finding subspace or her pent-up sexuality. He'd doled out the pain like it was bait for his trap. He would give her enough to ensure she stayed around and did what he needed her to do.

This wasn't the same thing at all.

"I don't want to cry in front of anyone, Kai."

"Then let me show them you can let go in another way." His deep voice was a wave of seduction, wrapping her up as securely as the bindings on her limbs.

If she gave them a little, they might forgive her. It didn't mean she was giving up everything. It didn't mean things between her and Kai needed to change. Tomorrow, they could go right back to the way it always was. Maybe this was a good thing. She could be more honest with her play partners. She could get an edge of what she needed from them.

Because she couldn't do this again with Kai. Kai was too dangerous.

"Yes. But this doesn't mean anything." She couldn't let it mean something.

"Like I said before. We'll talk about it tomorrow." Kai loved to talk.

She was sure he would sit her down and they would go over their feelings and come to the logical and compassionate conclusion that they would remain friends. Everything would be civil. It always was with Kai.

Except for now. Now he leaned over and she could feel him whispering in her ear. "I'm going to make you scream. I said I was doing this for their benefit and your own, but understand that when you scream, you're doing it for me. When your pussy clamps down and your whole body shakes, no one else matters but me. They can watch all they like, but I'm the man giving you what you need."

She felt something sharp and wicked against her earlobe. He'd bitten her, a nice little stab of pain that seemed to go straight to her pussy.

That sharp bite likely left a mark she would be able to see if she pushed her hair back. Everyone would be able to see it and everyone who knew her would know it was Master Kai's mark.

Yeah, that did something for her, too.

The cane came down on her ass again, another volley to survive, every single stroke pushing her higher and higher. All those lovely endorphins were starting to flow, making the world seem heightened and fuzzy all at the same time.

"So when you have a submissive who has betrayed her partners, an apology must be made," Kai said. "An act of contrition, so to speak. I'm going to show Kori that it's all right to let go here."

Something shifted and she felt Kai's finger move into place. He was touching her clitoris, the warm pad of his finger perfectly positioned.

"That doesn't seem like punishment," Jared said with a chuckle.

"Like I said, it's more of an apology and a lesson. I'm not going to make it easy on her. My hand is going to remain still. If Kori wants something, she's going to have to ask for it." The crop struck her thighs.

Bastard. It was one thing to let it happen, but Kai was a nasty sadist who likely knew begging wasn't something she normally did. She hated it.

"Or take it for herself," he offered as though he could read her thoughts.

He was giving her an out. If she didn't want to verbally beg, she could rub herself against his finger and everyone would know that she'd been so hot for Kai it didn't matter who was watching.

For some that would be a horrible humiliation. For her it was kind of exciting. Who the hell wouldn't want Kai Ferguson? No one could look at that man, get to know his way-too-intellectual heart, and not want him. Especially the dirty Dom side of him.

It went briefly through her head that if she did this with him, there would be no going back, no way to turn the clock setting to just friends again, but she shoved that thought out of her head. Kai was the most level-headed man in the world. If anyone could compartmentalize, it was Kai. He likely wouldn't see anything weird with playing every now and then and having a perfectly professional relationship at the office.

This could work out. She was being pessimistic. This could be good for both of them. He didn't have a play partner who genuinely needed what he was offering and no one could give her what Kai did.

A hard *thwack* brought her out of her thoughts. "Don't you leave me. You stay here with me."

His finger pressed up and around and she could feel him sliding against her clitoris.

She moved against him. Everyone would be able to see it. Everyone would see that she wasn't willing to simply lie there and take what he gave her. She needed more. Craved more. This was how Kai would give them their bit of revenge—seeing the most controlled sub in Sanctum lose her shit over an orgasm.

Her hips moved, and without another thought, she gave over to Kai. It was oddly easy since she trusted him completely in this. He would never give her more than she could handle. She started slow, letting herself feel him. Her skin was still flushed and hot, an ache in her bones that spurred her to want more.

"Not enough?" Kai asked before smacking her ass with his free hand.

She groaned at the pain and then the pleasure as her hips slid over his finger again. She felt something teasing at the outside of her pussy. Likely his thumb. Over and around and the tiniest bit inside. When she moved against him, she got more.

"This, Jared, is what I like to call a dirty little masochist." Every word out of Kai's mouth sounded like sin. He smacked her again and she gave up even pretending to not want it. "She needs the pain to allow herself the pleasure. She's been holding out on herself, not allowing anyone to give her what she craves." Another smack. "She needs a sadist who cares about her, who won't let her go too far because when she gets going she'll be like an addict. She'll want to prove how much she can take. This pretty girl needs a Dom who can handle her."

She rode his finger, giving over for the first time in what felt like forever. It didn't matter—all the reasons why it was a bad idea, all her good intentions—none of them mattered. All that mattered was the feel of Kai's finger rubbing against her, his thumb penetrating her.

They found their rhythm. Between the ache his slaps brought and the pleasure of his fingers, she couldn't hold out. It had been far too long since she'd indulged, truly indulged in submission this way. She groaned as his thumb arced up at the precise right time, mingling with the sensation of her clitoris being rubbed, and she did it. She cried out, not holding back. Her fingers sank against the padded benches and her toes curled and she let loose.

Her whole body relaxed as she started to come down. The lovely fog she hadn't felt in years settled over her as she felt Kai remove his hand.

"Now I think I'll indulge in a bit of aftercare. Jared, pass me the hand wipes and then I'll get on with ensuring her skin isn't too bruised tomorrow," Kai was saying.

"Don't take it all away," she complained.

She felt a hand on her back. "I wouldn't dream of it, but you should hush now. I'm leaving you tied until I'm done with you."

She sighed and settled back in. It wasn't time for reality yet.

* * * *

Kai was ready to punch something. Hard. Maybe if he punched his brother his dick would calm down. Violence could be his friend. "No, I don't want to go to some dance club."

Jared seemed invigorated by the night's lesson. He seemed unable to sit still, but his energy wasn't restless or upset. Kai had been surprised. He'd kind of expected baby brother to judge him, but Jared had been totally helpful, even being quiet during most of Kori's aftercare.

God, he'd started that scene telling himself it meant nothing beyond a way to honor his contract with Jared. When he'd realized she'd lied about her needs, he'd almost lost his damn mind. She'd lied to him, kept her inner nature from him. He'd wanted to smack her ass, twist her nipples, put a clamp on her clit. There had been a moment when he'd wanted to break her and truly show her that he was her natural Master.

There had to be a reason she hid it. Kori wouldn't play games or lie for the sake of lying. She was still hiding something from him and he was smart enough to know that he couldn't demand some truths. Some truths had to be earned with trust.

And he didn't want to break her. That was the nasty bastard inside him, the one he fed small bites but never full meals. He wanted to free her.

She'd been perfectly submissive, her whole body soft and relaxed from the orgasm he'd given her. She'd complied with his every instruction and allowed him full access to her body. If he'd wanted to he likely could have had her. He could have opened his leathers and forced his stiff dick deep inside her. She wouldn't have complained that he was rough. No, she would enjoy his hands on her, his cock thrusting hard.

Who the fuck was he kidding? Wanted? He'd been dying to get inside her, and one thing and one thing only had held him back. It certainly wasn't the crowd. He'd meant what he'd said. He wasn't the exhibitionist Kori was, but he wouldn't have minded showing every single person there that he was the one she submitted to. He was the only Dom in the room who could handle her. Damn but that had been a high. No, he would have viewed fucking her as a badge of honor with the singular exception that he wasn't about to get his freak on while his brother was watching.

He'd finally found the one thing that icked him out. He was damn near impossible to truly offend. Some chick got off getting peed on? Good for her. Dude liked to spend his off time eating out of a dog bowl? Nice going, buddy.

He couldn't have sex in front of his brother. Even when he really, really wanted to have sex. And that made him pissy.

"Come on, Kai," Jared said. "You're going to love this place. I've been told it's the hottest club in Dallas. They've already roped off the VIP section of the club for us. You showed me some of your world tonight. Let me show you some of mine."

He turned to explain to his brother that he didn't need to see a world where drunk chicks fawned all over his brother and the paparazzi made their living getting pictures of him. He ended up shaking his head because Jared was folding his clothes. Stark naked. "How about you show me less of your junk? God, do you have to leave that out there to swing around like that?"

Jared grinned and held his arms out. "What can I say? The beast likes to be free."

"Looking good, man." Chris Roberts gave his brother a thumbs-up.

"Thank you," Jared replied with an open smile.

Kai gave Chris a stare. "Won't your Dom be interested in knowing you think that?"

Chris smiled, though his head did go down submissively. "My Dom asked me to sneak pictures, but I'm more afraid of Big Tag than I am of him. Sorry."

Chris didn't look up again as he walked back toward his locker.

"This is a fully integrated locker room. Straight, gay, and bi. That doesn't bother you?"

Jared shrugged and didn't go for his clothes. "This body is a work of art in all worlds. When did you turn into such a prude? And while I'm straight, I have zero problems with my gay brothers and sisters. I was named Gay Fantasy Male of the Year two years running. I have the giant dildos on my mantle."

He should have known. "And I'm not a prude. Not normally. You're just…you're my brother and I don't want that thing swinging around in front of me."

When had it grown to monstrous proportions?

"All right, I'll give you that." There was the sound of a locker opening. "I'm putting on pants because you were nice and actually admitted that you're my brother."

"I haven't lied about it." He hadn't advertised it either.

"You tried to tell my publicist that you were my lifestyle expert."

"Well, that's what the contract calls me." It wasn't like he'd lied. He'd been trying to speak as little as possible to Thad or Brad or whatever asswipe Jared had brought with him. "And it's not like you advertise. You changed your name."

"You can look up. I'm perfectly covered now," Jared said.

Kai turned and rolled his eyes. Jared's version of covered didn't match with his. "Shirt? Did you even bring one with you?"

"Do you shake your fist at kids who walk on your lawn?" Jared sighed and pulled out his T-shirt, dragging it over his head. "There. I'll bring a turtleneck tomorrow. And Jared Johns sounded more professional than Jared Ferguson."

"It makes you sound like a porn star." He was not a grumpy old man. He wouldn't let his brother turn him into one.

Jared nodded, completely missing the point. "I know, right? It's cool. And you were definitely trying to distance yourself from me when you were talking to Brad. You didn't want him to know you're my brother. It didn't work because I already told them all."

Kai leaned back against the locker because it looked like this was going to take a few minutes. "I wasn't trying to distance. Not the way you think."

"All right, what were you doing?"

"I was trying to get away from that asshole as soon as possible. He's obnoxious and shallow and I'm worried because every single person you spend time with seems fairly despicable as a human being."

"I will admit that entertainment types don't rank high on the lovely human being list. Don't get me wrong. I've found some great people, but they don't tend to be the type of person who's willing to spend all their time following an actor around." Jared ran a hand over his close-cropped hair. "Look, I had a great publicist at one point. She was a wonderful woman, but I need someone who can travel, and oddly enough, she loved her husband and two kids. Same thing with my first agent. Great guy. He retired so he could play golf and get out of the war, as he would say. He'd taken enough bullets. I loved them. They took care of me after…well, they were there for me when I needed them."

"Why hire the assholes you've got now?"

"Because it was hard to lose them. Because at the end of the day, I needed more than Janice could give me and firing her was a horrible moment in my life. If I fire Tad, it won't hurt. If Brad suddenly disappears, I'll find another trainer and move on. I often think about firing Lena because she annoys the shit out of me on a daily basis. Which is exactly the reason I keep her around."

Was his brother actually trying to stay grounded? Jared wouldn't believe the fawning praise of people he didn't like. He wouldn't be able to get lost in his own fame if he was always questioning the people around him. Of course he also couldn't be comfortable, couldn't truly enjoy all that his success had brought him.

Maybe Jared's life wasn't as fulfilling as it seemed. Of course he always had his abs. "I can understand that. You move around a lot, don't you?"

Jared sat down on the bench in front of the lockers. "I spend a good deal of time in Vancouver, where we shoot the show. I love it up there. The cast is fun. The crew is like a family. I like the house I bought."

But there was hesitation in his voice. "And that's wrong, why?"

"Because shows end and I'm being pressured to take this next big step and move fully into movies."

"I thought the show was doing well." It seemed completely crazy to him that whole populations of human beings wanted to spend their time watching his brother throw darts at people while finding the thinnest reasons for shedding his shirt, but *Dart* was a popular show.

"It's good, but my seven-year contract is up in two years and my agent is already talking about leaving the show so I can get more film work. Even if the network reups the show, they can't force me to sign a contract. It might be the right time for me to get out of the TV business."

"Do you like the TV business?"

His brother's lips turned up. "Yeah. They let me direct a couple of episodes last year. I loved being behind the camera. I mean yes, it's fourteen-hour days, but at least it's in the same place. When I make a movie I live out of a suitcase. I'm not home for more than a few days before I start it all over again. Between filming, training, promoting, I spend very little time in any one place. What I like about TV is we all stay together for years at a time. It feels more stable."

Which his brother would need given their chaotic childhood. Jared had gone to four elementary schools alone. Their mother moved whenever the going got tough. She was a wonderful mom, but she was always looking for the greener pasture. "Then don't leave. It's a simple issue. You don't want to leave, you stay."

Jared nodded. "Of course. Well, that's that."

He started to turn away, but couldn't help but think about all the times Jared had come to him when they were kids, asking for his advice because he didn't know what to do. Jared often worried about what the people around him thought. He listened to too many voices when he was a kid. Kai blamed it on his popularity when they were younger. Now he understood that Jared needed to please the people around him. It was part of him.

"You also pick people you don't like so they don't have as much influence on you. You don't necessarily listen to people you don't like."

Jared stood, straightening out his clothes. "I suppose you would call it a coping mechanism."

"Yes, but it's not one that's going to make you happy." From a therapist's perspective, he knew no one really changed who they were at the core of their being. The choices a person made, those could be changed. Thoughtful decisions could change a path. Jared was trying. "Is this a decision you're making between what you think is best for your career and what you truly want on a personal level?"

Jared didn't turn. "Yes."

Then the solution was simple. Careful inner awareness would bring about the proper conclusion, one Jared would be able to live with. He'd interned with a therapist in high school as part of a work program for inner city kids. It had set him on his path. Even back then, he tried to make careful decisions. "All right. We need to sit down and make a pros and cons list."

When Jared's head turned up, there was a little smirk on his face. "And then we'll assign each item a variable weight."

Had he really sounded so pretentious? He did believe in the practice, but over the last fifteen years he'd perfected a less technical explanation. "Not everything is even. You can't look at five cons and two pros and decide to nix an idea if those two pros are deeply important. We can sit down and discuss it if you would like."

"I would like." Jared reached into his locker and grabbed his jacket. "Maybe we can talk about it tonight at the club."

"I'm not going to the club." He had something else he needed to do. He needed to get out of here and catch Kori. They had some serious talking to do. "It's almost one in the morning. Why would you go to a club now?"

"We're not all early risers, brother. Lots of fun things happen after midnight. I'm surprised you decided to hang it up so early. The rest of the club is still hopping."

He'd overheard Kori telling Sarah she was ready to go home. He meant to stop her in the lobby. It would take her some time to get dressed and Sarah had been in full fet wear. That worked in his favor. "I need to talk to Kori."

He'd taken his time untying the ropes that had bound her. He'd played with her along the way, pulling the rope taut and then smacking her with it. He'd loved the squeals and the way she'd squirmed. He'd loved running his hands over her pink flesh. But when it was over, he'd gone to get her a robe and she'd disappeared. He'd tracked her down to the bar where he'd heard her talking to Sarah and Mia and made the decision to talk to her outside the club.

They would sit down and discuss what had happened rationally and honestly. He would rationally and honestly explain to her that there was no fucking way he was going to let her go.

Hell no.

"Are you going to talk to her? Or are you going to kiss her?"

"Are you five years old?"

Jared shrugged. "I can't tease my big brother? Because from where I was sitting you were totally into that girl. Literally, at one point of the evening. I was surprised. I thought you were going to fuck her. I would have."

"Don't even talk about it."

"Sorry, she's lovely. That Sarah is pretty, too. She's got a mouth on her. Little brat."

"Getting into character?" He grabbed his kit.

"Uhm, yeah. Definitely. So why haven't you and Kori hooked up before?"

He'd thought about this question incessantly since the moment he touched her. "Because I don't hook up with anyone. I have relationships. Some are shorter than others. My relationship with Kori has been platonic."

"That didn't look platonic."

It hadn't felt that way either. "It's something we need to talk about."

"You've liked her before tonight though, right?"

Why was he asking about this? "Like I said, we were friends."

"Because you didn't seem happy to find me talking to her,"

Jared pointed out.

"Well, I have my reasons for that." He wasn't going to bring up his insane curiosity about how they knew one another. Thinking about it made his gut roll with jealousy, and he hated that feeling. There was no logic to it. Even if she'd slept with Jared, it had been long before she'd met him, worked for him, become his friend. It had been another lifetime, but the thought made him want to punch his brother in his perfectly symmetrical face. "You shouldn't bug her at work."

Jared's eyes widened. "You can't honestly tell me that's your reason. I was bugging her at work."

He didn't want to go into the real one. The real reason would lead to a family counseling session and while he was willing to talk to his brother about his career goals, he wasn't willing to go there. "I owe it to her to provide her with a workplace where no one harasses her."

"I wasn't harassing her. I was talking to her and you went twelve kinds of possessive. Come on, Kai. We both know why you did that, and I'm worried it's the very reason you kept your distance from a woman you obviously wanted." Jared wasn't letting up. He started to follow Kai out of the locker room.

"You just got here. You haven't seen me in years. Don't act like you know what's going through my head." He wasn't ready for this conversation.

"You're still angry with me for what happened. I get that. Don't take it out on Kori. She's not Hannah." Jared was hot on his heels.

"I never said she was and you shut the fuck up. You think you know me so well? Then you remember that I don't air my dirty laundry in public. You're making a scene." He couldn't stand it. He wasn't the guy who posted his every fucking feeling on social media. Some things were private, needed to be dealt with in quiet and thoughtful fashions, but his brother had never met a public argument he didn't love. He would throw down in front of anyone.

Jared stopped as they walked into the lobby. Up ahead, Kai could see his entourage was waiting for him. And look, his assistant had shown up. Lena was dressed for clubbing in a way-too-short skirt that would very likely show off all her assets as she got out of the limo they would surely take.

"Fine," Jared said, his voice hushed. "But since I'm living with you for the next couple of weeks, don't think this conversation is over. Maybe I'll make an appearance at this club and then call it an early night because I think we should talk about this."

He turned and joined his group. High-fives all around. Jared smiled like they hadn't just gone from being fairly cool with each other to nearly having a public knock-down, drag-out, but then that was how his brother rolled.

"Hey, Kai, you coming with?" Squirrel had traded his leathers for the equally awkward jeans that seemed painted on his body and a V-neck shirt that proved he was way less serious about working out than Jared.

Brad or was it Tad? He couldn't remember. They were dressed in the same douchebag outfits as the rest of the crew, as though they were all trying so hard to be Jared. One of the "_ads" gave him a nod. "The more the merrier. We've got plenty of room in the limo. Come with us. You've never gotten trim the way you get it when you're with this guy."

The asshole was patting Jared on the back like it was his duty to ensure every guy got laid by some chick who really wanted Jared but would take whatever they could get to be in a star's orbit.

The other "_ad" nodded and got a wolfish leer on his face. "Yeah, these chicks will do the craziest shit to get near him. And the drunk ones are easy pickings."

"Ah, date rape. It's the call of the lesser, more criminal male." Yeah, his brother needed to find another way to cope. "You'll excuse me if I choose better company."

He walked off toward the bar where he saw Vince hanging out with Mistress Jackie. Hanging out was a euphemism. He was actually curled up at her feet, his cheek against the leather of her boots that had come straight from Dominatrix.com or wherever Jackie was buying her outrageous getups these days. She looked lovely, but he couldn't imagine having to be stuffed into a corset. Some days he genuinely thanked the universe he'd been born with a dick. And now that he thought about it, his dick wasn't that much smaller than his brother's. It was simply that his dick had some humility, some modesty and refinement.

"I thought you would be in a privacy room by now," Jackie said, a knowing smile on her scarlet lips.

With Kori. How was Kori going to deal with the fact that everyone would think they had moved their relationship past the friend zone? How would she handle the fact that they actually *had* moved past it? That was the better question. It wasn't like she'd hung around. There could be serious issues for them to work out.

But he wasn't going to let that stand in his way. She was perfect for him. She complemented him.

And the truth of the matter was it was way past time for him to move on and settle down and start to build something. He could do that with her.

Was he being rash? Probably, but this decision didn't make him antsy. It didn't feel like something he should meditate on.

She made him feel alive.

"Where did Kori go, Vince?"

Jackie sighed. "Did the little coward run away?"

"I'm sure she'll have a reasonable excuse." And he would listen to it. "Mistress Jackie, could you please ask your submissive where my submissive went."

Vince's head came up off Jackie's fuck-me-hard boots, his eyes lighting up. "I knew you two made a connection. It was so easy to see in the way you caned her. That was beautiful. She needed that so badly. And she ran away like a coward. She even forced Sarah and Mia to leave with her. I think they went home, but I stayed here with Mistress. Mostly because I love Mistress, but also because when those three complain about men I get scared."

He was sure lots of things scared Vince when Jackie was around. She placed her well-manicured hand on his head and eased him back down. "You did well, pet. Perhaps later I'll reward you with an old-fashioned pegging. I do enjoy going old-school. Spank that brat when you find her, Kai. She deserves it."

It was said with an affectionate fondness. At least he knew Kori's play partners had accepted her apology. Not that they would be playing with her again.

His cell phone buzzed and he looked down. A text came through from an unfamiliar number.

Where is your brother heading for the evening? He lost me at the light.

Ah, the feds were quietly hanging around. That text made his stomach turn. It reminded him that he wasn't simply fulfilling a contract. He was spying on his brother. He was trying to figure out if a killer had gotten close to Jared. He would go through their files again, check their histories against his instincts. His brother's entourage was one fucked-up group of people.

He could do that tomorrow. For tonight, he was done. Let the feds do their thing. He had his own fucked-up human to deal with.

Some club. I don't know. Check his social media. I'm sure he's announced it to the world.

He shut his phone off for the night. The doctor was out.

He had other things he needed to do.

Chapter Six

"What do you think of Case Taggart?"

Kori turned to the woman who had asked the question. Mia was sitting on the couch, her legs curled under her and a glass of wine in her hand. Sarah sat next to her, a frown still on her face. She hadn't wanted to leave the club, but there had been the small problem of Kori's tires getting slashed. She'd explained to Sarah that she couldn't drive home without tires and getting someone out to fix it would have to wait until the next day. That was what she got for parking outside of Sanctum. She'd forgotten her keycard to get into the parking lot, but there was a nice gate between the parking lot of the building Kai owned and Sanctum that only required a code, so she'd parked by her building and walked over.

And some asshole had taken a knife to her tires. All four had been slashed. She'd had to run back into Sanctum, trying to hide from Kai the whole time, and then convince Sarah to give her a ride home.

If anyone knew she'd gone out by herself, there would have been hell to pay. She'd snuck around the bouncer because she hadn't wanted to wait for an escort out. Kai could have found her and then she would have been forced to talk about her feelings.

Apparently Mia was having feelings for a guy, too, though she seemed inclined to talk about them.

"He's a nice man." Kori answered Mia, who had come along for the ride. Her training Dom had gotten stuck at work and she'd gone home with Kori and Sarah. It looked like they would have a guest on the couch tonight. "He's been through a lot."

"I know he recently lost his brother." Mia took a long drink of the rich ruby liquid. "He seems to hate me. I don't get it. I'm nice to him and everything."

She hadn't seen them interact, but she knew Case. Big Tag had called her and a couple of the long-term subs in for a crash course in BDSM with Case. She wasn't sure why Case Taggart had suddenly needed Master rights at Sanctum, but she'd been game. Anything to help a friend. "I think he's hurting. Theo wasn't only his brother. He was Case's twin. They shared everything. When they graduated from high school, they went straight in the Navy together. They got separated in the beginning but were in the same SEAL training class before the CIA yanked them both and they somehow ended up here."

She didn't know the whole story. One day McKay-Taggart had way more employees than it had the day before.

Mia put down her glass. "That's fascinating. So the Taggart brothers went straight from SEAL training into Agency work? And they talk about it? Shouldn't that be classified?"

Shit. Was she not supposed to know that stuff? She'd gone to dinner one night with a bunch of the McKay-Taggart crowd and they talked pretty openly. Then of course they probably didn't think she would mention it to people outside the circle. Maybe they thought she was like Kai and what they said was covered under confidentiality. Charlotte might shoot her. "No, they don't talk about it and you shouldn't either. I shouldn't have mentioned it."

"Why?" Sarah asked. "He's not a spy now. I personally think way too many things are classified."

"I don't think he was ever a spy." Now that she thought about it, if Charlotte Taggart didn't want someone to know something, she wouldn't talk about it. "I think he was always a soldier."

Mia looked thoughtful for a moment. "And his brother died on a mission? I thought McKay-Taggart worked for businesses. I guess I thought that was things like finding corporate spies. Not many of those in the islands I would think."

"They work everywhere from what I can tell." It wasn't surprising that Mia was interested in Case. He was an amazingly attractive man. Like all the Taggarts, Case was a Viking god. "They do lots of kinds of work. I haven't heard the story about how Theo died. I only know a job went very wrong."

"No one wants to talk about it." Sarah set her glass down. "It hurts too much."

"I find it interesting that he died on the same island as Senator Hank McDonald. Did y'all see the news on his death? He died on the exact same island and around the same time. I always wondered about the story of his death," Mia said.

"Are you talking about the dude from Houston? Didn't he have a heart attack?" Sarah poured herself another glass of wine.

Mia was often interested in politics, but Kori couldn't help her here. "I have no idea. Once we all realized Theo was gone, I don't think any of us thought much past him, and Big Tag doesn't talk about work outside the office. If that's true then I suspect something was happening and the team was likely working to protect the senator. They do a lot of security details. We'll never know. That side of the Sanctum world keeps its secrets."

She couldn't help but think about Erin. Erin had been there when Theo had died. Kori knew that much. Had she held him as he died? Felt him take his last breath?

She'd run away from Kai today, and now that felt like a cowardly thing to do. Kai was her friend, her best friend really. Erin had lost the man she loved, had a hard road ahead of her, and Kori was sneaking out so she didn't have to have a difficult conversation with the number one man in her life.

Mia's eyes narrowed. "But don't you think…"

Her question was interrupted by a knock on the door.

It was one in the morning. Who the hell would be here at one in the morning?

"I'll get the bat." Sarah stood up, slapping her hands together like she'd been waiting for an occasion such as this to kick some ass.

Mia was up on her feet. "Who would come over this late? And what is she planning on doing with that bat? I have a gun if we need one."

That surprised her. The blonde was bubbly and fluffy and didn't look like a chick who carried concealed. "How about we find out who it is before we murder them?"

"It's not murder. It's self-defense here," Sarah corrected.

Wow, she'd never suspected her friends were so blood thirsty. "Fine, if there's a crazed killer on the other side of the door, self-defense murder him. I'm going to find out."

Sometimes their neighbor from next door got confused. He was an elderly gentleman with the sweetest wife in the world, and every now and then he thought it was 1955 and showed up asking where Elvis was playing. Mr. Swanson needed neither a bat to the head nor one of Mia's bullets.

She looked through the peephole and stepped back. "Oh, shit."

Sarah had her bat in hand. "I'm ready."

Mia was staring her way. "Who is it?"

Kai. It was Kai standing out on her porch looking completely hot and professorial with his jeans and button-down and sport coat. It was the one with those patches on his elbows. He'd put his glasses on and his hair was back. Nothing to see here, ladies. Just a super-smart man who could spank a sub until she cried out in complete surrender.

He was also a man who wouldn't walk away. There was no way he would leave because they didn't answer. The lights were on so if she didn't want the entire McKay-Taggart crew called out to investigate why she wasn't answering the door, she'd better open it.

"Stand down, warrior princesses. It's only Kai." She unlocked the deadbolt. Sometimes it was better to rip the bandage off quickly. They would have a short talk where she would reassure Kai that they would be fine tomorrow and he would head back out. She'd been so wrong to leave.

She opened the door. "Kai, I'm so sorry I didn't tell you I was leaving. I got involved in some things..." Like worrying about how I was going to look you in the face again. "...and I should have texted you."

"You should have stayed around so we could talk. I went to get you a robe. Did you run around the club naked?"

She gave him what she hoped was an impish grin. "I might have mentioned that I'm an exhibitionist."

He nodded slowly as though taking in her words. "Well, you could have told me you were leaving. I worried about you."

"Hi, Kai." Sarah waved his way.

"Are y'all playing baseball at this hour?" Kai nodded toward the bat Sarah was holding.

"Nope," Kori replied, eager to get him out of the house. Now that she thought about it, it was great that he'd stopped by on his way home. Well, driven several miles out of his way since he lived next to the club, but it was good. The awkward first interaction would be gone and they would be back to normal in the morning. No muss. No fuss. "They were prepared to take you down should you have turned out to be a creepy stalker guy. Mia's got a gun."

Mia held up her hands as though caught. "Licensed and stuff. All totally legal here. We should let you two talk."

Kori shook her head. "Not necessary. Kai came here to make sure I got home okay."

"You two should definitely talk," Sarah said, replacing her baseball bat and backing toward the kitchen. "Night, Kai."

"Night," Mia said with a wink as she followed Sarah back.

Ah, betrayal. Her old friend. Not that she wouldn't have done the same damn thing. She sighed and turned to Kai, who had to be super tired and longing to get home to his bed. "They're going to tease us mercilessly."

He moved toward her. "About what?"

Was he going to pretend nothing had happened? It didn't seem a very Kai thing to do. "About the scene."

"Why would they tease us about the scene? The scene was beautiful." He kept coming, crossing the space between them.

Maybe he needed a hug. Still, something about the way he was watching her made her suddenly feel like a rabbit in the presence of a very academic wolf. She backed up and tried to stop her stupid heart from thudding in her chest. This had to end. It was the adrenaline left over from the scene. That had to be it. She couldn't feel light-headed and giddy every time this man walked in a room from now on. "It was an awesome scene. You were great."

"I wasn't looking for praise." He was so close now and he didn't seem to be interested in personal space. "We need rules."

She nodded and found herself backed up against the wall. His words made total sense to her. Rules. They were all about rules and boundaries and all the things that made the world around them safe and sane. "Of course. Don't think I'm going to turn into some clingy thing, Kai. I understand what happened."

"Do you?" He stopped a few feet from her, but she could practically feel his heat.

Despite the fact that there was some precious distance between them, she couldn't help but feel the tiniest bit stalked. "I do. We're cool, Kai."

"I'm not cool. There is nothing cool about me right now. I need to make some rules. Rule number one is when I give you a mind-blowing orgasm, you have to at least stay around long enough to kiss me."

Her first thought was—what? Kiss him? Her second was a little easier to handle. The arrogance of that man. "Mind blowing? How do you know it was mind blowing?"

His lips curled up in the wickedest smile. "I think it was the way your pussy clenched around my thumb and how you screamed. Do you want to tell me you faked that? Because I won't believe you and I might have to prove it to you all over again. This time we'll be in private and I can show you exactly how nasty I can be."

"What are you doing?" She realized with dawning horror that her nipples had gone hard, like they were saluting the Master.

"Like I said, I'm making some rules. Are you going to follow them or not?"

She couldn't think long enough to follow them. "I don't understand what's going on here. Kai, we still work together. Unless you fired me. Did you fire me?"

He reached out and brushed her hair off her shoulder. The minute his fingers brushed her skin it was like she was back on that stage waiting for him to smack her ass hard. Her whole body had softened the minute he touched her. Except for her nipples, which still stood in a full-on salute, and the thin material of her tank wasn't helping.

"I would never fire you. I would be lost without you. Which is precisely why we need rules."

"I thought one of the rules was we didn't play together because we work together." She'd thought friendly Kai was dangerous. Who the hell was this guy?

"We broke that tonight and now we need new rules."

"Or we could forgive ourselves and go back to the old rules."

He stopped, his stare pinning her to the wall. "Are you afraid of me?"

Yes. She was terrified of him. He was everything she couldn't have, and he knew exactly how to work her because she wasn't about to tell him that. "Of course not."

"Are you embarrassed by what happened?"

"Not particularly." She was only worried about how it affected her relationship with Kai. Because Kai was too important to her. "I'm not willing to risk our friendship, Kai."

"By adding to it?" He took a step back and some of the tension seemed to go out of the room. "We shouldn't talk about this tonight. I'm too tired to be rational."

Thank god. She had no idea how to respond to him. Well, she did. It would have been the easiest thing in the world to do what he wanted. Rule number one—she owed him a kiss. A kiss. She could have gone up on her toes and brushed her lips against his and then she would know what it felt like to kiss Kai Ferguson. Somehow it seemed more intimate than what they'd done in the club. It was sweeter. If she kissed Kai she couldn't say they'd only been performing a scene for Jared's sake. Jared. She latched on to that question. "Shouldn't you be with your brother?"

He turned away and walked over to the couch. "Yeah, that's kind of why I'm here. He's apparently gotten extremely good at breaking and entering and he took over the guest room. Hell, the way he's going he might have moved into my room, lock, stock, and entourage. He's going to some nightclub but he's planning on coming back to my place. I can't get a full set of those laser things that chop off arms and stuff until tomorrow."

She couldn't help but laugh. "You are not wiring our office with lasers to keep your brother out."

"Okay, how about we go tomorrow morning, pick up three Dobermans and train them to eat anything that smells like Axe body spray."

"We're not killing your brother. Can you imagine the public mourning of his abs? You would have women from all over the planet showing up with wreaths and teddy bears, laying them out as a shrine to your brother's hot bod."

Kai made a gagging sound. "Don't forget the gay guys. I was told Jared doesn't discriminate against any gender that wants to worship him. I don't want to go home."

Something about the slump of his shoulders made her heart nearly break. This was Kai. He was always strong, always resilient. He was the one everyone came to for advice or help and he gave it immediately, even to people she knew he didn't like. "Where would you go?"

"This couch looks comfy," he said quietly.

"That couch is more of a love seat, and there's zero chance of your six-foot-two-inch body fitting onto it." He would have to bend that body in half to fit on it or most of his legs would be hanging off. Either way, she couldn't imagine he would be comfortable.

He still didn't turn, as though he wasn't ready to face her. "Okay. I can sleep on the floor. I've slept in worse places."

"You want to avoid your brother that much?" It wasn't like she didn't understand. Her sister had shown up in Dallas a few months before, wreaking havoc on Kori's existence. She'd been high and angry, and who had Kori turned to when her sister got to be too much to deal with? Yeah, Kai had gotten Shawna into a rehab center. Kai was the one who traveled with Kori on family visitation days. Kai was the one who was going to help Shawna transition when she completed the course. Kai was the one who helped Kori finance it all.

"Just for tonight." There was a weary tone to his voice. "I have to deal with him eventually, but I don't want to do it tonight. All I need is a pillow."

"I think Mia's had too much to drink. She's staying here tonight. I don't know how comfortable she'll feel sharing the living room."

"Oh." He nodded. "All right. I'll see you in the morning."

She stopped him before he made it to the door. Somehow her hand found its way into his. "Or you can stay with me. I have a queen-sized bed so there's plenty of room. I think I snore though."

It was a horrible mistake, but she couldn't let him walk out that door. She couldn't. After everything they'd meant to one another, she couldn't be the one who shipped him back to somewhere he didn't want to be. He would never do that to her.

"I can handle a little snoring," he said, his eyes warm. "The way I feel I'll sleep like a log."

Something about the way his fingers curled around hers made her mushy. She hated feeling mushy and weepy and like something was happening that was way more important than it should be. "This doesn't change anything between us."

He nodded his head solemnly. "It only adds."

"Kai, I'm not sleeping with you tonight."

He frowned. "You're taking the couch?"

He could be so obtuse at times for a man with a genius level IQ. "No. I was talking about sex. I'm not going to sleep on the couch. It's lumpy and horrible. I'm not having sex with you tonight."

"I promise to keep my hands to myself."

That sounded terrible. "Come on. We have a long day tomorrow."

She would set an alarm and maybe if she hustled him out of the door early enough tomorrow morning she could convince Sarah and Mia that nothing happened. Which was true because absolutely nothing was going to happen except some serious sleeping. That was totally going to happen.

She led him back to her bedroom. They'd been friends for a long time, worked together most of the time she'd been here in Dallas. He'd never been in her bedroom. She'd been in his a hundred times before, mostly since he worked and lived in the same building. First at Sanctum and then in their own place after the explosion. At least twice a year she would come into work and find him a ball of snot and sadness curled up in the middle of his futon. Yes, he was a grown man who slept on a futon. He claimed it helped his back or something but mostly she thought he couldn't afford much else. She would have to spend days bringing him chicken soup and babying him.

Her bedroom was a bit plain, but it had some windows into her soul.

"Who is this?" Kai's eyes almost immediately found the pictures on her dresser.

She closed the door behind her, locking out the world. The fact that she was alone in a bedroom with Kai was not lost on her. Alone and with every intention of getting into bed with him. Her room seemed smaller than before, with his big body taking up most of the space. "It's me and my mom and my dogs. The pug was named Jinx, the pit bull mix was Cuddles, and the one I'm holding was named Butch."

"You named the tiny Chihuahua Butch?"

She shrugged. "Better than that. He was a girl, but she humped everything she could so I think she was gender confused. I had a lot of dogs growing up."

He nodded to the other pictures of pups she had framed around the room. "Obviously. Were you the girl who picked up strays?"

"I guess I tend to like animals more than people. I'm the person who stops traffic to move the turtle out of the road. I always wonder if the turtle is pissed because maybe he knew where he was going and I take him someplace different." She'd always wanted to write a kids' film about that possibility.

"You don't keep animals here."

She missed them with all her heart and soul, but it was another piece of herself that seemed lost. "Well, I work a lot."

"You work at a place where the boss would pretty much let you do anything you like. If you want to bring a dog to work, do it. As long as the pup's trained, it would probably be nice to have around. Which side do you sleep on?" He pulled off his jacket, laying it over the small chair tucked under her desk.

"Uhm, the right mostly. I think I move around a lot."

"Then this should be fun. I'm very warm and cuddly, so if you end up wrapped around me, it's going to be your fault because I'm a polite sleeper. I'm very Zen when I sleep." His shirt was next to go.

Oh, that man was gorgeous. He might not be as cut as his brother, but she preferred his lean body. He did as much yoga as he lifted weights. Kai was flexible in more ways than one.

"Are you all right? I can go," he offered.

"We're friends. Friends can sleep together without sex. I'll be

From Sanctum with Love

right back. I'm going to brush my teeth. Make yourself comfortable." She fled into her tiny bathroom even as she saw his hands go to the waistband of his jeans.

What was she doing? Was she actually going to hop in bed with Kai? Maybe she should sleep on the floor.

Like Kai would accept that. She looked at herself in the mirror. Kai obviously needed a friend. He wouldn't be here if he didn't need her. He didn't make a habit of showing up and needing a sleeping buddy. If she'd shown up on his doorstep and needed a cuddle, he would very likely open his arms and give it to her. Instead, she'd shown up with a junkie sister and he'd handled it, so she was going to brush her teeth and get her ass out there and sleep with her boss.

Five minutes later she walked out of the bathroom having made herself as hygienically ready for a sleep cycle as possible. Kai had turned off all the lights with the exception of the one by her side of the bed. He was lying back, the sheets halfway down his chest, and he was not wearing a shirt.

"Please tell me you've got something on under there."

"I'm in my boxers. Do you want me to wear jeans?" He turned toward her, propping up his head in his hand.

He looked like the best man treat ever offered to a girl. "No, it's fine." She could handle it. He wasn't wearing anything except his likely very thin boxers. It would be good. This would prove once and for all that they were friends and no amazingly hot spanking could change that. She slid into bed and turned out the light. "Good night, Kai."

She lay there for a second. It was so odd to have someone in bed with her.

"Why didn't you tell me you were a masochist?"

Should she snore? Maybe if she gave him a couple of good snores, he would think she was asleep.

"Were you afraid of me? Don't answer with arrogant Kori. I'm honestly asking. I told you I was a sadist when I first met you. You nodded and ignored me the rest of the day. I thought you would quit. I was a little surprised when you showed up the next day."

Thank god for blackout shades. Somehow it was easier to talk in complete darkness. She remembered the day he was talking about. It had been before her first night at Sanctum. She'd started the job with Kai and Big Tag had sweetened the pot by offering her a membership at Sanctum as part of her salary. Back then, Big Tag had funded Kai's practice. Kai had warned her that he would be in the dungeon that night and explained in perfectly academic terms his status as a sadist. She'd nearly gotten to her knees right then and there.

How should she explain this to him without giving away everything? She stared up at the darkness. "I'd just moved here. I'd been in a relationship that was unhealthy to say the least. I didn't know you. It seemed easiest to keep the two things separate."

"Was he your Dom?"

"Yes. For several years. I was in the lifestyle before he was and then he took over everything. My life. My career. I moved to Arizona for a couple of years and then I came out here. I didn't want to get back to that place again."

"So that's why you don't let anyone give you what you need."

She didn't say the truth. The truth was no one at Sanctum with the exception of Kai could give her what she needed. She needed more than a hard hand on her ass. She needed Kai's unique brand of dominance. "I think it's dangerous for a person like me."

"He abused your trust. Not every Dom would do that. I wouldn't even call him a Dom. A Dom puts his sub's needs first."

She'd spent the last five years of her life dissecting that relationship. "I know that intellectually, but I don't think I can ever go back. I can't get in that deep again. Tonight was fun, but I have to leave it there."

"So you're leaving Sanctum? Because the other Dominants aren't going to let you get away with faking anymore."

She hadn't even thought of that. Silence filled the dark as the real ramifications of the night hit her. She was stuck. Now that everyone knew, no one would play with her. Not the way they had before. She'd been outed. Even if they forgave her for keeping the truth from them, most of the Dominants wouldn't want to play with a sub who had zero interest in ever letting them in.

"I'm going to move my arm out," Kai said, his voice carefully polite. "I told you I wouldn't lay a hand on you but if you rolled over and cuddled up against me and then my arm kind of turned in, that wouldn't be the same thing, right?"

He was offering her comfort without asking for anything in return. She was sick of overthinking, sick of constantly putting up boundaries and barriers. Kori rolled to her side and sure enough Kai's arm wrapped around her, drawing her against the warmth and strength of his body. "It's not the same thing at all."

He cocooned her in the dark, his hand holding her head against his chest. "I'll talk to them. I'll make sure you have a safe place to play."

Or she could accept that she had a play partner. It wasn't like she'd been there alone tonight. Kai was excellent at compartmentalizing. She let her head rest on his chest, hearing the beat of his heart. Slowly she relaxed, her arm winding around his torso so they were wrapped together. It didn't have to mean anything beyond they were friends and she needed comfort. He needed comfort, too. It was obvious his brother's appearance threatened Kai's much needed calm. What if she could give him some of that peace back through play? He hadn't found a play partner who met his needs either. They could help each other. She could stay at Sanctum and nothing had to change with the singular exception of getting to go to her happy place a couple of times a week. Kai wasn't Morgan. Kai wouldn't take her freedom and turn her into some kind of pathetic acolyte who gave up her own credit to please the Master.

No one could do that to her. No one except herself. She'd made those choices. She'd let herself slide.

If she was vigilant about keeping herself in check, she could have what she needed. And it wasn't like Kai was looking for scripts he could pretend were his own. Kai likely wouldn't insist he got full credit for watering the plants or keeping his schedule organized.

"Kori? Talk to me. I'm getting afraid."

She nestled closer to him because somehow in the safety of the darkness it seemed all right to cuddle. Especially with a man who wasn't scared of saying he was afraid. This was one of the things she adored about Kai. He was open with his feelings. She could trust that he was always honest with her. "Afraid of what?"

"Afraid that you're going to push me away because of what

happened tonight. I don't want that. I enjoyed our scene, but if it scared you that much, I won't ask you to play again. This relationship is important to me." His fingers moved over her, running across her hair.

This was what she'd missed earlier, the connection, the sweet intimacy. She'd been wrong to run away. Kai just wanted the connection that came from a scene. That was all. "I wasn't thinking of pushing you away. I was wondering if it wouldn't make sense for us to be play partners."

He moved, his lips brushing her forehead in a sweet gesture of affection. "I think that makes complete sense. We're obviously well matched. I haven't met anyone who needs me the way you do. I call myself a sadist, but I don't really want to cause pain that isn't necessary. I suppose in the strictest sense that makes me more a rough Dom than a sadist. I enjoy the play. I sometimes think I need it so the part of me that gets fulfilled by hurting someone doesn't take over my life. I can keep it at bay, be the man I want to be. Lately I haven't…well, let's say I haven't fed the beast and I worry he's coming out in little ways. I'm short with everyone if I don't think about what I say."

She understood. She'd spent years keeping everyone at arm's length because there was a part of her that she'd hidden away. It was out now and the choice was to accept what she needed or run away again. "I think we can make it work. This relationship is important to me, too."

So important. They could make this work. They could stay friends. She played with friends all the time.

"We need rules."

Rules. Kai was a big fan of rules. At least he wasn't talking about a contract at this point. The idea of signing a contract again made her antsy. "Sure, we can talk about some common sense rules in the morning."

He would likely want to talk about compartmentalizing. He would want to keep the play strictly to the club and that was fine with her.

He was quiet for a moment. "Thank you for telling me why you worry."

It had actually felt good to tell him. It made it easier for her to tell him other things. "I knew your brother in Los Angeles. I worked for a production company before I came out here. Strictly professional. I didn't date him or anything."

"I'm glad to hear that. Maybe it makes me a bad guy, but I'm glad you didn't date him. My brother and I have history when it comes to the women in our lives. I think I push away women I could care about because he slept with my fiancée. I thought I'd gotten over it, but now I have to wonder. I wish he hadn't come here."

He was not practicing what he preached. "Hey, you're the one who always says you have to face your issues. I think Jared is one big issue for you."

His chest moved as he chuckled. "But if I'd faced him tonight, I would be arguing with him instead of being warm and in bed with you, so in this case deflection works in my favor. Go to sleep. We'll deal with all of this in the morning. It's going to be all right. We're going to be all right. You'll see."

Nothing had to change except she got to cuddle up with the most beautiful man she'd ever met.

One day he would meet the right sub. One day he wouldn't need her anymore and he would want to be with someone who could fulfill all his needs, every one of his sick and glorious desires.

But for now she could find some peace with him. She moved her leg up, putting her thigh over his...what the hell was that? She'd touched something hard and thick and impossibly long.

"Kai?"

"Yeah, that's my penis. He's not going to attack. He's just...reacting. He needs some time to calm down. Go to sleep. He'll still be there in the morning. You do have a cold shower, right?"

"Yeah."

"Excellent." He shifted so his cock wasn't right up against her anymore.

His really big, really erect cock.

It was the longest time before she got to sleep.

Chapter Seven

Kai neatly flipped the omelet. One of the helpful things about being the son of a mom who had worked two, sometimes three jobs at times was the fact that he'd learned to cook at a very young age. He stared down at the ham and cheese and spinach omelet and a memory came rushing in. He'd been eight and trying to cook eggs for Jared and they'd burned because…he was flipping eight years old. Jared had sat at the table and eaten every bite, insisting they were awesome even though Kai knew they sucked. He'd told Jared he had to eat them anyway because it was all the food they had. Jared could have been a brat, but he'd smiled through the whole thing.

"You should stay over more often." Sarah grinned at him from her chair at the bar. There was a plate in front of her waiting for that omelet he was working on. "Kori can't cook for shit. Well, she cooks but it's all vegetables and nasty stuff."

He was grateful for the distraction. He flipped the omelet one last time before easing it on to her plate. "Kori's a vegetarian. I always thought that was a health thing until I saw the pictures of her dogs last night."

Being inside Kori's bedroom had answered a whole lot of questions for him. Of course it had brought up a whole bunch more. She didn't talk about her past. He'd thought she was embarrassed by her sister and an underprivileged childhood—he could understand that. Now he wondered if it was something more. He knew he would have to play dirty to get under her armor.

He'd started last night. He'd walked in thinking he would basically tell her that now they were a couple and they would work things out. One look at the fear in her eyes had made him completely change his plan. He needed a mix of hard and soft play with her. Sure she enjoyed a rough hand on her backside, but she craved someone who cared enough to be gentle with her, too. Not that she would say that. She likely didn't recognize the need in herself, but then she wasn't the most self-aware woman he'd ever met. It was all right because he was honest enough for both of them.

"Ooo, breakfast." Mia hopped onto the seat beside Sarah and clapped her hands together. "Is this made to order or should I accept anything you put in front of me? Because I can do either. I am not picky when it comes to men feeding me."

He could use this time to get to know the mysterious Mia better. "I'm here to serve Kori's friends whatever they would like. Unless you want a meal that requires anything more than eggs, cheese, ham, and a surprisingly healthy amount of veggies."

"I will take what Sarah's having. Yum." Mia smiled brightly, belying any hangover she might have. "You're up bright and early this morning. I thought the two of you might sleep in."

Sarah shook her head. "I'm telling you they didn't do the nasty. I heard absolutely nothing." She blushed. "Not that I was trying to, but the walls are thin."

"We were tired last night. It had been a long day." He wasn't about to tell them that he'd actually planned on trying to seduce her, but he'd decided she needed comfort and security more than another orgasm. He started cooking the ham and spinach. It was a trick Sean had taught him. Cook the ingredients first and then add the eggs around them. Back when he was a kid, he'd simply thrown a bunch of stuff into a pan and prayed it didn't catch fire.

You make the best grilled cheese, Kai. Jared would stand beside him, his eyes wide because the kid had always, always been hungry.

He'd been a bottomless pit.

Take care of your brother, Kai. He needs you more than you know. You've been his father his whole life.

He forced his mother's dying words out of his head. She hadn't known exactly how well her youngest son could take care of himself.

And there it was. There was that nasty kernel of anger. He thought it had gone away, thought time and distance had healed the wound, but the flame had merely been banked.

There was a knock on the door, pulling Kai back from his thoughts. That was happening a lot this morning. He'd thought about staying in bed, but he wasn't sure he would be able to stop himself from kissing her and he had plans for that later on today.

Kori was going to find out what being his sub meant.

Because he damn straight wasn't about to be her "play partner," whatever that meant. He was fairly certain "play partners" got no kisses.

He wanted some kisses. Like stupidly wanted them from her. It seemed wrong to him that he'd touched her pussy, brought her to orgasm, and hadn't kissed her yet.

"I'll go and see who's here at a ridiculously early hour." Sarah hopped off her chair.

"I should go." He was the guy here. The neighborhood was safe enough, but bad things still happened.

"No, breakfast boy, you're needed here. Trust me. I've opened the door many times." Sarah flounced off. He wondered if she wore a full-length satin gown and robe with fluffy feathers and kitten-heeled slippers every morning. Sarah looked like she'd rolled out of a 1950s pinup girl's bed. If said pinup girl wore full makeup and had perfect hair every morning.

"So you and Kori are an item now, huh?" Mia was wearing what she'd had on the night before. When he'd woken up earlier, she'd been using Sarah's shower, the blankets and pillows neatly folded up.

He wished he could have gotten into her purse, but then again, he wasn't an investigator. That didn't mean he couldn't help the cause. "I don't think she would put a label on it."

Mia smiled and nodded. "Ah, so you're playing around. I guess

I didn't think you were the playboy type."

So she was protective. That was interesting. Or she simply didn't like men who weren't committed. He shrugged. "I definitely wouldn't call myself the playboy type. I kind of hate that type. Rich. Privileged. I've known a few. They're practically their own stereotype. You know what I'm talking about, right? The young billionaire who thinks he owns the world because he thought up some silly app. Yeah, I'm definitely not like that."

Her brother was though. From what he'd read, her brother had gone from foster care to the richest man in Austin in a short period of years. Of course he'd also found out that her father had killed himself and Mia's mother in a murder/suicide. That kind of childhood trauma could fuck a person up.

Her mouth turned down. "They're not all that way. Some of those developers work hard. Some of them use that money to pull their families out of poverty. You can't always judge a book by its cover, you know."

Definitely protective. But definitely not honest. "I don't know. I only know what I see in the media."

"The media often paints people in a bad light," she said primly. "It depends on what they think will sell. They're all about making money these days. No one seems interested in real journalism."

"How's the job going?"

According to her paperwork, she was a receptionist at a dental office. He, of course, knew her status as a freelance reporter. He had to wonder about that. He thought Big Tag and Case were too quick to think she was a Collective plant. Their own tragedy might be clouding their judgment in this case.

"Great. It's really nice. Keeps me busy." She leaned forward, her eyes on the pan. "I think the work you do is extraordinary. It's important to help people. Not many people get that. It's a calling, I think. People like doctors and therapists and the ones who put themselves on the line to get to the truth. Sorry, I'm still waking up. I'm probably not making a ton of sense. I just wanted you to know I admire you."

And she felt guilty about lying to him. He would also bet she felt a kinship with him. It was there in the way she held herself as though she wanted to tell him her secret, thought he perhaps would understand. He added the egg mixture now that the spinach had gotten nice and soft and the ham was warm. "It's important to help people in more ways than one. We all do our part. I'm sure you're very good at helping people who are scared. A lot of people hate going to the dentist. You give them the proper facts and then they're not so scared."

She nodded. "Yes. Information is very powerful. I'm glad you get that."

"Information can transform the world." He was definitely getting to her. She was dying to tell someone. He wondered if she'd told Sarah, but he would bet she hadn't.

"It can be very important. Sometimes people aren't what they seem and it takes someone willing to stand up and tell the truth to make justice work the way it should."

"What are we really talking about, Mia?"

She bit her bottom lip, but a light came into her eyes. He knew that light. It was determination, pure and simple. She'd made a decision. She was going to spill.

"Hey, brother. I thought I'd find you here." His brother strode in, a smile on his face like he hadn't been out partying like a rock star into the wee hours of the morning. Hell no. Not Jared Johns. He was practically glowing.

He was fairly certain his brother used some serious moisturizer. And Kai wanted to punch him in his cosmetically perfect face. He'd almost had Mia talking and now she was shut down. It was right there in the stiffness of her body, the way her arms crossed over her chest as though she needed protection.

"Aren't you supposed to be at McKay-Taggart this morning?" He'd made a schedule for his brother, one that kept him busy most of the time and out of Kai's hair. He'd also thought about the fact that if Jared bugged Ian too much, Big Tag might take care of his problem.

Jared gestured back toward the living room. "Your friend came looking for you so he gave me a ride here. I'm trying to get into character so I'm avoiding limos like the plague. According to Big Tag, they're for douchebags."

So Ian was already fucking with Jared. That was inevitable. He glanced back and Case Taggart was standing in the doorway, his massive body filling the space.

"I went to your office to find out if Kori's all right," Case said, his eyes going to Mia. "Hello, Mia. I'm surprised to find you here. Shouldn't you be at work?"

She slid off her barstool. "I was getting ready to go. Kai, it turns out I don't have time for breakfast. Thanks, anyway. I have a train to catch."

Case didn't move. "Or I could take you. I'll drop you off wherever you like."

Mia stopped, as though wary. "Really?"

Case nodded. "Of course. I'm sorry. We got off on the wrong foot. I've been sharp with you and I apologize."

"You've been a complete asshole," she argued.

"Then let me make it up to you. Let me give you a ride to work." Where he would likely follow her to see where she went because Mia didn't work at the place she said she did. It looked like Case was taking a play from his brothers' book. Charm. It was so much easier to catch flies with honey or a smile and the promise of pleasure.

Mia softened, her eyes lighting a bit. "If it's not out of your way."

"Not at all." Case was working. Kai was certain she could have said she needed to go to Oklahoma and Case would have claimed he was going that way, too.

Thank god. One less thing for him to deal with. Where the hell was Kori? If she'd slipped out, he was going to spank her.

He flipped the omelet and then slid it on the plate.

"It's raining men in here today," Sarah said with a smile as she looked over at Jared. "Can I get you some coffee?"

There was no way to miss how Jared's eyes slid over Sarah's curves. "I'll take anything you have, honey. And I like it strong."

He was going to vomit. "Mia, do you want to try to take this with you?"

"I'm late, but thanks anyway." Mia was following Case into the living room.

"Thank god," Jared said, taking her place at the bar. "I'm starving. All you had at your place was granola and shit. I need some protein. I can start with that, but I'll probably need two or three of those."

Sarah set the coffee mug in front of him. "Because you burn so many calories when you're doing all that workout stuff. I subscribe to all your YouTube channels. My favorite one is Jared's Abs of Steel where someone spliced all your *Dart* workouts together and set it to Marvin Gaye's 'Let's Get It On.' I watch it at least once a day."

He was definitely going to vomit. There was a reason he didn't spend much time on the Internet.

"So you can give Kori a ride?" Case said as he held the door open for Mia.

Sarah sat down beside Jared as he dug into Mia's omelet. Kai was fairly certain he heard her saying something about how perfectly masculine Jared's eating practices were.

Kai was confused and not only by his brother's innate ability to attract fawning women. "I can but why would Kori need a ride?"

Case looked out the door as though making certain Mia didn't get away. "You don't know? I thought that was why you came over here. I was sure when I saw your Jeep in the driveway that she'd called you. Dude, did you and Kori get it on last night? Because I've got some money riding on it and it would be better for me if you held off a few weeks."

Fucking assholes. "When did this start up?"

"After that scene last night," Case admitted.

"This is excellent, Kai," Jared said with a nod. "I don't suppose you could whip up some pancakes. It's been a long time since I had your pancakes. I'll run 'em off, if you know what I mean."

"I'll watch you run," Sarah vowed. "I'll set up a couple of lawn chairs, make some mimosas, and you can run all around the block."

"Shut that shit down, Case." He wasn't about to have it get back to Kori that there was a damn betting pool concerning when they were going to sleep together. Still, something was definitely missing in all the chaos his brother had brought with him. "And why were you coming over here to check on Kori? Did you honestly think I would hurt her?"

Jared shook his head. "No. My brother would never hurt her. All that sadism stuff is strictly for the dungeon, and it looked like she was having fun, Case."

"Kori was having fun," Mia said, her purse over her shoulder as she stepped back in the doorway. "Case should understand that. I know he's a baby Dom, but he's been around Sanctum for a while I would think."

"I am not a baby Dom. I hate that term. It makes me sound soft and fluffy." Case stared Mia's way.

"Well, I was told you don't have Master rights at Sanctum," Mia returned. "If you're in a training class you're a baby Dom."

"I think we use that term in the script." Jared seemed to warm to the conversation. "It's cute."

"And it doesn't apply because I do have Master rights," Case argued.

"I don't care about baby Doms. I want to know why you thought I would hurt Kori." It rankled. He would never hurt her.

"I think he's talking about her car," Sarah explained.

"Some French toast would be good if you don't want to make pancakes." Jared was already finished with omelet number one and had reached for one of the muffins Sarah had made earlier. Where the hell did he put all those calories?

"You should have more respect. They're Doms in training." Case was still trying to make his point.

This was why he lived alone. Chaos. So much of it. "What about Kori's car?"

"Someone slashed her tires last night," Sarah explained, passing Jared another muffin. "The secret ingredient in these is love. Well, and chocolate chips, so you'll definitely need to lift some weights. I have hand weights in my room. Never been used before."

Someone slashed her tires? What the hell? She hadn't mentioned that. Not once. They'd talked and cuddled and slept together wrapped up all night and she hadn't once slipped that tidbit of information in.

They had rules. Oh, they needed new rules, but they had a few rules that had been set down when she'd become his assistant. Try to be on time. Call if you're late or sick. She had free run of the building, including his living quarters if she needed anything at all. And if she felt herself in danger, she was to call him.

He hadn't gotten a fucking call.

Everyone was talking at once. Mia defended her use of the word baby while Jared talked to Sarah about his workout plans. Kai turned to walk down the hallway. It was time he and Kori had a serious talk. He'd meant to be patient, to ease her into this whole couple thing, but he needed to make a few things plain.

She stood in the hallway, her eyes wide. She was wearing a tank top and those pajama bottoms that clung to her curves. She looked soft and sleepy and infinitely fuckable. Also confused. "Why is everyone here?"

"Why didn't you tell me someone slashed your tires last night?" Kai shot back.

"Damn it," Case said. "Ian's going to win. He took the 'within twenty-four hours' slot."

Kai shot Case his middle finger as he prowled down the hall toward Kori. "We need to have a serious talk."

She backed up, her eyes steady on his face. "We do?"

"Your room. Now."

She scurried back. At least one person was willing to obey him.

* * * *

Kori ran back to her room and gave serious consideration to locking the door behind her. She could live here now. Sarah could stuff protein bars under the door and she could live off tap water. This could be her home for many years. As long as it took for that wicked look to get out of Kai's eyes.

Or he would find a way inside anyway and then her ass was grass because that man looked serious.

She should have told him about the tires. She'd made that promise a long time ago. In her attempts to avoid him the previous evening she'd decided that calling and telling him her car had been viciously attacked was counterproductive to the whole point of avoiding him. Now with a night's wisdom behind her, she could see that it might have been a mistake.

Locking him out of her room would probably be another mistake.

She turned on him. Maybe she could get out of this. "Hey, you know in all the craziness of last night I totally forgot to mention that my tires got messed up. Maybe that was a manufacturer defect or something. It's hard to tell in the dark."

He stood in the doorway to her bedroom. Past him, she could still hear a lot of talking since it seemed her normally quiet house had been invaded. It didn't matter. They could talk all they liked because all Kori could see or really hear was Kai. "Are you certain that's the tactic you want to take with me?"

"Nope. I'm not certain at all." She wasn't certain of anything. When she'd woken and realized he wasn't still in bed with her, she'd been disappointed. She'd reached out and his side of the bed had been cold, and for a second she'd felt tears cloud her eyes. Then she'd decided it was a good thing. He'd done what she wanted him to do. He'd snuck out and avoided all the embarrassing morning after stuff. Except he hadn't. Apparently he'd invited friends over to witness the embarrassing morning after stuff. "What are you still doing here?"

He crossed his arms over his chest. "What am I still doing here? I was making you and your friends some breakfast. I was attempting to be a good…houseguest."

She was almost certain houseguest wasn't what he'd meant to say. What other words would he have used? Boyfriend? Dom? Master? Every single one of them got her heart racing. Was she thinking of trying with Kai? Could her heart handle that? "How did everyone else get here?"

"My brother seems to be stalking me and Case came over because he was worried about you. Apparently he knew about someone vandalizing your car."

That was news to her. "He did? I didn't tell him."

"Who did you tell?" The question came out with an edge of irritation.

"Sarah and Mia. I decided to wait until this morning to call someone because it was late last night." *And I'd been trying to avoid you only to end up having the best sleep of my life because I was wrapped around you.* Yeah, she wasn't going to say that.

"How about the police? Were you going to call them? If you're going to make an insurance claim, you'll need a police report. Or are you going to claim that your tires died of natural causes?"

She held her hands up, attempting to placate him. Why did her room seem so much smaller when he was in it? It was a good-sized room, but Kai took up all the space. "You're right. I should have called last night, but I was tired and I wanted to get home and get in bed."

His gorgeous eyes narrowed. "You weren't in bed. You were sitting up with your friends drinking wine. Try again."

"Kai, what's going on here? It's a couple of tires."

"You were supposed to call me if you got in trouble."

"I wasn't really in..." What was she doing? Before yesterday she would never have lied to Kai. Not right to his face. "I was nervous about seeing you after the scene."

"Finally some honesty. I'll handle it. I'll deal with the police and get you what you need for your insurance. The boys from McKay-Taggart will set up some discreet surveillance cameras around our parking lot."

There was a reason they didn't have that. "I thought you didn't want the patients to feel like they were walking into a secure zone."

Some of them had serious issues with people watching them. They dealt with a lot of PTSD patients.

"I will deal with them. Your safety is more important. Now turn around, pull your pants down and place your palms flat on the bed. It's a count of thirty."

She could actually feel her womb spasm. "What?"

Nothing about his face or stance conveyed that he was anything but dead serious. "This was a condition of your employment. It has been from the beginning."

If she wasn't careful her damn jaw was going to hit the floor. "I remember the conditions of my employment. Are you saying if I'd been late and hadn't called, you would have spanked me?"

"I suppose we should be happy you're a very prompt girl. And you tend to be good about calling. We'll never know. What I do know is that after last night, I will definitely spank you and you'll enjoy it. You might start showing up late just so you can walk into my office and present that juicy ass to me." He moved in front of her, staring down at her with heat in his eyes. "I want you to think before you tell me no. I want you to question which side of the Kori I know is going to win this battle. Is it the funny, happy, brave Kori who never stands down from a challenge, or the one who's denied herself for years because some idiot asshole Dom made her feel small. I won't ever make you feel small. My job in life will be to lift you up, to help you be strong."

His words cut through her. "What are you saying, Kai? Is this about you being my boss or acting as my play partner?"

She thought they'd worked it out last night.

His hands cupped her cheeks, forcing her to look up at him. "I'm acting as your Dom, Kori, and you know it. You can pretend all you like. You can call it whatever you want to, but you know how this ends. This ends with you and me."

She shook her head. "Kai, yesterday we were nothing more than friends."

"Yesterday I didn't understand you. Today I do, and I want you more than I want my next fucking breath. I'll go slow. I'll give you all the time you need to wrap that gorgeous brain around the idea. I'll be indulgent as hell with the exception of two things."

"Do I dare ask?"

"You play with me and only me. I won't play with anyone but you. And when something goes wrong, you call me. You give me the chance to protect you, to shelter you."

"I thought we agreed to keep it to the club."

"I didn't agree to that and why should we?" He sounded so reasonable. "What does scared Kori say?"

"Scared Kori thinks this is all moving too fast, but she's kind of drowned out by Wants to Kiss You Kori."

His lips curled up in the sweetest smile. "I know who I'm voting for. Come on, baby. We've been dancing around this since the day we met. I've put up stupid boundaries because I was scared, too. I've pushed away a lot of good in my life because I couldn't trust it. I cuddled you last night and all I could think about was the fact that I trust you. Of all the people in the world, I trust you most. I want to be with you. When I'm with you I'm not lonely."

The man knew exactly what to say to shut Scared Kori up. When she was with him, she didn't feel the hole in her soul the way she did before. Somehow even simply being friends with the man had filled her in a way no one had before. Was she going to let him go because Morgan had been a giant massive asshole?

If he hadn't been, she wouldn't have found Kai.

She went on her toes before she could talk herself out of it and brushed her lips against his. Warm, soft. Those lips were plump and sensual and he somehow made them masculine. They were like the rest of Kai. Utterly beautiful and on someone else perhaps a bit feminine, but Kai was all man.

He was still as she kissed him, her lips moving softly over his. It wouldn't last long. He was giving her this time. He would take over and her whole body thrilled at the idea. He was right. They couldn't go back after last night. They'd connected in such an intimate way that she didn't want to. Yes, she was still afraid, but this man was worth the risk.

When she eased back down, he was smiling at her. "Do you know how long I've waited for you to kiss me?"

"Probably since last night."

His hands smoothed back her hair, making her feel so wanted and cared for. "Since the day I met you. I was too stupid to understand that. Now, we have the issue of your infraction."

Yes, they did. Why had she ever thought they should keep this to the club? She turned, her hands shaking as she shoved the pajama bottoms and bikini panties off her hips and down her legs. Leaning forward, she found the position he'd asked for, palms flat on the bed, her ass in the air.

"Look at that," he whispered. "I thought I'd been rough with you but this morning your backside is fresh and perfect. It's like no one spanked you. Just this one tiny mark here."

His fingers brushed over a spot on her left cheek that made her gasp. He might not have left marks, but damn she was sore. She was about to be sorer. God, this was going to hurt. Her whole body softened at the thought.

She'd denied herself for so long.

"I'm going to give you the choice this time." Kai's fingers scraped lightly along her flesh, sending shivers up her spine. "Normally I love hearing you scream for me, really the more the better. Some tears and pleas and I'll be a very happy Dom, but there are still people out in the living room. It's not going to bother me at all, but I want you to be comfortable."

"Please gag me, Kai. Please."

"With pleasure, baby."

She could hear him moving around behind her, and when he came back he had a fresh pair of her undies in his hands.

"Unlike a lot of Doms, I personally enjoy pretty panties. They make such good gags when we need to keep our games private. Open. Since you won't be able to talk through this spanking, all you have to do to get me to stop is hold up your left hand."

He was giving her a way to safe word without speaking. She had to admit that the idea that her friends were right down the hallway and Kai was about to do dirty things to her aroused her unbearably. "I can do that."

"Stand up and ask me to gag you again. Does my sub need a gag in her mouth so she won't cry out?"

Her nipples were rigid against her tank top. "Yes, Sir. I need it."

"Open your mouth." His right hand caught her, forcing her head up. "And I damn straight meant what I said about stopping me if it's too much. I know you like it, but I won't damage you for anything. Take it."

He was rough as he shoved the panties into her mouth. She would never be able to look at those the same way again. He pressed them, filling her mouth and making her jaw ache. It was the right side of pain, exactly enough to start up the chemical reaction in her brain. Some people got runner's high. She found such peace in this place.

And it was better this time because she could trust Kai.

Because Kai was the one.

"Back down," Kai ordered.

She turned again, placing her hands down on the bed. She could scream as much as she liked now. For the first time in forever, she could actually let loose.

"Have I ever told you how beautiful you are? I like having you gagged because you can't talk back and argue with me. Did you think I didn't notice that every single time I give you a compliment, you negate it somehow? When I told you that dress was lovely on you last Monday, you told me you had borrowed it from Sarah and I should see how she filled it out." His hand smacked on her ass, fire skimming her skin. "I don't care how Sarah fills it out. I care about you. I watch you. I fantasize about you."

They were not words she'd ever expected to hear from him. Not once. She'd dreamed about him, but she'd convinced herself that nothing could ever happen between them. Tears pricked her eyes, sweet and pure emotion running through her.

He rained down on her skin, the soreness from the previous night making every strike more visceral. She groaned around the gag.

"So that's a new rule. When I tell you how pretty you are, you'll thank me. Maybe if you hear it from me enough, you'll start to believe it, though I think you should know that while you're gorgeous, it's not the thing that attracts me to you the most." Another long volley where all she could hear was the sound of his hand hitting her flesh and then the flash of heat that sank into her bones.

Fuck but she felt alive.

"No, what attracted me to you was the fact that you are the single kindest person I've ever met." He smacked her on the underside of her ass, making her jump slightly, the sensation so close to her rapidly moistening pussy. "You try to hide it, but I see you. I see how you treat people, how you protect them and take care of them. I also see how you never ask for anything yourself."

He made her sound like a martyr, but it wasn't like she could defend herself. There was nothing to do but take Kai's discipline and listen to his words. Over and over her skin lit up and she took in the pain before shaking it off and letting the sensation change deep inside her body. Metamorphosis. It was how she always felt when playing. Like she began as one person and changed somewhere in the middle into someone else—someone stronger, more at peace.

"I'm going to take care of that because I'm going to take care of you and you're going to let me. You're going to trust me to take care of you emotionally the way I'm taking care of you physically. I know that's hard, but I promise I won't let you down. After last night, after the connection we had, I can't let us go back to what we were."

She could see that now. How had she thought for a second that she could breeze back into the office and pretend nothing had happened between them? What happened the night before was more meaningful than simple play. They'd needed each other, filled something that had been missing deep inside.

The pain focused her, helped her to push aside those voices that always seemed so close to the surface. All her nasty doubts and self-loathing melted away when tested against Master Kai's discipline. She knew so many people who would judge her a freak for needing this, but she'd learned long ago that smart people accepted who they were, what they needed.

She needed Kai and in more ways than one.

Her backside was on fire as he continued, his rough voice keeping a count. Ten and then fifteen. Twenty and more. Somehow he knew exactly what to give her to make her ache for more.

"Thirty." His hand moved over her skin, holding the heat in as he stroked her flesh. "I don't want to be finished with this, Kori."

Neither did she. There was no reason to hold him off. They'd had years of friendship to build a trust like nothing she'd known. She wiggled her ass against his hand because she couldn't talk and hadn't been told she could move yet. Rubbing against him was the only way she had to communicate that she wanted him.

He hauled her up, turning her to face him. "You know what I want. I believe I told you the first rule I wanted to change."

Kisses. He'd claimed he wanted kisses. He gently pulled the panties out of her mouth, tossing them to the side. He lowered his mouth to hers, lips pressing down. He didn't allow her to control this kiss. His hands sank into her hair and tugged her head back, giving him full access to her mouth. His tongue plunged deep, rubbing along her own in a silky glide. He kissed her over and over again, sinking deeper. She didn't give a crap that her pants were still around her ankles. All that mattered was the feel of his lips on hers, the way his hands gripped and dominated her. There was power in how he held her, how he moved her, and it made her submissive and willing.

"Please, Kai," she whispered. She'd spent years without and it had been all right. She'd survived and not even thought about sex. Now she couldn't stand the thought of him not being inside her. Not one second more. She needed him.

"Tell me you want me."

"I want you." She could feel how much he wanted her. His erection rubbed against her belly, long and thick and so enticing.

Her whole body hummed in anticipation. He was her Master, her natural match.

He kissed her one last time. "Get naked."

He turned and walked out the door.

What the hell? She was left standing there half naked as Kai went and did… What the hell was he doing? Still, he had given her an order. He'd looked at her and growled the words "get naked."

Should she get nakeder? Or pull up her pajama bottoms and go figure out what he was doing?

The door came back open and there was Kai, his face tight, his eyes going straight to her body. "I told you to get naked."

Naked. She was going to be naked in front of Kai. But then he'd seen her naked. He'd thought she was pretty.

If she didn't do what he asked, he would very likely do something super nasty to her. What was in his hand?

"Tell me you didn't walk out to your car to get a condom? Did they see you?"

"I didn't have one in my car. If you aren't naked in the next three seconds, you'll wear a butt plug to work today."

She pulled her tank top over her head as quickly as she could. There were some things even her masochist's soul couldn't handle. "If you didn't get it from your car, where did you?" The truth made her gasp. "Please tell me you didn't ask your brother for one."

"Good, I won't tell you. Kiss me again. I can't get enough of your mouth. I want to feel it everywhere." He leaned over, pulling her to him. The rough feel of his denim stroked against her naked skin. "And it doesn't matter how I got the condom. From now on, I'll have them on hand."

His brother knew they were about to have sex.

Kai slapped her ass, a hard, nasty strike that brought her back to him. "Focus. I don't care who knows. I don't intend to keep this hidden and if you're embarrassed by being with me, you better let me know now."

Embarrassed because she was about to have sex with the most amazing man she'd ever met? She went up on her toes and pressed her lips against his. "I don't want you to gag me this time, Sir."

His arms went around her, lifting her up so their mouths could fuse together. His tongue invaded and Kori couldn't think about the

From Sanctum with Love

fact that they weren't alone in the house. Jared had been standing there the previous night when Kai had made her scream. It didn't matter that he was outside now. Not when she'd made the decision to try with Kai.

Fear ran through her at the very thought, but she shoved it aside. Brave Kori. She was going with it. Brave Kori got all the orgasms, and that was worth the risk.

Brave Kori might end up with Kai. That was worth anything.

"Take my shirt off." He growled the words against her lips as he set her back down.

She let her hands find the buttons on his shirt, carefully easing back each one. He was a present to unwrap, his masculine beauty a gift for her eyes only this morning. Kai stood still, his gaze steady on her as she pushed back his shirt and let her hands roam. Soft skin over smooth muscle.

She started to move on, but he stopped her, his hand coming up and moving over hers, holding her palm to his heart. "Go slow. It's the first time."

"The first time?"

"The first time you've touched me. Do you know how long it's been since this meant anything to me?"

She was not going to cry. His warmth suffused her, seeming to spread from his hand through her system. He wasn't letting up. If he'd walked in and demanded her submission, she could have told him to go to hell, but she couldn't walk away from this. He made her meaningful and that scared her. Scared her and made her heart swell like it hadn't in forever. "Not as long as it's been for me."

Quick would have been easy, but nothing was simple with Kai and that was a good thing.

When he eased off, she let her hand slide over his chest, learning the feel of his skin, the way his muscles moved under her touch, how his heart thudded against his ribs. She leaned forward because touch wasn't the only thing she wanted. She kissed the curve of his neck, worshipping the body she'd watched and wanted for so long. Honoring the man she'd needed since the day they'd met.

Slowly she worked her way down his body, touching and kissing and exploring. He hissed when she licked at his nipple.

Kai's chest was smooth with only a few scars marring his perfection. She kissed those, too. It didn't matter where he'd gotten them. It could have been in the Army or little reminders of carelessness from his childhood. They were a part of Kai and she accepted them. Flaws and imperfections made humans who they were, so his were lovely in her eyes.

She unbuttoned the fly on his pants. His cock was already tenting the jeans. She eased the jeans down and saw the head of his cock was poking out of the waistband of his boxers. Eager thing. The idea that beautiful cock was hard for her slammed into her brain.

"Touch me," Kai growled. "You can be rough."

She didn't want to be rough with him. She gently pulled the boxers free, his cock springing forward. "I thought that was your job."

"We need to talk about what you really like."

She dropped to her knees before him. This was something she definitely liked. His dick was perfect, long and thick and made for giving pleasure. She brushed her fingers over the velvety head, examining the pearly drop pulsing from his slit. "I like you."

His hand found her hair, twisting and lighting up her scalp. "I like you, too, baby. I'm talking about hard and soft limits. We don't have any. I don't want to scare you or hurt you in a way you don't enjoy."

He was being way too careful. If she didn't like something she would tell him. "It's fine, Kai. I like the hair pulling though. That is definitely doing something for me."

He twisted her hair again, sharper this time, making her moan. "I like the way that sounds."

So did his cock apparently. It stiffened further right before her eyes. She glanced up. "I like being controlled during sex. I haven't in so long, but you have no idea what this is doing to me."

His eyes went hard, his hand pushing her where he wanted her to go. "I can do that. I'm going to ask for permission until we get in a groove. Just know that all you have to do to stop me is tell me no."

She was afraid she might never say that word to this man. "I'll tell you."

"Then kiss me. You know where I want it." His fingers gripped her, moving her head toward him.

She loved that. If he tied her up and manhandled her, the world would be perfect, but for now she gave over and let him show her what he wanted. She licked at his cock, letting her tongue run over it. He tugged and yanked. Every movement of his hand, twist of his fingers, made her shiver and shake.

"Suck me." He pushed his cock toward her.

Yeah, that did something for her, too. She wasn't sure why rough sex lit her fire, but it did in a way no amount of sweet vanilla lovemaking could. It wasn't that she didn't want tenderness. She'd loved lying in Kai's arms the night before. She'd felt protected and safe. This was all role-play. If she couldn't stop it at any moment, it wouldn't work. But here in the safety of their relationship, she could give over to her desire.

She let his cock invade her mouth. He tasted clean, smelled like soap and arousal. He tugged her head back. His cock slid deeper. So big. He was so big. He filled her mouth, making her jaw ache as she worked to get her tongue around him.

"Take it all. It's for you. One day I'll fuck this mouth hard. I'll fuck it until I find the back of your throat and press down. I'll fill that pretty mouth with more come than you can handle." His voice had gone rough, gravelly.

She sucked at his cock, relaxing and letting him guide her. His hands eased out of her hair and cupped her skull. Ah, the better to fuck her. He used her mouth, pounding inside. She tried to avoid it but her teeth scraped over him. It made him groan and fuck her harder.

He finally pulled away, his breath sawing from his chest. "But I'm not doing that today. Get on the bed. Spread your legs for me."

She scrambled up. It was so easy now that she'd given over. She wasn't worried about whether she was doing it right or pleasing him. He would tell her and he would expect her to tell him if something wasn't pleasing to her. She sank down on her comforter, the softness curling around her back that still ached from the spanking he'd given her. Her jaw ached, too. By the time he was done, she would feel him everywhere.

He kicked off his jeans and stood looking down at her. He was so stunning with his hair around his shoulders. "Arms above your head."

She let her arms drift up. Her body was on display for him, utterly open and vulnerable.

He walked around the bed, leaving her sight for a moment, but she didn't move. It was all part of the glorious mind fuck she'd missed.

She could hear him moving, thought the bathroom door came open and then closed again. What was he doing? What was he planning? Her heart was racing. All the other sex she'd had in the last five years—not that there had been much of it—had been surprisingly vanilla. The Dom she'd tried with had enjoyed play before sex, but he'd been pretty traditional in bed.

Not so with Kai. She should have known he would be the bastard, son of a bitch, so hot she could barely stand it Dom who played with her brain as well her body.

"I thought I remembered seeing this in your bathroom." He came into her line of sight, standing over her. In his hands was the long-handled body brush she used in the shower to soap and exfoliate her back.

Oh, shit.

He tapped her knees with the solid side. "Further apart."

She complied, her skin coming alive with anticipation. The brush was plastic, one side flat, the other bristled. She would bet what he was about to do with the flat side.

"I said further." He brought the brush against the inside of her thigh with a short, decisive swat.

That sound cracked through the air. He'd brought it down on a delicate part of her skin. He hadn't held back. She moved immediately, forcing her legs as far apart as she could so her pussy was completely open to him.

He struck her other side, balancing out the pain. "The first one was to get my point across."

"And the second?"

"That was for good behavior. So is this." He rubbed the bristly side over her abdomen. Soft and silky, the bristles ran up her torso. "And this."

With a swift flick of his hand, he brought the brush up and back down hard on her left breast, right over the nipple.

Kori screamed out and then braced because he seemed to be a very symmetrical Dom. Sure enough he tortured her other breast in the same manner. Now her boobs were on fire.

Like he was caressing them even as he lowered himself down on the bed. Her body was his at that moment, every inch of skin connected to him in some way, and the beautiful ache would remind her of that connection all day.

"I want to taste you." He brought the flat side down again, another slap to each breast. "But I don't want you to be bored. We do this at my place next. I have a hundred ways to tie you up and make you cry at my place."

So the office was going to be fun from now on. "I'm not bored, Kai."

He kissed a spot above her right knee, where he'd brought the brush down. The skin was still stinging so when he ran his tongue there, the heat was almost too much. He dropped the brush to the side. If they ever showered together he would probably give her a heart attack. "Are you bored now?"

"Nope." His tongue was moving along her thigh, getting closer and closer to her pussy. "Definitely not bored."

"I want to bite you, Kori." The words rumbled over her skin. "I like to bite and leave a mark, but you have to tell me if it's too much."

Her pussy pulsed at the very thought. "Go for it, Kai. It's been a long time, but I used to like it."

His teeth scraped against her inner thigh as his now free hand moved, teasing against her labia. "I could give you a nip." He gently bit her. The sensation sizzled and faded. A little disappointing. "Or I could take a nice bite."

Pain flared and she shouted out as his teeth bit into her, sharp and jarring. Her whole body shook and there was no way that sensation would fade for a while. He'd gone hard and would leave a mark. His mark. He eased his tongue over the bite, soothing it as his thumb ran over her clit.

"Now that got you juicy and wet." He covered her pussy with his mouth.

That was all it took. The minute she felt his tongue move

through her, she came. Like a bottle of champagne being uncorked after far too long on the shelf, her whole body tightened and released. Pleasure coursed through her.

His tongue plunged deep inside as his thumb kept up the slow circle on her clit. It was almost too much, but she knew she wouldn't settle. She needed more from him, needed to give back to him.

"Kai, please." Her voice was breathless, her body already prepping for the next wave to come. She didn't want that to happen without him inside her.

He growled against her. "Only because I want it." He kissed her one last time and got to his knees, reaching for the condom he'd brought back with him. His body was rigid, every muscle defined and toned. He stroked his cock before rolling the condom on.

Kai was going to fuck her. He was between her legs and he was going to cover her with his body and everything would change.

Nothing would change. Either he was being honest and he'd wanted her, or he was the single meanest human being in the world and he was willing to toss away everything they had for a lay.

She reached up to him because she wasn't living in that world anymore. Just because one man had done her wrong didn't mean she couldn't find one who mattered. Kai mattered and she could believe her fears or she could believe him. "You're an indulgent Dom."

"You have no idea. Don't expect this to always go so quickly. I'll want to take my time, torture you for hours. But not this morning. This morning I need to get inside you." He moved between her legs again, his hands on her knees. He looked down and his thumb ran over her inner thigh. His eyes heated, lips curling up when she winced at the pain from his mark. "That's going to be there for a couple of days."

"When it's gone, you'll do it again?" She let her hands find his lean waist.

His cock was right there at her entrance. "I'll mark you any way you'll let me, baby. I'll bite you a hundred fucking times because I love how you taste." He pressed his cock against her. That gorgeous face of his contorted, his eyes on her. "And you're going to feel so good."

From Sanctum with Love

He stretched her as he pressed inside. Kai didn't go slow, didn't wait for her to catch up. He invaded. His cock ruthlessly gained ground. So long. It had been so long and the stretch felt so good. Pain and pleasure. Her cocktail.

He groaned as he fucked his way inside her. "I didn't tell you to move your arms. You'll pay for that later. For now, dig your nails in. Make some marks of your own."

She let her hands run up his back, scraping along his muscles. He hissed and thrust harder.

"That's what I want." He pounded into her, ensuring she would feel every stretch and pull for hours.

She fought for her pleasure, the tension rising again as Kai continued to take her higher and higher. The first orgasm had been nothing compared to this. This was a wave pounding against her again and again, and it was so much better this time because she could see him getting close. His gorgeous eyes held hers. He wouldn't let her close her eyes or look away.

"Stay with me." He pumped into her, his pelvis grinding on her clit as he looked into her eyes.

She was so connected to him. Never before had she felt so much, and tears welled in her eyes as Kai managed to send her flying over the edge again.

Kai stiffened above her and he thrust in again and again, his orgasm heightening her own.

He dropped down on top of her, his weight pressing her into the mattress. His lips pressed to her cheek, wiping away the tears there. "We're all right, baby. We're okay. This is going to be good. I promise."

Two seconds before he'd been savage. This was the man who'd marked her so well. He'd made her scream out in pure erotic pleasure and now he wrapped her up in his tenderness.

She hugged him, unwilling to let there be any space between them. "I know."

He kissed her nose. "You don't yet, but you will. We're going to be good together."

They'd already been spectacular. It wasn't the sex that scared her. It was the fact that her heart was so full. The words had played around in her brain.

I love you. I'll love you forever.

Morgan had nearly destroyed her and she'd never loved him. Not the way she loved Kai. If Kai ever...

Kai wasn't Morgan. He didn't cheat or lie. He wasn't perfect, but he was perfect for her.

She let her head rest on his chest as he shifted, rolling off her but keeping them cuddled together.

"I think I'm going to be late for work today, boss." She curled into his warmth, her whole body languid.

"I'll cut you some slack. I'm going to be late, too." He kissed her forehead and they were blissfully quiet for a moment.

It didn't last long. There was a knock on the door and then a familiar voice spoke. Jared cleared his throat. "Hey, Kai. I was hoping you could give me a ride up to McKay-Taggart. I don't want to be late and it sounds like you're done and stuff. Not that I was listening or anything."

"I wasn't listening either, but the walls are thin," Sarah agreed from what sounded like right outside the door.

"Very thin," Jared said. "So how did the condom work out? Held up under fire? You know I was happy to help."

"I'm going to kill him," Kai whispered. He'd gone the sweetest shade of pink.

She might help.

Chapter Eight

Kai pulled into the McKay-Taggart parking lot an hour later, thinking about the fact that Big Tag had completely ruined his plans to dump his brother at the soonest possible moment. He'd intended to drive Jared's ass straight to the nearest bus stop and explain that if he wanted to play someone from Dallas, he should get used to the city's mass transit system. He would see how Jared enjoyed that research. Maybe if Kai was lucky, he'd get lost and Kai could spend the day making his new sub scream, but no. Instead he'd been forced to drop Kori off at the office because Big Tag wanted a meeting.

Stupid meeting. He could be meeting with Kori again. The first meeting had gone spectacularly well right up until the moment his brother had knocked on the door and started asking about condoms.

"I get it, you're mad," Jared said. "You wanted to do the whole happy, postcoital, we-finally-did-it thing. I do get that. There was once this girl I liked a lot and she held out three days on me and when we finally did it, it was like I'd climbed Everest. But it was getting late. You're the one who always taught me to be on time. By the way, I called Lena and she's already been out to document the damage to Kori's car. I called the police, but there's no history of vandalism in the area so they'll file a report so Kori can get insurance to cover it, but that's about all they'll do. Lena's taking care of that, too. All Kori will have to do is sign the report."

"I was going to handle that." He'd gotten a glimpse at her car. Someone had done a number on the tires.

"You had plenty to deal with this morning and I didn't mind. I didn't have time for a run. I'm scheduled to work out this afternoon anyway." His brother had hopped into the passenger seat when he'd dropped Kori off. Jared had done it quickly, slamming the door as though pleased he'd managed to make the switch.

If Kai had been faster, he could have driven away then, but no, he'd been kissing his assistant.

His assistant who also happened to now be his sub. The thought of all the nasty things he could do to her at the office played through his brain. Not that he would get to do any of it since his brother was a tick who'd dug in and wouldn't be removed. "Three whole days. That must have been hard for you."

Jared sighed. "I really wanted her. Naturally it turned out she taped the entire thing and tried to sell it."

Kai felt his jaw drop. "You made a sex tape?"

This was why it worked with Kori. They were the adults of their families. They both had horrible siblings.

Jared waved it off. "Lots, but that's the only one that almost made it out. All those celebs who claim the maid stole our sex tape and leaked it, it's all bullshit. Sex tape is one of the first things a good publicist will tell you to do. Well, unless you've got a small penis."

He thanked god he'd been given a brain and didn't have to live in Jared's world. "Why didn't you let yours get out? Apparently you might have an Oscar by now."

"I liked her. I thought she liked me. I paid a lot of money to keep it off the Internet." His brother sounded serious for once. "Everything I'd saved up to eighteen months ago. I'm good at starting over."

Well, it wasn't like his brother had ever been a financial whiz. Kai parked the Jeep in the McKay-Taggart visitor slot. He couldn't help but notice there was a limo hanging out a couple of rows down. "You'll make it back. It seems like you're doing pretty well. I thought you had given up limos."

"I let the guys use it. The studio pays for a driver. It's part of my contract."

Kai turned the engine off. "Your entourage is here? Upstairs? With Big Tag?"

"Not sure if they're with him, but I asked Squirrel and the guys to start taking some notes, maybe some pictures so I can get in the character's head. Don't worry. Everyone loves to answer questions about themselves."

"How many actual spies have you known?" Kai opened the door and hopped out, praying he could get up there fast enough to save some lives.

Jared was right behind him as he strode to the elevator. "I played a corporate spy on a Lifetime movie once. Have you seen it? *Cyber Eyes Are Watching Her*. It wasn't as bad as it sounds."

It sounded spectacularly crappy. "I don't watch a lot of TV. Or movies." Luckily there was an elevator open. He hopped on. "You can't treat Ian like some movie consultant. He's the real thing."

Someone shouted out Jared's name. He turned before he got on the elevator, his face going movie star bright as he waved. "Yes, it's really me."

Kai reached out and hauled his brother inside. "No time for autographs." He pushed the button for McKay-Taggart. They now occupied the top two floors. "I'm serious about Ian. You have to be careful. Even now he's involved in classified stuff. The company he runs still works for the government from time to time and they take those secrets seriously."

Like the fact that Theo Taggart was alive somewhere. If Jared threatened that mission in any way, Tag would happily bury his body.

Jared grinned. "Real spy stuff. That's cool. And I'm sure my guys are sitting in the lobby somewhere looking at their phones. It's kind of what they do."

"How are you still with Squirrel? I can't see that kid does anything real for you."

"You always hated him. And I gave him a job because he stuck by me when no one else did." Jared looked straight ahead, his eyes on the elevator doors. "He's not stupid. He can run errands."

"I thought that's what Lena did." Kai knew it didn't matter, but he wanted Jared to admit that Squirrel was mooching off him. He wanted to at least get that out into the open. So often Jared looked at the bright, shiny side of everything, refusing to see anything could possibly be wrong.

"He's my friend. Just drop it, Kai," Jared said in a stubborn tone. "You wouldn't understand."

"I wouldn't understand friendship?" They were good at falling back into old patterns. Kai would come out accusing his brother of acting like an idiot and then Jared would say Kai never understood. Nothing had changed in fifteen years.

"Not really. How many friends do you still have from childhood?"

It was a decent point, but he had one of his own. "I didn't have a lot of them. I was too busy taking care of you."

"Fine. Blame me. How about from the Army? Have many friends from those times?"

He didn't. He had some guys from his unit he called from time to time to check in on them. "They live in different parts of the country and most of them are at different stages in life. And I've made a lot of friends here."

"Well, when they've been around for ten years or so, get back to me."

There was something deeper going on in his brother's head, but at that moment, Kai didn't care. His inner therapist voice was only a whisper really, telling him his normally sunny brother was hiding something. Jared didn't push this way. But right then, Kai didn't give a shit. "Just because I don't pay a group of people to stay around me all the time because I can't stand to be alone with myself doesn't mean I have a problem making friends."

Jared turned and his eyes were lit with an anger Kai had rarely seen in his younger brother. "I wasn't talking about making them. You're good at that. Everyone wants to be your friend. I was talking about keeping them. Is anyone good enough for you? Is there anyone in your life who measures up to the Great Kaiser Ferguson's standards? Or do they all end up being stupid and human and flawed like me?"

"Flawed? You call sleeping with my fiancée a flaw?"

Jared shook his head. "You hated me long before that."

Hate was a strong word and not one he used often. "I don't hate you."

"Bullshit."

He took a deep breath and realized maybe he had issues with Jared, but Kori was right. He needed to face them. He had to stop getting surly every time the chance to deal with Jared came up. "I don't hate you. I might not have fully forgiven you for what happened with Hannah, but I don't hate you."

"You don't even know what happened with Hannah. You have no fucking idea what happened to me while you were gone. You left me behind."

"I went into the Army so I could help support you, you asshole." How did his brother do this to him? With anyone else he would brush off the accusations and try to find the heart of the matter. He was trained to do this. He'd been called every name in the book by his patients, who often mistook anger at the world for anger at him. He could handle it. In some ways, it was part of the healing process. But the minute his brother walked in, Kai was right back, standing in that living room where his brother had betrayed him utterly.

God, maybe he did hate Jared a little.

"I didn't need money," his brother ground out. "I needed someone who gave a shit whether I lived or died. Hell, I didn't even see any money."

"What is that supposed to mean? I sent it to you every month. It's not my fault you spent it on hair gel or whatever the hell you spent it on."

His brother's eyes widened. "Are you fucking kidding me? The great and mighty Kai has no idea. Well, that's rich, brother. I guess you don't know everything."

What had happened? "I sent the money, Jared."

The elevator doors opened and Lena was standing there. She was dressed in what looked almost like a copy of the dress she'd worn the day before, though this was a slightly different shade of black.

"Thank god. This place is horrible," Lena complained as Jared stepped off the elevator. "Everything about this particular movie is simply awful and you need to think about that proposal I sent you. You're better than this."

Jared gave her a smile, but Kai was starting to realize that Jared smiled at everything and everyone and in every circumstance. There was a difference though. This smile was tight and didn't come anywhere close to Jared's eyes. "It looks pretty nice to me."

"Ugh, they have babies and everything. It's like a suburban nightmare in there. And they could use a decorator." Lena looked down at her phone. "I've already gone by and done all the stuff for the police report and Ms. Williamson will find I've filled out all the insurance forms as well. Someone is coming at one this afternoon to pick up the car and she'll have it back by four. The tires will all be top of the line, but there's nothing I can do about the fact that the car itself is pathetic and sad."

"Less opinion, please," Jared said.

"Fine," Lena continued with a sullen sigh. "I've set everything up for the club next Tuesday, but the big scary guy asked if he could be included along with some chick he's trying to bang."

"Scary guy?" Kai asked. That could likely be anyone at McKay-Taggart.

"One of the big Viking dudes. The young one. Chase? Maybe. I called him Sven, but he didn't answer to that." Lena continued checking off things on her phone.

"Case Taggart. He's been very helpful so far. If he thinks hanging out at the new nightclub will help him get laid, he's more than welcome. Call the manager and tell them to expect two more. Also find out what his lady drinks and make sure it's available." Jared stepped up to the main doors. "I got the schedule you sent me. I'll be here most of the afternoon if anything changes, but I don't particularly want to be interrupted. And work on the hospital thing."

Lena made a gagging sound. "Fine, but I'm taking the limo and going shopping."

She stepped into the elevator Kai had been holding for her, and never once had she looked his way. She seemed to have the preternatural ability to walk in high heels without ever looking up from her phone.

"What hospital thing?" Watching his brother with Lena had been interesting. Jared had shoved all the emotion from the elevator down and dealt with her professionally. He would bet his life Jared hadn't fucked her. They seemed to keep a certain distance.

Jared's jaw tightened as though now that they were alone, the emotion was back. "I like to visit children's hospitals in the cities I'm in. A lot of kids watch *Dart*. It makes them happy."

"I've never seen articles about you doing that." All the articles he'd seen were about Jared's love life. Not that he really read them. They sometimes came into view on the Internet.

"I keep it quiet. The kids are terminal or very sick. They don't need reporters in their faces. Look, I can handle hanging out here on my own. I'll rent a car so I don't inconvenience you again."

"Apparently we should talk. I think there's something I don't know about that day."

Jared was about to speak when Grace walked into the lobby. Jared immediately plastered a brilliant smile on his face. This one definitely reached his eyes. Jared's smile for all the pretty women of the world. "You must be Mrs. Taggart. I can't tell you what a pleasure it is to meet you. I've heard so much about you and let me say, Serena's descriptions of you in *The Mercenary I Loved* don't do you justice."

Grace flushed a pretty pink and let Jared take her hand. "That is very sweet of you to say but don't believe everything you read. Serena makes us look more exciting than we really are. Please call me Grace. Welcome to McKay-Taggart." Grace looked over and seemed to notice Kai. "Hello, Kai. How are you today?"

Confused. Elated. Excited. Wary. All the good emotions had to do with the woman he'd left at the office and the bad ones with the man standing in front of him. He had to admit that his brother was different in some ways. The old Jared wouldn't have thought to visit a bunch of kids. "I'm great, Grace. I'm supposed to meet with Ian. Is he here?"

"Go on back to his office. He's waiting for you." Grace smiled back at Jared. "And how can I help you?"

"You could get me reservations at your husband's restaurant for starters. I have to warn you, though, I'll probably have some photographers following me." Jared frowned as though it would be an imposition. "If that's trouble, I can order takeout, but I've heard your husband is an amazing chef."

"Who would stand to gain so much from you eating at his place," Grace replied. "We would love to have you. We'll keep a table open for you while you're here. Feel free to walk around and ask anything you like. Your friends are already here. I set them up in an empty office, but apparently Brad decided to run up stairs or something."

"He's very active. Thank you for putting up with all of us." Jared turned back after giving Grace a wink. The minute she was back at her desk, he leaned over. "I'll go and see if I can shadow someone since you're meeting with Ian. I'll stay out of your way."

He stopped Jared when he turned to walk away. "Hey, that's a nice thing you're doing for Sean. Top will get a lot of publicity if you're seen there and you know it."

"I like to be seen in all the hot places."

"Top is small. There are a ton of other restaurants in Dallas with higher profiles, some that would likely pay for you to walk past the front of the place."

Jared shrugged. "They seem like nice people."

Maybe his brother wasn't so shallow. "Like I said, I appreciate it. I know I might not have friends from childhood still hanging around, but I do have friends and I am grateful when someone helps them out."

Jared nodded. "Anything I can do."

His brother had done a lot for him today. For him. For Kori. "Thanks for helping with Kori's car, too. What was Lena talking about when she asked if you'd looked at her proposal?"

He had to admit, he was curious.

"Her mother runs a studio. Lena thinks I'm wasting my life making comic book TV shows and movies like *Love After Death*. She's not into genre entertainment. She wants me to do a bunch of small indie films. Something with award bait to it."

"Why not?"

"Because I have fun making *Dart*. I'll have fun doing this. I know a lot of people in the industry look down on genre stuff, but it has something to say, too."

"That a douchebag with a bunch of darts can do push-ups?"

Jared stared at him for a moment. "That ordinary guys can be heroes. That it's not all bad out there. I can pick up a newspaper to tell me the world is shit. I don't need a film to tell me that, but there are days when I need to turn on the TV and be reminded that it can be good, too. That's what I do. That's what I want to do. I want to make people happy. I don't see how that's a bad thing to do. I don't see why that makes me less of an artist."

Kai stopped, looking at his brother in a slightly different light. Maybe there were times he'd been the asshole. "It doesn't. It's good, Jared. You need to do what makes you happy." If he didn't stop, he was going to get emotional, and he didn't have time for that right now. Still, he couldn't leave Jared like this. "Why don't I show you around here? Ian's office is in the back. I can give you a quick tour."

A cautious smile this time. "I would like that. This is the top floor, but I read that there's a second floor."

The tension seemed to go out of the room. Oh, Kai had no doubt it would rear its ugly head again, but they needed time and privacy for that conversation. "The second floor is fairly new. It used to be a law office. They moved to a private building and Ian took over the space. The business covers a lot of security needs, but they're broken up into different teams now that MT has gotten so big. The main floor is for the central team. They work for corporations and do some government work. Downstairs there's a team specifically for physical security, both buildings and people. There are five highly trained bodyguards on retainer and the nerd squad specializes in security systems. On this floor, we have several conference rooms, the main one right here on the left. What the hell?"

Adam and Jesse both had a leg up on the conference room table, stretching their big bodies as Brad pressed a hand to Jesse's back.

Yes, he had to figure out what was going on there. He opened the door. "Dare I ask?"

Jesse looked up. "Hey, Kai. Brad here is showing us how to properly stretch out our hamstrings. I keep pulling my left one when I run. Nearly took a damn bullet in LA last week when Si and I were on assignment. It stiffened up on the flight last night. I'm getting old."

Adam shook his head. "I'm not old. I just spend too much time behind a desk. Brad's going to give me a comprehensive workout plan. Jake doesn't believe in intellectual pursuits and somehow he never gains sympathy weight. Serena's pregnant again. I have to keep off the weight or I'll be the less hot but still intellectually superior husband."

So it was a typical day at McKay-Taggart.

"You can come and work out with me," Jared offered.

Adam gave him a thumbs-up. "That would be awesome."

"I'll get these two in better shape. Let's go run some stairs. See how that hammy holds up now that you've properly warmed it." Brad clapped his hands together like it was the best thing in the world.

It sounded horrible to Kai. Of course, he'd always accepted that he was the less hot but intellectually superior brother. Kori didn't seem to mind that he wasn't a gym rat who pounded pavement or lifted weights four hours a day.

Jared watched as the trio started toward the stairs. "That has to be Axel from *The Doms with the Golden Whips*. It was one of my favorites."

"You've seriously read all of Serena's books?" Somehow he hadn't seen his brother as a big reader.

"They're cool. Very sexy. Again, you wouldn't like them because they're not intellectual," Jared shot back. "I started them as research but I ended up thinking they were awesome. I like Serena a lot."

Tad strode out from the far hallway, a phone to his ear. "I know. I know, but I need Franco here next week. I don't care if he's taken a vow of silence. I don't need him to talk. I need him to work his magic and take some pictures and video. And get a good stylist. These people are very…military. I don't mean rah, rah military. I'm talking they could use some serious flair."

Jared groaned and stepped up, grabbing Tad's phone. "Cancel everything." He jabbed at the phone's screen, hanging up the call before handing it back to Tad. "I told you, we're not asking the company to let documentary crews in."

"Not unless they get to kill the documentary crew afterward," Kai agreed. It was the only way Big Tag allowed that to happen.

Tad's eyes widened. "What?"

From Sanctum with Love

"They're very private," Jared explained. "Where's Squirrel? Did he stay at the hotel?"

Tad shook his head, edging away from Kai. "No. He's been following that Tag person around trying to take notes for you."

Jared nodded and looked back at Kai as if that made some kind of point. "That's nice of him."

"No. No, it's not. Shit." A million and one scenarios ran through Kai's head—all of them bad. "Has anyone seen him lately?"

Jared would likely get upset if his best friend ended up stuffed in a box somewhere. That was the least lethal scenario he could think of.

"No. Not for an hour or so." Tad was dialing his phone again. "Can we at least bring a reporter in? 'Actor plays decorated military hero' would be a great visual. It'll be good for the company too. Please let me bring in a stylist for the chick with the freckles. I can deal with the other women, but she's too severe."

"That's because Erin will murder you and not think twice about it. I have to go find Ian." Before he eviscerated Jared's friend.

Jared jogged to keep up with him as he strode down the hall toward Ian's office. "You think Squirrel could annoy him to the point of violence?"

"I think violence is Ian's default state." And he was in a piss-poor mood as it was. He passed Eve's office and then Alex's. He hoped he didn't piss off Ian too much, but he knocked once and then went in just in time to see Ian lifting Squirrel up by the neck and shoving him against the wall.

"I swear to god if you don't stop following me I will split you open, pull out your insides, and let my baby girls play in them. My wife will get all pissy because she thinks the girls shouldn't play in entrails, but I say they're free. Do you have any idea how fucking much toys cost?" If Tag was at all bothered by Squirrel's weight, he didn't show it. The man simply held him up, the poor dude's sneakers kicking slightly. "A lot. A metric shit ton of cash, so I'm always looking for something cheap to keep them entertained."

He needed to bring the level of potential death down to a manageable portion. "Hey, Ian, I want you to think about how much the girls would miss their dad if he got shoved in a prison."

"He followed me around all morning," Ian bit out.

"Sorry." Squirrel managed to whisper the words.

"Ian, is it really worth it to murder him? Jail is a real possibility." Ian would respond to logic.

"He followed me into my fucking bathroom."

Kai turned to his brother. "I'm sorry. You're going to have to find a new best friend."

Big Tag had a private bathroom. He took that shit seriously.

"Do you understand what it means to be the only man in the fucking house? My kids don't care about privacy. My wife thinks intimacy means I shouldn't be able to spend an hour alone in the bathroom. I like my personal time, motherfucker. The only time I get it is here. Have you ever had to take a piss with not one but two babies in your arms?"

"It sounds terrible, sir. I would want to piss in peace, too," Squirrel managed.

"Ian, he's turning blue." More logic. He hoped it got through.

Ian's hand released and Squirrel hit the floor. "Go away."

Squirrel dragged air into his lungs. "That dude is crazy."

Jared reached out a hand and helped his friend up. "I'll take him out. Sorry for the disruption, Mr. Taggart. It won't happen again."

Jared held Squirrel up and helped him stumble out. The door closed with a thud and he was left with Ian, who walked to the big floor-to-ceiling windows that marked his corner office. He crossed his arms over his chest and looked out over the Dallas skyline.

"Ian, are you all right?" It was a stupid question. He was obviously not all right, but this was a way Kai could allow Ian to control the conversation. He could say yes. He could say no. This wasn't a therapy session and Kai wouldn't press the issue.

A long silence followed. Kai let it lengthen, the quiet not bothering him at all. Sometimes these things took time.

"He was taking fucking notes. I hate that. Why the hell was he taking notes? Does he think he's going to learn something? I get that the film is about a security company but that asshole was acting like it was all about me. Dumbass."

They were right back to Ian's self-awareness issues. "I think he was trying to help out Jared. You know the character he's playing has a lot in common with you."

"Fine, but that kid is annoying as fuck. And he talks about your brother like he walks on water. I swear the kid has a crush on him. I know I agreed to do this, but it's too many fucking people. There's Death in a Dress who complains about everything and wanted to know if the water in the coffee had been blessed by holistic monks. Then there's that smiley, happy fuck who seems to have worked out so much he's OD'd on endorphins. I want to kill the guy who told me I need a stylist. I don't need a fucking stylist. I don't even know what they're supposed to fucking style."

"I'll get rid of them." Ian deserved some peace. "I'll take care of this. From now on it's going to be Jared alone and he'll simply observe."

Somehow he knew Jared would keep that promise.

Ian ran a hand over his head, a long sigh coming from his chest. "I don't want this. I don't want any of this. Do you have any idea how shitty I feel about bringing this down on us?"

It was a good bet Ian wasn't simply talking about the film crew. He was talking about the investigation. "It's all right. We'll keep everyone safe."

"I have my reasons."

"I know you do."

Ian's head turned, eyes narrowing. "Do you?"

Kai merely smiled. "I know that you would never endanger anyone here or at the club without a good reason."

"You know."

He wasn't going to lie to the guy. "There's only one thing you could possibly want from the feds."

"Shit." Ian moved from the window, pacing like an angry, caged lion. "I don't want Erin to know."

He understood that. He'd considered it after finding out about Theo and he agreed with Ian's decision. "You don't want to give Erin false hope."

Ian had turned a nice shade of red. "Shit and fucking shit, you really *do* know. Goddamn it. I always said you were too smart for your own good."

It was definitely time to stop playing games. "Just so you'll stop testing me, I know you have reason to think that Theo's alive and you have the feds working on it. I suspect Liam's sudden desire to take a family vacation to South America has something to do with it, too. And I agree with you on keeping it from Erin. She needs to concentrate on the baby and having a healthy pregnancy."

"Erin's too reckless. If she thought for a second there was the slightest possibility that he was out there, she would go off alone. She asks me every single day if I've found Hope McDonald. Erin would go after her, too. So I lie to my sister-in-law. I know they weren't married, but it's how I have to think of her. I swear to god if it weren't for Charlie and the girls…"

He would be in a hole somewhere, doing what he was attempting to keep Erin from doing. Ian would invest the rest of his life in killing one woman. "And if Case didn't have you and Sean, he would be lost, too. Ian, you're doing what you have to do. There's no judgment from me. If everyone knew, they would pitch in."

"They can't know. I don't even like you knowing, but I trust you not to give it away."

Kai knew how to keep a secret. "It's not an issue. Now why did you need to talk to me?"

His shoulders eased down marginally. "It's about Mia Danvers. She's been talking to some interesting people lately. Hutch pulled her phone records. She's been calling a number in Argentina. I need to know who she's talking to. I need to listen in on that conversation the next time it happens."

"Li's in Argentina, isn't he?"

Ian nodded as he slumped into the big chair behind his desk. "Yes. It's the last known location of a medical group called Project Remembrance. It's a small group funded by a known Collective company. They move around doing research on memory and how global and political conditions affect neurological function. What they're actually doing is something very different."

He'd read the reports. Normally he wouldn't, but he'd insisted in this case because of the stress damage the operation had caused on members of the team. He'd also insisted every single person who'd been there come in for sessions. Some had been surprisingly willing to talk. Case was angry, but he'd sat and talked about his brother and the hole in his life. Erin had been utterly shut down until Kori broke through to her. At the London offices, he was coordinating with a fellow psychologist Damon Knight had hired to help the other members of the team.

Ian had refused all sessions. He'd handed his girls over to Alex and Eve and disappeared into Sanctum with his wife for two days. The club had been locked up and when he'd come back out, he'd been calmer, more focused. Charlotte was Ian's therapy.

"I suspect they're testing out the time dilation drug Dr. McDonald used on Ten." Tennessee Smith was a former CIA operative who now worked for McKay-Taggart. The op had been his and it had gone straight to hell. Hope McDonald was something of an evil genius. She'd designed a drug that tricked the brain into thinking time had passed, time that Hope filled with the experiences she chose to give the subject. In Ten's case, it had been days of pain and torture all wrapped up in a single dose of her drug.

Kai worried that even if they found Theo he wouldn't be the same smiling, happy man who had been taken. That drug would twist his soul.

He should do some serious research because if Theo was alive, he would need help reintegrating into the real world. They all would.

"Yes, I've had reports that Hope is up to her usual tricks. By the time Li got to Argentina, they had moved on. He found their base of operations."

"Did he find evidence that Theo had been held there?"

Ian shook his head, his eyes infinitely tired. "No. The whole place had been cleaned from top to bottom." Ian was quiet for a moment. "Am I being too optimistic? There were bloody sheets found at McDonald's place in the Caymans. I had them tested."

"And the blood was Theo's," Kai surmised. "Given that Hope McDonald is a gifted surgeon and she had an obsessive interest in your brother, I think we can say there's a chance that she saved his life and now she's taking it again. Ian, if she's giving him that drug, she's basically reprogramming his brain."

"I know that. I also know that once we get him off the shit, he should remember who he is. I can't leave him." Ian's hands fisted at his sides as though they needed to hit something, anything.

"I'm not saying you should. I'm simply preparing for every

eventuality. You have to understand that finding Theo and bringing him back won't be the end of the problems. He'll need medical and therapeutic care, and I need to be ready for that. I know you didn't want to bring me into this, but unless you're planning on bringing in another therapist, I need to plan now. Has Eve thought about a possible course of treatment? There are people working in the field she could reach out to."

"No," Ian replied. "I want you. I love Eve, but she's dealt more with the academic end of things. She's more of a profiler than an active therapist. I need you to help my brother if he comes home. When he comes home."

He would feel better knowing it was in his own hands. "I'll start prepping and Ian, you have to know anything you tell me stays between the two of us."

"Don't consider my silence on the subject a statement about you. I do trust you, Kai. I guess I'm trying to manage everyone's expectations. The only people who know are me, Charlie, Chelsea, Li, and Alex and Eve. My brothers, of course. Now you. I need this circle to stay tight. Grace doesn't even know, and until such time as I need them, neither does the rest of the team. I've asked Chelsea to keep it from Simon. I know I'm asking a lot. Avery doesn't know. All she knows is her lovely vacation to the beach turned into an op, and do you know what she said?"

He could guess. "She would never complain."

"She said she and Aidan would have fun learning to tango. I fucked up her only vacation and she thanked me." Ian shook his head.

"Avery has faith in you and faith in Li. And so do I. My mouth is closed. Now what do you need me to do to help with the Mia situation? Can't the feds get a warrant to bug her phone?"

"The feds are scared of her brother. We have to tread lightly. Drew Lawless has the money and power to take on the government, and the company is beyond reproach as far as the feds can tell. If he's Collective, then he's in deep cover."

"They all are after McDonald went down." The Collective was a shadow group, a collection of high-powered corporations who worked together to mold the world to their liking—and their profits. "They're very quiet because they know certain agencies are looking

From Sanctum with Love

into them. They'll regroup and be back and more deadly than ever. How can I help with the Mia situation? I haven't heard from Special Agent Rush." Except he had. He felt himself flush. "Okay, I dodged him last night. Is that what this is about?"

Ian frowned. "You dodged him? Why would you...where'd you go last night after the club, Kai?"

He should tell Ian to shove it. It wasn't Ian's business, but it was the first time the big guy had smiled during the course of this meeting. Kai could handle some ribbing if it made Ian forget his trouble for a few moments. "I stayed at Kori's last night and obviously yes, we're very much together now."

Ian slapped his hand on his desk and then leaned over and touched a button on the landline that controlled the floor's PA system. "Pay up, bitches. I told you that scene wasn't over. It was just hitting the road."

Even through the closed door, Kai could hear the collective groan from the office. He rolled his eyes. "Yeah, fuck you, Big Tag."

A single shoulder shrugged as he sat back. "I'm happy for you. You should have been doing that girl for over a year now. I'm also happy she's going to get the attention she needs. Kori's good people. We need more like her. Which is why what I'm about to ask you to do isn't fair."

Shit. There was only one thing he could ask that would involve Kori. He'd thought about doing it earlier today himself. "You want me to use Kori's friendship with Mia to get her phone."

"I want you to tag her phone, not steal it. I need her to make a call from that phone. She doesn't bring it to Sanctum and she doesn't leave it in her car. That in and of itself is suspicious. Charlie's tried everything and she can't get close. Mia has a thing for Case. It's why I sent him in. He's asking her to go out with Jared and his crew the next time they hit a nightclub. When she's got her purse with her, she tends to have her phone. I hope Case can make her feel comfortable enough to let her guard down."

"I think her attraction to Case is real," Kai explained. "I also think she wants someone to talk to. She stayed the night at Kori's last night and she had her phone, so she's actively hiding it at the club."

"I think she might feel safer if she wasn't at Sanctum. If she was at a nightclub with friends around her. I was thinking she might even forget to be so vigilant if the man she had a crush on asked her to dance."

Now Case's request made sense. "You want me to tag her phone when she goes out with Jared on Tuesday. That's what that was about. They'll all be at Sanctum for the next few nights."

Tag nodded. "Hey, if Case does his job and gets the girl in bed, you might not have to do this, but I want you to be ready. I also worry that it's going to look odd if you go out with your brother alone when you've so publicly claimed a sub."

He had to bring Kori with him and he couldn't tell her what he was going to do or why he was doing it. Shit. He hated the spy stuff. His life was about being open and honest and still...he owed Ian. He owed everyone on this team and he definitely owed it to Theo and Erin and to that baby who might never meet its father. If Mia was working for The Collective, they needed to know. If she was innocent, they could focus on other leads.

It would also give him a chance to observe his brother's friends in their natural habitat.

"I'll do it. Someone's going to have to show me how. I've never tagged anyone's phone before."

"Thank you, Kai," Ian said somberly. "Case and Rush will be at your office sometime Tuesday to talk about the op. Like I said before, it may not be necessary at all. Be careful though. I wouldn't let Kori find out. Women can get downright mean when they think they've been betrayed."

He wasn't betraying her. It wasn't like that at all. Still, discretion being the better part of valor, he would try to keep it on the down low.

The good news was Big Tag had very likely scared his brother off. Maybe now Jared would keep his research to the club. Kai stepped out of Ian's office and moved down the hall. He had a few days before he would have to play the spy. He would keep an eye on Mia and watch his brother's entourage.

He would spend all the time he could with Kori.

"Holy shit, did you see that?" Jared was standing in the lobby, his eyes wide and a smile on his face like his baseball team had won the World Series. His voice went low, a damn fine approximation of Big Tag. Jared's face hardened, his jawline squaring off as he held an invisible man up in the air. "I swear to god if you don't stop following me I will split you open, pull out your insides, and let my baby girls play in them." He dropped the act and went right back to sunny. "He's so awesome. I'm going to work night and day to get into that character. I think I love him."

Maybe his brother didn't scare so easily. "Is Squirrel still peeing himself somewhere?"

Jared waved that concern off. "We managed to catch Lena. He's going to tag along with her today. I'll send everyone home. Now I understand that Pierce Craig needs his solitude. He needs peace and quiet because the world is so chaotic for him. He's a deep man."

He wasn't sure how deep Ian was. Kai had seen Big Tag blow up shit for fun in his backyard, but he didn't mention that to Jared. He might find himself hauling Jared out so he could sit in Tag's yard and soak up his vibes or some shit. "I've got to get to the office. I have patients to meet."

He knew he was running away, but he couldn't seem to stop himself. He needed to sit his brother down and have a long talk, but his gut was rolling after the talk with Tag. He needed something else more than closure with his brother and he found himself anxious to get it.

"I'll hang out here for a while," Jared replied. "That Alex guy said I could follow him on a couple of client meetings. He's bringing his wife with us. She seems nice. It's going to be good to get to see what the job is really like."

Eve would be profiling Jared the entire time. Somehow, the idea rankled. He actually thought about telling Jared not to go.

His brother wasn't a killer and that's what Eve would discover. "Have fun."

"Kai," Jared called out when Kai got to the lobby doors. "Thanks for not kicking me out."

Kai nodded and walked to the elevator, but he couldn't get the nasty feeling out of his gut that he was missing something. Something big. Something he would have to deal with before this was all over.

* * * *

Kori relished the quiet. No appointments until after noon. No one in the building at all from what she could tell. All she could hear was the hum of the fan overhead and the rushing water of Kai's office fountain. She took a deep breath and was grateful for the peace. It gave her time to think about what had happened.

Kai had happened. He'd kissed her and spanked her and adored her body. She could still feel the ache deep in her bones like a reminder of how well he'd loved her.

Was she thinking that word already? She knew she shouldn't, but the pesky word wouldn't leave her alone.

She said it all the time. She loved her friends, loved certain books and TV shows, loved the club. But this was a different love. This was a forever and drown in it and lose herself love.

It scared the holy crap out of her, but she also had to be reasonable. She didn't have to "lose" herself. She simply had to find the Kori who loved Kai. No one stayed the same. To cling to that idea was childish. She wasn't the same person she would be ten years from now. Time and experience would shape her. Loving Kai would change her, but that didn't mean it had to be for the worse.

Losing herself wouldn't be so bad if he was with her. That was the key. She had to figure out if Kai felt for her what she felt for him.

And it wasn't like she didn't have time. She moved through the office, watering the numerous plants that Kai kept. He was right about all that green. It was soothing.

There was time. They were starting to explore, having fun but within boundaries.

He was very likely going to ask her to sign a contract with him.

The thought of that made her feel a little caged. She'd signed contracts with Morgan. She'd convinced herself she was safe and that it was all right to give up those pieces of herself to a man who took care of her. She'd given him far more than the contract ever required. Every day she would give more, sign away something else, let some piece go until she'd had nothing left.

Was she willing to let another man take from her?

What would Kai want?

She looked around his office. It was simple, lovely but in a very Spartan fashion. He had a desk, the computer tucked away inside the top drawer. There were no photos or keepsakes marking the top of the desk. The whole office was a shrine to peace and serenity, as though personal history or individual memories had no place here. Beyond the desk, there was a chair and large sofa patients could choose from. Some, Kai had explained, preferred to lie down when they talked, looking up at the ceiling instead of directly at him. It was a way to distance. He often knew he was making progress with those patients when they finally looked at him. There was a rolled up yoga mat tucked into a corner. Even that was a soothing green color.

This was the place where Kai worked, but he lived here, too, and his personal spaces looked an awful lot like this office.

As if Kai lived merely to serve those around him.

He rarely went out beyond his nights at Sanctum. She knew he went to parties the MT group threw, but the only people he regularly saw outside of work and the club were her group when they would have their late night meals. Even then he wouldn't talk much. He sat back, watching the people around him. He always, always sat next to her. When someone took his place, he made up ridiculous reasons why he needed that particular seat.

Had Kai been trying to get close to her all this time?

She heard a bell chime, the one that indicated she was no longer alone. With a long sigh, she stepped out of Kai's office and back into the lobby. Her desk looked nothing like Kai's. There was a picture of her mom framed on her desk and a docking station for her laptop. She had a pile of bills and receipts left to log. And two coffee mugs because Kai hadn't cleaned up yesterday. Which was a surprise since she could always count on Mr. Clean to ensure everything got scrubbed down.

She waited for the lobby door to open, wondering if it was Kai coming back. His meeting had obviously not taken too long.

He'd kissed her when he'd dropped her off. Apparently they weren't doing the professional thing.

Would he kiss her again? Should she insist that they kept up some kind of distance at the office? Her heart sped up and she tried to smooth down her hair.

The door opened but it wasn't Kai who came through. Lena strode through like a diva taking the stage. She had a massive handbag on her elbow that would likely cause nerve damage some day and a phone to her ear. "I need three in the V-neck. Not the crew neck. The crew neck makes him look like an old man. I want only dark colors and one hundred percent cotton. If you try to show me a blend I will have you fired on the spot. Do you understand me?"

Squirrel wandered in behind her. He was wearing skinny jeans and one of the V-neck T-shirts Lena seemed to be very specific about. He looked quiet, shy. His hair was a bit longer than Jared's, but it was obvious he tried to emulate his friend. "Hi, Kori. Sorry about that. She's been on the phone for twenty minutes with some store because she doesn't like the colors Jared brought with him. The stylist called from LA and said the pictures from the club last night made Jared look old. Like he was thirty or something." Squirrel smiled. "He is thirty something."

Kori rolled her eyes. "I'm so glad to be out of that world. You know thirty isn't old."

"It is in our world."

"Not for men."

Squirrel shrugged. "Maybe not, but boy they make you feel it. They're already trying to put Jared on something called a maintenance schedule with a plastic surgeon. Like he needs Botox or something."

Yeah, she'd heard the phrase before. "He doesn't need it. I think Jared is one of those men who'll likely look amazing at seventy-five."

Like Kai would.

Squirrel gave her a half smile. "We brought by the insurance paperwork for you to sign. Naturally it's in her bag and I'm afraid to put my hand in it. I have no idea what she keeps in there. It's probably only going to be another couple of minutes."

Lena groaned into her phone. "Neutral colors. I said neutral. Purple is not neutral. Give me to your supervisor. Do you even know who you're dealing with?"

"Or not." Kori nodded toward the small kitchen. "I'm going to get some coffee. Can I get you anything?"

"I'd love a soda if you have one."

"Of course." Squirrel seemed quiet but sweet. She gestured for him to follow her. "So how do you like Dallas? You're lucky you're here at this time of year. Summer is a bitch. I, for one, kind of like having brief seasons."

"It's nice enough. It's good to be home for a while. Back in the States, I mean. Whoa, is that what I think it is?" He peered into the fridge. "This is real, actual soda with real sugar."

She hadn't thought about that. Jared's crew didn't seem big on carbs. "I can find you a diet somewhere. I stock this place. Kai only drinks tea and the occasional glass of wine."

Squirrel grabbed the red can and popped the top as fast as he could. He took a long drink. "God, that tastes good. No one allows sugar around Jared. His trainer banned it. I don't think Jared minds, but I miss it."

Kori grabbed her coffee mug and fit the pod in the machine. Kai didn't believe in caffeine but a few days after she'd hired on there had been a shiny new coffee maker and a box of almost every blend the store carried. She preferred a medium roast but she'd found it nice that the boss wanted her to have her favorite morning drink.

Had he been taking care of her even then?

"So you grew up with Jared?" She had to admit she was deeply curious about Jared and Kai's relationship. Kai never talked about his family. She knew he'd grown up in Seattle and his mother had passed away young. He'd gone into the Army to support his brother. Then he'd made his way through college and grad school very quickly once he'd gotten out. That was all she knew. If Squirrel could shed some light, she'd take it.

Squirrel leaned against the counter. "Oh, yeah. We've been best friends since we met in junior high. Jared's a great guy."

"Did you live in the same neighborhood?"

"Pretty close. I was a couple blocks away, but it was easy to get there on my bike. I liked Jared's house better than mine. His brother was kind of a tool though. Luckily Kai was always working or studying and their mom was never there."

"A tool?" She was well aware of the chill in her tone.

Squirrel's hands came up as though in apology. "Sorry. He was kind of the father figure in our lives back then and he wasn't exactly easy on us. He was always pushing Jared. I don't think he liked me much."

"Kai likes everyone. Well, he tolerates everyone."

"All right, let's say Kai didn't think I was a good influence on his brother. Not that I was into drugs or anything. We didn't do stuff like that. We played football and worked out. Kai thought those were stupid things to do."

She had to smile because he hadn't changed that much. "Kai works out plenty and he plays basketball with the guys, but I understand. He likely told Jared that football wasn't a profession. I can imagine he pushed academics."

Squirrel's eyes rolled. "You have no idea. He was always on Jared to take all these froufrou classes. Like the kind that get college credit."

So even as a kid Kai had been a good parent. "He was trying to watch out for his brother. I tried to do the same for my sister, though my mom was around more. I didn't have the same responsibilities Kai obviously had."

Her mom had worked, but she only worked one job, and every other moment was spent with her girls. After her dad died, her mom made sure to be around for all the important stuff.

She tried to picture Kai as a kid. He would have taken the responsibility seriously. He would have tried to be the man of the house.

"Yeah, well, Jared wanted to be left alone. He didn't need any of that shit. I think that's why he liked me so much. I didn't try to make him be something he wasn't. He could chill around me. Jared and I been tight ever since. We used to have a big crew, but a lot of them moved on after high school."

She remembered what it felt like to watch her friends all go off to college while she'd been left behind. She'd gotten into a prestigious writing program, gotten a decent scholarship, but it hadn't covered enough. She'd been the one left behind. "Yeah, I know how that feels. It's good that you had a friend."

"We're a good team. You know in the beginning I was his manager. I was the one who set up all his auditions and stuff."

"That's nice. Did you ever think about becoming an agent? I'm sure you've got a lot of contacts by now." She wasn't sure how efficient he would be, but stranger things had happened.

"Oh, no," Squirrel said. "I couldn't leave Jared. He wouldn't know what to do without me. He'd be left with people like Lena and that asshole, Tad. Brad's pretty cool, but then he doesn't try to change everything. You have no idea how much pressure he's got on him."

She remembered. "Are they already pushing him to leave TV?"

Squirrel smiled as he nodded. "Oh, yeah, I forgot you used to be in the biz. Jared reminded me that you worked for the producer of *Dart*."

She'd been the one who brought the original treatment to Morgan's attention. "One of them, but I left before production actually started."

"You wrote some movie scripts though, right?"

There it was, that nasty feeling in the pit of her stomach that she got when she thought about her former career. "A couple."

"Yeah, I think I saw some of your horror flicks. Good stuff."

She didn't want to talk about this. "Well, I like the job I have now better."

Did she? She told herself it was easier to be out of that life, but lately she missed the peace that came with writing.

"Yeah, I get what you're saying. When you find something good, you gotta hold on. Too many people don't get that. They're all trying to change him. I don't think Jared wants to do those dumb films where everyone's in historical crap. He's happy where he is. I don't get why we can't be happy where we are."

Because that wasn't the way Hollywood worked. "He needs to decide what he wants. He can actually have a great career doing nothing but TV and genre films. That fan group is very loyal to the actors who treat them well."

"See, that's what I say. I don't think he'll be happy doing all those fancy movies."

The door to the kitchen came open and Lena walked in, a long-suffering sigh issuing from her mouth. "Are you on that again? God, get with the program. In order for Jared to move up in the world, people have to take him seriously. That's never going to happen as long as he's wearing superhero costumes and spanking girls onscreen. Let the rest of us handle the career part." She looked over at Kori. It was kind of the way Kori suspected she would look at a bug on the floor. Or a non-designer shoe. "As for you, here's the paperwork. I need you to sign and send it in, and then the work on your car will be paid for. I have no idea why anyone would want to trash your car. It's pathetic enough as it is."

Squirrel took the papers out of Lena's hand and gave them to Kori. "I think it's a nice car. I actually thought it was Kai's car when I first saw it. It looked like something he would drive."

Kori took the papers, looking them over. It wasn't anything she couldn't have done herself, but Jared seemed to want to make things easy for her. "No, Kai drives a Jeep. He likes to get out of the city as much as possible. He spends a lot of time hiking."

Maybe that was something he could do alone since nature wasn't really her thing. It was pretty and all but she was a city girl. Kai could go hiking and she could...

Write. She could write.

She shoved the thought out of her head. "Thanks for this. I appreciate it."

"Squirrel, could you go and have the limo pulled around? We have an appointment with the manager of the men's department at Neiman Marcus in a few minutes and then we'll have lunch." She actually gave him a small smile.

"All right, but I want to go by a game store. There's a new game Jared wants. Bye, Kori." Squirrel waved as he walked out.

The minute the door swung closed, Lena turned on her, that pretty face of hers going arctic.

"Am I about to get the mean girl speech?" Kori sipped on her coffee, waiting for whatever would happen next. She was pretty sure this was the part of the scene where she got told to stay away from someone's man. Lena had the look down, but Kori wasn't sure she'd be so good with dialogue.

"I have no idea what you're talking about, but I do have some things to say to you. I looked you up last night. I know that you used to be someone."

Not bad. As hits went, it would be pretty good if Kori gave a real shit about that life anymore. She'd figured out a long time ago that if the "someone" she had to be was dependent on others, she was cool being "no one." "Please continue."

Lena frowned as though this conversation wasn't going the way she thought it would, but she soldiered on. "You're not going to use Jared to get back in the business. I know Morgan King. I called his wife last night. She told me all about you. How you pathetically clung to him for years. How you claimed to have written all his scripts. You would force him to put your name on them, too."

She had to clear something up there. "Except that last one. I had very little to do with *Our Time Together*."

Oh, it had been the script she'd left him over. Those ninety pages had chronicled what it had been like to grow up as Kori Williamson. It should have been a small film about how one young girl survived, about her tenuous relationship with her sister, how she'd come to finally admire her mother. She'd meant it to be an indie film. When she'd envisioned it, she'd thought about filming in real locations, the real neighborhood she'd grown up in. It was set during her high school years, during that time when she found out only she could lift herself up out of poverty and she had to do it by believing in her own talent.

The studio had turned it into a teen rom-com that had bombed so spectacularly it had taken Morgan and his new wife, Claudia, years to get another film in production.

Sweet, sweet karma.

"That film was so stupid," Lena said with a sneer. "Anyway, Claudia warned me about you. You get your hooks into men so they'll take you places. She says you're going to try to sleep with Jared."

Kori bit back a laugh. "Not at all. I have a relationship with his brother and I'm perfectly happy there. The idea of stepping into the spotlight gives me hives."

Lena looked her over and obviously found her wanting. "The press would tear you up. Do you understand what they would do to you? Even if you could get into Jared's bed, you would be the fat chick he was banging."

"Absolutely," she agreed. Anyone over a size zero was the fat chick in Hollywood. "More importantly though, I'm not interested in sleeping with Jared. I'm happy with Kai."

"She also told me you lie. Apparently you were Morgan's assistant but you tried to get into bed with him, too. You thought you could control him with sex. Do you even look at yourself in the mirror? Jared doesn't want you. He's only being nice to you because you work for his brother. I don't believe you and he have anything going on. He's not as hot as Jared but he's attractive. He's never going to be with you."

This was so sad. "Okay, let me tell you all the ways you're going wrong here. First, I'm mostly bored by this dialogue. I can turn on a *Real Housewives* episode and hear this crap. At least flip a table or something."

"What?" Lena's eyes went wide.

She was likely used to running off lots of women with her rapid fire but deadly dull dialogue. Like that was the first time someone had told Kori she wasn't attractive enough. She'd lived in LA for years. She'd been told a thousand times she wasn't smart enough, attractive enough, thin enough. If she'd believed any of it she would never have gotten a film made.

"I'm going to give you some advice. Here's the key, when you're trying to intimidate someone, you have to make them believe you're the tiniest bit batshit crazy. This 'you're not pretty' crap is only going to work on girls who just got off the bus. For real women, you have to dig deeper. You have to scare them. Like you'll do something really bad. I'll give you an example. Lena, if you don't get out of my face in the next two minutes, I'll make sure Jared never speaks to you again. You see, I have some actual leverage. He wants a relationship with his brother and I can give that to him. You're a piece of crap in last year's Pradas, and he can pick up another one of you in the lobby of any production office. So maybe you should turn around and walk out of here and the next time we see each other, you'll smile and be polite because I can have your job in two minutes."

It was an empty threat. She would never once do that. She wouldn't come between the brothers like that.

"You wouldn't. You couldn't do that," Lena sputtered.

"See, now we're having a smack down. It's so low to go after a woman's looks. She gets that from every side. You have to go after her intelligence or her job, or sometimes you can score points by

From Sanctum with Love

sounding like a crazy bitch. That prostitution-whore stuff can throw a girl off because she's trying to figure out what the hell you just said. Like if I called you a skanky ho-bag who's one step above assistant crack whore, you would try to figure out if I was calling you a slut or a prostitute. Mix it up. It throws people off."

"You're a bitch," Lena said, proving she couldn't even do comebacks well.

Kori sighed. "Yeah, I've heard that before. And now I'm bored again. Scurry off, sad woman. I'm sure you've got something to do with your time."

Some people couldn't learn. It took the right amount of intelligence and pure quick wit to be able to truly insult someone.

The door opened and Lena gasped.

"You should probably leave now," a familiar voice said.

Shit. Kai was here. Kai had heard her. Oh, shit. How the hell was she going to explain what she'd said? She heard the clack of Lena's shoes against the floor and then the door swung open. Kai stood there still wearing yesterday's clothes. Somehow he made the walk of shame look so damn good. The shirt he wore was slightly wrinkled, but she couldn't help but think about the chest underneath it. His hair was pulled back now and his glasses were perfectly placed, but she knew what he looked liked right before he bit her, when he was predatory and fierce. And she knew what he looked like when he was mad.

Like now.

"Are you all right?" His voice was quiet, but she could hear the edge to his tone.

"Kai, I was telling her off. She was being a bitch. That was all there was to it."

He held a hand out. "I need you. I've had a disturbing morning. I need…you."

Her body already ached. She wasn't sure she could take more. Still, she found herself reaching for his hand and letting him lead her to his office. What was he going to do? Spank her? Bring out his whip?

She'd agreed to a D/s relationship with him. This was what she was supposed to do. She was supposed to give him what he needed even as he gave to her.

She could handle it. Hell, she might like it. If she spent the rest of the day not being able to sit down, maybe she would remember that she shouldn't even joke about using Kai's brother to further her own ends.

He strode through the door and right to the big couch in his office. He sat down and she was certain he would command her to lift her skirt and let him spank her. Instead he dragged her down, laying her out before wrapping himself around her.

"Stay with me for a while." His head found its way to her breast and he sighed as though he needed the contact. "Did you think I was mad about what you said to Lena?"

Almost immediately all her stress fled and she found herself relaxing. He wasn't the only one who needed this. They'd been disrupted this morning. They hadn't spent enough time exploring the new intimacy between them.

Because she had to face the facts. She hadn't simply started a new D/s relationship with Kai. She'd started a relationship with Kai. A real relationship where they played and worked and relied on each other. One where he needed comfort and could ask it of her.

She smoothed her hand across his head and kissed his forehead because it was her right now. She cuddled against him. "I didn't mean it. And yes, I was worried you would punish me."

"No punishments," he said with a sigh. "I don't want that, baby. I want to play but I don't want to be responsible for you. Not in that way. Shit. I'm fucking this up."

He wasn't. He was saying all the right things. She kissed him again. He was responsible for so many things, so many people. He needed a safe place. She could be his safe place. "I want that, too, Kai. I've been in a relationship where I bowed to the Master. I can't do it again. I want to play with you but I also want to be your partner. I want you to value me and what I have to say. I want to be able to say it whether you want to hear it or not."

He brought her free hand to his lips. "I don't think you could be any other way, baby. As for what you said to Lena, I knew exactly what you were doing."

"How?"

"Because I know you," he replied. "Now cuddle with me until my next appointment. Talk to me. I want to know about the scripts you wrote."

"You heard too much."

He looked up at her. "If you don't want to talk, we don't have to."

Didn't he deserve to know who she'd been? And what was so wrong with who she'd been? "All right, but it's not all pretty."

Kai settled against her again and she began to talk.

Chapter Nine

Kai closed the door to his office as Case and Ethan Rush took their seats. It had been days since his last meeting with Ian and he hadn't been looking forward to this instructional session. Not at all. He'd been kind of praying it wouldn't have to happen.

"I assume since you're here that you've been unable to tag Mia's phone."

Now it was Tuesday, the night he was supposed to run his "op." There was only one reason he would still have a damn "op" in the first place.

Case had the grace to flush. "I'm sorry. I've tried with her. I've been as charming as I know how to be. We've had dinner twice. She never leaves her purse alone. I offered to try breaking in when I'm sure she's gone to bed, but Adam said her security system is so high tech it isn't even on the market yet. I guess that's what happens when your brother is some kind of technological genius."

Drew Lawless wasn't merely a genius. He was a billionaire. When he'd taken his software company public a few years before, he'd become the youngest billionaire in the country. He was also known for being reclusive and mysterious. Her family had an interesting history. Their inventor father had killed himself, their mother, and according to all police reports, he'd meant the children to die in a fire he'd set. Drew had led the four siblings out of the home. He hadn't been able to keep them together afterward. The siblings had been split up and sent into foster care. Mia, the youngest, had been adopted, but her three older brothers had lived in the system.

It looked like her older brother still cared about her. "If he's protecting her, what makes you think you'll be able to tag her phone without him knowing?"

"What we're planning on uploading to her phone looks like a harmless app. Actually, it doesn't show up on her screen in any way. He would have to physically find the program and even if he did, he couldn't be sure it was us. This kind of malware is all over the place," Case replied. "If he's Collective, I'm sure he's ready for us and the next time she does a check on her phone, she'll find it. Even if it doesn't work, it's another piece to the puzzle. We'll know more than we did before. I think we'll have some time before she finds it. I think her brother is the one who would run that check. She fumbled with her security system the one time I managed to get into her place. I don't think she's particularly tech savvy."

"Why couldn't you do it then?"

Case groaned. "Do you think I didn't try? She immediately put her purse in the bedroom and let me tell you, I didn't come close to getting back there. I haven't managed to kiss her yet. I think she's playing me."

Interesting. Kai would bet that frustration came from more than a job Case hadn't been able to do. "I noted she spent all her time at Sanctum with her training Dom."

Though he'd also noticed she stared at Case when she thought no one was looking, and the one scene Case had run with another sub had sent Mia straight to the locker room. So why would she hold Case off?

"She won't scene with me. She claims she owes some kind of loyalty to her training Dom and that when she graduates she'll think about it, but she's playing me."

"Does she question you about McKay-Taggart?"

"Not really," Case replied. "We've mostly talked about baseball. She loves baseball. We've talked about movies and stuff. She never mentions her brothers, but she talks about her adoptive parents a lot. Her moms. She put that out there like I was supposed to freak out or something. I don't get her. She's not my type at all."

And yet he was struggling with his attraction to her. That was easy to see. Kai wasn't about to explain that often times opposites attracted because they gave each other something important that was missing. Like Kori brought him a peace he couldn't find in a fake waterfall. And he could bring her a partner who didn't scare away easily.

This wasn't a therapy session, however.

"Has she agreed to go out with you tonight?"

Case nodded. "Yes. I think she's interested in spending more time with your brother. He might be the one who gets her up and dancing and then I'll handle it."

"I doubt that." Mia didn't watch Jared. She watched Case. The few times she'd been in a room with Jared, she barely noticed him, but damn the girl lit up when the young Taggart walked in a room. If she was holding out on him, she had her reasons.

Could Mia be turned? Would she go against her family for a man she loved?

While he waited for a chance to tag her phone, he would also talk to her. He would try to get a better feel for the woman.

"Case is going to teach you what you need in order to follow the Lawless woman, but I'm here for a different reason," Rush said, looking a bit impatient. He was out of place in the peaceful confines of the office. He sat on the couch, his big body rigid in a space that was supposed to be relaxing.

God knew he relaxed there. At least once a day for the last couple of days, he called her in and cuddled against her, their bodies tangled together while she talked to him about her life, her past, her friends, her everything. He would rest his head against the softness of her breast and spend an hour simply being with her.

He loved to scene, but those hours of peace and calm were so precious to him.

"You want me to tell you my brother is a serial killer." This was precisely why he needed the calm with Kori so badly. Jared had

From Sanctum with Love

flown back to Vancouver to shoot some promotional spots for his TV show, but he'd shown back up this morning.

They still hadn't talked. He'd fully intended to sit his brother down and find out what he'd meant in the elevator that day at McKay-Taggart. Not everything Jared had said made sense. But the next time he'd seen his brother had been at Sanctum and he'd gone into teaching mode, and then Jared had been called away.

It had been so much nicer to concentrate on his new sub. His new girlfriend.

With Jared out of town, he'd been able to focus on her. All his nasty attention. Night after night. Twice during the afternoon.

It should have made him chill, but somehow fucking Kori simply made him want her more. Even now he was thinking about her and wondering if she'd gotten his gift yet. She was outside in the lobby at her desk. Sitting there. Waiting for him. Fuck, he wanted her.

"I want you to do what we discussed. I want you to get involved in your brother's life so you can figure out if he's the one killing these women."

He wished he could stop thinking about this. "He's not. I grew up with him. I would have seen signs. I was responsible for him the entire time we were growing up. He wasn't a bully. He wasn't bullied. He was the kid everyone else loved."

"He also grew up without a father and I suspect his childhood wasn't as rosy as you claim. He had several visits to the emergency room and a couple of brushes with the law."

Did the special agent think he didn't know his own brother? "He got into some fights and he was always a clumsy kid. He had a couple of football injuries. I think he broke his arm during a game once."

Rush's eyes narrowed. "Yes, I've made a study of your brother. You're talking about an incident in high school. A spiral fracture of his left arm. The only problem was he didn't play that night. I checked the actual hospital records. He was taken to the ER long before the game that night. I suspect your brother suffered some abuse at the hands of a coach. Sometimes that can make a man like Jared feel small. Did you know that there was a rash of small animal disappearances around the same time he was in high school?"

"Don't be ridiculous. My brother took in strays constantly." Why would Jared have lied about how he'd broken his arm? He remembered the day. He'd been working and he'd come home to his mother worrying over Jared. She'd been sick at the time, too. It had been the early days of her cancer, the first rounds of chemo that had left her body devastated. Even as her hands shook because she hadn't been able to keep anything down, she'd taken care of her youngest child.

Kai remembered how pissed he'd been because they didn't have money for more fucking medical bills. He'd had an argument with Jared about how much playing a stupid game was going to cost him.

Take care of your brother, Kai. He needs you more than you know.

Had his mother known something he didn't?

"You know as well as I do that many serial killers start with small animals before moving to humans," Rush said, a nauseating sympathy in his voice.

"Yeah, well, we lived in Washington state. You can throw a rock and hit a serial killer." It wouldn't do any good to argue with the special agent. He had preconceived notions and the only way to fix the situation was to prove it couldn't be Jared.

Because it wasn't. No matter what the man said, he couldn't buy that his brother was a killer. He could buy that Jared was keeping secrets. It was time to acknowledge that his childhood wasn't as cut-and-dry as it had seemed. Tomorrow morning he and his brother were going to have a long talk.

After he got through tonight. One clusterfuck at a time.

"You're being awfully narrow in your thinking, Special Agent," Case interjected. "I've studied those files too. The brothers, Brad and Tad, they came from an abusive home. From the time their father left them, their mother went through multiple men, several of whom abused both boys according to CPS records. The boys went to live with their grandparents, but both of them were in and out of trouble. The grandmother had enough money and power to cover a lot of it up, but they both had some violent encounters."

Rush shook his head. "Yes, I've read the files. I also know that the publicist has had some complaints of sexual harassment filed against him, all of which have been dropped."

"Settled," Case corrected. "The cases were settled and the records sealed. There's a big difference and you know it."

"Not to mention the fact that his assistant has an obsessive interest in him, and I would say she's got some narcissistic tendencies." Kai had come to a few of his own conclusions. All it had taken was a single ten-minute conversation with her to realize Lena was a vengeful woman. She'd talked a lot about the people who had done her wrong and how she'd dealt with them. "Everyone's got issues. If you truly look at any single person's background, you can make a case for violence. All of us are damaged in some way. Until you have some real proof, I don't want you focusing in on my brother. For all we know this is coincidence."

Rush's eyes rolled. "If you can't do the job, let me know now."

Kai took a deep breath. He was getting sick of the whole thing. There was a reason he worked by himself and not in a practice where he would have a boss. He had some authority issues of his own. "My job is to teach my brother about BDSM."

"Your brother has been in the lifestyle for years. God, you haven't even figured that out yet?" Rush stood up, his big body stiff with frustration.

"What are you talking about?" Kai asked, Rush's words not quite making sense.

Case shot the special agent an arctic stare. "I thought my brother asked you not to mention that."

"Your brother also told me this guy could do the job," Rush retorted. "So far all he's done is his secretary."

"I can do more," Kai promised, visions of his hands around the asshole's throat playing through his brain.

Case stood and got between them. "He means that, Rush, and don't judge him by his looks. He could take you on and he would very likely enjoy hurting you."

Kai didn't move. "See, we've all got issues. As for my brother, I'll go with him tonight and I'll watch everyone carefully. After I tag a woman's phone."

If it weren't for Ian, he would tell everyone to go to hell. Well, likely not because if he wasn't doing this for Ian, he would be doing it for Sean. Or Case. Or Erin.

He was locked in and there wasn't anything he could do about it. Maybe what his brother had said was right. He'd spent the last few decades of his life trying not to have ties only to find himself bound tightly again. He'd run from one brother only to find an entire family, and he'd slid into it because it seemed like Ian was the only one with real responsibility. But in a family, everyone had responsibility. It was only a matter of time before it reared its head.

The responsibility was chafing. It reminded him of all the reasons he'd walked away in the first place. Sometimes it took him back to that place where he was twelve and his mother was working an overnight shift and Jared had fallen and hit his head. There'd been so much blood and it had been his fault because he wasn't watching his brother properly. His mother hadn't yelled, but the point had been made.

"Ferguson, I'm sorry. I'm under a lot of pressure. I don't like bringing family members in. Not ever." Rush ran a hand over his hair as he walked toward the door. "Do what you can. I don't want anyone dying on my watch. Know that we'll be sticking close tonight."

Jared was surrounded by vultures and men who wanted to see him in prison. Once again it was up to Kai to save his brother.

The door closed behind Rush and he was left alone with Case.

"I'll do everything I can to make sure you don't have to do this. Hell, why don't I bring along Hutch? I can introduce him as a friend and you can be out of this altogether," Case offered.

There was a problem with that scenario. "If she's Collective, then she knows who Hutch is and she'll likely be vigilant around him. I'm the non-threatening one. I'm the therapist who rarely works for McKay-Taggart and never in the field. If she sees Hutch or Adam or any of the tech guys, she'll figure out what's happening and we'll lose her. This will work because she'll think you can't get anything done if you're out dancing with her. She'll leave her purse with Kori because she's Mia's friend and Mia trusts her, and I'll very quietly get the job done because we'll make sure someone distracts Kori. I can get Jared talking and he tends to command the room when he does. We'll get what we need. I can handle tagging the phone, but Rush is right about one thing. I'm too close to the murder case. I can't conceive of a world in which my brother is a serial killer."

"Honestly, having spent some time with him, neither can I. I have to wonder if this isn't some unfortunate coincidence. I think we should concentrate on the situation with Mia and let the feds do what they need to do. Once you tag this phone, all you need to do is fulfill the contract you have with the studio and you're out of it. No more spy stuff."

There was one more matter to settle. "Apparently my brother doesn't need training. What do you know about that? Is it true? Has Jared been in the lifestyle for a while?"

Case's jaw tightened as though he didn't like this line of questioning. "According to the file the feds have on him, he's been going to clubs for years. He started in his early twenties."

Had Hannah been the one to introduce him? Wouldn't that be a kick in the groin? "Thanks for telling me the truth."

"I think he's lying because he wants to get close to you and this was a good way to ensure your attention," Case said. "Look, man, you've never been the little brother. I've been both. I know what it means to have to look out for your younger brother, even when he was only a few minutes younger than me. Theo was…reckless. I always knew that. In some ways the fact that he was always so reckless made me more careful."

Kai knew this story. He'd lived it. It had to have been worse for Case since Theo had been his twin. Was his twin. "You had to be his more reasonable half. I was basically Jared's father figure, so I understand. It doesn't make it easier to swallow that he's lying to me again. He made me spend hours going over contracts and talking about different forms of play when he likely knew everything I was saying."

"Ah, but that's where I do understand him. Look, maybe I was the oldest growing up, but it's different now," Case explained. "I was the leader when Theo and I were young. I was the one who decided to go into the Navy. Theo followed me. I was the one who decided we would join the CIA team. And then I met Big Tag."

The Taggart brothers hadn't grown up together. They shared a father, one who had walked out on Ian and Sean when they were young. Papa Taggart had found a new family, fathered Case and

Theo, and moved on from them as well. Tennessee Smith had been the one to connect the dots. The brothers had finally met, but it hadn't been an easy family reunion. "You didn't like him at first."

"No. He was a challenge to everything I knew about myself. If it had been up to me, I would have walked away and never looked back. When Ten got burned, I would have stayed with the Agency and I probably would be an operative by now. I would have no family. No future. Nothing but the work. Theo wouldn't leave. Theo wanted to know Ian and Sean. He was the leader in that. Now there are times I would do anything to get their attention. Ian and Sean's, that is. I'm not a kid so I don't act out, but I'll show up on their doorsteps with the thinnest reasons possible. They never turn me away. Jared thought you would turn him away. I would bet anything he enjoyed going over things he already knew because he would do almost anything to get to spend time with you."

Case was right. He likely would have turned his brother away. "Jared and I have history you've never had with your brothers. It's not the same."

Case's jaw tightened. "No two relationships are ever the same, but you're brothers. No matter what he did, no matter what you did, you're never going to get another one. Do you have any idea what I would do to get another chance? To go back and do it again? To get another shot at watching my brother's back? Anything, man. I know it's not the same, but it is. Think about it, Kai. That's all we're asking. And thank you for everything you're doing."

"I'm doing it so maybe you do get that shot."

"I don't know if he's out there or not. I think Ian might be optimistic."

"He has his reasons and he won't be satisfied until he's made every attempt to find Theo."

Case slumped down. "I had to tell our mother he died. I had to tell her I didn't protect my brother."

Kai's chest tightened. He didn't know what he believed about the afterlife, but he wondered sometimes. Was his mother angry with him? She hadn't asked him to look after his brother, but only if Jared didn't piss him off. She hadn't put a clause in her dying wish that released him from the obligation in the case of fiancée stealing.

Had he taken the first chance he had to distance himself? To be free?

Had he really been that selfish?

"You were not responsible for what happened to Theo any more than Erin was. It was an operation that went very wrong."

Case's eyes were so weary when he looked up. "I can say that as many times as I like, but my gut will never believe it. I can smile and say the right things and I can pretend like I'm moving forward with my life, but there's a part of me that died when he did. I felt it. I fucking felt him die."

Sometimes twins had amazing connections. "Do you feel like he's alive?"

Case shook his head. "All my life I've had this connection to my brother. Not some psychic shit. It's like a low hum. White noise, maybe. It's something that's always there. Now it's gone and I don't know what to do about it. There's this place that's totally empty. And I can tell myself that I'll find a way to fill it. I can put my heart and soul into helping Erin raise Theo's kid. But at the end of the day, I think that place will always be there, a hole inside me. If Ian's right and Theo's alive, something's gone horribly wrong with him because I can't feel him anymore." Case took a deep breath and shook his head as though trying to shake off his emotion. "Let me show you how this works."

He reached down and picked up the small laptop bag he'd shown up with.

"Case, if you need to talk, I'll move my morning sessions to this afternoon."

Case shook his head. "I talk too fucking much these days and I've got lunch with Mia. Hell, maybe I'll manage to get her phone this afternoon and you won't have to."

Kai doubted it. He leaned in and listened as Case began to explain what needed to be done. He took it all in, but he couldn't let go of the thought that he'd failed his brother somehow.

* * * *

Kori looked up as the big, hunky dude in the suit stalked out. He'd shown up with Case, so she was betting he was an applicant at McKay-Taggart. Looked like the psych evaluation had gone poorly.

"Are you still there?" Sarah asked over the phone.

"Yep," Kori replied, looking at the "bouquet" that had been delivered not moments before. "Still here and still looking at my present."

It was a beautiful array of torture implements surrounded lovingly with well-placed daisies and chrysanthemums.

"He sent you an entire bouquet of sadisticks? Are you kidding me? He's the most romantic sadist ever," Sarah said with a happy squeal. "Send me a pic. It will liven up my super-boring day. Believe it or not the ER is actually quiet for once. We've got a couple of boring broken bones and a chick who thinks she's having a heart attack but it's actually gas. Give me a good trauma any day of the week. Which brings me to why I'm calling."

Kori stared at the present. The little instruments of torture called to her in a way no bouquet of lilies ever would. She brushed her fingertips across the round pink tips. The carbon rods were flexible and the tips when they hit flesh stung like hell. They would leave a matchstick-shaped mark that she would wear for however long it lasted. She would touch them and let her fingertips play and remember how much fun she'd had. How much her Master knew her.

Kai. How well Kai knew her.

He hadn't asked about a contract. At first she'd been happy to not deal with it. Now, as the days went by, she wondered why. He was a man who would want a contract. The few times he'd taken on even a training sub, he'd signed a contract and slapped a collar on her.

She got sadisticks.

"Are you even listening to me? Or are you already playing with your toys?" Sarah groused.

"I wouldn't dare." Kai had given her one rule. She wasn't allowed to play unless he was there or he'd vetted her partners. He'd been very clear that by partners he meant he didn't mind her playing with her friends. Sometimes the girls and Vince got together and played around with a violet wand or spanked each other. It was all in fun and there was nothing at all intimate about it.

She knew damn well she wasn't allowed to scene with anyone except Kai.

So why did the fact that he hadn't asked for a contract bother her? It was perverse. She knew she didn't want one. The threat of having that conversation with him hung over her. She was waiting for the fight, going over it again and again in her head.

"Yes, I'm listening. What's going on?"

There was a pause on the line before Sarah began. "You're going out with Jared tonight, right?"

Kori winced. She didn't particularly want to go, but Kai had asked her to and it was good he was spending time with his brother. Why he had to do it at some dance club, Kori had zero idea. At least Mia was going. If she had to spend all her hang time with Lena, someone was going to get murdered and hard. "Yeah. We're going to Top for dinner and then out to some club in Deep Ellum. I was told I have to wear heels. I don't know why."

"Because the paparazzi is going to be there," Sarah explained. "Do you think there's any way you could see if I can go, too?"

Kori had to smile. "Because you like Jared."

It wasn't a question. Sarah hadn't been able to stop talking about him. He'd run his first scene the night before he'd left for Vancouver and he'd chosen Sarah as his sub. He'd spanked her in a way that proved that man was a born Dom. He was a natural. She'd seen them later, Sarah wrapped in his arms in the bar.

"I do. I know it's insane. I know there's zero chance of this working long term, but I want to see him again and I don't have his number."

"Sure." Speaking of the devil, Jared walked by the front doors, his bag slung over his shoulder. He was wearing his normal uniform of a V-neck T-shirt, jeans, boots, and a pair of aviators, but she could see how tired he was from the slump to his shoulders. "Actually, I'll go and talk to him now. I'll call you back."

"Thank you! I've got the perfect outfit. I'm totally seducing him." The line went dead.

Kori ran to catch Jared before he walked up the stairs to the residence portion of the building. He'd been sleeping on Kai's bed since Kai had started spending every night at her place. The door swung closed behind her as she caught up to him.

"Jared!"

He stopped and turned, and that brilliant smile of his was on his face. If she hadn't seen him when he'd thought no one was looking, she wouldn't have thought anything was wrong. He was damn good at hiding his emotions. "Hey, Kori. How's it going?"

She stopped. This was the time to decide if she was ready to drop into the deep end of the pool. She could pretend she hadn't seen that look on his face, ask her question and move on. Or she could be his brother's girlfriend and try to figure out what was going on. "What's wrong?"

Jared frowned as though no one ever asked him that question before. "What do you mean?"

If she let him, Jared would talk his way right back into everything being fine. She got the feeling Jared would do a lot to keep the peace around him. "No bullshit, Jared. I'm not a fan or a reporter or a flunky. You look tired and worried. What's wrong?"

His lips formed a flat line. "It's nothing."

"Nope. It's not nothing. It can be something you don't want to talk about, but it's not nothing."

He let his bag drop and sat down on the second step. "You care?"

She moved toward him, dropping down beside him. "Of course I do. You're Kai's brother."

"Yeah, well, he doesn't care." For the first time since she'd met him, a hard look came into his eyes. "That's something you have to understand about Kai."

He didn't know Kai now. A lot had happened to both brothers over the time they'd been apart, but she softened her response. Jared didn't need a lecture. He did need the truth though. "I can care enough for both of us. You have to give Kai some time. You were an asshole."

"It's been twelve years."

"He's smart in many ways and slow in this one. Trust me. Kai always does the right thing. He'll come around. Is this about Kai?"

Jared shook his head. "No. It's about everything. I hate conflict. We all got into a massive fight on the plane and I don't like it when things get nasty."

"What was the fight about?"

"Whether or not I sign a new contract with *Dart*."

That was one problem she did understand. "Ah, your contract is up but the show is going strong. Your career is going strong, too, and they think you'll have a million and one offers after this movie hits big."

"You have forgotten nothing of your time in Hollywood." He turned to her, giving her a smile that likely could melt the heart of any woman he chose. "I've got a little time, but I have to make the decision. I have to give them time to wrap up the show or find a way to transition it away from me."

"It sounds like you've made your decision."

He shook his head and leaned back, his elbows on the stair behind him. "Not at all. I like the steady work of television. I like playing the same guy. I get to really get into the role. The producers have been cool about letting me work in our off time. Hell, when they found out I was up for this role, they offered to work around me."

She understood the problem he was facing. "But you have a shelf life."

"Most actors do. I'm never going to be a character actor. I'm not that good. I've got ten years maybe before I have to transition."

"TV is kinder," she pointed out.

"It is. But if I have a shot at doing something more, shouldn't I take it?" Jared asked.

"It depends. What do you want? Stop listening to all the other voices. I get that you have about a hundred voices playing through your head at any given moment. You've got the people who work for you. You've got the producers. You've got an entire small industry that has built itself around you and you feel the weight of it. You've got the inner voices. The ones that tell you you're not good enough and all this is going to go away tomorrow. The ones that tell you if you make one wrong move, you'll be done."

"Heard those, have you?"

She'd been an artist once. She still heard some of them. And some of them, the ones that had felt dead and gone, those had started whispering to her. They'd started telling stories again. "Yes. So now I'm going to tell you what you have to do. You have to shut them all out and hear the only voice that matters now. Yours. What do you want? Not what's going to placate the most people. What does Jared John Ferguson want?"

He was quiet for a moment. "Is that what you did? Is that why you walked away?"

"Hey, we're supposed to be talking about you here."

His voice lowered and she realized he was taking the whole Dom training seriously because he suddenly sounded like one. "And you are suddenly the only link I have to my family. Family opens up. Family talks. You want me to follow your advice, then tell me why you left. You were smart and your scripts were good. And everyone knew you were the one writing those scripts."

This was something she'd been avoiding thinking about for years. "I wasn't strong enough then. I didn't believe enough in myself, and maybe when I think about it deep down inside, maybe I didn't want it enough to fight. I thought that was my dream. I was wrong. I'm happier here."

Though lately she'd begun to wonder if she wasn't missing one tiny thing.

"It's a rough lifestyle. No one gets that. They see famous people and think about how good they have it." Jared sat back up. "It's hard. It's going to get harder from here."

"How much money do you need, Jared? How much fame? I walked out because I realized how much of myself I'd given up. I didn't recognize myself anymore. It's taken years, but I'm me again. I'm not the me I'll be ten years from now, but I'm the me I chose."

He was quiet for a moment. "I want to stay. I like the show. I want to see where it goes. I'm smart with my money now. And honestly, if it goes away tomorrow, I'll still be okay. When I look deep down, I want to stay on the show as long as it lasts. I'm happy there."

"Then that's your answer."

A grin lit his face. "Do you have any idea how many people I'm going to piss off?"

"That brings us to step number two in becoming a real live boy, Jared. You can't allow that to sway you. This is your decision. It's your life. You can't live it for other people."

He nodded. "You're really happier here?"

"Oh, yes. I can breathe here and it's not about a place. The location means nothing. I found the right people. I found people I care about who accept me for who I am. It made me accept me. That's the hardest part. It's too easy to find fault in ourselves. I'm still scared. I'm scared of what's happening between me and Kai to tell you the truth." He was oddly easy to talk to. Once a woman got past how beautiful Jared was, he was a great guy, willing to listen, willing to talk about something other than himself. "I think if I get in too deep with him, I'll lose myself all over again."

"Or you'll find something even better."

"There's that fine line I'm trying to walk. I do get that. I'm trying to be reasonable. Hell, it might not even be as serious as I think it is."

Jared shook his head. "Nope. It's serious. He's in love with you. It's a perverted freaky love, but it's love."

She couldn't help but think about what Kai would do with that gift he'd given her. "I like perverted, freaky love."

"Good because I think you're the woman he needs," Jared said, but his smile faded. "The problem is Kai doesn't always know what he needs."

"What do you mean?" She wasn't going to discount his opinion. Jared had grown up with Kai. Jared had lived with Kai when his core was being formed. He understood things no one else could, had seen pieces of Kai no one else had.

Jared sighed and was silent for a moment, as though thinking through what he was going to say. Or deciding if he was going to say it at all.

"Hey, just put it out there. Like you said before, we're practically family."

"That's what I'm worried about," Jared admitted. "I like you a lot, Kori. I think you could be so good for him, but Kai puts a lot of things before his relationships. He also isn't very quick to forgive."

"Jared, you slept with his fiancée."

He held a hand up. "I'm not only talking about me. You tend to get one shot with Kai. He can be huggy with all the people in the world who don't really touch him. He can hold them at a distance and be tolerant, but with the people he's closest to, he can get pretty judgmental. I worry he's gotten worse over the years. The Kai I used to know would already have a ring on your finger."

Her stomach turned at the thought, but not for the reason she would have guessed. "How long was it before he asked his fiancée?"

"He'd known her a month and then he wanted to actually get married before he went into the service, but she held out. She said she wanted a big wedding. I overheard. He argued that he simply wanted her. Be careful, Kori. One of the few times I tried to talk to him after the incident with Hannah, he promised me he would never get serious with another girl. The good news is he seems to have broken that promise. Now, I'm going to sleep for a while because when I make this announcement, I'm going to piss off everyone in my life with the exception of Squirrel." He gave her a grim smile. "Hey, I've always got Squirrel. But maybe I'll put off the announcement for a while. After we wrap this film I've got a couple of weeks vacation. I'll go someplace none of the bastards can find me. Then I'll tell them."

It sounded like a perfect plan to Kori. He stood up and Kori remembered why she'd run out here. "Hey, I was wondering if I could bring a friend along tonight."

He stopped, his jaw forming a hard line. "Sarah?"

That wasn't a good look. "Yes."

He paused for a moment before answering. "I would rather you didn't. I like her."

"That would seem to be a reason to invite her along."

"I like her. She's a lovely woman and I could spend time with her, but I couldn't bring her into my world."

She had no idea what was going on in his head. "I don't know that she wants to go into your world. I think she wants to spend time with you."

"Yeah, well, I can find a lot of women who want to spend time with me. Do you know the funny thing? Most of them don't bother to call after they've gotten what they want. Even the ones who seem so nice and sweet, they run once they get a taste of what it's like to be close to me. Over the last couple of years I've found some women I thought I could get close to, really talk to. Once I left town, they never called."

"Did you call them?"

His head shook briefly. "I try to leave it in their hands. I don't want to pressure anyone. Sarah is different. She's vibrant and cool and fun, and if she was my girl I would have one of two choices. I could hide her away or I could let the vultures have her."

God, he really was Kai's brother. "Sarah is a strong woman."

"They break down everyone." Jared lifted up his bag, a hollow look on his face. "I can't do that to her. She's stunning. She's so fucking beautiful I can barely look at her, and they'll make her feel like she's nothing. How can I do that to a woman I like?"

"Shouldn't that be her decision?"

His shoulders squared and he seemed to grow a damn foot. "No. It's mine. She needs to stay out of this life. She'll be happier. I'm sorry, Kori. The last thing I want to do is disappoint you. It's an actual ache in my gut to do it, but I have to. She deserves better than what they would do to her. They shame anyone who isn't a size zero negative. I've seen them hurt women who are a fucking size two. No woman can win with them. Sometimes I think they live to hurt people."

"Shouldn't she decide if she can handle it?" Sarah was strong. She believed in herself. Sarah was smart and self-sufficient.

"She doesn't understand what could come for her. Not really. I've had several women who understood how bad it could be."

"Maybe you've found not-so-strong women."

"Maybe, but they taught me. I like Sarah too much to put her in harm's way. Please come up with a reason she shouldn't come. If you can't, I'll have to ignore her and that's going to break her in a way I never would. I like her. Please don't make me hurt her."

Kori understood him. She got that he was trying to save her from herself, but her heart ached for her friend. And for Jared. It seemed like an awfully lonely life.

The door opened and Kori recognized the young man walking toward the office. He was a patient of Kai's.

"I'll think about how to handle it," she said, standing up. "Maybe I'll convince her to stay in and watch some movies with me."

"Oh, yeah, I guess that would work. Though if you don't come, I can't imagine Kai would. I'll leave it in your hands." Jared turned and walked up the stairs.

Kori walked back to the office to make a call. If she told Sarah she couldn't go, it would break her friend's heart. She walked through the door in time to see Case walking out as Kai greeted his patient and allowed him into his office. His eyes found hers as he began to close the door.

Heat flashed through her system because there was promise in those eyes. Was the promise only for now? Did she have a future with him?

She settled in behind her desk, her thoughts on how to handle the Ferguson brothers.

Chapter Ten

Kai closed the door that led to the lobby behind his last patient of the day. He now had a couple of hours before he would be expected to go to some dance club where he would likely be the closest thing to an adult in attendance. He hated those places. They made him feel old, but then it wasn't like he'd frequented them in his younger years.

Maybe he'd been born old.

There was one person who could make him feel young though. One activity that could make him not care about any of the pressure that was building inside him.

"Are you going to lock up?" Kori asked. "Because I was kind of hoping we could have a talk."

That didn't sound good. "About what?"

"Tonight."

Shit. It wasn't like Kori wanted to go to the nightclub. She loved Sanctum, but other than that, she tended to be a homebody. He'd spent the last couple of nights curled on the couch with her as she watched TV and he read a book. He thought it would annoy him. He didn't even own a TV, but something about how much it seemed to please her made it all right. He'd even watched one of the mystery shows with her. It hadn't been half bad. Modern day Sherlock Holmes was a nice way to spend the evening. He'd had to talk her into going to the nightclub with him. "You've changed your mind?"

What the hell was he going to do if he didn't have Kori with him? Would Mia still go? She'd seemed so happy to have a friend going with her.

"I was thinking about staying home and spending some time with Sarah."

"Why doesn't she come out with us?" Sarah would be excellent at distracting Kori. The more he thought about it, the better he liked the idea. Sarah might distract Jared, too. The lovely brunette was exactly his brother's type. That way Kai wouldn't spend the entire evening thinking about murdering his brother because if it was only Kori and Mia, Jared's attention would laser focus on Kori. "Sarah loves to dance."

Kori frowned. "Jared doesn't want her to come."

"My brother doesn't want a pretty, curvy girl around?" Who the hell were they talking about?

"I think he's worried for her. I also think he's gotten hurt one too many times."

"Jared doesn't get hurt. Jared parties and plays and has fun." And lies. Lots and lots of lies. His eyes caught on the present he'd sent her earlier today. The bouquet of evil sticks was sitting on her desk for all to see. His girl wasn't one to hide herself away. She didn't pretend to be a masochist like other subs he'd met. She was a pretty little pain slut. His pretty pain slut.

Fuck. He was hard again. He'd spent every night since that first scene at her place, making her come as often as he could, and the beast still wasn't satisfied. He had to admit, it felt good to want someone as much as he wanted her. Craved her. Needed her.

Now.

"I don't think so, Kai. I don't think you know him as well as you think you do. He's changed over the years. Are you serious?" She was staring at his crotch, one brow up over her pretty eyes.

He couldn't help it. He locked the door and drew the blinds. "Ms. Williamson, I'm afraid I need to talk to you about your performance."

She sighed. "Kai, I think we need to talk about your brother."

That was the last thing he wanted. "It's been a rough day, baby. Can we play for a while? I'll understand if you don't want to and then we can go have a nice dinner and I'll go out with Jared by myself."

He hoped guilt worked on her. He threw in some puppy dog eyes to make the point clear.

"I can't believe you're giving me that look," she complained. "You think I don't know that look? Because I do. That's your sad puppy look and it always works, damn it. It's so freaking cute on you."

He let his fingers brush over the pink tops of the sadisticks before selecting one. Yeah, they would leave nice marks on her skin. She would squirm and cry when he worked her over. Maybe if she was happy with him, she would plead with him to stop. Not use her safe word, of course. It was all part of the game. She would pretend she couldn't take another second and his cock would respond. "If you want Sarah to come out with us tonight, invite her along."

"I told you, Jared doesn't want her there."

"He does want her. I assure you I know what type of women my brother likes, and I'm surprised he hasn't jumped into bed with her yet." He moved behind her, relaxing because he was sure he was about to get what he needed. He put his hands on her shoulders, fingers running under the edge of her blouse so he could feel the heat of her skin. He loved how her shoulders immediately relaxed, as though submitting to their Master.

"He doesn't want to subject her to his world," she replied, her voice dropping.

His fingers massaged the muscles of her shoulders as he started to work the blouse down. "Sarah's a strong woman. She can hold up to the scrutiny. What she won't be able to handle is not knowing if it could have worked. Did Jared forbid her from coming?"

"Not exactly. He said if she came, he would ignore her. What am I supposed to say to her? She knows damn well Case and Mia are going and that Jared doesn't have a date. It's going to hurt her feelings if I tell her she can't go, and it'll hurt her if he ignores her."

"Ah, but if he ignores her, she'll be able to say she tried at least." He needed Kori with him and he wasn't saying anything he didn't believe. Sarah would be happier with a direct confrontation than she would being left behind. He didn't actually think Jared would be able to ignore her, but if he did then Sarah could call him a dick and move on. "Being left completely out without an explanation will hurt her more than Jared ignoring her."

He ran his right hand up her scalp, tugging lightly. This was a dance and he needed to warm her up.

She sighed as he pulled her hair. "I think Jared really doesn't want her to come."

"Then he can turn her down. It isn't right to make you do it. He's the one who showed up at your house and flirted with your friend. He's the one who made her think she had a shot with him."

"Something happened in Vancouver. God, that feels so good, Kai."

This would feel even better. He leaned over and kissed her ear, running his tongue over the shell before he nipped her earlobe. Her whole body shivered under his touch. So responsive. So perfect for him. "I'll handle it. I'll make sure none of this blows back on you. Sarah can come with us. If Jared ignores her, she'll find someone else and she'll have fun. Sarah isn't a girl to sit idly around waiting for her prince to come."

"You can't be mean to Jared," she said firmly.

He bit her again. "How about a please? We're playing right now, unless you tell me to stop. When we're playing you don't give me that ballsy, take-charge voice. You get to be in charge most of the time. This is my time."

He needed it. The truth was he needed both Koris. He needed the Kori who took charge of the office and made things run smoothly, the one who he didn't worry about because she could take care of herself when she needed to. He also needed the Kori who submitted to him, who needed what only he could give her.

Damn but he needed that Kori right now.

She turned in her chair, the one he'd bought for her because after their first office had blown up, he'd enjoyed shopping for new furniture with her.

Why had he wasted all this fucking time? Was he going to

waste more? Was it too early to get her tipsy and on a flight to Vegas and oops, where did that wedding ring come from? Damn, guess we should make the best of it.

He had to play it cool with her. She was the elusive, free-range sub and he had to get her to understand she was safe with him.

"Do I even want to know what's going through your head right now?" Her eyes lit with mirth as though she could read his thoughts.

"Probably not."

She stood up and wrapped her arms around him. Her head came to his shoulders because somewhere along the way, she'd kicked off her shoes. "Thank you for dealing with the Sarah situation. I don't want to cause anyone trouble. It's why I thought staying home would work."

He cradled her against him. "She would know something was wrong. She still will, but confronting the problem is almost always the best way to move forward."

Her head tilted up and she proved she could give him some puppy eyes of her own. "Like you're doing with Jared?"

"I'm going to talk to him. Let's get through tonight and tomorrow morning, we'll have a nice knock-down, drag-out fight the way only brothers can. Will that make you happy?"

She nodded. "Yes. I want you to be happy, Kai. I don't think you can be until you deal with this situation."

Case's words from earlier had haunted him all day. "I'll talk to him. Now can we play?"

"You said you had a problem with my work duties. Did I do something wrong, Sir?" Kori stepped back, biting her bottom lip as she stared up at him. "I didn't mean to."

"Boss and secretary will work so well on me today, baby."

"Assistant." There was his brat.

He shoved a hand in her hair, drawing her back so she was forced to look up at him. "Are you correcting me? If I say you're my gorgeous secretary, then what are you?"

Her eyes had gone hot. "I'm your dirty little secretary, Sir."

He let go of her hair. "You're not in uniform, Ms. Williamson."

Her hands immediately went to her blouse, undoing the buttons one at a time. "I'm sorry, Sir. I'll fix that as soon as possible."

"And I'll be waiting in my office for you. Bring along the

present I gave you. I think you're going to require some discipline." He strode into his office. It was so much more comfortable than the lobby, with its hardwood floors. He had carpet in his office. He'd done it for the sound reduction, but now he was happy because his sub was going to spend some time on her knees.

He sank into his chair and watched as she walked in. She'd taken off every stitch of clothing and moved toward him with the grace of a goddess offering him a prize. She was the prize, of course, but she held out the bouquet for his selection. She dropped to her knees before him, holding up the instruments of her torture as though they were gifts. Which they were.

"Did I say a proper thank you for my present, Sir?"

"I think you forgot, but we'll get to that. Spread your legs wider. I want to see my pussy."

Her knees splayed, though her spine remained perfectly straight. He watched as the pink lips of her pussy were revealed for him. She had the prettiest fucking pussy in the world, plump and ripe and always so creamy for him. Her breasts were thrust out, nipples already tight.

She was ready to play.

Kai took the present from her and set it on top of his desk. All day long he'd had this nasty feeling in his gut. It had been about what he had to do tonight, about what was left unsaid with his brother. It was about not letting the Taggarts down. He let it all flow away now.

If Kori wanted him to talk to his brother, he would. He might never be close to Jared, but for her he would try. And after tonight, he would be out of the spy business and he could concentrate on what he did best. He would put all his training into finding a way to help Theo when he came home.

Because Theo Taggart would come home.

"Take off my shoes."

She went to work on his loafers, pulling them off and dragging the socks with them. He nearly sighed when she ran her fingers over the arches. It was a service he usually provided for her. The last few nights when they sat together, she would put her feet in his lap and wiggle them until he finally gave in. He loved the sounds she made when he rubbed her feet.

"That feels good, baby."

"Anything for my boss."

He wanted to be so much more than her boss. "Really? Because I think you think you're the boss."

She shook her head, all that gloriously curly hair tumbling around her shoulders. "No. I'm only a secretary."

"What did I order for lunch, Kori?"

Her cheeks went the sweetest shade of red. "A steak salad with bleu cheese dressing."

"What did I get? And don't try to tell me they were out of beef."

"You eat too much red meat. I thought you might like the salmon. The light dressing was a mistake on the restaurant's part."

He reached out and selected one of the sadisticks, turning it over in his hand. He'd known exactly what she was doing and he hadn't complained. It was hard to complain when someone cared. He'd spent too much of his life without anyone giving a damn that he ate too much red meat. But it did give him a perfectly fine reason to torture her. "Lean back, hands on your ankles."

A fine shiver went through her body as she complied. In this position, she was on full display for him. Her pussy was exposed, her torso leaning back, hands balancing against her ankles. She was a gorgeous example of submission with her breasts thrust out, her eyes on him.

"When I say I want something, you will give it to me." He gave her a wink. "Unless you're willing to pay the price."

"Anything to save my Master from the inevitable heart attack that will come."

Gorgeous brat. He flicked the pink tipped rod over her breast and she gasped. Immediately the skin reddened, a matchstick mark on her tender flesh. "You're very giving, baby. Let's make a deal. You feel free to save my arteries and I'll happily mark you."

She groaned as he flicked her other breast. "Yes, Sir."

Her eyes were already dilating. How could he have spent all that time with her and never seen this part? Had he seen it deep down? Was that why he'd been so attracted to her? "And we'll make another deal. I think part of your day should be spent in a creative exercise."

She frowned. "What do you mean?"

He flicked her again and then again, loving the way her flesh responded. Seeing those marks swell made his dick jump in his slacks. "I've been thinking over the past few days." He dropped down behind her because he was fairly certain that leaning back against her own ankles was probably starting to get hard for her. "Lean back against me. Hands on your thighs."

She leaned her weight back and he felt her sigh. He wasn't going to let her rest for too long. Being in this position made it easy to flick the stick against her thighs.

"Oww, oww."

He could feel her breath, the way her skin jumped when he flicked her. "Tell me what it feels like."

"It stings. It burns. It lights me up and goes straight to my pussy. Please, no more."

That was not her safe word. He flicked her again, the marks showing up against the ivory of her skin. She wouldn't be able to wear too short a skirt or someone would see. He was okay with that. Those legs were his along with every other pretty piece of her. She jumped against him as he struck again, a bit harder this time because she was warming up nicely. He used his free hand to cup her breast. "You'll take as much as I give you."

"Yes, Sir."

He rolled her nipple, tweaking it as he pulled back the stick and let it fly. "As for your creative time, I want you to write for me."

She went still in his arms.

He'd thought about this a lot. "Whatever you want. If you want to write nothing more than how awful I am, then that's what you do. But I want you to write because I think you miss it. I saw Serena's script on your desk."

"I'm just helping out a friend. Please don't stop, Sir. I'll talk about this, but please don't stop."

He understood this woman. This was her safe place. She could talk here because this was a space where there was nothing but honesty. She accepted herself here. "I won't. I won't ever stop. Do you have any idea how beautiful you are to me?"

"I feel beautiful with you, Kai."

He twisted her nipple and was rewarded with a squeal. "You

From Sanctum with Love

are always beautiful. I want you to have everything you need, everything you want. Do you want to be my assistant for the rest of your life?"

"I could be happy. That's something I've learned. I can be happy in many places. I don't have to be one thing, but I'm starting to miss it, too. I don't know what I want beyond being here with you."

"Will you try?"

She nodded. "Yes. I think I might write about this. I might write about us."

"As long as names are changed to protect the innocent, I'll go along with that. Are you going to write about how wet your pussy is?"

"It's always wet when you're here, Sir. When you walk into a room, my body gets soft and ready, and I always want you inside me."

Every word was like a drug. "Write about how hard I get when I think about you. Write about how much pleasure it brings me to see you wearing my mark, to make you squirm and scream for me. You don't ever have to put it out in the world if you don't want to, but you should write it down. Every day. A little bit more."

Her head fell back against his shoulder, her body offered to him. "Yes, Sir."

He flicked the stick over her breasts, raising pretty welts as she shook and cried in his arms. She never cried before, but she did now. That was an offering he would take, too. Her tears, her pain, her pleasure, her every emotion. They belonged to him.

"Touch yourself," he ordered. "I want to play with you while you make yourself come."

Her hand moved, sliding over so her fingers could reach her clit. Kai watched, his eyes roaming the length of her body as he flicked her skin from time to time. Every time the stick would impact, she would jump slightly and go breathless in his arms.

Her finger was immediately slick with her own moisture. He watched as she ran the pad of her finger over and around her clit. He pinched her nipple and bit her ear again, sliding his tongue over it to soothe the ache. He could see the spot where he'd bitten her the night before. It would fade by tomorrow, but she would have fresh marks, all those matchsticks that proved how much fun they'd had.

"One more time, please, Kai." Her finger rubbed hard, in furious motions.

He didn't have to ask what she meant. He knew. He knew her and what it took for her to really come. He flicked the stick hard, right on her thigh, and her whole body stiffened. She called out his name, turning her face up for his kiss. Even as her fingers slowed, he fused their mouths together.

Perfect connection.

Now it was time to get what he needed from his sub. He would relax, spend all afternoon inside her, and once tonight was over, they would be home free.

"Up, baby. Time for you to serve me."

Her face was flushed as he got to his feet in front of her. Playtime was over and he needed the feel of her mouth on him.

She seemed to understand exactly what he wanted. She let him help her up. He took her hand in his and when she was steady on her feet, he brought it to his lips. Those pretty fingers were coated in her own arousal, and damn but he loved the way she tasted. He sucked her fingers inside, giving her a bite that made her shiver all over again. He sucked her fingers clean, enjoying the sweet taste of her essence.

"Undress me," he said when he was satisfied those fingers were perfectly clean. "Tell me how you feel."

She gave him a smile as she started to work on his shirt. "Happy. Relaxed."

He watched her, enjoying the graceful way she moved and how the marks on her body formed patterns he could touch, patterns that spoke of her trust in him. "I don't want you to worry about tonight."

She smoothed the shirt off him and placed it around the back of his chair before running her hands over his chest. "I want everyone to be happy. I hate the thought of Sarah feeling bad, but I also hate the idea that Jared will think I betrayed him."

"I'll talk to him. He'll understand that it was one hundred percent my call." He cupped her face in his hands, staring down at her. "I know you like Jared, but you have to understand that once this film is through, he likely won't be back."

Her hands moved on his waist as though she drew comfort

From Sanctum with Love

from the contact. "I don't know about that. I think if you would let him in, he would be close to his family."

He kissed her nose and then her lips, tenderness welling inside him. "He was never close. Not after we got to be teenagers. He went his way and I went mine. You're my family, Kori. You're the one I need close."

"You know exactly how to manipulate me," she whispered.

"I'm not manipulating you. There is nothing but truth here. I will talk to my brother, but I don't want you to get too close to him because he disappears. Have fun tonight, but always know he's going to go away again. Your sister is much better and you've learned to distance from her."

She frowned. "Not really. She drives me insane, but she's my sister. She's family."

"Family is what you make it," he whispered.

"I...I..."

He knew that look. She didn't want to say something because she thought it would make her look foolish. Kori struggled with any emotion that wasn't bravado. There was only one thing she could want to say that would make her blush that hard. He could spank her ass all day, inflict torture on her and fuck her sideways, but only one thing would make her blush. "Say it."

Her mouth formed a stubborn line.

He moved in, his lips hovering above hers. "Say it."

"I love you, Kai."

That was what he wanted to hear. "I love you, too. Always have."

He kissed her long and hard, his tongue tangling with hers. He let his hands slide down her back, cupping her cheeks and dragging her against him. He didn't need anyone else. He didn't need Jared or the rest of the world as long as he had her.

"I want you to suck me, Kori," he whispered against her ear. "I want you on your knees, sucking my cock hard, and then I'm going to fuck you right here on my desk. I want to look down at this desk and always be able to see you there waiting for me, naked and wanting."

She dropped to her knees, her hands unbuckling his belt. She pulled it from his slacks and looked up at him, her eyes wide, hands holding it out.

Wicked girl. What was he going to do with her? "Kiss the belt and ask me nicely."

She kissed the belt, her eyes never leaving his. "Will you please spank me while I service you, Sir?"

"No. I'll do it after. I can't be accurate while I'm getting a blowjob and I won't hurt you without purpose."

She frowned. "It could be fun."

"So could me shoving an anal hook up your rectum." He'd been eyeing them lately.

"After would be so lovely, Sir." She let him take the belt and worked the fly of his slacks, his cock springing free. She took him in hand. "And thank you for handling the situation with your brother. I wasn't sure of what to do."

He wasn't about to tell her that he would have moved mountains to ensure she would come with him, though not for the reasons she would suspect. He didn't like the twist of guilt in his gut. It was so much easier to focus on her. He would make it up to her. Hell, he would make it up to Sarah. When all this was over, he would take Kori and her friend out to dinner and maybe start looking around to see if he could pair Sarah with a good Dom. One who would treat her right.

Then he wasn't thinking at all because Kori leaned over and dragged her tongue over his dick. Heat flashed through his system, threatening to set him of fire. No one else could manage to do this to him. He'd had plenty of sex, but she was the only one who could truly touch his soul. Only this brown-haired beauty with her blue eyes and saucy mouth.

She used that mouth to drive him fucking insane. She played with the head of his cock, teasing licks that made him want to stop her, to force her to take all of him. He could throat fuck her until she begged for mercy. But he held off, letting her play. Sometimes watching her enjoy her service was more important than taking control.

She licked around the head of his cock, sucking lightly. He watched as her lips moved over him. Her hands ran up the length of his thighs, nails scratching lightly. Yes, she'd figured out he liked it when she was a bit rough with him, too.

Her tongue found the underside of his dick and he hissed slightly as she ran over and over it, focusing on the place where his cockhead met the stalk.

He watched as her lips moved over his cock, pink tongue making an appearance from time to time. She dragged it up and over his shaft. Her hands came up to cup his balls before moving around and tracing the curves of his ass.

She settled in and started to work his cock deep inside, taking more with each pass. She hummed around his dick, the sound sending vibrations through his most sensitive flesh. All the while he was getting harder and hotter until he couldn't take another second.

He sank a hand into her hair and forcibly tugged her off. "On the desk. Now."

She scrambled up, laying herself out in a submissive position she had to know would test him. Instead of placing her back flat on the desk, she leaned over it, breasts down, facing away. Vulnerable. Trusting. She spread her legs and glanced back. "Is this all right, Sir? I want you to have a good memory of how I look spread out on your desk and waiting for you."

She actually wiggled that hot ass.

He was a goner for this girl. He picked up the belt. She was going to get her way. Again. He couldn't help it. He saw those gorgeous cheeks and realized they were perfectly unmarked. He'd worked over her breasts and thighs, and now she presented him with the one thing he couldn't fucking turn away. A pretty blank canvas waiting for his handiwork.

"You know you're a brat." He doubled the belt in his hand. She was rapidly taking over his every thought. Now he wouldn't be able to buckle this belt without thinking of her and how sweet she looked begging for his discipline.

"I'm your brat," she replied with a smile.

He brought the belt up and down, the nasty slap sounding through the room and followed by the sweetest sound of all—her gasp and groan. He gave her ten quick licks, watching as she shuddered and braced herself each time.

They could drown in each other and it would be all right with him.

Another ten and then he placed his hand over the stripes that now covered her backside. "Like I said before, so fucking gorgeous." He opened the drawer to his left. He was prepared now. Years he'd gone without needing to have protection around him because sex had become routine and scheduled. It wasn't that way with her. With her he needed to stash the fuckers everywhere because he wanted her all the damn time. He'd put them in his wallet, his briefcase, his car. He'd placed a box in her bedside table and hidden a couple around the office.

All so he wouldn't have to wait, so he could have her whenever he wanted her.

He tore it open and rolled the latex on. When all the craziness settled down, they would talk about commitment and monogamy and better protection because he definitely didn't want to wear a condom for the rest of his life.

She was the rest of his life.

"I love you, baby." He liked saying the words. He liked meaning them. He gripped her hips and lined his cock up. She was so wet and ready. The spanking had gotten her hot and bothered all over again. All he had to do to get his little pain slut ready for his cock was give her a couple of good slaps to her ass. All he had to do to get ready to fuck her was think about her.

"Love you, too, Sir."

He thrust in hard, knowing exactly how difficult it was for her to say the words. He hadn't expected them so quickly. They were a gift. Kori didn't trust easily, though once she gave her loyalty, it took a lot to break it.

She felt so good around him, so perfect and tight.

Her pussy wasn't the only thing he wanted. "Let me take your ass."

"Oh, god. Kai, it's been so long."

"Let me." He wanted everything from her.

"Yes. Take it, Kai."

Luckily, condoms weren't the only things he'd stashed in his desk. He grabbed the lube as he pulled out of her hot pussy. He parted her cheeks and dribbled the lube over her tight asshole. Pink and perfect. It was going to grip him like a vise and better, he would feel her squirming as he forced his dick inside. He lubed up his cock and circled her rosette with the head of his dick. "Tell me if it's too much."

"I like it, Sir. I haven't done it in a while, but I know I enjoy it. I'm going to admit you're bigger than the other guy."

He smacked her ass. "I don't want to hear about the other guy. I want to talk about us. You and me. Take me."

He worked his way in, her ass flowering open in little passes. He looked down, watching the way the tight entry fought to keep him out. It wouldn't work. He would fight his way in.

Kori's spine shuddered, her hands reaching out to grip the edge of the desk. She was a gorgeous sacrifice, offering herself to him in every way imaginable.

"Tell me if you like it now." He shoved in hard, forcing her to take more.

Her breath came out in shaky pants. "I love it. I love the burn. It feels so good."

He could see tears on her cheeks. She gave them up, too. She gave him everything, which meant he owed her everything, too. He stood firm as he impaled her on his cock, pulling her hips back as she took his full length.

"You're killing me, Kai." She'd lifted herself up, pressing back against him so there wasn't an inch of distance between them.

She clenched around him and it took every ounce of his willpower not to come then and there. The heat was different in her ass, the muscles so tight around him.

He dragged his cock back out and Kori gasped, trying to move against him, to keep him inside.

He pressed her down, ensuring her pelvis was rubbing against the edge of the desk. He knew he'd hit the right spot when she started pressing forward, her breath catching. It gave him the chance to find the perfect rhythm. In and out. He thrust deep and dragged out, his balls starting to draw up.

He pounded inside her and felt the moment she came. She clenched around him and sent him hurling into his own orgasm. It sizzled along his spine as he poured himself into her.

Kori dropped down, the left side of her face pressed against his desk. A satisfied smile curled her lips up. "If that's what I get for a bad performance, I can't wait to see what good girls get."

He pulled out of her and tossed the condom in the trash. The cleaning lady was going to love him. Kai sank back into his chair. He would have to clean it later, but he wanted his cuddle time. Kai pulled her into his arms and couldn't help but smile when she winced.

"Good girls get sore asses in our world." He wrapped his arms around her. They would shower in a minute. The building was empty and everything locked up. He would carry her upstairs and if his brother got a show, well, he should have thought about that before he invaded Kai's place.

"It's been a long time," Kori complained, snuggling against him. "I forgot how much it hurts afterward. How am I supposed to dance tonight?"

"Very carefully, my love." Like everything had to happen tonight. Very, very carefully.

Chapter Eleven

Kori looked out over the dance floor and wondered why she wasn't at home cuddled up with Kai on the sofa. She could be in PJs, drinking a nice cup of hot chocolate and reading Serena's script. Before bed they would hop in the shower and she would wash her Dom's hot body before he did the same for her.

But she was here, sitting in the VIP section of a crazy luxurious club where the music was way too loud.

Kai sat beside her, his arm around the back of her chair. He looked over at her and sent her a look that let her know he was thinking about what he'd done to her in his office.

If she was at home, she could be sitting on a nice bag of frozen peas. That would be so soothing.

Sarah stood up suddenly, smoothing down her dress. "I'm heading to the ladies' room. I'll be right back."

Jared looked up from his conversation with his fourth blonde of the night. Lena sat beside him, a dour look on her face while she talked to Squirrel and Tad. Brad was walking around somewhere and Mia seemed to be ignoring Case as much as she could.

And everyone in the damn club was staring at them. Like every single person had been watching them since the moment they'd strode through a bunch of reporters and been shown to this suite-like portion of the club.

All in all, it would be so nice to be home.

"There's a private VIP bathroom right behind us," Jared said. "It's through the door that leads to the private bar and buffet. Look in the back and you'll find it."

Sarah gave him a brilliant smile. "Thank you so much."

She stared down at Kori. Yep, that was her cue that it was time for girl talk. This was precisely why Kori had done the women's bathroom at the office up like a damn luxury lounge. She so very often got hauled into some bathroom for a life chat, and half the time they were nasty. Life chats should be conducted in nice, glamorous surrounding with pictures of cute dogs and babies and shit. Not surrounded by random tampon vending machines.

"I'll join you." Kori sent her best friend a stiff smile because she'd found a comfy place. Anal sex was not something to be taken lightly.

Of course neither was the fact that she'd told Kai she loved him and Kai had said it back.

Scary, scary, amazing and wonderful stuff. Kai Ferguson loved her. It was almost surreal. He loved her and he wanted her to write. Not for his sake. Not because she could bring in income or further his career. He wanted her to write because he loved her and she needed it.

Sarah sighed and held a hand out, helping Kori get up. She leaned in. "This is what you get. Who the hell lets their superhot sadist boyfriend talk her into anal before going to a dance club?"

"Me," she admitted. At the time, she'd only been thinking about how hot it was and how good that burn felt. She'd loved the way Kai tasted and she'd wanted to give him everything.

Mia stood up, her shoulders squaring as she secured her purse over her shoulder. "I'll go, too."

"Obviously, because you all go in a flock," Case said with a frown.

"Girls stick together." There was a whole lot of tension going on that Kori didn't get. Mia had been tense ever since they'd picked her up in the limo. Case had gone to her door and she sat beside him, but she wasn't acting like they were on a date.

Jared had already turned back to one of his blondes.

"Some have to because they don't have any confidence in themselves," Lena said, taking a sip of her skinny cosmo.

It was the most calories the woman had consumed in days, it seemed to Kori.

She wasn't about to engage. She sucked it up and put a smile on her face because not everyone in the room needed to know what she'd done with her superhot sadist boyfriend only a few hours before.

Kai stood up beside her and drew her in close. All evening long he'd been attentive, sitting with her and generally being around if she needed something. He'd calmed so much from earlier in the day. He drew her away from the crowd, leaning over to whisper in her ear. "Can you do me a favor, baby?"

For that face, she would do almost anything. She let her hands run up his torso. It seemed insane to her that she'd spent so much time watching him and not touching him. It felt so damn right to touch him. And she'd made the decision to chill about the contract. He'd told her he loved her. If he wasn't ready for a contract, then she wouldn't push. And all that talk Jared had given her about how fast Kai moved when he was truly in love, well, Kai had grown up a lot since then. He wasn't a man who would ever lie to her. There was absolutely nothing truly manipulative about Kai Ferguson. "Of course."

"Talk to Mia. Case is going crazy. He wants to spend some time with her. I've seen the way she looks at him. Find out why she's so scared and calm her down," he whispered. "Just one dance. I think that would help Case a lot."

Okay, so he was only manipulative in other's best interests. Kai was right. Mia was twelve kinds of hung up on Case. So why wasn't she paying attention to him tonight? "I'll do what I can."

He winked and brushed his lips over hers before she joined her girls.

The minute they walked out of the VIP lounge and into the private bar, the music volume dropped and Kori could hear again. Thank god.

Sarah turned the minute the door closed. "He's a dick."

Jared had been true to his word. He'd accepted Kori's request that Sarah be included and then proceeded to ignore her in favor of any other woman who wanted to talk to him.

"I'm sorry." The whole night was one big waste. Why anyone would want to sit in a club all night where they couldn't hear well and no one seemed to be getting along was way past her understanding. "I think maybe he's more of a player than we thought he was."

She'd hoped Jared would come around. Sarah was strong enough to handle the press. Kai was right about that, and he'd been right about letting Sarah make her own decisions.

Sarah shrugged and walked over to the bar. Earlier there had been a bartender present, but Jared had explained that he preferred to mix his own drinks and tipped the guy to go away. Kori was certain that was because Jared was fairly paranoid that everyone was some kind of undercover reporter waiting to sell him out to the tabloids. He might be right, but it would have been nice to have a bartender.

"I thought we were going to the ladies' room," Mia said, looking back toward the door.

"Oh, that was my way of not having to bring anything back for the guys," Sarah explained. She uncorked a bottle of tequila and poured out a shot. And then another. And another. Luckily the limes had already been sliced and someone had thoughtfully left out a saltshaker. "Drink with me. Please, I need my bitches. I got the cold shoulder from Hollywood hottie and now I have to watch him flirt with skanks all night." She pointed Mia's way. "Don't you start with they might not be skanks. I'm not in a fair or forgiving mood."

Mia's shoulders squared and she stepped up to the bar. "They are obviously skanks."

Ah, the solidarity of womanhood. Kori picked up the remaining shot glass, but not before giving her thumb a nice lick and letting Sara salt her up. There was a proper way to do a shot even in times of distress. It's what lifted them up from the barbarians. Not the animals. Animals were often nicer than people. But she was fairly certain barbarians didn't properly shoot tequila. She held her glass up. "May he get an STD from sleeping with skanks."

"Here, here," Sarah agreed. "And may this liquor help Kori's asshole feel less inflamed."

Unfortunately, Mia had already started her shot when that little line was uttered. She nearly spit out her tequila.

Damn, but she might need more than one. Kori did her shot, managing to not choke before she bit down on her lime and sent Sarah a look that hopefully could freeze over hell. "Really? We need to advertise?"

"You let Kai do that?" Mia grabbed a bottle of water. "Seriously?"

"He's my boyfriend and we're…very open to certain types of play," Kori admitted. "I'm going to take it this is one of your hard limits?"

She wasn't going to get all bent out of shape. Mia wasn't looking at her like she was the whore of Babylon or anything. The pretty blonde was fairly new to the scene. She was finding her way and that often meant asking questions.

Mia took a long drink. "No. I made it soft, but I don't do any of the sex stuff with my training Dom. Javier is nice and all, but I'm interested in a relationship, not casual sex."

Javier was a line chef at Sean Taggart's restaurant. He was known as Top's manwhore du jour. "Yes, you should keep it friendly with him. I don't think he does relationships."

"What about Case? Are you trying to bag a Taggart?" Sarah asked, pouring herself another drink.

"I don't know. I'm going to admit that I am very attracted to him, but he scares me, too. I don't like the fact that he seemed to hate me one day and the next he's asking me out," Mia admitted. "It seems fishy to me. He's been almost too nice lately."

"Cut him some slack," Kori said quietly. "He's still in mourning."

"I get that, but I think something's going on. And I'm not sure I completely trust Jared's crew." Mia leaned against the bar.

"Because he's a dick," Sarah agreed.

Mia shook her head. "No, I've been doing some digging. His entourage has some serious issues. Did you know that Lena chick threw hot coffee all over a woman who was hitting on her last employer? She was working for a big-name actor and the rumors are she had an affair with him. Well, at a promo junket, she decided one of the reporters was getting to close to her man and she tossed a Starbuck's in her face. Lena spent some time in 'rehab' after that."

That was some juicy gossip. "How do you know that?"

"I have friends in LA," Mia admitted. "Look, I don't talk about this a lot, but my brother does some work for important people. He has connections and I used them to look into the new guys."

"Paranoid, much? Not that I'm blaming you," Sarah said, finishing her second shot. "It's totally cool because your paranoia is the most interesting thing that's happened all evening, but it's weird. Normal people don't investigate newbies."

Mia shrugged. "Consider it a hobby. I think we should stick together while we're hanging out with Jared and his crew. It's fine to dance and everything, but maybe we shouldn't wander off alone."

"Okay, now you're scaring me." Kori stared at Mia, who suddenly looked like a girl who knew something she shouldn't. "What is this about?"

"Look, I had a friend who knew Jared a couple of years back," Mia replied. "We went to college together. She was murdered after she visited one of his sets."

Sarah's eyes went wide. "You think Jared killed her? Because I'm not seeing that. I was voted girl most likely to be murdered by my senior class and he's not interested in me at all."

"You went to a weird school," Kori said with a shake of her head before turning back to Mia. "You've got to be kidding me."

Mia's eyes were clear and serious as she spoke. "About my friend? No. I'm not kidding. She really liked him and then one day I didn't hear from her. A week later they found her body. I don't know if it was him, but I started doing some research..."

The door opened and Mia's mouth closed fast. Brad and Lena walked in, Lena's head shaking as she walked toward the bar.

"I told you, I've already got everything set up," Lena was saying. "My mother is going to be producing several high-quality, Oscar-worthy films and I'm going to get Jared in them. He's leaving the whole TV shit behind him and he won't look back."

"Lena, don't push this. You know how this goes. If he moves out of superhero shit, he won't need me," Brad argued, his face florid.

Lena waved that worry off. "He'll always need a trainer."

"But he'll get one of those easygoing ones," Brad argued. "Look, no one trains this hard if they're not taking their shirt off five times a day. Do you have any idea how long it's been since that man had carbs? No one wants to live like that. They have to because their careers depend on it. You want to make him over into some bullshit actor. Have you seen him really act?"

Lena rolled her eyes. "I have more faith in him than you do. He'll learn, and yes, I'm going to make sure he gets a new trainer. And a new agent because your brother sucks. He spends all his time hitting on women when he should be managing Jared's career. Now get away from me. I'm going to the ladies' room. Alone. Because I'm an adult."

Sarah shot her the finger, which Lena ignored.

"Bitch," Brad said before slamming out the door.

"Okay, so we'll keep an eye out for each other," Kori said. She wasn't sure she bought Mia's theories, but people who lost friends didn't always see things clearly.

"I'm going to find a hot stud and dance the night away, and Jared can kiss my juicy ass good-bye," Sarah stated, holding herself regally. "This house of pleasure is closed to him."

"I guess we should head back out," Mia said.

Kori let Sarah go first and held Mia back. "Give Case a chance."

Mia glanced to the door. "I want to. He's so…overwhelming and I worry about his family."

"The Taggarts are some of the most amazing men I've ever met in my life."

"I've found appearances can be deceiving," Mia said quietly.

"How do you know if you don't try? I'm going to ask you something. What's going to make you happy? Trying and failing with Case—who could honestly use some happy things in his life right now—or being too scared to try at all?"

Mia frowned, thinking for a moment. "I worry that I'm crossing a line I can't come back from. Kori, I haven't told you everything, but now isn't the time. Let's say I have an ulterior motive for being here."

"The stuff with your friend?" It wasn't a hard leap.

"Yes."

"Case has nothing to do with that."

"He might," Mia replied. "McKay-Taggart has worked for some interesting people."

"I assure you Case Taggart would never do anything to hurt you. He's not that kind of guy. If he's interested in you, it's because he wants to spend time with you. He's not working. The man wants a dance. I wasted so much time with Kai. I didn't read the signs. I held off showing him I was interested and I did it because I was scared. Then we lost Theo. I think that made every single one of us realize how short life can be."

"I've lost a lot of people in my life. I lost my parents when I was very young. I lost my brothers for a long time after that."

"What would your parents want for you?" It felt good to be helping someone. She couldn't help Sarah and Jared, but Mia and Case were a different story. If they liked each other, there was zero reason for them not to try.

Somehow being in love with Kai made everything seem possible.

Mia sniffled. "They would want me to be happy. My friend would want me to be happy. But Kori, until I figure this thing out, be careful."

She leaned over, giving her friend a hug. "I will."

Mia straightened up and smiled. "I'm going to go ask that cowboy to dance. Can you hold my purse?"

It was the job of a good girlfriend. "Will do."

Kori took Mia's little bag and followed her out, sure at least one thing had gone right tonight.

* * * *

Kai watched as Kori walked out with Mia. She looked over and gave him a wink and that was when he realized what she was carrying. Mia's purse. It was one of those tiny things that was mostly a wallet with some bling on it. It wouldn't carry more than some cash, credit cards, and her phone. He was only interested in one of those things.

Mia stopped in front of Case and held out her hand.

Shit. Kori had done it, and she looked so happy for her friend. Kai's gut twisted.

"What is she doing?" Jared asked, staring out on the dance floor where Sarah was commanding attention.

"I think she's dancing, man," Squirrel said as he stood up and slapped Jared on the shoulder. "Face facts. You lost that one. Guess you can't win 'em all. I'm going to grab a beer from the bar. A real beer. All the crap they have in the VIP lounge is artesian crap. I'll be back."

"Have you seen the others?" Jared glanced around as though he realized his crew had deserted him.

Squirrel shouted over the music. "They're out and about, brother. Don't worry about them. Find another lady and have some fun. I know that's what I'm going to do."

Kori sank down beside him, settling her purse and Mia's away from him. He would have to reach over her to get to it. Damn it. He wanted to tell Case to fuck the whole op. He wasn't doing this. If Kori found out, she could get hurt, and the most important thing in the world to him was that Kori didn't get hurt.

But he owed more than Kori. He owed them all. He had to make this work.

Case stood up, taking Mia's hand in his. He towered over the blonde, and even from where Kai was sitting it was easy to see how the couple leaned into each other, how their bodies couldn't seem to stay apart. The smile he gave Mia wasn't all about the op.

Case looked over at Kai and nodded. "We're going to go dance for a while. Be back in a bit."

Mia clung to his hand, looking up at him like he was everything she wanted. She winked Kori's way.

"I think that's going to work out," Kori whispered in his ear. "Thanks for pointing it out to me. I hope at least one of my friends finds a happy place tonight."

Actually, it looked like Sarah was doing a pretty good job herself. The brunette beauty was commanding the dance floor, with not one but two guys vying for her attention. Her hips moved sensually, her eyes flashing.

And Jared couldn't look away. Kai noticed all the women had given up and walked off while Jared frowned toward the dance floor. "Does she know either of those men?"

Kori flashed an impish grin. "It depends on what you mean by the word 'know.' Because the way she's twerking on that one dude, she could know him biblically soon."

What was he going to do? How long would Case keep Mia on the dance floor? He only needed a few minutes to properly upload the software to her phone if the device Hutch had rigged was half as good as he said it was. He had a small thumb drive attached to one end of the device. It contained the upload information and a program designed to get through any security she had on her phone. He would plug it into the phone's port and it would upload the cloning application while it downloaded any information she had on her phone. In minutes they would have all her contacts, her e-mails, texts, pictures, anything and everything a person kept on their phone. If she used one of those training and fitness devices, they could potentially know when she was asleep.

It was a scary invasion of her privacy, but if she knew where Theo was or had any contacts who might know, they had to take the chance.

He wouldn't get that chance if Kori kept sitting next to him.

It ran through his head to tell her. He could tell her everything. She wouldn't break his trust, but doing that would violate Ian's and Case's. It could potentially put her in danger.

He had to find a way to keep her out of this altogether.

He leaned over to his brother. "Are you sure you're all right with letting her get away? Sarah's not the kind of woman who will hang around and hope you notice her."

Jared's jaw firmed stubbornly. "It's better this way."

"Really? Because it looks like the lady is going to have fun with or without you," he pointed out. "I saw you with her the other day when you scened. Are you going to find another sub to practice on?"

Jared's hand tightened around his water bottle. "She's drinking. She can't make a proper decision while she's drinking and she's my responsibility. She came here with me. I'm not going to allow her to go home with someone she doesn't even know."

Now he was thinking like a Dom. Of course, according to the FBI, Jared had been one for years. "Maybe you should talk to her.

Or better yet, get out on the dance floor and ease up to her. Women love dancing. You can tell her you were wrong to ignore her. If you're worried about hurting her feelings, I think you hurt her more by not being honest with her."

"Do you think so? I like her, but I'm leaving in a couple of weeks. Hell, once filming starts I won't have time anyway."

"So tell her what you're willing to give, what you can give," Kai said. "Explain the situation and let her make her own decision. If the two of you want to play for the duration of your time here, I'll help you work out a contract with her."

"I've never tried it that way. It might work if we both know the boundaries."

This was his chance. "So take Kori out for a dance and ease up to Sarah. You know I have two left feet. It's going to be the only time Kori gets out there on the dance floor. Can you do me that favor?"

Jared stood up. "Yeah. I can do that. And thank you for the advice."

Once this thing was done, he was going to sit down and tell his brother everything he knew about the stupid FBI investigation. It wasn't Jared, but Kai was starting to wonder about the other members of his entourage. Watching them this evening, it was obvious they all had their issues. It was time to take his baby brother in hand and clean house. Jared needed people around who were there for the right reasons.

Hell, it was time to sit and listen to what his brother had to say. It was time to be a family again.

One day he and Kori might have some of those stinky, adorable baby things everyone else was so into. Shouldn't they know their uncle?

"Be easy on my girl," Kai said with a smile.

Jared held a hand out to Kori. "Hey, do a guy a favor and dance with me? I think I've changed my mind about Sarah and I need some advice."

"Advice can totally be given while sitting down," Kori said with wide eyes.

Jared reached for her hand and hauled her up. "Not when there's dancing going on, darlin'. We'll be back."

Kori looked back as Jared hauled her toward the dance floor. That was a murderous look in his love's eyes. He was going to pay later.

For now, he had a job to do.

The minute Kori was out of sight, he grabbed Mia's bag. He picked up Kori's too and headed for the lounge. If anyone asked, he was unwilling to leave the bags out in the open while he headed for the men's room.

As fast as he could, he slipped into the lounge. It was quiet and empty. He strode behind the bar and opened Mia's bag. He'd been right. There was very little in it. A credit card, her ID, a tube of what looked like lip-gloss, and her phone.

He pulled the small device Case had given him out of his pocket and quickly connected it to the phone. The screen flicked on, the security login coming on.

And a picture. It was Mia's screen saver. Mia and three men, obviously her brothers. She stood in the middle, nearly overwhelmed by the three big men. They were smiling for the camera, though one man's smile didn't meet his eyes. Kai would bet anything that the one in the back, the only one who wasn't touching the others, was Drew Lawless. He had the haunted look of a man who'd seen too much. Done too much.

Was he a member of The Collective? Did that man on Mia's phone know where Theo Taggart was being held? If he did, he didn't understand pain yet. He would after Ian Taggart got hold of him.

Or Mia could be completely innocent and then this would clear her and Case might find some solace.

He was doing the right thing.

The door came open and Kai slipped the entire phone and device into Kori's big, open bag. He would have to fit it back into Mia's. It was far easier to hide it in that tank of a bag his girl carried. He grabbed a bottle of something and pulled the cork as his brother's agent walked into the room.

"Oh, it's you." He frowned and looked back down at his phone. He likely didn't need to hide crap from these people. They wouldn't notice anything at all that didn't have something to do with them. "Have you seen Lena? I can't find her."

Kai poured himself a glass of…ugh, vodka. He actually hated vodka. Why couldn't he have reached for bourbon? "Nope. She walked away with your brother a while back."

"She said she had something to tell me," he muttered. "I guess it can wait. I'm going to head back to the hotel. I've got some things I need to handle. Tell Jared to call me if he needs me. Or if he needs me to find him a girl. It looks like the one he wants is playing hard to get."

Kai nodded, praying for the fucker to leave the whole time. Maybe he should have gone into the bathroom to do this. It was behind him and through the hall, but he needed to get back out to the couch. He had to be sitting there when Kori came back.

The minute the door closed again, he glanced down. The software was still loading. A green light would flash when it was done. He could see the screen flashing as the code took over. If everything worked properly, she would never know it was there, but he could see it taking over all her systems, sending copies back to the thumb drive.

Another few minutes. That was all he needed. He needed his luck to hold out a few more minutes.

How long could the damn thing take?

The green light flashed and he pulled the drive out of Mia's phone, pocketing it.

The door opened, loud music blasting inside the quiet of the lounge.

"There you are." Jared was carrying Kori in his arms. "Your girl had some trouble with her heels. Can you fix up an ice pack?"

Shit. He couldn't slip Mia's phone back in her purse. He let it drop into Kori's open bag again and prayed they hadn't seen it in his hands. "What happened?"

He didn't like the look of Kori in his brother's arms. Even though he knew damn well Kori had zero interest in Jared physically, he didn't like anyone holding her except him. He'd done this. He'd insisted she go out and dance and now she'd gotten hurt.

"Set her down on the couch and I'll take a look at it."

The minute Jared turned his back and started to settle her in, Kai switched the phone over and closed Mia's bag.

Done. Finished. It was over.

The door came open again and Kai realized he'd managed it just in time. Chaos erupted as the entire crew seemed to file in.

Sarah rushed in, holding Kori's shoes. Squirrel walked in with Brad. Mia and Case followed, a frown on Case's face as Mia immediately went to Kori's side.

Yep, that had been good timing on his part. He looked over and nodded Case's way. The big guy breathed an obvious sigh of relief.

Kai quickly got the ice pack ready and went to look at his girl's ankle. Maybe it was time to call it a night. All he had left now was the handoff and then he and Kori were home free.

Chapter Twelve

Kori stood up and her ankle held. No doubt about it. She was never going to be the world's most graceful dancer, and if she never had to see those damn heels again, it would be way too soon. She'd twisted it as she was dancing with Jared, who turned out to be an amazing dancer but not the most attentive of partners since he'd had his eyes on Sarah the whole time.

"Is it okay?" Kai glanced down as though he could see through to her bones. He'd been sweet and very gentle with her, but he hadn't thought she'd done more than twisted it slightly.

It felt like he was right. She wasn't sore after a couple of minutes with the ice pack. Well, her ankle wasn't sore. The rest of her was deliciously, delightfully sore. "It's all good, but I think I'm ready to head home."

Kai had ordered everyone out so he could look her over. It was nice and quiet in the lounge now. She had to admit that if one was required to be in a nightclub, having a lounge and bathroom all to oneself was really the way to go. When the door closed, she couldn't hear the thudding music from outside.

Kai leaned over and kissed her. "I'll go and call us a taxi. Give me a few minutes, though. I need to talk to my brother and make sure everyone else has rides home if they want to go. Can you stay here? I won't be long. And stay out of those shoes. I'll carry you out myself."

She nodded. Staying put seemed a good thing to do. "Did Mia get her purse?"

"Yes and yours is sitting on the bar. Do you need it?" He glanced over to where he'd placed her bag.

"I'm good." She settled back down. She was ready to go home, get in PJs, and cuddle with her man. Nothing would be nicer than sleeping in Kai's arms. It had only been a few days, but she was already worried about how she would sleep when he wasn't there with her. Inevitably, he would want to stay at his own place when his brother cleared out.

Then they would have to figure out how to settle into their relationship. The last few days had been bliss, but all relationships inevitably moved past the flurry and excitement of those first couple of weeks. When Kai was back at his place and they were still working together and playing together, she would see where their relationship could go.

Of course the way Jared and Sarah had been arguing, there might be more than Kai at her place tonight. They were the reason Kai had ordered everyone out. Sarah had accused Jared of deliberately running off her two dance partners and Jared had shot back with a lecture on how dangerous it was to play around with men she didn't know. He'd come damn close to calling her behavior promiscuous, which likely would have gotten him Sarah's pump right in his balls.

They were probably making out somewhere.

Kai walked out and Kori took a deep breath and sat back. It hadn't been the worst night ever and now she could relax.

The door came open and Mia slipped inside. "You okay?"

Kori smiled. "I'm fine, but I think we're going to head home. This is not my scene."

She preferred Sanctum, where she knew everyone and they all watched out for each other.

Mia nodded and sank down beside her. "That's what Kai told Case. They went off somewhere. I guess Case had something to say to Kai."

"What's wrong? Did you not have fun with Case?" Kori was watching her and she didn't look like a woman who was happy with the way her evening had gone. It surprised her since when they were out on the dance floor, Mia had clung to Case and her eyes had lit up.

"I think someone went through my purse. Did you need something in there? It's totally cool if you did. I just want to make sure it was you."

"No, I didn't touch it except to pass it off to Kai. I'm sorry. I know I said I would look after it, but Jared was kind of insistent on dancing."

"It's okay." She pulled out her phone. "It's weird though. It says I put the security code in ten minutes ago. I haven't touched it all night."

"Phones keep track of that stuff?" She mostly played Candy Crush on hers. She didn't even realize they had security codes. Not that she would put one in. If someone wanted to play Candy Crush that badly, she would let them.

"This one does. It's something my brother built in. He's paranoid. Now I'm getting a little paranoid, too. I was dancing with Case ten minutes ago." Mia flicked her finger across the screen, obviously checking it.

"Maybe it's wrong. Or the screen came on when the bag got moved."

"I don't think so. I think someone got to my phone. Why would Kai want to get into my phone?"

Kori thought Mia was definitely paranoid. "He wouldn't have a reason to do that and Kai would never do something like that. Sweetie, is there a reason you think someone's spying on you?"

Mia frowned. "Look, there are some things you don't know about me. I think I should probably tell someone anyway. You know how I told you about my friend?"

"The one who was killed?"

Mia nodded. "Yes." Mia's eyes squeezed shut, and when she opened them again there was a determined look on her face. "I'm a reporter. I used to work at a paper in Austin, but once I put together the pattern surrounding the murders, I decided to dedicate myself to this story, to getting justice for my friend."

Her night had taken a surreal turn. Had she taken a worse fall than she thought? She didn't remember hitting her head. "Murders?"

"Yes, I've been tracking Jared for the last year. I think it would be best if you came home with me tonight. I can show you everything I have. I can lay it all out for you. I need you to listen to me because I think you could be in danger."

Kori mentally recounted the shots she'd taken. Nope. Not enough to make this conversation go away. "How am I in danger?"

"In the last couple of years, several women have been murdered, all with connections to Jared Johns. All with the same MO and all shortly before Johns left the area. I tried to quietly get myself on his set in Canada, but I couldn't get hired on."

Pieces began to fall into place. "So when they announced *Love After Death* would be filming here, you decided to move to Dallas? Not because you got a job at a dentist's office?"

"That's a cover. I don't actually work there. When I realized the connections between Jared Johns and Kai Ferguson and McKay-Taggart, I knew I had to come here. I had to imbed myself here. Sanctum was a good bet since the rumor in the publishing world is that's the club the whole series is based around. I knew Jared would come and stay with his brother. He would come and hang out at Sanctum and McKay-Taggart."

She wasn't sure what she was feeling. Shock. A bit of betrayal. "You lied?"

"I had to. No one will listen to me. The FBI blew me off when I took this to them. I need solid proof to get a newspaper to print the story. They're all terrified of getting sued."

"Yes, I think if you ruin a man's career and reputation with no real evidence, you're likely to get sued." Anger started to thrum through her system. The club was a place where everyone got to be safe. Sometimes it was the only place in the world where she felt safe. Mia had lied and manipulated her way in. She hadn't come to Sanctum for the right reasons. She'd come to investigate, to report. Privacy was tantamount in a place like Sanctum, and all the while Mia had been investigating them.

"Please don't be mad at me, Kori. I didn't do this to hurt

From Sanctum with Love

anyone. I can't stand the thought of him taking another woman's life. It's going to happen. He can't seem to go more than eight months without killing. He's a predator and I've started to think that he's got powerful friends covering for him. Something's up at McKay-Taggart. They're involved in some very shady business dealings. That thing that happened in the Caymans with the senator, I don't believe the official reports. Someone's hiding something."

Kori stood up. Screw her ankle. "The only thing that happened was we lost a friend. Case lost his brother and I refuse to believe they were doing anything wrong. You don't know them. You have zero idea who these people are. How dare you come here and lie to us. We were your friends. Case really liked you and now I've got to tell him you were playing him for information."

Tears welled in Mia's eyes. "I wasn't. I like him, too. It's why I haven't done anything with him. I haven't let him kiss me because I refuse to start a relationship with a lie between us. But Kori, can't you see? He's the one playing me. He knows. He knows I've been lying and I think he asked me out so he could spy on me. I think Kai knows his brother is a killer and they're all covering for him."

Kori shook her head, her mind rejecting every single word that came out of Mia's mouth. "Why would they do that?"

Mia put her hands up as though trying to calm the situation down. "Because I think McKay-Taggart works for a group of corporations that run the world. I know it sounds crazy and paranoid, but I've been putting it together. I've managed to talk to some people who got out. These are beyond one percenters. They're the richest of the rich, and so powerful no one knows their names. What if the production company Jared works for is involved? They would cover up his crimes. What if McKay-Taggart is one of the ways they control things?"

"Do you have any idea how insane you sound right now? You think Ian Taggart runs some sort of Illuminati?"

"I think he's involved somehow," Mia explained quietly. "His name comes up too often. I've found at least four operations that he was involved in with companies I know for a fact are in The Collective. That's what they call themselves."

"You're insane." How had she not seen that Mia had been hiding a whole bucket full of crazy?

Mia stood her ground. "They asked my brother to join them. Oh, it's not like they sent out an engraved invitation. They're subtle, but they've felt him out. They've made it plain that he can get with the program and things will be easy or he can work against them."

"Who the hell is your brother?"

"Andrew Lawless. He started 4L Software."

Mia's brother was one of the richest men in the world? The youngest billionaire in the country? One of the most reclusive men on earth. Well, that explained how she could afford her Sanctum membership. She wasn't listening to another word of this crap. It was time to make her intentions plain. "You've lied about everything. Don't contact me again and understand that I'll be talking to Kai and you won't be allowed back at Sanctum."

"Do you think I did this for fun?" Mia asked between clenched teeth. "I didn't. I did it because I can't allow him to do it again. He's after Sarah. Can't you see that? He's watching her. He'll hop in her bed and then she'll be another victim by the time he leaves. And your boyfriend is helping cover it all up. He's manipulating you. He's using you."

"You're wrong. He loves me." He wouldn't have said it if he didn't mean it. "And he didn't want his brother here in the first place."

"No, he's doing it because he's a loyal McKay-Taggart man," Mia agreed.

"He's loyal because they're good people."

"Good people don't cover up murders. Good people don't protect corrupt corporations."

She was done with Mia. She strode toward the back of the lounge. She would go and clean up in the bathroom so she didn't punch Mia in the face. "Don't talk to me again."

She pushed through the door, and the back of the building was blissfully quiet. How could this have happened? How could they not have properly vetted her? McKay-Taggart Security checked everyone who came to Sanctum. How had Mia gotten through?

"This is done, Case."

She stopped, her hand on the bathroom door. The sound was coming from her right. She glanced down the hall. It ended in an exit door, but it looked like it veered off, a hall leading back into the club. The sound reverberated off the stained concrete of the floors. Likely they thought they were being quiet, but she could hear them plainly. Of course, if she'd been wearing her shoes, they would have heard her walk in.

"You take that and give it to Adam or Hutch or whoever needs it. I downloaded her whole phone the way you asked me to. I want out of this. Don't get me wrong, man. I'm happy to help, but this stuff with Kori has to stop. It makes me sick. I can't keep this up."

"This is everything we need to figure out how to proceed with Mia. You're out of this. Handle Kori however you like," Case's deep voice said. "I'll deal with it all from here out. Kai, I know what kind of sacrifices you've had to make to get this intel. It won't be forgotten."

"Yeah, well, it's not over yet. I still have things to deal with."

Her. He was talking about her.

So many things began to make sense. She stood there in the hallway, her body going cold. He had to deal with her.

The door came open and Mia walked out. She was wearing shoes and they clacked against the concrete. "You need to listen to me, Kori." Mia stopped. "What's wrong? You're so pale. Are you all right?"

All conversation around the corner had stopped.

Maybe she'd misheard. Maybe they were talking about something else entirely. Except Kai had admitted he'd cloned Mia's phone. Or downloaded it. She didn't understand all the technical stuff. She did know when she'd been had.

There was a reason he hadn't offered her a contract. He'd never intended for it to last very long. Case hadn't been able to get close to Mia, so they'd changed tactics. They'd decided to go through one of her friends. Kori had been a fairly easy mark once Kai realized what she really wanted from a Dom. Kismet. It must have seemed like pure kismet that she turned out to be such a masochist.

But then he'd likely seen that in her all along. Kai wasn't the kind of person who was easily fooled. He'd likely known what she wanted and hadn't acted on it because he hadn't honestly wanted her. Not until he'd needed her easy compliance.

She'd fallen into the trap again. This time she hadn't even realized it.

Stupid. She was always so stupid.

"Kori?" Mia said.

She heard him move before she saw him. His loafers thudded over the floor. Yes, this was why they'd thought they were safe. All sound echoed through here. She'd closed the door quietly behind her, not wanting to let Mia see how angry she'd been. They'd never expected she would hear because Kai had told her to stay put and she was a good fucking sub. He'd never thought she would disobey him.

He stepped out from the corner and she saw it right there on his face. Guilt. Anger. His hands were clenched at his sides. Case stepped out behind him.

"Kori, we need to talk," Kai said quietly.

"Did you do it?" She stared him down. She wasn't going to let him see her cry. She'd cried enough for one lifetime. God, she'd actually believed him. This was why she'd hidden herself away, why that part of her that cried out for a Dom needed to stay buried. That part of her was an idiot. That piece of her got her into trouble time and time and time again. She never learned.

Would he lie to her? Again. Since he'd been lying to her for a very long time it seemed.

Mia went still beside her. "Kori, I think we should go."

Case crossed his arms over his chest. "Did he do what, Kori?"

Case's eyes pinned her as though daring her to say it out loud. Or pleading with her to keep silent. She wasn't sure.

Was she in the middle of something she didn't understand?

What she wanted to do was walk right up to Kai and kick him in the balls. She wanted to rage at him.

She needed to figure out what was happening because she didn't understand anything. She knew what she'd heard. She knew what Mia had said. If she raged at Kai right now, she could blow up whatever Case had been doing.

And that would be good. Yeah, angry Kori was definitely in the house. Vengeful Kori was ready to blow up everything and everyone and take them all down in the process. It didn't matter if they were guilty or innocent. All that mattered was her rage.

"I was asking Kai if he'd called a cab. I got dizzy all of the sudden." She couldn't do it. Not until she understood what was happening. Being an adult fucking sucked sometimes.

Kai was suddenly right beside her. "Baby, it's all right. I'll get us out of here. I'll take care of you."

Yes, she was sure he would try to ease out of her life. Kai didn't do big scenes. He would slowly ease her out and likely find a way to make her think it was all her idea in the first place because he was a manipulative bastard.

God, how many ways had he manipulated her to get to tonight? She hadn't wanted to come out, but he'd talked her into it because she was the only one who could talk Mia into it. When she'd wanted to stay home to comfort Sarah, he'd gotten her to believe it would be better for Sarah to confront Jared.

Who was he? This wasn't the Kai she knew. This wasn't the man she'd fallen in love with.

He'd said he loved her, too. Wasn't that the greatest manipulation of all?

He touched her, his hand gripping her arm more tightly than he needed to, as though he was afraid to let her go. "Come on, I'll get us home."

"Mia, are you ready?" Case asked.

Mia looked over at Kori. "I think so. Maybe we can catch a cab with them. I just need to be dropped off at my place."

"I thought we could hang out for a while," Case offered, his smile turning high wattage.

Manipulation. She'd thought Case wanted Mia. She'd thought Kai wanted her. All manipulation.

She pulled away from Kai. She needed a minute. "I need to use the bathroom. I'll be right back."

The door was cool under her hands as she pushed it open. Mia was hot on her heels. Kori didn't want to deal with any of them at this point. Not one of them. Maybe there was a window she could crawl out of.

"What happened?" Mia asked. "Don't tell me nothing. You went so pale."

She couldn't tell Mia what she'd heard. Not until she found out what was going on. There was a mirror to her left. It looked like the ladies' bathroom was divided. They were in a lounge portion with a huge vanity stocked with everything from mini hairspray bottles to perfumes to condoms. Nice. True VIP service. Yes, it was like she was back in Hollywood all over again. VIP luxury and all she had to do was sell her soul out.

"I feel sick. It's fine. The guys were down the hallway talking."

"About what?"

"About how fast a cab could get here." She hated lying but she needed time. Mia was too close. Kori moved into the second section where there appeared to be three large stalls. In the low light, she could see the marble floor. It was white with some kind of dark stain to it.

"Kori, stop. Don't take another step," Mia said, her voice tight.

"I told you I'll be right back." She would hide in the stall. Hell, she would call her own cab and sneak out and deal with Kai in the morning when she handed in her resignation and then kicked him in the balls. Maybe shove a sadistick up his asshole. See how he liked that.

The minute she hit the stain on the floor she realized why Mia had told her to stop. Something had spilled and for the second time that night, Kori felt herself sliding and falling to the floor.

"Damn it." She was going to sue. She was going to sue whoever thought it would be cool to coat the bathroom in…what the hell was that?

She started to push herself up, and that was when she realized she wasn't alone on the floor. Lena was lying across from her, a gaping hole in her neck, her eyes staring at Kori with absolutely nothing to illuminate them.

She heard someone scream and then the lights seemed to fade to black.

Chapter Thirteen

Kori shivered as she looked around the small, utilitarian room. She glanced up at the clock. Two a.m. How the hell had it gotten to be two in the morning? She was supposed to be asleep by now, cuddled up in Kai's arms. All her friends were supposed to be happy because she'd worked hard to make sure they got what they needed.

They weren't supposed to be sitting in a chilly interrogation room.

"Why are we here?" Sarah asked. "If they think we did something wrong, shouldn't they split us up?"

Kori looked over at Sarah, who sat beside her. "They took Mia away. Maybe they'll come and take us one at a time to somewhere else."

Sarah kicked off her shoes. "Are you all right? Because you look like hell."

"Thanks so much." Naturally Sarah looked damn near perfect. Her hair was still silky and smooth, and the woman knew how to set makeup so it lasted forever.

Kori had caught a glimpse of herself in the mirror when they'd allowed her to clean herself up. She looked like shit.

Sarah's hand slid over hers. "I'm sorry. I'm worried about you. You've barely said a word since the police showed up. Why wouldn't you talk to Kai?"

She'd hoped Sarah hadn't seen that single exchange with her ex-boyfriend. Should she call him that? Did he count as an ex when everything he'd done had been to manipulate her to the point that he gained access to her friends?

The door opened and Kori was grateful because she wasn't ready to answer that question yet.

Please, let me talk to you. Let me explain, Kai had said, his eyes pleading with her, his mouth against her ear.

She'd looked up at him. *Tell me you didn't do it.*

He'd simply stared and she'd walked away, and a few minutes later she'd found herself being taken to this police station and giving a statement as to how she'd found the body. She'd expected to be let go, but they'd been left here for hours.

"Good evening, ladies." The man was tall and well built, dressed in an immaculate suit. Even at this time of night, he looked well rested, energetic even. He had dark hair and piercing eyes that seemed to look right through her. "My name is Ethan Rush."

"You're a fed, right?" Kori asked, the words feeling dull in her mouth.

"How do you know that?" Sarah asked. "He could be a lawyer. Do we need a lawyer? Are we in some sort of trouble? When I got coffee ten minutes ago, I could swear I saw a couple of guys from the club walking around. Mitch and Harrison. They're lawyers, right? Are you their friend?"

"No," Rush said, still looking at Kori. "I'm Special Agent Rush with the Federal Bureau of Investigation. I believe you'll find the lawyers aren't here for you."

"Did Kai call them?" She'd known he was a fed from the suit and how he handled himself. At this time of night most police officers looked as haggard as she did. The detectives who'd come out on call to the club had worn suits, but not one as expensive as this man's. She would bet he had money on the side, money that hadn't come from the FBI.

"Yes." Rush set a folder in front of them and settled his big body across the table. "And neither one of you is in trouble."

"But Kai is?" Sarah sounded a little panicked.

Kai was in a lot of trouble. Kai was in trouble Kori would never have suspected, but then she was a very dumb girl. Always so dumb. "What do you need from the two of us? I already gave a statement."

"Yes, you gave a very brief statement about finding the body. I need to know more. I need to know what went on tonight with Lena and the rest of the group. Lena's body was found within an hour of her murder according to the medical examiner. I need to account for everyone's movements during that period."

She was so damn numb. Shouldn't she care more that Lena was dead? It was like discovering Kai's betrayal had left her utterly hollow and nothing could quite reach her. "Check the security cameras."

"Kori?" Sarah leaned in. "We should be more helpful." She looked up at the special agent. "I'll tell you everything I remember, but I was on the dance floor for most of that time. I know Lena walked away shortly before I left. She'd been arguing with that guy. One of the brothers. Brad or Tad. Have you talked to them?"

"They're being questioned even as we speak. Why don't you go and grab another cup of coffee. I need to speak with Ms. Williamson alone."

"Maybe she should have a lawyer." Sarah's hand was shaking this time when she placed it over Kori's.

Obviously whatever Rush had to say, he wanted it to be for her ears only. It was time to start protecting her friends. She'd done a fucking poor ass job of it up until now. She'd never seen the web they'd stepped into until the spider had come out all ready for dinner. Kori gave Sarah what she hoped was a confident smile. "I'll be fine. I don't need a lawyer. Special Agent Rush knows I didn't horribly murder anyone."

"Ms. Williamson is not a suspect," Rush affirmed. "She is, however, a very important witness. There's an officer outside who will take your statement and record anything you can remember. Thank you so much. I'll be done with your friend very soon and you'll be free to go home."

"Okay." Sarah picked up her shoes and gave Kori a pat on the back. "I'll be waiting for you."

The door closed and she looked at Rush. "Say what you need to say."

Rush's sensual lips quirked up. "Tough girl, huh? It's funny because I happen to know you aren't a McKay-Taggart agent, but you sure behaved like one tonight. That statement you gave was very careful. Normally witnesses to a murder are all over the place. Their statements are difficult to follow because they haven't processed yet. Not yours. You were careful, as though you knew someone you cared about would be accused of the crime and you wanted to mitigate any damage you might do."

Jared. Kai's brother would be looked at. If Mia had managed to gather that much information, it stood to reason someone else would, too. Hell, the very presence of the FBI led her to believe they'd likely been watching Jared. "Why are the feds here so soon?"

If this wasn't a serial case that crossed state lines, there would be no feds. This should be handled by the DPD. The body wasn't even cold yet but here was a guy in a suit. She'd done enough research to know when and where the feds would be called in. Likely the Rangers would be called in if the murder case was big enough or crossed county lines, or the locals weren't equipped to handle them. The Texas Rangers acted like a state bureau of investigations for Texas. The FBI would only be called in for special reasons.

Like the search for an international serial killer.

Was all of this about hiding something Jared had done? How well did she truly know him? He was sweet and funny and charming, but then she suspected Ted Bundy had probably been, too.

"What do you know about Jared Johns?" Rush asked, obviously getting down to interrogation mode.

She shrugged. "He showed up last week. I've spent some time with him. He's living at my office right now. That sounds weird. Uhm, you see my boss owns the building and his office is downstairs and he lives upstairs."

"Your boss or your boyfriend? Or is he better described as both?"

She felt herself flush. Some exhibitionist she was. It was funny how she could be naked in front of a crowd at Sanctum and it didn't bother her at all, but having someone know her emotions made her feel so damn vulnerable. Still, it was apparent that he knew what was going on. "Kai and I have a relationship outside of work."

Had, she amended silently.

"Did you know he had a brother? How often did he talk about him?"

She shook her head. "Never. I didn't know about Jared until he showed up."

"Do you think he would cover for his brother?"

"I don't know." She would have said no. Absolutely not. She would have said Kai was incapable of protecting a killer. But then they came to the problem of Mia and her phone. What other reason could he have? Mia was investigating Jared. Case and Kai had worked very hard to figure out a way to bug Mia's phone. The only reason Kori could think of was they wanted to know how much Mia had figured out. "They aren't close. I can't tell that Kai has anything but negative feelings for him."

Which would be a good front to put on if he wanted to help his brother get away with murder.

Had she really thought that? It was inconceivable. That wasn't Kai. But then she would have said Kai wouldn't use her, wouldn't manipulate her emotions in order to get what he wanted and then dump her.

I'm happy to help, but this stuff with Kori has to stop. It makes me sick. I can't keep this up.

Sleeping with her made him sick.

"Would you cover for your boyfriend? Would you allow his brother to go free?"

She wanted to go home. "I don't know anything."

Rush flipped open the folder, turning it so the photos were facing her. "This is why I'm here. These women are why I'm here, and I want to make sure you don't allow your soft heart to aid and abet the man who killed them. Kori, I'm here to make sure you're not next, that your friend Sarah isn't next."

She looked down and her stomach flipped. The women in the photos were all dead, their vacant eyes staring up. They'd all been stabbed like Lena had been. Kori couldn't forget the way the white shirt Lena had been wearing had turned to a bloody color, the way it smelled.

There were so many of them. So many.

She couldn't help it.

"There's a trash can to your right, sweetheart," Rush said.

She stumbled out of her seat and dropped to her knees, emptying the contents of her stomach into the can. She could hear Rush at the door calling for someone as she heaved.

Who could do that? She'd worked on movie sets and they always laughed as they poured blood on the "dead" actress, who usually joked and complained the whole time. She'd played around with retractable knives and goofed off with prop guns.

This was real. Those girls were dead. Mia's friend was one of them. Someone had stabbed her over and over and left her behind like she was nothing more than trash to be picked up.

She didn't know Jared. She didn't know Kai the way she thought she did. She would have said Kai wouldn't hurt a fly, would never do anything secretive. How could she think she knew Jared if she didn't even know the man she'd fallen in love with?

An emptiness swept through her. How could she know anyone if she couldn't know Kai? He'd been everything to her.

Maybe this time she would go somewhere and be truly alone. She had some money saved. There were places she could go where no one could ever touch her again.

"Here." Rush stood over her, a washcloth in his hand. "When you're ready, I've got a cold soda for you. It should settle your stomach."

She took the cloth and ran it over her face. It was cold and it seemed to seep into her skin. She rose, refusing Rush's hand up.

She was alone now.

Kori made it back to the table. Loyalty had kept her mouth shut, but there was something more going on now. Those girls were real.

"Kori, when we found Jared, he was with Sarah," Rush said, his voice gentler than before. "He'd taken her to a private room. I don't know what would have happened if we hadn't gotten there in time. There might have been two victims."

She still wasn't sure it was Jared. Her heart ached at the

thought, but she shoved it aside. Her heart was a stupid thing.

Justice. That was all that was important now.

"I'll start at the beginning of the evening. Jared had a limo pick us up. Me and Jared and Kai." She settled back and began her story.

* * * *

"What the hell is taking so long?" Kai demanded as he paced.

He'd been separated from Kori for hours. Every minute that dragged by was a minute too long. What the hell was happening and why were they being detained by the police? There was zero question in Kai's mind that this was a detention. Oh, there might not be a lock on the door, but he suspected if he or Jared tried to leave, they would be stopped and quickly.

"I don't know." Jared sat in one of four metal seats, his head in his hand. "I can't believe she's dead. I didn't see her. You did. Are you sure it was her? Maybe it was some other woman."

"It was her." He'd never forget the sight. He'd run in at the sound of Kori's scream, and for a moment he'd thought it was Kori's blood that coated the floor. For a moment he'd thought something horrible had happened to his Kori, and his life had stopped. He'd fallen to his knees, ready to do anything to save her when he'd caught sight of Lena out of the corner of his eye. She'd been laid out in the largest of the stalls, likely falling where she'd been murdered. She'd been on her side, her knees close to her chest, so Kai could believe she'd tried to protect herself.

Something horrible had happened to his girl. She'd heard him betraying her and then she'd seen something no one should ever have to see. Now she wouldn't accept his comfort.

Fuck, even Mia had clung to Case afterward. She'd cried and held on to him. Kai had picked Kori up and carried her out while Case called the cops. He'd held onto her, praying she hadn't hit her head. When her eyes had fluttered open, she'd seen him and for a moment it was like nothing had happened.

Then she'd come to her senses and moved away from him.

Tell me you didn't do it.

He'd known in that moment that she'd heard everything and there wasn't much he could do. He couldn't lie to her again. It wasn't in him to do it. He couldn't lie and he couldn't tell her the truth. He was caught in a trap and she was the one who would pay the price.

"Why?" Jared asked. He looked up and for the first time Jared looked tired, weary even. For the first time he could see how his brother had aged. "Why would someone kill her? I know she was a bitch, but she never deserved anything like this."

"I don't know." He was tired, too. Tired of everything. Case had been taken to a room to visit with his lawyer. Mitchell Bradford was here, and Kai wouldn't be surprised if he'd brought Harrison Keen along for the ride. Mitch was McKay-Taggart's attorney, but Harrison was one of the top criminal defense attorneys in the state and he happened to be a sub at Sanctum. While Harrison might enjoy submitting to Dommes in his free time, the man was an animal in the courtroom. An alpha animal.

McKay-Taggart was busy protecting their own. And he couldn't protect Kori at all.

He was starting to believe he needed to protect his brother, too.

"When was the last time you talked to Lena tonight?" Kai asked. He couldn't talk to Jared about the FBI investigation. It would go against McKay-Taggart's deal with the feds and could stop the flow of information. He couldn't risk that, not when they were in the middle of an interrogation room. Anyone could be listening in. They could be taping the two of them for all Kai knew. Without a lawyer present, the cops could do what they liked. He would feel better if they'd been taken to Derek Brighton's precinct. Lieutenant Brighton was a Dom at Sanctum and he'd taken care of issues before, but he wasn't here tonight.

Jared's shoulders slumped. "I don't know. It was hard to talk to anyone. The club was so loud. I talked to her before we went in and she said she needed a couple of hours of my time tomorrow because she wanted to talk about a staffing issue. She said one of the guys had to go. I don't remember who she said because the reporters were in my face by then."

Maybe he was thinking about this the wrong way. Maybe this had nothing to do with the serial case. "Okay. So Lena had a problem with one of the guys."

Jared sighed. "Lena always had a problem. She's tried to get me to fire every one of them at least twice. She hated everyone. She was always asking for private meetings so she could talk shit about the guys."

"But if one of the guys thought she was a threat to his job, he might have wanted to take her out."

"I can't imagine that. They all knew she talked about them behind their backs. They expect that behavior. Why aren't we talking about the patrons of the club? Someone likely followed her back there and tried to take her purse or something."

"This wasn't a crime of opportunity." Lena had been killed in the same fashion as the others. Even with only a brief glance he could see the same MO. "Besides, it would be difficult to get back there without going through one of the two ways into the VIP lounge."

The lounge was cordoned off from the dance floor, but there were two ways servers and staff could get there. There had been the direct route to the bar and bathrooms, and then there was a specific entrance to the right for staff that led back to the bathrooms but not through the lounge. It was the way he and Case had gone to discuss the op.

If only they'd been smarter and not discussed it at all.

It was his fault. Not Case's. Case had tried to make the handoff and leave it at that, but Kai had to push. Kai had to get his two cents in there. Now Kori knew and she hated him.

He needed to see her. Maybe if he could get her alone, he could make her understand.

Understand what? He couldn't tell her anything. He couldn't do anything but apologize.

He was so fucked.

Kai sank down into the chair beside his brother's. "I'm sure they've got security cameras. They'll be able to tell who went back there and at what time."

Jared nodded. "I only went back once and it was to go to the bathroom. I didn't see Lena back there at all. I have to admit though that I skipped the lounge and went the back way because I thought she was in there at the time. She was arguing with Brad and I didn't want to get in the middle of that shit."

"I would like to know if Brad followed her to the bathroom.

You don't remember anything?"

"No. I got up right after Sarah took Kori in the back. When I returned, I realized Sarah was practically humping some asshole on the dance floor and then I acted like a douchebag the rest of the night. I know I ignored her. I know it hurt her. I was actually trying to apologize to her when they told me Lena was dead."

"You were trying to apologize? Verbally?" He knew his brother pretty well.

"Fine, I was trying to kiss her. The cops came in just as I got my hands on her. They acted like I was trying to murder her or something. For a minute I thought someone was going to shoot me. Who's the guy in the suit? Is he the lead detective? He's the one who damn near shot me."

Rush. Of course Rush had come to the scene. He'd likely been shadowing them all night. He'd been waiting for something to happen and it had. Kai guessed he should be happy Jared wasn't under arrest yet. He needed to tell Jared who Rush was and why he was here, but he glanced toward the mirror that covered a good portion of the room. Somewhere behind that mirror they were watching. He wasn't sure if it would be Rush or one of the FBI's profiling team, but they were watching every move his brother made. It was likely why they'd left Kai in here with him. They wanted to see if Jared would screw up and say something.

They might want to see if Kai was more loyal to his brother than he looked.

If they were listening in, he would give them a show. Jared wasn't showing any signs of lying. There was nothing in his manner that led Kai to believe Jared was anything less than devastated by what had happened. So maybe if there was a profiler on the other side of that mirror, they would see it, too. "Has anything like this happened before? Any women you knew who went missing or got killed?"

Jared's eyes widened. "No. I've never known anyone who got killed. Like murdered. I knew a guy who died of a brain tumor, but that's about it. And missing? No. I meet a lot of people though. Why are you asking?"

His brother didn't even realize he'd left a trail of bodies during his travels. "Do you keep up with the women you sleep with on the road?"

His brother turned a nice shade of pink. "That's none of your business, Kai. And there aren't as many as you would think. Every now and then I'll hook up with someone, but when I'm on the road, they very rarely ever call. I give them my private number, but no one calls. I think they probably see me as a collectible."

"You don't call them?"

"I don't want to pressure anyone. I'm also not real great about using my damn phone, okay? One of the guys programs it. It's easier to give them my number."

"You honestly believe that you've had sex with a bunch of women who don't want to have sex with you again? Because I've heard some of the stories. Hey, my fiancée left me because apparently you're better in bed."

Jared stood, his shoulders squaring. "She left you because she was a bitch and you didn't see it. She left you because she couldn't stand to have you walk away from her. She left you because just like the rest of us mere fucking mortals, she couldn't quite live up to your standards."

Shit. He did not want to do this here. "Fine. All I'm saying is I find it highly unlikely that none of those women called you back."

"Seriously? This is what you want to talk about? Are you trying to solve a murder or fix my love life?"

The door slammed open and Kai was surprised to see Erin Argent standing there. She was dressed in jeans and a T-shirt, her face makeup free and her wild red hair up in a messy bun, as though she'd rolled out of bed to come here. "Is Case with Mitch?"

"Yes. They called him out a while ago. He's not in trouble or anything," Kai explained. "He was there when we found a body."

Erin's left brow rose, a queenly gesture. "So it was a fun night. Big Tag wasn't answering his cell so Case called me and told me to get the lawyers down here pronto. Then he told me to go back to bed and not worry. Yeah, like that was going to happen. I called Mitch, who called the subby boy, and then I got Hutch on the case. He was on guard duty."

"Guard duty?" Jared asked, looking Erin over as though trying to figure out if she was a threat.

She was. Erin was deadly when she wanted to be. Years in the

Army and then private training with Big Tag had turned her into a deadly weapon, but she wasn't a threat to them. "A couple of months ago an op went wrong and Big Tag is simply making sure Erin's safe."

"He's making sure crazy pants Doctor Evil doesn't come back for seconds." Erin rolled her green eyes. "Which she won't since she's off happily fucking around with unsuspecting victims somewhere that's not here. But Big Tag, Little Tag, and Should Have Covered His Tracks Better Tag decided I should have protection, at least at night, so they all take turns sleeping in my guest room. I swear I'm going to be pissed if someone breaks in and I don't get to kill someone. No one ever lets me have fun anymore."

Erin's idea of fun could get grisly. And Big Tag had been worried about more than Hope McDonald. He'd been worried about her being alone, worried she might hurt herself or run away. So far she'd been pretty solid. Tonight she even sounded like the old Erin. She was apparently seriously amused that Case had gotten caught. "You didn't have to come down here. We're not in any real trouble."

She gave him a sour grin. "Maybe not with the police, but I'm intrigued. You see, Hutch is a very smart hacker and he works for candy. I wanted to know what had gone down here that would require not one but two lawyers for our boys. So I shoved a bag of gummy bears his way and he managed to find some very interesting video of the hall outside the private lounge."

"What?" Kai moved in close. What the hell was Erin thinking? "This is a police investigation."

She shook her head. "I'm sure the murder is. I'm not concerned about some Hollywood chick. I'm concerned about what the hell you handed Case and why he's running an op that isn't on the books. Don't tell me it wasn't an op. Case had his op face on. It's a little like his I-ate-too-many-fries face but with a hint of his vicious-badger face. I love my broth…I like the guy, but he's pure muscle. He can't play a role to save his life."

It wasn't inaccurate. Of the two, Theo had been the better operative while Case could kick ass and take names all day. "You should take it up with Case."

"What does she mean about an op?" Jared asked, looking

between the two of them. "And why would she hack into the video feed from the club? Is the hacker five? Who else eats gummy bears?"

Naturally that was what Jared would hit on. "Don't worry about it. We need to worry about making a statement and getting the hell out of here. We can talk more when we get home." He frowned Erin's way. "You do realize someone is likely taping us even as we speak."

"Fine, I'll drop it for now, but why does Kori look like she lost her best friend?" Erin asked. "We'll get back to Case later, but Kori's sitting out in the station waiting for a ride. Shouldn't you take her home, Doc? Or is this part of the sadist stuff?"

If they'd been at Sanctum, he would have called her on that. Erin had played before. Hell, Erin had played with him. Erin was one of the few women who could handle his form of play, but it had been apparent even in the beginning that she'd had a connection to Theo. Once the youngest Taggart had come on the scene, Erin hadn't been interested in play anymore. Not with him. So he found it very annoying that she was accusing him of neglecting his sub.

Except Kori wasn't his sub anymore. She never had been since he hadn't managed to find a good time to talk about contracts with her.

"She's not going anywhere." It didn't matter that she was pissed at him. All that mattered was taking care of her. "You go out there right now and tell her she's not to leave this building. I will be very angry if she tries to go home without an escort."

Jared stood up beside him, a stubborn look crossing his face. "And Sarah isn't an escort. She's not going anywhere either."

Erin looked between the two of them. "Wow, for a minute there you two actually looked like brothers. Tell me something, Jared. How did you get the masculine name and Kai here got the hippy name?"

"My mom simply liked it." Let it stay there. Please.

A slow smile split Jared's face. "He hasn't told anyone, has he? Kai is short for Kaiser. Kaiser Ferguson. And before you think maybe we had a German relative in our background, you're wrong."

"Jared," he began.

Jared didn't skip a beat. "When he was born, the doctor handed him over and the blanket slipped off his butt and Mom said his backside looked like two perfect Kaiser rolls. And that's what she named him."

Erin burst into laughter, her whole body moving.

Damn but it was good to hear her laugh. He shot his brother the finger, but Jared smiled as though he'd known the woman in front of him needed a reason to momentarily let go.

Before Erin could finish laughing, the door came open and Special Agent Rush strode in. He was followed by two uniformed officers, and there was no way to miss the handcuffs in his hands. The metal glinted in the stark light of the room.

"Jared John Ferguson," Rush began. "You're under arrest for the murder of Lena Klein. You have the right to remain silent."

Jared went pale as Rush continued to Mirandize him. As they hauled him out, he looked back Kai's way, his eyes wide. It was the same damn look he'd had on his face the day Kai had driven away and not looked back.

Desperation and then acceptance. Jared's face went blank as though he knew Kai wouldn't help him and he was alone.

Fuck. Kai strode out the door. "Don't you say a fucking word, Jared. I'll have a lawyer here as soon as I can. Not a word to them. Do you understand me?"

He didn't respond, but suddenly his brother's spine straightened and his head came back up.

"I'm going to need to talk to Harrison." He had no idea who had said what or why the police thought his brother had done this, but he knew one thing. He wasn't walking away this time.

"He's still here," Erin said. "I talked to him on my way in. He was planning on talking to you. He isn't only here for Case. I sent him for all of you. It's what Big Tag would want, if he wasn't busy fucking his wife. He'll likely get my texts soon and he'll be in here like an angry bull, so enjoy the calm now."

Two things. He knew two things. He was going to save his brother and he was going to take care of Kori. No matter what. "Will you take Kori back to your place? I fucked up with her, Erin. You have to talk to Case about what we were doing, but Kori overheard something I said and now she thinks our entire relationship was about an op."

"Girls get pissy about that. It's why honesty is always best."

"I couldn't." He couldn't say anything. His hands were tied. "Please take care of her."

Erin nodded. "All right, but only because I'm tired and I can get a couple of tacos on the way home. I throw up all day and I'm hungry all night. Pregnancy sucks." She stepped out into the hall. "And tell Case that we're not through. I'll figure it out in the end."

Erin walked away and Kai started looking for the lawyer. It looked like they were definitely going to need him tonight.

Chapter Fourteen

"So, I'm betting I get the couch." Hutch frowned as he locked the door behind them.

"I think one of the girls is taking the couch," Erin said, pressing the buttons on the control pad for her home security system. "You should feel free to sleep in a corner, or you could go home, buddy."

Kori watched them, taking in the byplay as she set her purse down on the table while Mia and Sarah did the same. Kori had tried to argue for going home, but Erin had stood pretty firm. Erin could be scary when she stood firm.

Apparently they weren't allowed to be murdered by a serial killer. No one cared that the cops were looking into it so any serial killer with sense likely would be laying low. That bit of reason hadn't worked. And it didn't matter that Hutch was going to lose his bed.

Hutch shook his head and yawned. "No way, sister. My spinal column will fare better against your floor than it would Big Tag's hands. I think he could do that *Predator* thing where he pulls it right out and hoists it over his head like a trophy. I'll grab one of the sleeping bags I saw in the hall closet. Thank god Theo liked to camp." He stopped and went still. "I'm sorry."

Erin stared at him, arms crossed over her chest. "That Theo liked to camp? Or that he liked to collect piles and piles of crap that I now have to deal with?"

Hutch sighed. "Night, Erin. Yell if you need me."

From what Kori could tell, Erin hadn't dealt with anything of Theo's. Theo's clothes were still hanging next to Erin's, his shoes on the floor, his toothbrush still in a cup in the bathroom.

Kai had brought a toothbrush over the second night he'd stayed at her place. Before they'd left, he'd run upstairs while she talked to Jared. Kai had come down with an overnight bag and not even a good-bye for his brother.

Had he been acting the whole time?

One thing was for sure, his toothbrush would not be staying at her place. She would toss it and everything he'd left right in his face when she quit. Without notice. He could keep his own appointments and stock his own groceries and shove all his Zen and calmness right up his muscled ass.

"I still don't understand anything," Sarah complained. "I don't understand why we can't go home."

Erin shrugged as though it was none of her concern. "Because you all signed contracts with Sanctum that state plainly any of the Master Doms can be overprotective dicks about you. The overprotective dick award goes to Kai 'Hot Buns' Ferguson this evening. So take it up with him. I'm merely the girl who happened to be there. The guest bedroom is back there. The couch folds out and I would bet Hutch is already asleep in my office. You would think all that sugar would keep him awake, but his body doesn't work that way. So everyone get some sleep. Except you, blondie. You and me, we're going to have a talk."

Mia's eyes widened. "I think I'm going to break my Sanctum contract. After what happened tonight, I won't be going anymore."

What the hell was going on? She'd been a little confused from the moment Erin and Hutch had shown up and hustled them all out of the police station and into Hutch's SUV. They'd been told they weren't going home. They needed to stay with Erin because the men had decided they were still in danger.

From a serial killer. That was what Special Agent Rush had

described, what he thought Jared Johns was. According to the FBI agent, Jared had killed all across the globe. He'd been vivid in his description.

Kori still hadn't explained things to Sarah. Mia and Sarah had been sitting on a bench in the station house when Kori had been released by Rush. He'd explained that he had other witnesses to talk to before he made a decision, and he might need to meet with her again tomorrow. She'd slumped down next to her friends and wondered what fresh hell tomorrow would bring.

Obviously tonight wasn't quite over. Erin could be like a dog with a bone. Kori was done pretending. After what had happened with Lena, it would all come out anyway. "Mia is a reporter. Case was investigating her. I don't think it's safe for her to go home since she's been tracking a serial killer and he struck tonight."

Sarah gasped. "I heard that rumor but I didn't think it was true." She shook her head. "It's not him. It's not. I'm going to bed because I'm not going to listen to anyone say he's a killer. He might be an asshole, but he wouldn't hurt me."

Sarah turned and walked toward the guest bedroom.

"Well, I've lost enough friends tonight. I'll call a cab. You won't see me again," Mia promised. "I'll go home and help the police from there. I'm sorry I hurt you, Kori. I never meant to do that. I only meant to honor my friend."

"Wow, that's some girl drama there." Erin stepped in front of the door. "You'll go and sit down and we'll work this out like two grown-ass females because the men have fucked up everything, it seems to me. The minute he found out you lied on your application, Case should have sat you down and had a conversation. You'll have to forgive him. He often thinks with his dick, and his dick is not smart."

Mia tensed, her body stiffening, and Kori hoped she hadn't managed to fit her gun in that tiny bag. "I don't think that's necessary. I have what I needed. At least the police know what's going on."

"Yes, they arrested Jared while I was there," Erin said calmly. "Did you convince them? I take it this is all about your friend. The one who died in Canada."

Kori felt her stomach flip. They'd arrested Kai's brother? Had

Kai known what was going on with Jared? According to Rush he'd been involved in this sting operation, but it was hard to believe. If he could give up his brother like that, why did she think for a second he would give a shit about her?

"How did you know?" Mia moved back in the living room.

Erin followed her. "Because I don't have a dumb dick that makes decisions for me. Case and Kai ran an op tonight. I figured that out because Hutch is the one who programmed that device that downloaded your phone. The minute I told him Case and Kai were at the police station, he gave himself away. That boy can't play poker to save his life. When he's trying to lie he frowns and looks totally ridiculous. Lying or subterfuge is the only time that boy gets serious. So when he reacted to Case and Kai getting hauled in for questioning, I knew I was on to something. It was a short hop and a few threats and Hutch was telling me everything. Your brother is Andrew Lawless. He's the CEO of a company called 4L Software. I think Hutch got a little horny when he said your brother's name."

So Kai had definitely been working for Case and McKay-Taggart to figure out what Mia had been up to. Why all the subterfuge? Kori sank down on Erin's couch. She'd been over here a couple of times, but only once when Theo had been with her. They'd only lived here together a week or so before they'd gone on the op that led to Theo's death. The way she understood it, Theo had surprised Erin with the house after they'd returned from working in Africa. Kori remembered the night she'd come out with some of the guys who'd installed Theo and Erin's fire pit. They'd made margaritas and ordered pizza and toasted the new house around the fire they'd lit. Those same guys she'd sat with that night had been in on the plot. They hadn't thought twice about Kai using her. She'd been a pawn.

One more memory ruined.

How many holes could a person have before they weren't really there anymore? How many pieces could she lose before she simply stopped trying?

"You should know that if anything happens to me, my brother will move heaven and earth to find me." Mia was still standing like a trapped animal ready to run at the first opportunity.

"Sit down, Mia. She's not going to hurt you." Kori was so tired of all the lies.

Erin sat down across from the couch, leaning back. "I wouldn't say that. If I don't find out what I want, I might cut a bitch."

"She doesn't mean that." Kori patted the seat beside her. Sometimes she thought Erin had been born to be a Taggart wife. Sarcasm and a little streak of violence had been bred into her DNA.

Mia ignored the couch and stepped up to Erin. Her voice went low. "Don't let the blonde hair fool you. I'm not about to back off a fight. You want to come at me, we'll see who wins. My brother might have all the money in the world now, but I didn't grow up that way. I fought for everything I have and I'll fucking fight you too, if I have to. I won't pull hair or try to bitch slap you. I'll go for the kill and I'll do it quick."

"She's pregnant, Mia." Kori thought that should be put out there before Erin and Mia started throwing punches. Or stabbing each other. Jeez, she didn't want to get in between a couple of alpha females. All they needed was Charlotte Taggart to show up and they could start their own wrestling crew.

Mia took a deep breath. "Damn it." She sat down on the couch. "I could use a good fight after tonight."

A smile of pure pleasure swept across Erin's face. "Oh, see, now I like you. You're going to need that fight if you take on McKay-Taggart. Now tell me why you're here and why you've lied to my people."

Mia's eyes narrowed. "So you can report back to them? How deep are you in? You can tell them my brother will never join them. They can block his access to resources all day. He'll find a way around them."

Kori saw the moment Erin realized what Mia was talking about and she got a chill. She didn't understand the spy stuff, but she did know when a moment got real. Really fucking real. She tried to laugh to bring the potential for violence down. "Mia thinks McKay-Taggart might be involved with some weird corporate thing. I think it's price fixing or something. I told her that's crazy."

"The Collective killed my husband. Theo. The Collective killed Theo," Erin said, her jaw tight. "Are you telling me they've come to your brother? Did they try to tell you we're involved?"

Mia took a moment and seemed to come to some kind of

From Sanctum with Love

decision. "They approached him a year ago, right after his stock soared. They were quiet about it, but my brothers started to do some digging. I have three brothers, Drew, Riley, and Bran. Riley's a lawyer. Drew found out where the contact had come from and then Riley connected that man to a couple of companies. Mega firms with so many arms it's hard to tell who's who, but Riley managed to make sense of most of it. Then Bran and I ran with it and figured out how they operate. They're responsible for a lot of crimes. This goes way beyond price fixing. They own politicians and start wars in Third World countries to advance their business and to crush their rivals. Ian Taggart's name came up more than once. And when I found out the very man I believe killed my friend was tied to this company, I knew they were involved."

Erin pulled her phone out of her pocket and dialed a number. "Tag, I need you to come to my place. Now. I don't care. Case is a big boy and he can find his way home. Ian, I'm serious. I need you here now."

She flicked her finger across the screen. Not many people in the world would hang up on Ian Taggart. Erin had balls. She sat forward and looked at Mia. "We've been fighting The Collective for years. I wasn't here in the beginning, but the firm's involvement goes back to a rogue CIA agent who attempted to use McKay-Taggart to help him steal technological plans for a drone that would have put the US military years ahead of every other country on the planet. He intended to sell them to China. McKay-Taggart stopped him. We've been fighting ever since."

"So I was right and Senator McDonald was a member of The Collective," Mia said.

Kori's stomach was in knots. What did any of this have to do with why Kai needed to clone Mia's phone? "But you're wrong about McKay-Taggart working for him. They wouldn't work for a corrupt senator. Big Tag is smart. He vets his clients."

"He also loves subterfuge," Erin said. "Once a spook, always a spook, I say. Ian vetted you, Mia. I'm sure he's known all along exactly who you are, and I suspect that he thinks you're working for The Collective."

"He thinks my brother is one of them?" Mia paled a little.

Erin touched her nose and gave Mia a wink. "Now you're

catching on. We've been in a Mexican standoff without knowing it because the boys are dumb shits who would rather play spy games than sit down and think this out rationally."

"Why wouldn't he ask her?" Kori didn't understand. She didn't understand why they wouldn't sit Mia down, and she definitely didn't understand why they'd gotten Kai involved.

Except that Mia had been Kori's friend and Kai had an in with Kori. If Case hadn't been able to get close to Mia, which it looked like he hadn't, then Kai could do the job. Which he had. He'd done his job with the cool precision of a McKay-Taggart operative and then he'd wanted out. He'd obviously found his work distasteful.

Erin sighed, her eyes a little weary. "Ian would love to believe that he's a mystery to all of us. He's not. I'll tell you exactly what he was thinking. He was wondering if Blondie here wasn't working for her brother. He hoped and prayed she was a plant so he could switch it all up on her and spy on Drew Lawless and maybe, just maybe Lawless would lead us deeper into the organization. He would have listened in, but only one name would have mattered. Oh, if Ian had really found something out, he would alert the authorities, but only if it wouldn't compromise his mission."

"I'm scared to ask what his mission is," Mia admitted.

"They didn't catch who killed Theo, did they?" There was only one thing that would drive Big Tag like this, that would make him single-minded and utterly ruthless.

"Theo was killed by some random asshole who got the jump on him because he fucked up," Erin replied. "That man was meaningless. Going after that idiot would be like stomping on the bullet that pierced Theo's heart. He was a tool. Maybe he died when we stormed the compound. Maybe he's still some asshole's lackey. I don't know. I don't care. I shot Senator McDonald through the brain. Put that in your story, Mia. I sat on a rooftop with a sniper rifle and waited until the perfect moment, and then I pulled the trigger. You would think I was angry at the time. That I was emotional. I wasn't. True revenge is cold. It means you've got nothing left and all that will satisfy your icy heart is killing another human being. I would very much like to kill Hope McDonald. So would Ian. So would Case. So would Sean."

Hell, Kori had no idea who Hope McDonald was but she kind

of wanted to kill the bitch now. "Erin, I don't think her brother knows."

Mia's face had hardened. "Ian Taggart is going to want a meeting with my brother. He's going to ask him to go undercover."

"Or to allow one of us to do it. I know how Ian thinks. I know what I would do. You're a gift, Mia," Erin said, her voice cold. "And you'll get a hell of a story out of it. I think you should call your brother. Ian's on his way over."

Mia stood, flipping open her bag and pulling out her phone. She frowned as she looked at the screen. "Damn. I've got five messages from him. One of them says I should stop using this fucking phone. Awesome. They already figured out I'm compromised. I hate Case Taggart. I hope his balls shrivel up and die. Son of a bitch. I'll never live this down. Do you have any idea what it's like to have three insanely protective alpha male brothers?"

"I got a Taggart in my womb. You're kidding me, right?" Erin snarked.

Mia calmed a bit. "I'm sorry for the trouble. I was suspicious. It's a scary world out there. I wanted to make things better."

Erin stood and held out a hand. "Then work with us."

Mia shook it. "All right. I'll get my brother on the phone. Apparently he's waiting up. Or he might be on a plane already on his way here. Maybe we can get him and Taggart on a call. Is there somewhere I can talk in private?"

Erin gestured to the left. "My bedroom is in there. You can use it. After we pass this off to the boys, we can get some sleep. I'll make up the couch for you and Kori can bunk with me. It's a king-sized bed. I can share."

Kori wasn't sure she would be able to sleep at all.

Mia walked toward the master bedroom and Kori stood up.

"I'll get the sheets and stuff. Are they in the hall closet?" She was willing to do anything to shut her brain down.

Why hadn't he told her? If Kai had told her he was trying to track down Theo's killer, she would have helped. She would have stood at his side and played her role, and they could have come out of this mess as friends. She would still have him in her life, still have a job, still have a home.

"I think we should talk before Big Tag gets here and the shit storm begins."

Kori shook her head. "There's nothing to talk about."

"Oh, there is. Kai fucked up. He fucked up badly and I can see in your eyes that you're going to run. I know because I would very likely do the same thing. What did you hear him say? I watched the tape, but there's no sound."

"He said he was done. He said he wanted all of this crap to be over so he didn't have to deal with me anymore," she admitted. "The thing is I would have done anything he asked. Why did he have to hurt me like that? And what did he think would happen afterward? Did he think he could walk in the next day and ask for a mulligan on the whole relationship thing? Did he think I wouldn't notice that we'd stopped fucking like rabbits?"

"That doesn't sound like the Kai I know," Erin allowed.

"Yeah, well, the Kai I know wouldn't lie to me. He wouldn't use me. He put us all in harm's way. Sarah didn't have to go tonight. She didn't have to fall in deeper with Jared, but Kai insisted because it suited his plans. He didn't think about the rest of us. He didn't care who got hurt as long as he did his job." It was obvious who Kai's loyalties belonged to and it damn straight wasn't her.

"Men get odd when they're working. Especially operatives." Erin seemed strangely calm, as though the events of the evening had soothed her in some way.

"Kai isn't an operative. He's a shrink. He's a yoga-doing, Zen-master shrink. He's not some kind of spy."

"Ah, but he's in the brotherhood and you would do well to remember that. He did his time in the Army. He fought for his country, and no matter how many downward dogs he does now, deep down he'll always be a warrior, and that makes him one of them."

"One of them?"

"The brotherhood," Erin explained. "I like to call it that. I'll be honest, when I first joined up at McKay-Taggart, I almost quit a couple of months in because I know what it feels like to be on the outside of the brotherhood. I've got a vagina so no matter how hard I fight, I'm never really going to be one of them. The Army taught me that. Don't get me wrong. The men I served with never treated me as anything less than one of the team. They valued me. The Army was where I found my worth. But the kind of men who willingly go and risk their lives for our country also tend to be the kind of men who throw themselves over a woman's body when there's a bomb in play. That's the McKay-Taggart guys to a *T*. They will value me for my skills and when the time comes they will also throw my ass into the last lifeboat with their wives and children."

Kori didn't see the problem. "That doesn't sound so bad."

Erin sat back, her head resting against the comfy chair that used to be Theo's. "I grew up trying to be a guy. I was the only girl among a family of men who didn't know what to do with me. Hell, they didn't really want me there at all. Some people would say my childhood bordered on the abusive. I went into the Army right out of high school because that's what all Argents do. I learned how to be a soldier there and it bugged me that the guys in my team protected me. I thought it meant they didn't respect me. I didn't understand how to be a girl until I met Charlotte and Grace and well, everyone. I know it seems like I'm closer to Li than anyone else, but that's because it's easy to talk to him. He's the brother I never had."

"I thought you had a couple."

"I had three. I had three awful, vicious, competitive brothers. Li is the brother I wish I'd had. And he's hiding something from me. I trust him more than anyone in the world and he's lying to me."

Kori knew how that felt. "About what?"

"I have my suspicions," Erin said softly. "Do you know what I'm going to do about it?"

With Erin it could involve violence. Lots of violence. "I think you should talk to him."

"No. I'm not going to talk to him. I'm going to smile and pretend like I don't know and then I'm going to stay the hell out of it because Liam would never hurt me. Case would never hurt me. Ian Taggart would rather die than hurt me. God, I wish I'd figured that out before my Theo died." Tears pierced Erin's eyes, but she held herself with a regal possession. "The men in our lives don't think we're soft when they protect us. They think we're precious. And protecting us can mean more than stopping a bullet. It can mean a lot of things. I look in the mirror the last couple of days and

I no longer recognize myself."

"Erin, you're still you." Kori couldn't imagine how hard this was for Erin to go through. She was still grieving and now she had to deal with a pregnancy. She had to face the reality of being a single mother.

"No, I'm not," Erin argued. "I'm more now. Do you know what my first thought was when I found out I was pregnant?"

"Probably horror and fear." It would be her first thought. She was happy Kai had at least protected her in that way. She wouldn't end up raising a child he didn't want.

"I thought I should get rid of it. I can't raise a baby. I didn't have a mom and my father was a piece of shit. What do I have to give some kid? Theo was the soft one. Don't argue with me about that. I caught him listening to Taylor Swift more than once. Theo was the one who could love and nurture a kid. Then I thought hell, Alex and Eve probably want another kid. I could do that. I would know the baby had a good home."

"Erin, I think you need to give this some time before you make a decision like that." Somehow she knew Erin would change her mind.

"My decision's made. It was made when I laid awake in bed a couple of nights ago and called this piece of Theo inside me TJ."

Kori felt her heart clench. "Theo Jr?"

She nodded. "Theodora if it's a girl. She might hate me for it, but that's her name. I don't think so though. I think it's a boy. When I started calling the baby TJ I realized something. I realized if I was actually going to do this, I have to grow the fuck up. I have to. I can't stay here in this place. I'm not talking about this house. This is my home. It's where he wanted to live so we'll stay here. I'm talking about me. I can't be so angry all the time. I can't rage at people who aren't even here. I can't allow monsters to hold me down anymore. My father was a monster. I'm still afraid of him. I'm afraid there's a part of him in me. It's the part that sees the worst in everything, the part that hates, the part that thinks the worst will always come because I don't deserve any better. The part of me that looked at Theo and thought nothing that beautiful could be true. I never really had a mom. She walked out when I was a tiny kid because she couldn't handle my dad. She left me there, but that doesn't mean I can't be a good mom. I've thought about this a lot. I thought about what I missed out on because she dumped me. I figured it out. Do you know what mothers do, Kori? They slay monsters for their children. Even the ones that live inside them. I'm not your mother, but I know when a person is wrestling with demons. This isn't just about Kai."

The tears were right there, but somehow they wouldn't come out. They sat there behind her eyes, gated and kept inside as though she was hoarding them. "He said he wanted this to be over with so he could end this crap with me."

"He used those words?"

"He told Case that he was happy to help, but this stuff with Kori had to stop. It made him sick. And then he told Case he couldn't keep this up. I don't think he was talking about his dick because he kept that up fine."

One side of Erin's mouth tugged up in a wry grin. "That's good to know. So you're pissed because he said some words that you might have taken out of context."

When had Erin become the damn voice of reason? Before the whole pregnancy thing, Erin would have been right there with her, cheering her on and possibly teaching her how to load a gun. "How the hell else am I supposed to interpret those words, Erin? I appreciate what you're trying to do, but I have to face the facts. He needed me in order to get close to Mia. Instead of asking for my help, he chose to deceive me. I guess he thought getting me into bed would make me more pliable or something. He went too far. He made me think he loved me. It doesn't make sense. Why would they hide this? Why would he do this? Did they know about the fact that Jared might be a serial killer?"

"I suspect so," Erin admitted.

Another betrayal. If they knew Jared could possibly be a killer, then they'd put everyone at Sanctum in harm's way. The Doms were supposed to protect them, not use them for an op. "Then they put us in danger. I get that you all want to find this woman, but there was another way. If all they wanted was Mia's phone, I could have gotten it for them a long time ago. I've been with her in training classes. I've been at her house. I could have done this."

"Which means what? Come on. You're a smart girl." Erin

stared at her and Kori was suddenly happy she'd never been in Erin's crosshairs because there was something deeply predatory about Erin when she got serious. "They put the club in danger. Big Tag had to be in on that. He's a reasonable man. If he thought he could get what he wanted by coming to you and asking you to do him a favor, wouldn't he? He didn't. Instead he kept his mouth shut and put everyone in danger. What does that tell you?"

She thought about it for a moment, a chill going over her skin. "There's something else. There's something bigger that they aren't telling us about."

"Exactly. It's whatever Li's hiding. Whatever keeps Ian locked in his office all day. The old me would barge in and demand to know everything. I would take it all as a sure sign that these people don't trust me. I would be so angry. But TJ's mom has to be more. I have to be the woman Theo thought I could be and that woman has something I've never had in my life. I might have found the one thing that's even better than love."

Kori couldn't think of what that would be. Love had briefly seemed to be everything. She'd relied on friendship to take its place for years, but being "loved" by Kai had blown all of that away. "What's that?"

"Faith," Erin replied softly. "I have faith in the people around me. I have faith that whatever they're doing is out of love for me. I'm going to concentrate on growing this baby. For once in my life, I'm going to trust my family because this one is the best family. This is the family I chose. This is the family I fit into. You fit here, Kori. You're part of this. So it's time to really look at Kai Ferguson. Is he the type of man who would use you?"

"I didn't think so." For so long she'd thought Kai was almost perfect. Even his quirks had called to her. She'd loved the fact that they worked as a couple, even when they'd only been friends.

"Your instincts told you he was solid. All the time you spent working with him told you he is honest and true. Your friendship with him taught you he's a great guy."

Her instincts had told her he was the one. That magical one everyone talked about. "Yes."

Erin's hand drifted down, resting on her belly as though she could already feel the baby growing there. "So why are you letting a couple of words he said change everything? You're actually allowing a few seconds you heard in a hallway to have more weight than all the other time you spent with him. Did you think for a second that maybe what he meant was he wanted you out of the op? That the 'crap with Kori' was about being forced to lie to you? Case could do that to him. Don't forget the brotherhood. They like their secrets, especially when it's all in the name of protecting the womenfolk. Maybe instead of him using you, he leapt at the opportunity to hop into bed with you because he's wanted you forever."

"He told me he loved me." That was the part that hurt the most. She'd opened herself up to him, made herself vulnerable. More vulnerable than she'd ever been before since she'd never said those words to a man. She loved Kai. She probably would always love Kai.

"Maybe he told you that because he loves you," Erin insisted. "Guys like Kai don't normally lie about that. Would you have slept with him if he hadn't said it?"

She could still feel his hands on her body, strong hands that dominated her, caressed her, made her feel alive. "I was having sex with him when he said it."

Erin's lips turned up in a knowing grin. "See. He didn't have to say it at all. At the end of the day, it's your relationship and your choice. You can stand tall and tell him to fuck off and never believe a word he says again. I'm sure that feels like the way to go. I know I did that to Theo more than once. I thought being strong meant telling everyone to fuck off, but I was a scared little girl. Be a strong woman and ask him what he meant. You can give him a chance. Do you have any idea what I would give to have taken that chance before I did? To be able to look back and have had more time with him. But I was stubborn and arrogant and I was so scared. He scared the hell out of me."

Her heart ached for Erin and for herself. For what Erin lost. For what Kori had never really had. "Would you take it back? If you could. Would you go back and erase it all so you don't feel the pain you do now?"

It was an actual ache in her body. The loss of Kai felt like emptiness one minute and agony the next. She wasn't sure how she would get through the next few weeks. How was she going to be able to face him?

"Not a second," Erin said, her face flushed with emotion. "Not one single second. If you would go back and erase Kai from your life, then walk away now because that's not love. If you would do that, then he's not the right man and you can move on. But if he is, then have some faith in him. Have some faith in you."

There was a short knock on the door and then the alarm pinged briefly as it came open. A few more beeps and Big Tag was walking in, his massive shoulders filling the hallway. There was proof that Erin trusted him. He had a key and knew her code.

"Okay, I'm here. Someone want to explain why I'm not springing my brother from the big house?" Ian asked with a frown.

Erin rose to her feet. "Case isn't arrested, the big baby. Besides, jail would do him good. Rough him up a little. Your whole line is soft, Taggart. Did you call Sean to pick him up?"

"Yes, and he was pissed about it. Why can't people get thrown in jail during business hours?" Ian nodded Kori's way. "Hello, Kori. Is there a reason you're running around in the middle of the night without your Master?"

"My Master turned out to be a total douchebag who can bite my ass." She was still thinking about Erin's words. She knew what she'd heard, but did she honestly know what Kai had meant? Was she filtering his words through all the crap from her past? "Maybe. I'm not sure yet."

Ian frowned. "You should talk to him. Kai's usually very careful. If he's fucked up, there's probably a reason for it. He's probably thinking with his dick. I don't do that. My dick is perfectly submissive to my brain."

Erin snorted a little. "Yeah, we all know who's in charge there. Come on and I'll introduce you to the woman who might get us to Hope McDonald."

Ian's expression went completely blank. "I'm listening."

"Hello." Mia walked in, her phone in hand. "My brother would like to talk to you. He thinks you're looking for the same people that he is. Sorry for the whole lying about my name thing and thinking you were part of The Collective."

Ian snorted. "Fuck a duck. Charlie's never going to let me live this down. She said you were too bright to be a part of The Collective. I hate it when she's right. Okay. Let's talk."

He took the phone and started to wander back toward the office.

"I guess now we're out of the loop," Mia said with a frown.

"No." Erin walked back toward her kitchen. "We're in a different loop. You see, I've found the only thing more powerful than the brotherhood is the sisterhood. Who wants some tea? I would offer you tequila, but I'm not drinking for a while."

While Erin boiled water for tea and Mia complained about Case, Kori sat and thought and wondered if she shouldn't call Kai.

Tomorrow. She would face him tomorrow.

Chapter Fifteen

How the fuck late was it? Kai glanced up at the clock, surprised to discover it was only four in the morning. Had it only been a few hours since that horrible moment when he'd realized what Kori had heard?

Had it only been two hours since he'd watched his brother being arrested for murder? It seemed as though he'd been here forever, waiting in this cold, stark room. Seeing Kori's blank face over and over again. He'd tried to call, but she wasn't answering. He'd texted. No reply. Now it was going straight to voice mail.

He sat in the police station on a bench right outside the men's bathroom, his whole body completely numb. What the hell was he supposed to do now?

"All right, here's what's happening." Case sank down on the bench beside him. "I've made a deal with several devils, including one crazy bitch ADA who I have to spank for the next six weeks."

Kai felt his eyes widen. "Maia? You made a deal with Maia?"

Maia Brighton was Derek Brighton's ex-wife and one of Dallas's most ambitious assistant district attorneys. At some point in the next few years, she would very likely be the district attorney. She was also a raging sex addict who knew where all the skeletons were hidden. Ian had allowed her into Sanctum because her contacts often got them out of hot water. But there was always a price with Maia.

Case nodded. "Yes. No sex, but I have to go hard core with her at least twice a week for the next six weeks."

There were several flaws in that scenario. "I don't think your new girlfriend is going to like that."

"Mia was nothing but an op and that op is over," Case said, his jaw stubborn. "I don't have to see her again since apparently now Ian's working with her brother."

"What?"

"Erin stuck her nose in and it turns out Lawless isn't Collective. He thought we were, and Mia's been trying to pin her friend's murder on your brother for years. Ian's going to handle the whole thing from here on out, and Mia's on her way back to Austin in the morning. I won't be seeing her again."

He'd watched Case with the pretty blonde for the last few days. There was no way this was only an op for him. "You like her. You have feelings for that woman. Don't let her go."

Case's head shook slightly as he sat back. "There's nothing to let go. All my feelings for her have to do with the fact that I haven't gotten laid in months. She's not my type. Hell, I don't think I have a type. I'm not cut out for the relationship thing. Besides, I've got to concentrate on Erin and the baby. I don't need that blonde fucking up my life. So the deal I made with Maia, who made a deal with the DA. It included getting a judge up at this time of night to set bail for Jared. Harrison got the judge to agree that the press will swarm once they hear about Jared's arrest and it's better for everyone if we get him out of jail and into a private residence where the city doesn't have to worry about liability. I swear I don't get the lawyer crap. Once Mitch and Harrison started talking about liability and something called optics, the DA caved like a wilting flower."

Because Jared would likely not do well in prison. Even

overnight. There would be a circus by morning because there was no way this news didn't get out. The press would be at the door. Hollywood executives would be calling in all their favors. Fans would show up outside the damn jail in order to get a glimpse of their hero.

What a fucking nightmare.

"So he's getting out in the morning?" It would be one less thing he would have to worry about. He couldn't stand the thought of his brother sitting in a prison cell. It wasn't right. No matter what Rush thought he had on Jared, Kai knew he was innocent.

"Do you honestly believe I would have given up six weeks for the morning? Like I said, the judge got his ass out of bed once Maia got on the phone with him. Apparently she's got shit on a couple of judges and she's not afraid to use it. Everything's already finished. Jared will be coming out in a few minutes and I'll drive you home. He's been released on a million dollars bail and into our safekeeping. He's not allowed to leave the state. Bail's already been posted and he's being processed out."

That was one issue down. At least his brother wouldn't spend days in jail. "So Harrison has agreed to take the case?"

Kai had worked with Mitch in the past, but this was a criminal case. Mitch was their go-to lawyer for all things business. Harrison Keen was the criminal defense attorney. Kai had been a bit scared Harrison was only here to make sure Case was fine. He'd been sitting on this stupid bench looking up attorneys.

Because he had to find a way to help his brother.

"Of course," Case replied. "Why do you think he's here? The minute we found that body I knew Rush was going to do anything he could to pin it on Jared. He's got a hard-on for your brother. I don't even know what evidence they have on him yet."

"Nothing," a deep voice said.

Kai looked up and Harrison Keen was walking down the hallway looking pristine and perfect in a three-piece suit. He was a large, muscular man with broad shoulders and stark green eyes. His deep black hair was slicked back and he carried what was likely a designer briefcase. Everything about the man was polished to perfection, his whole presentation screaming power.

Kai had seen him in nothing but boy shorts and a leather collar, being whipped by his Domme of the night. Everyone had their kinks. No one was truly as they seemed. He'd learned that long ago.

God, he hoped Kori knew that not every word should be taken at face value.

"They've got nothing on Jared but a couple of eyewitnesses who say they saw him walking out of the hallway that led to the bathroom where Lena was killed," Harrison explained. "It's the thinnest piece of shit case I've ever seen. They don't have prints or a weapon. They don't even have CCTV coverage of the doors to the bathrooms. He was walking down a hall."

"How can they arrest him for that?" Case asked.

Harrison shrugged. "Mitch heard a rumor that one of Jared's friends told the feds Jared and Lena have been fighting and that Jared had threatened to kill her. It's complete speculation. There hasn't been time to run any evidence yet. This is all bullshit and Mitch is ready to sue the department for false arrest once they admit they've made a mistake. Ah, there he is."

Kai looked down the hallway and his brother was walking toward him. He'd never seen Jared look so grim. There was a darkness to his eyes that made Kai wonder what the hell had happened. Jared stared blankly past him and it hit Kai that no one was waiting on Jared. All those people who clung to him, who fed off him had fled. They were likely back in the hotel suites Jared paid for and they'd taken the limo he'd rented to do it. Jared—who always seemed to need people around him—was completely alone for the first time since he'd come to Dallas. No friends. No employees. None of them had called him a lawyer. Apparently one of them had tried to pin this on him.

But he had his brother. For the first time in forever, Kai was going to make sure that Jared had his brother.

"Thank you for getting me out of there." He held his hand out to Harrison, who shook it.

"The pleasure is mine," he said with a smile that reminded Kai of a hungry tiger. "I look forward to taking this one on. Jared, you understand the terms of your release?"

Jared stopped, briefly looking Harrison's way. "I do. I won't leave the city. I'll check in with…who am I checking in with?"

"His name is Simon Weston. He's going to be the McKay-

Taggart contact," Harrison explained. "He and his partner are already on the case. They'll want to talk to you in the morning. Hey, you can watch them work and maybe get some research out of it while they clear you."

"I won't need it. The production company will fire me in the morning. I'll be lucky to come out of this with my TV job intact," he stated flatly. "They'll likely fire me, too. Or the network will cancel the show and everyone will be out of work."

"You didn't do this," Harrison replied. "If they fire you, we'll sue them."

Jared shook his head. "Doesn't work that way in Hollywood. Oh, we can sue and they'll pass me some cash, but my career is over. I'll always be a killer to some people no matter what the outcome is. The cloud will never go away. I'm going to catch a cab and find a hotel. Mr. Keen, if you could send me a bill for your services tonight, I'll pay it. I'll find my own lawyer tomorrow."

Jared pulled his phone out of his pocket and started walking toward the front of the station.

Kai turned to Harrison. "He doesn't know what he's saying. We need you on this case."

Harrison shook his head. "Explain to him that he needs to talk to Big Tag. Until Big Tag fires me, I'm not off the case. That is one Dom I'm not about to piss off. Night all. I'll be in contact in the morning."

"Fuck," Case said with a frown. "They can't fire him. Can they?"

Kai was already moving, following his brother. "I'm sure they can. Go on ahead of us. I'll get my brother home."

"No can do," Case shot back. "I promised Ian I would see you home safely. He put up the million for Jared's bond."

Shit. Although it made sense because how the hell had Jared been expected to do it in the middle of the night with no one helping him. "I'll make sure Ian gets his money back."

"He's not worried about that, damn it. He's worried about you. He's worried about you and your brother. Sean brought my truck up here so I'll pull it around and I'll wait for you in the front. Talk to Jared and then you need to get your girl because she was pissed and right now she's at Erin's. I can only imagine how that's going to go for you. Erin could be teaching her how to take your balls off."

He didn't have time to worry about that right now. One massive cluster fuck at a time. It's what his life had become. He needed to deal with his brother first and then he would figure out how screwed he was with Kori.

Kori, his sweet girl with so many walls he'd only barely managed to climb the first couple. She was likely erecting more. Higher walls. Stronger walls. These walls would be fortified against him.

Did he even deserve a second chance with her? He stalked out of the station and saw his brother staring down at his phone.

He'd walked away and left Jared alone. What would Ian have done if he'd found Sean with a woman Ian thought he'd loved? Would he have walked away and never spoken to his brother again? Or would he have beaten the shit out of Sean, dumped the girl, and started over again?

Because they were family.

For so long family had seemed like a cross to be borne, like a stone dragging him down. He couldn't look at his brother without seeing their mother in her hospice bed, wasting away. There'd been nothing to do. No magic tricks, no amount of discipline and work had made her better. Tired. He'd been so fucking tired. Tired of poverty. Tired of worry. Tired of the feeling in his gut that he was useless. He'd walked away the first chance he'd gotten and he hadn't looked back.

"Jared?"

"I'm not leaving town," Jared said, his voice tight. "I know your friend put up the cash for my bail. I'll have it back to him in the morning. I'm going to a hotel. I won't leave until my new lawyer says I can. You're safe. Your friends are safe, so you can leave me the fuck alone."

What had happened? "I don't think I deserve that. I'm trying to help you."

Jared turned, his eyes staring right into Kai's. "Are you? Or are you helping the FBI?"

He was going to kill Ethan Rush. "Jared, I have never once believed you did this."

"Five women. Five women I liked. Five women I spent time

with and talked to and thought they used me. They hadn't. They couldn't fucking call because they were dead. Someone's killing the women around me and you didn't bother to mention that you were a part of an investigation into me. I thought you were finally ready to talk. I thought, wow, after all this time Kai's going to show me the ropes. He's willing to be part of my life in some way. I should have known the only way you would ever let me back in was for some revenge."

"This isn't about revenge, Jared. Goddamn it, you're never going to believe me, but I was going to tell you about the investigation tomorrow. Today. I don't know. I was going to lay it all out for you, but I owed some people first."

"Of course. Everyone comes before me," Jared agreed sullenly.

"Don't pull that shit on me. I spent my whole childhood putting you first."

"And didn't I know it?" Jared shot back. "Do you think I didn't hear you tell your friends how much a burden I was, how you wished I didn't exist half the time?"

"I didn't mean it. Or maybe I did, but I was a kid, Jared. I was a child trying to fill an adult role. I also loved you. Maybe I didn't show it enough, but I loved you. You were my brother. I'm sorry for what happened that day with Hannah. I can see now that you were acting out, trying to get my attention, and the truth of the matter is you deserved my attention. After Mom died, I shut down. I left you with Aunt Glenna and I shouldn't have. I should have found another way to make money."

Jared's eyes narrowed, the first hint of dark emotion he could remember seeing in his brother. "Yes, you left me with Aunt Glenna. Such a lovely woman. Did you know she pimped me out to her friends? She took all the money and the only way I could stay in the house was if I entertained her friends. It was subtle at first. Just talk to them for a while. No big deal. And then one of them made a move on me. I turned her down. Our sweet aunt explained that if I didn't fuck her friend she would kick me out."

Kai felt like his whole world flipped over. "What?"

"She turned me into a whore," Jared enunciated. "She did it to move up in her world. She said she was an event planner, but what she actually did was provide escort services for some of the wealthiest women on the West Coast. When she realized what a gold mine I was, she wasn't about to let go."

"What?" Kai could remember coming home and screaming at Jared for wasting money on designer clothes and all the shit he had in his room. Now it made sense. His brother didn't care about suits. He preferred jeans and T-shirts. "Why wouldn't you tell me?"

"I was ashamed. Why wouldn't I tell you? Let's see. Why wouldn't I tell my high and mighty judgmental brother that I was stupid enough to get caught in a trap? I didn't even realize what was happening. Why wouldn't I tell you I was a whore? Because I knew what would happen. You would walk away from me. It still fucking happened."

"Was Hannah a client?"

Jared laughed, but there was no humor at all in the sound. "No. Hannah was a drunken mistake. I met her at a bar. I wanted to obliterate myself. I wanted to get so fucking numb I couldn't feel anything. And Hannah walked in and we started talking about you. That was the good part. The bad part was waking up and realizing what I'd done. The whole night was a blur but I did it. I know I did it. I can remember thinking I wanted a couple of moments that were mine. I wanted a woman who knew me, who wanted me and not some image she had in her head of me. How foolish do you think I felt the next morning? When I woke up and realized it had all been about you and I'd finally done something worse than selling myself for a roof over my head?"

"Jared, I had no idea." Because he hadn't bothered to truly know his brother. Because he'd been like everyone else in Jared's life. He'd seen the handsome exterior and fooled himself into thinking there wasn't anything else there. He hadn't wanted anything else to be there. After watching his mother die, he'd wanted to not care. He'd managed for years and years.

Jared turned, staring out into the night. "It doesn't matter now. I left the day after you did. I packed a bag and walked out and I slept on the streets for a month or so before I got my first contract. Squirrel went with me. Only person in the fucking world who ever cared about me."

"Jared, I'm sorry. I'm so fucking sorry I didn't see it. I didn't see what was happening to you, and I damn straight didn't look closely enough at what was happening to me. I distanced. I retreated after Mom died." It was so easy to see what he'd done now.

"She died on me, too. She died on me and when I turned around to the only family I had left, you were gone."

"I know. I did that," Kai agreed. "I've been doing it ever since. I'm the asshole in this play, Jared. I find it easier to care about strangers than my own brother because their problems are intellectual. I don't have to feel them. I don't have to care. I don't have to wonder if they're going to walk out on me. If they're going to die on me."

Jared shook his head. "The work you do is good. Don't sell that short. You're successful."

"Successful? I'm only here because Big Tag believes in my work. Hell, I can barely afford the building I'm in. I had to take a loan out. A couple of months ago I had an anonymous donor give us enough to keep going for a while, but if I don't keep finding ways to fund the practice, I'm going to lose it all."

"You won't." Jared cursed as though remembering something bad he'd forgotten. "Fuck, or maybe you will now."

There was something in the way Jared said it that made Kai wonder. "I rely on several charity groups for funding."

"No. I've been funding you since the explosion at Sanctum."

Why did that suddenly not surprise him? He didn't have to ask why his brother hadn't told him. He knew. Jared had been afraid Kai would have turned the money down if he'd known where it came from. And he might have. He wouldn't now. He couldn't. "Then I need to thank you for that. I need to thank you and I need to apologize."

Jared's head shook again. "No. Not so fast. Not until you've heard everything. Let me lay it all out for you, brother. I've been lying. I've been in the lifestyle for years. After what happened at home, my first agent took me and Squirrel in. She let us stay in her guesthouse and after a few months, she invited me to go to her club. At first I thought, well, you know what I thought."

He'd thought he was going to have to work for his room and board all over again. "That's not the way our world works. She'd seen you needed the training, hadn't she?"

"I was lost. I was so fucking out of control but I couldn't admit it."

When he thought about it, he could see what his mind had hidden. "You were never out of control. You might have felt that way, but even at a young age, you were in control. You never got angry. Mom talked about it. One year all you got for Christmas was a couple of used toys and you sat there and I thought you would throw a fit, but you got up and hugged her and thanked Santa Claus."

Jared leaned against the railing, his shoulders slumping as though tired of carrying so much weight. "I knew there wasn't a Santa, but she liked to pretend."

Now that he looked past his own issues it was easy to see that there were a hundred times when Jared could have lost control. "She cried that night. She told me it would have been easier if you'd thrown a fit. If you acted like a brat she could have held it together."

"She told you all that? I shouldn't be surprised. You were her partner. After Dad left, she turned to you. That wasn't fair."

Something lifted deep inside him, some stupid piece of him that needed acknowledgement. Some selfish piece left over from childhood. He hadn't realized it, but there had been some small part of him that required that Jared know what he'd sacrificed. The minute he had what he needed, he realized the truth. "Life wasn't fair to any of us. I'm so sorry. I should have stayed. I should have kicked your ass and sat down and figured out what was going on because my brother wouldn't have done that to me if he'd been in his right mind."

It seemed to Kai that there was an awful lot about his brother that Jared had hidden. Had he hidden those things because he'd been ashamed? Because he'd been desperate for Kai to accept him?

"I never once in all of this believed that you could have hurt those women. Not for one second. I kept it from you because there's more at stake than you and me and I have to beg you to understand that I can't talk about it. Not because I don't trust you, but because I made a promise. I'm going to make another one. I'm going to stop being an arrogant, unforgiving asshole and start being your big brother. So listen up. You will get in that truck with me and Case and you'll go home with me. You will accept Harrison as your lawyer and you and I are going to fight this with everything we have. You will not give up. Not on yourself and not on the career you've built. They can't hold us down. Not if we go into this together."

He'd been so stupid. He'd been foolish and hurt and selfish and he'd wasted so much damn time. He'd wasted time with Jared and he'd wasted time with Kori. He should have wrapped her up in his arms the minute he'd met her. He should have pulled her close and thanked god he'd finally found her.

He should have thanked god he hadn't been alone anymore. He should have figured out that he'd never been alone. Not really.

He moved in and faced his brother. He was so fucking intellectual. It had been his refuge, a way for him to rise above the misery he'd been born into, but now he could see it had been a wall, too. His childhood hadn't been all misery. It had simply been easier to see it that way because losing his mother had been so painful. He'd lumped Jared in with that loss and walked away. He'd held everyone off until one little brat had wormed her way into his soul, and now he couldn't hold back a second more. Kori was in his heart, and his heart suddenly seemed like such a massive, open thing, full and yet wanting more.

He put his arms around his brother and hugged him close.

This, this was what he should have done that day. He should have hugged his brother and asked him why he was acting so out of character. He should have had some faith.

Jared was still for a moment, his body unmoving, but it didn't take him long before his brother wound his arms around him and a shudder went through Jared.

"It's so fucked up, Kai." His brother squeezed him tight.

"We'll make it right," Kai vowed. He would get his brother out of this. He would do whatever it took as long as it didn't hurt the only person in the world he had to put above all others—his love, his other half, his Kori.

Jared took a step back. "All right. I'll do what you want. But you have to do something for me."

"Anything." After all this time, he owed Jared something.

"Go after Kori. I saw the look in her eyes. You can't wait. She's angry and you have to make it right."

"I don't know that there's any way I can make it right."

Perhaps this was payback for all the years of turning his back on his brother. Maybe it was nothing more than he deserved.

Case pulled up, his big truck taking a large portion of the round drive. "Let's go. I'm supposed to head over to Ian's after I drop you two off. I swear to god I'm not getting any sleep tonight."

"Maybe we should drop my brother off at Kori's," Jared said, swinging his body into the cab.

And wake up Erin? Not even he was that much of a sadist. "I'll see her tomorrow."

He hoped.

Chapter Sixteen

Kai stared at the computer. Every single news headline stated the same thing. Jared Johns arrested for murder. TV hero kills assistant. Hollywood actor slays women.

God, it was a bloodbath.

He flipped the computer closed and went back to staring at the screen that hadn't pinged once all night or morning. His phone. Kori hadn't called. She hadn't texted. She hadn't sent him an e-mail.

He loved her. He knew he'd fucked up royally, but what could he do about it if she wouldn't talk to him? And didn't that say something about the way she felt about him?

"You still waiting for her to call?" Jared asked, walking into the kitchen. Baby brother looked worse for the wear this morning, his hair all askew and his eyes tired. He moved toward the coffeepot. Usually Kori had already booted the thing up by now and was working on her second cup.

"Call back. I've left her many messages. I don't think calling her again will help. Did you sleep at all? I thought you didn't touch caffeine." He watched as his brother navigated the coffee machine with the ease of an expert.

Jared popped the cup into the mechanism and pressed the screen. "That was when I had a career. The good news about no longer having a job is that I can eat and drink whatever I like. Can we get pizza at this time of the morning? Do you know how fucking long it's been since I had pizza? And like five burgers with real, actual cheese on them. I'm going to need a bunch of sugar and cream for this coffee. Oh, and we need to have someone deliver a case of beer. I'm going through that tonight."

"I thought you told Kori you loved cheesecake and pasta."

"I love them," Jared shot back. "And I totally lied about eating them. No one wants to know how hard it is to keep this body. I have to stay relatable and that means lying about eating pizza and cheesecake. The great news is I don't have to do that anymore. I can be really relatable and gain fifty pounds of pure flab."

When had his sunny brother turned into Mr. Pessimism? Probably right around the time he'd been falsely accused of murder. Kai didn't like it. Jared was supposed to be the eternally optimistic one. "You don't know that. Have you talked to the network? Hell, for that matter, have you talked to your agent?"

"Earlier this morning. He explained he couldn't work with me anymore. At least he had the decency to actually talk to me on the phone. Tad texted me his resignation. Said it wouldn't look right for him to stay. And then he sent me a teary emoticon. I want to punch him in the face."

Kai could totally understand that, but it might have to wait. "Karma is your friend in this, brother. Just wait and he'll end up getting his. Let Simon and Jesse do their jobs. You never know. Maybe Tad killed her. Or his brother."

Someone in Jared's entourage had offed Lena. There was no question in his mind. The only real question was why. He'd thought about it all night long and well into this morning.

"Karma stinks then." Jared opened the fridge and rooted around until he came back with a carton of milk. "I try hard to do the right thing. I give money to charity. A lot of it. I visit sick kids. I try to help the people around me. You know what I get? Arrested for murder. Awesome. Yay, fucking universe. Where's the sugar?"

"Cupboard above the coffeepot." Where Kori had stashed it. "Sometimes the world works in mysterious ways. Just because you're down doesn't..."

"Mean you're out." They finished their mom's favorite phrase together, a moment of harmony only siblings could understand.

No one else in the whole world knew what it meant to be loved by their mom. No one knew what their shared world had been like. He'd pushed his brother away for a lot of reasons, some understandable, others selfish. Only now did he realize what he'd missed. He'd missed the comfort of familiarity, the warmth of understanding.

"I miss her. Every day," Jared said solemnly.

Grief welled inside Kai, as pure and visceral as it had been the day she'd died. His mother had been complex, as complicated in her methods and meanings as any human being. She'd made decisions that put them all in a hard place, and yet she'd managed to give them exactly what they needed. Love. Each other.

Take care of your brother, Kai. He needs you more than you know.

She could have said something different, likely would have if she could have seen the future.

Take care of your brother, Kai. You'll need him more than you know.

"I do, too. Jared, you won't believe me, but I missed you, too."

Jared nodded. "I do. You were always a little slow."

Kai laughed and thanked god he'd had a brother because a sister would have made that moment way too real. He stood up and shook his head. "Yeah, that's me. Is there any coffee in that coffee?"

Jared spooned in way more sugar than any adult should start their day with. "Doesn't matter. I no longer have a trainer either. Besides, if I get really fat, maybe no one will want me to be their bitch in prison."

"You're not going to prison. And you would still have that face. You would totally still be someone's bitch. No way around how pretty you are."

That got Jared grinning. "I can't help it. I was born this way."

"I'm not letting you go to prison. I've already talked to Harrison this morning. You have to let him help you."

Jared nodded. "I will and I'll answer any questions the McKay-

Taggart guys want me to. I've been thinking a lot about this. I'm sick over it. I knew those women. I liked them."

"Yes and that's a key. That's something they all had in common. I need you to think about them and your relationships with them. What else did they all have in common?"

Jared held up a hand. "But that's what doesn't make sense. I had flings with those women. Most of them brief, one of them lasted a month or so. I've never touched Lena. Not once in my life. She's not even close to being my type. It's one of the reasons I hired her. I didn't want to get attached. So why break the pattern now?"

"Unless she figured something out. Or she challenged him. I'm going to go back over all the files and see if I can come up with something. The obvious fact is this is a man who hates women."

"Or he hates me in particular. With the exception of Lena, losing every single one of those women hurt me. Everyone around me knows my 'call me' rule. When they didn't call, I got hurt. What if this is all being done to hurt me? It seems to me I'm the real common denominator in this equation."

Kai stared at his brother, wondering who the hell had said something so very insightful.

Jared rolled his eyes. "I've got a brain, Kai. I just don't have to use it often."

Not often at all. It was refreshing. "I think you're right. In fact, I was thinking about this last night and while I believe this man hates women, I think he hates you, too."

"Well, then take a closer look at Brad and Tad because Squirrel is practically in love with me. We've been friends for so long we're like an old married couple."

But old married couples could get jealous. Old married couples sometimes found all that love and familiarity turning into hate. "When was the last time Squirrel had a girlfriend? Any of them, really?"

Jared thought about it for a moment. "Brad usually has a girlfriend in LA, but he cheats any time we're on the road. And it's not like the arrangement I have with Jess."

"What is the arrangement with Jess?" How could he have forgotten about Jessica Hamilton? Jared's super-couple other half? Somehow it was easy to forget her since Jared rarely mentioned the woman he spent much of his off time with. She was a stunning beauty. He'd seen her on the covers of magazines. What if she wanted to take her relationship with Jared past their arrangement? Would she kill to do it?

Jared sighed. "I'm telling you this because you're my brother and I trust you, but don't ever mention this to anyone else. Jess has some issues with her sexual identity that she would rather not explain to the press. I like women I would rather not expose to the press. We came up with the idea of helping each other a couple of years back and it's worked quite well. Every now and then I'll get caught talking to some woman, but Jess always goes out and explains that she loves and trusts me and it dies down."

That was a lot for a woman of her station to take on. But there was also the issue of timing. From what Kai understood, Jessica hadn't known Jared when the killings began. Unless she was obsessed with him. God knew plenty of teenaged girls had been. They'd shown up at the house at all hours of the day trying to get his attention. "What is the identity issue she's dealing with? Is she a lesbian, because that's quite accepted in Hollywood today. Given that she tends to star in intellectual films, I would be surprised if she would lose work over that."

"She's asexual."

"Ah," Kai said, understanding the issue. There was a small amount of the populace that simply didn't have any kind of a sex drive nor did they find themselves sexually attracted to either gender. It was oft discussed as to whether this was nature or nurture, so to speak, but admitting she was so far out of the status quo likely would bring her unwanted attention. "I understand. And you're sure she's not in love with you?"

Asexual people could love as easily as anyone else. They simply didn't care for sexual intimacy. Kai wouldn't eliminate her because of her preferences though.

"It's not Jess. She's in Hong Kong filming as we speak. I doubt she flew here, killed Lena, and then made it back for AM call. I want to know who told the feds Lena and I had that fight. Because we didn't. She told me she needed to talk to me about firing someone. I avoided her. That's not a fight." His cell trilled and Jared frowned again. He stared down at the screen. "This is my private line. No one has this number. I crushed my professional line earlier because it's nothing but reporters. How do I know that number? Janice. Shit. I think that's Janice. My old publicist. I've got to take this."

Jared put the phone to his ear and stepped out.

Kai looked back down at his cell. Shit. Nothing. He picked it up and quickly texted.

Are you coming to work?

Kori always had her cell with her. Maybe if he kept it professional, she would reply. He waited a minute and then two more. Nothing.

She was done with him. A few thoughtless words and she was through. Guess her feelings hadn't been as strong as he'd thought.

He had to face some real truths. She'd lied to him about what she wanted. She was a masochist. He'd never once lied about being a sadist. They were a match to have at the very least played together. Yet she'd stayed away from him, preferring other dominant partners. Maybe she'd been looking for an out. He'd threatened her that first night. He hadn't meant to, but the fact that she'd been lying to every partner she played with could have gotten her escorted out of Sanctum. He might have played that to his advantage because he was a selfish bastard who'd wanted her so badly he couldn't stand it. She'd seen the opportunity to get out of the relationship with her Sanctum membership intact and she'd taken it.

But she'd said I love you.

Kori didn't lie. She couldn't be bothered to. If she'd said it, then she meant it, and not in terms of "I love what you do to me." She'd said I love you and that meant she loved him.

So why was she ignoring him?

Talk to me, he texted her. *Please talk to me.*

He sat and stared at the screen as though he could will her to reply. The phone buzzed in his hand.

I'll be in the office in an hour. We do need to talk. I don't know how we move past this.

He took a deep breath. Okay. At least she was replying to texts. He would give her that for now. *We will move past this. I love you. No matter what you heard, I love you. Let me try to explain.*

I'll be there soon. Just got home and have to deal with your brother's friend first. As soon as I've figured out what he wants, I'll be there.

Jared's friend? *Who's there, baby? I don't want you opening the door to anyone. Anyone.*

It's the weird one. He's trying to find out if we saw Lena last night. Don't be a drama queen. I'm not alone.

So Erin or someone else was likely with her. He could breathe a bit easier. Still, he wanted to know what the hell Jared's friend wanted with Kori. Squirrel didn't need to be running around trying to do the cops' jobs.

The door opened again and Jared walked back in, an odd smile on his face. "That was Janice. I told you about her. She was my publicist when I first started out. She's in LA with Bernie, my old agent. They called to say I wasn't alone and they'll take over now. She's fielding calls and Bernie talked to the production company for my TV show. I still have a job for now. He's going to put in a call about the movie, but he's optimistic."

Ah, there it was. Sweet karma at work. "I'm glad. I really am. But I think I'm going to head over to Kori's. She said she's coming to the office, but I would feel better if I could see her."

"Of course." Jared crossed his arms over his chest and seemed to come to some decision. "I like Kori, but you're my brother so I'm going to tell you some things I know about her."

"What things?"

"There were rumors back in the day that she was involved in a Master/slave relationship with a producer who used her."

"She told me." Thank god. For a moment he thought his brother was going to bring some dirt up on her.

"She likely didn't tell you how bad it got. Morgan King is still an exec on *Dart*. He's an asshole of the highest level, and I deal with Hollywood assholes so let me tell you it's a whole new level. What everyone talks about behind his back is the fact that without his former writing partner, he's useless as anything but a moneyman. Kori was the brains of that operation and he basically traded her in for a thinner, more acceptable model. Kori was a good business partner, but not wife material. He never took her on the red carpet, not even when they were together. He would walk it alone rather than hold her hand. He lied to her about pretty much everything, and the rumor is that he stole her last script and gave it to his new wife."

Kai would really like to meet this man. Preferably in a dark alley. "How can he do that?"

"He had all the power and she chose not to fight him. I'll be honest, at the time she likely would have been crushed. She could have gone to her union, but he was too powerful. No one wanted to take him on because he was involved in so many hot productions. He could have lawyered her to death and she wouldn't have been able to find work. I'm only telling you this because she was brilliant. She wrote stuff you would never watch, but there was such humanity in them. You don't expect that out of horror films or action films, but she put it in there. She should be writing. It's a gift, and her not using it makes me sad. I don't know what went down between the two of you last night, but she's got reason to be distrustful. You need to be open and honest with her."

And there was the problem. "And what if I can't?"

"Why wouldn't you?"

He couldn't be completely honest with Jared either. "What if I made promises to other people?"

"Are those other people more important than she is?" Jared asked.

"No, but I promised."

"And you wouldn't be Kai if you broke that. I understand. I guess we have to hope she does, too. I've got a meeting with Harrison in an hour or so. Maybe he's figured out who spread those rumors about me. I'd like to know if it was Brad or Tad."

"Or Squirrel." He wasn't willing to eliminate anyone.

"It's not Squirrel. Of all the people in the world, he's the least likely to be a serial killer. Come on. I've practically lived with the man since we were teens. Wouldn't I have seen something? Wouldn't there have been a rash of girls being murdered back in high school?"

An idea started to play around in Kai's brain. "Serial killers tend to start small. They often start by torturing small animals." And around the time they were teens, there had been a rash of small animals reported as missing in their neighborhood. Kai and Jared's, not Squirrel's. And they'd lived in a poor neighborhood. Pets went missing. They got out of crappy fences and got lost.

Or they got caught by the blossoming killer.

Kai stood up, the hair on his arms standing on end as he remembered some of the things Jared's best friend had said. Not to him but to Kori. She'd mentioned it because she'd thought it was odd and she'd been annoyed at the time. He'd asked about Kori's car, saying something about how he'd been surprised that it hadn't been Kai's. That had been the day after Kori's tires had been slashed. She'd told Kai she'd wished it had been his car, too.

"What are you doing?" Jared moved in behind him as he started to pull up his search engine.

He typed in the name of his neighborhood and the years between Jared's last year of high school and the time he got signed on for *Dart* and the words missing girls. "Following my instincts."

He waited for a minute while the screen whirled, pulling up stats and news stories. He had to move around because there were years of data but he came up with two names. "Do you know these women? Emily Glass and Patsy Huss?"

Jared leaned over. "I went to school with Emily, and Patsy was a model in the first agency I signed with. I lost touch with Emily, and Patsy left the agency."

"They went missing. Patsy's body was found three years ago with the same MO as the other women. Emily was raped and only saved because a couple of joggers came along. Jared, did you have a relationship with these women?"

Jared had taken a step back, his face going white. "He wouldn't. He's my best friend. He's the only person in the world I've been able to count on."

But sometimes those people went bad. And now that man was at Kori's. Oh, he might be after Sarah, but he wouldn't hesitate to kill Kori. Kai stood. There was no time to waste.

"Sarah," Jared said. His phone was already in his hand.

Kai's was too. He dialed Kori's number as he moved toward the front door. Nothing. He went straight to voice mail. At least he was fairly certain someone had gone with her. Erin wouldn't have let her leave alone.

That was when he got the text from Big Tag. *Your sub needs a* spanking. *Get to her place because she and Sarah snuck out of here and I've got a meeting. Tell Sarah she's up shit creek and I will find a Dom with a paddle for her.*

"Shit." She was there alone. She was there with a killer.

"I'm calling the cops," Jared said, following him.

Kai started running. They would need the cops because there was no way he allowed anyone to touch his sub.

He'd played the spy this week. But it was time to be a warrior again.

* * * *

Kori stepped inside her place with a heavy heart. How long would she stay here? How long before this house was nothing more than a memory and the people she'd come to care for were distant and faint in her head?

What was she going to do? Go and pack and run right this second because she was such a damn child that she was going to let another man run her out of her own fucking life?

She might have spent too much time with Erin. And Charlotte Taggart and Chelsea Weston, who had shown up for breakfast this morning. Phoebe Murdoch had been there, laughing and joking about how tired Big Tag looked. They were all waiting on Drew Lawless, who was flying in and was planning on meeting them.

"I think we're going to get in trouble for this," Sarah said with a sigh. "Like real, not erotic trouble."

"You didn't have to come with me."

"Yeah, I did. If you're going to defy the Doms and do something stupid, then I am obligated to be stupid with you." She set her purse on the bar. She was still wearing her clothes from last night, which she tried and failed to smooth out. "I think I'm going to argue that we've had enough punishment. We had to do the walk of shame public transportation style. I had a guy offer me a hundred bucks for a hummer. Ewww. I would charge way more than that."

"Yes, you should." Coffee. She would be putting on some coffee at work right now. Kai wouldn't drink it. She would put a kettle on for his tea because apparently proper tea didn't come from K-cups, the pretentious bastard.

He would have to make his own tea. It was okay. He was a big boy.

"There was another reason I had to come," Sarah admitted.

Kori could guess. "You have to be at work in a couple of hours."

"I got Lila Daley to swap shifts with me. No. I had to come to make sure you're still here at the end of the night. I heard what you said to Erin."

"You were listening in?"

"It's a hobby," she admitted. "Also, no one tells me shit. I know you don't tell me shit because I gossip like a schoolgirl, but you have to know I wouldn't gossip about this. Kori, there's no way Kai meant what he said."

She'd heard this argument. She was still considering it, but she didn't particularly want to talk about it at the moment. "It doesn't matter. I've been thinking about finding a new job for a while."

"What are you going to do now? Sling some burgers?" Sarah frowned her way. "Oh, maybe you can get a job as a maid."

"My mother was a maid. I'm not sure where you're going with this."

"There's nothing wrong with hard work, but this isn't your job. It's not what you were born to do. I've seen your movies."

She felt her cheeks go pink. "I told you not to watch those."

"Yeah, well, as we've learned this morning, I don't always follow orders," Sarah pointed out. "I've watched all of your movies because you're my best friend and that means I'm your biggest fan. You're so good. You're funny and real and I love your characters and I want to know why you're wasting it all? Why would you throw away your career and god, I need to understand why you would throw away Kai. I need to know those things because I'm pretty sure you're also ready to throw away me."

"It's not like that." But wasn't it? Hadn't she had friends in California that she'd distanced from? They'd done nothing wrong, but she'd stopped calling, stopped sending e-mails.

She'd simply stopped. Was she doing that again?

"I think it is. Serena gave you that script last week. Have you even picked it up? You told her you would help, but you shoved it to the side."

Guilt sat in her gut over that. She knew she should be further along. "I read it. I made a few notes."

"Then why haven't you called her?"

Because getting back into that world meant opening herself up again. "You don't understand what it's like."

Sarah stared at her. "Then tell me. Make me understand why you would ignore such an obvious gift. I thought about it all night. I think everything comes back to what happened to you in Hollywood. It's why you won't fight now."

"I was criticized every single day."

Sarah shook her head. "You had a shitty Master."

"It wasn't just Morgan. It's everyone. You put your heart and soul into your work every day and once a year you get called in for a performance review with your boss. I got fifteen performance reviews every hour of every day, and it's all on the Internet. My dialogue is stupid. The plot of this film desperately needed to find a writer whose head wasn't stuck up her ass. Do you know what that's like? And every minute of every day I was terrified that it would all be over."

There was very little sympathy in Sarah's stare. "That's tough on you. No one in the whole world has ever had that happen."

"Don't be a bitch." Very few people had to deal with that level of scrutiny.

Sarah waved her off. "I'm simply saying that we all have our issues. You had the greatest job in the world. You got to make a living doing what most people would kill to do. You don't see Jared out there crying and quitting because some people think his show is stupid. That man gets told every single day that he's a bad actor. Guess what—he doesn't believe them. He gets up and does his job and he's thankful for it."

"No, apparently he murders people when the going gets tough." Kori closed her eyes in shame. "I didn't mean that."

"I'm glad because he didn't do this and if he'll let me, I'm going to stand by him. I care about him and damn it, I'm going to fight for what I want," Sara said passionately. "I'm never going to let a few shitty voices stop me. And I've read your reviews. You don't mention the ones where they talk about how much they loved the script, how close they felt to the characters, how the films you wrote gave people something to think about other than the bad things happening in their lives. God, Kori, you don't get the gift without the curse. It doesn't work that way. You don't throw away the gift because it comes with some strings. And you don't throw away a man like Kai because you're still a scared girl who thinks no man will ever love you. Love is hard. Love isn't guaranteed. It's something you work at and you fight for. Happily ever after is something you earn every damn day of your life. You want it easy. There's no such thing."

Emotion welled inside her. "But I did this. I let myself be controlled. You're right. I wanted it easy. When I first started my relationship with Morgan, I think I wanted him to take over everything. I wanted to do nothing but write. I didn't care that he took most of the credit because I lost myself in it. It was the first time I felt free." Because she'd had to deal with parents who fought constantly. Because she'd thought the worst thing in the world was listening to her mom and dad fight until she'd been forced to listen to the utter silence after her father died. Those first few years in LA had been a revelation, and then she'd been forced to deal with the world she herself had made. "I let him use me. I let him take from me. I let him turn me into someone I didn't recognize."

Sarah's eyes softened. "God, Kori, you grew up. That's what happened. Stop trying to turn this into some grand drama. You grew up and you looked back and hated who you were. Every single one of us does that at some point. Forgive yourself. Stop hating yourself and stop running because you can't outrun yourself."

Was that what she was trying to do? Was she trying to run from who she'd been? From who she was afraid she could be again? Why had she wasted all that time when she'd known she wanted to be with Kai? Because at the end of the day, she wasn't scared of him. She was scared of herself.

Her gut knotted and she was about to explain to Sarah what was going through her head when she heard a knock on the door. Damn it. Well, at least it saved her from having to answer some difficult questions.

Sarah frowned and stalked over to the door, peering out the peephole. "It's Jared's friend. Maybe he has news on Jared since you won't call Kai to find out."

That had been a serious point of contention between them on the ride home. Sarah had seen some of the press concerning Jared's arrest and wanted to go over to see him. Kori had stopped her, saying they didn't know if they would have to get through a crowd of reporters or if Jared even wanted to see them.

At least now maybe she would get some answers. Sarah opened the door and let Squirrel in.

He was shorter than Jared and likely weighed fifty pounds less, but it was obvious he worked out with his buddy. He had a wiry strength to his lean frame. "Hey, I was hoping I could talk to you. I know you're pissed at Jared, but you have to understand."

Sarah shut the door behind him. "You don't have to plead his case to me."

Kori's cell trilled as they spoke. She looked down. God, there were ten voice mails and twenty texts from Kai. And one very angry note from Erin swearing she'd already told Ian they'd left and there would be spankings aplenty in their future. She quickly texted Erin to let her know they'd made it home all right and not to worry. And then she looked at the messages from Kai.

Please talk to me. Don't go to bed without talking to me. I'm waiting here for my brother. I'll be up all night.

Kori, do not believe everything you hear. Talk to me.

Baby, I'm so tired. I just want to hear your voice.

Tears blurred her vision at that one. How alone had he been? Should she have stayed despite it all? Guilt wrapped around her. He'd been there worried about his brother and she'd been warm and safe and bitching about him.

She'd been so angry at the thought that he'd helped make her safe place dangerous. She'd been angry at them all. Sanctum was the one place she could be herself. Or was it the only place she trusted herself to be herself?

"I know he's not guilty. And I don't care what that FBI dude says," Sarah continued. "He wasn't trying to hurt me. He was about to kiss me."

"Jared was going to kiss you?" Squirrel asked.

"He put his hands on my face, not around my neck. I don't think FBI guy could see much past his gun. He acted like he'd saved me from certain death. All he did was stop me from kissing my one true love for the first time. He's an asshole. Why am I surrounded by assholes these days?" Sarah complained as she moved to the coffeepot.

Squirrel followed her. "So you and Jared are still tight? Even after he got arrested?"

Kori read the last text Kai had sent her just a few minutes before.

Talk to me. Please talk to me.

That didn't sound like a man who didn't care. Was he trying to win her back or trying to keep his secretary?

When had she gotten so damn cynical? Sarah's words and Erin's advice from the night before swirled around in her head. How much time did she have with Kai? Was she willing to let last night be the end? Or was she brave enough to try?

I'll be in the office in an hour. We do need to talk. I don't know how we move past this.

His reply pinged mere seconds after she'd sent hers. *We will move past this. I love you. No matter what you heard, I love you. Let me try to explain.*

Did an explanation truly matter? It suddenly struck her that she'd been making this about Kai. Yes, he'd done something underhanded. Never in the time she'd known him had he done it before. Shouldn't she wonder why he would do it now? Why would Kai place her in danger? Why would Kai lie? What would motivate him to do that?

Love. Friendship. Brotherhood.

And what would motivate Kori to turn away from him? Fear. Self-loathing. Cynicism. Only one thing could make her stay. Faith. Faith in Kai. Faith that this time she'd chosen wisely, that this time she could love herself enough to not lose herself entirely.

I'll be there soon. Just got home and have to deal with your brother's friend first. As soon as I've figured out what he wants, I'll be there.

Who's there, baby? I don't want you opening the door to anyone. Anyone.

She keyed her reply. *It's the weird one. He's trying to find out if we saw Lena last night. Don't be a drama queen. I'm not alone.*

She put the phone down. She could hear Squirrel talking to

Sarah. Naturally they were discussing Jared. She peeked into the kitchen. "I don't suppose we have any muffins left."

Sarah shook her head. "No, but I can mix up a batch."

Squirrel smiled. "I love it here. We get carbs here."

"I'll help you in a minute. I'm going to check the laundry and see if I have anything clean to wear." She walked out, making her way to the small laundry room. Luckily she'd done a load the day before and there was a dress hanging in there. She scooped it up after making sure it didn't need ironing. She was going to need to look good if she was going to face Kai.

She really didn't have a ton of time now that she thought about it. She needed to get to work and get this over with. She would listen to him this time. They would talk and get everything out in the open.

"Hey, I probably should get ready and go into work." She pushed through the door and into the kitchen.

And stopped in her tracks. Squirrel held a knife at Sarah's throat.

"Don't you run. If you take another step, I swear I'll slit her throat."

Sarah stood still in his arms, but tears flowed down her cheeks. "Get out of here, Kori."

Shit. They were really were going to get spanked for this.

Chapter Seventeen

Kori put her hands out, trying to show the creepy serial killer dude that she wasn't a threat. Not in any way. "Let's talk. What do you want?"

"I'm pretty sure he wants to kill me," Sarah said, sarcasm still in her voice even in a life and death situation.

"I do. I want to kill you so bad. I thought killing Lena would quiet the voices, but it didn't because she wasn't the right one. I've been trying to figure out for a week who the right one was. He's always got someone, you see. Jared always has. Ever since we were kids. I swear he was diddling girls when we were in fifth grade and not a fucking one of them would ever look at me. Not while he was around." The arm he held Sarah with wasn't empty. He had a pistol in that hand. It looked like he was ready for anything.

"Then why didn't you leave him?" Kori wished she'd brought her phone with her. She was fairly certain crazy guy wouldn't let her go back and text Kai a 911 message. So that left her with the only option she had at the moment. She had to keep him talking until she figured out how to save Sarah.

Squirrel's arm tightened around Sarah. "I can't leave Jared.

What would he do without me? What would I do without him? This isn't about Jared. This is about you bitches who can't see past him."

"He wasn't interested in Lena."

"No, but Lena found out. That bitch went through my shit and found all the press clippings of the murders. She was going to go to Jared and tell him I was a pervert."

Kori wished Lena had been a little faster with her tattle telling. "He wouldn't have believed her."

"No, but he would have known those names. Do you know how hard I've worked to keep him from even thinking about those girls?"

She had to keep him talking. "Sarah hasn't rejected you."

"She would." His tone dripped with disgust. "She wouldn't let me touch her. She only wants Jared like they all want Jared. Like they all try to take him away from me."

God, he was insane and she wasn't sure what she could do. He was too close to the knives, and unlike Mia she didn't tote a gun around, though now she did see the value in owning one. Just in case crazy serial killer who's in love with his best friend and doesn't like women turning him down decides to show up. That's what a gun was for.

But he had given her something to work with. "You're not thinking this through, Squirrel. Jared is going to know about this. He's with Kai right now. You can't pin this one on him."

"I didn't mean to pin Lena on him. I swear I didn't. He's my best friend. I can't let him go to jail, but I can save him from one more gold-digging bitch. Now I can get rid of you and then off myself and everything will be made clean for Jared again," he said.

"Please think about this." She couldn't stand here and watch Sarah die. This couldn't be how she ended. "Sarah hadn't even kissed him. They aren't close."

"I wasn't thinking about marrying him. Actually, I was lying and I don't find him attractive at all," Sarah managed to wheeze.

"Liar," Squirrel spat. "I saw how you looked at him. It's the same way all the others looked at him. You wanted to use him like those women did when we were kids. I watched it. I saw how those old ladies would use him and he was helpless. I thought I could help him. I offered to take his place once but that bitch sneered at me and told me I could never be worth a dime. I killed her. She wasn't my first, but she was one of the best. I loved the way she screamed. I wish I had more time with you, gorgeous. I wish I had time to show you what you missed out on. Do you know that most of the women begged me to stay with them after I showed them how good I was?"

"They weren't begging you to rape them again, dumbass. They were trying to survive the experience," Sarah shot back.

"Will you shut up and stop irritating him?" Sarah's mouth was definitely going to have to go. "Squirrel, I was wrong. If you kill Sarah and then kill yourself, they'll think Jared did all of it. They'll think Jared was jealous that you stole his girl. That's what the cops will believe. It's going to be so bad for Jared in prison. He'll probably die."

Squirrel's eyes went wide. "Can't you see I did this all for him? I did this to take care of him. If only I'd had more time with Lena. I should have hidden her body. Why would they think he killed Lena?"

She needed to make him see some kind of reason. "Because the feds have been on to you for a while now. Well, not you. They think Jared did all of this, and if you don't talk to them, he'll go to jail."

"He'll get the death penalty," Sarah corrected. "They'll stick a needle in his arm and everything he's done will be tainted."

"He won't be a hero anymore." Kori was willing to try anything to keep this from happening.

"I think I should kill you, too. For good measure," Squirrel said. "You're his type, you know. You and this one. You're exactly the type of women he adores to fuck, but Jared wouldn't ever make it real. He wouldn't be seen on the red carpet with a woman like you. You're too fat. He'd be a laughingstock."

"Then why kill her? Why kill me? He won't ever love us. For that matter, I'm involved with his brother and Sarah was just a girl he almost kissed. We can't hurt your place with him." He'd done that all on his own when he'd decided to start killing women.

Squirrel stared through her. "Once he starts taking fancy roles, he'll drop me, too. Now that he has his brother back, I don't think he'll need me anymore. I never wanted that fucker to come back in our lives."

"You're the one who slashed my tires." He'd thought the car

was Kai's.

"I hate him. He always told Jared I wasn't good enough for him. He's still fucking saying it. For years he ignored Jared, and the minute he's willing to talk, Jared dumps me with the rest of the crew. Like I was another employee. I couldn't stand it. It eats at me. I can usually go a year or so before I really need to hurt someone, but the minute he started talking about his brother, I knew I would have to do this. I thought I could hold out, but the pressure's too much. I can't wait."

"Please stop." She could see a thin line of red on Sarah's neck, see the pain in her friend's eyes.

And that was when she heard the wailing of a siren. It was distant but becoming more and more distinct every second. Was it nothing more than a cop chasing down an errant driver? Would that sound rush past them and be gone again?

Or had someone known she needed help?

She caught the sight of something moving past Squirrel, just a glimpse of sandy hair darting across the kitchen window. Kai. Kai had figured it out and he'd come for her.

Soon she wouldn't be alone. Of course, it also put Squirrel in the position of fight or flight.

She was worried about the choice he would make. He didn't seem ready to go down alone.

"I can't stop," Squirrel said, his eyes going dark.

"Then take me instead," a deep voice said. Jared walked in from the living room, his palms out, showing he had nothing in his hands. He was wearing a T-shirt and jeans, sneakers on his feet, and he looked positively haunted. His eyes took in the scene, going to that place on Sarah's throat where the knife dug in. "Let her go and we'll talk about this."

She seriously doubted that. Kai was out there. He wasn't in here and that meant something nasty was likely to happen. Kai wouldn't wait on the police. Not if he could help it. He stepped up to the back door, apparently realizing there was no way Squirrel could see him from where he was standing. The only trouble was the door was locked.

Kai stared inside, his gaze finding hers. He put a finger to his lips, asking for her silence, but offering her hope. He wouldn't allow this to happen. He wouldn't let her die.

Squirrel faced off with his best friend, his arms tightening as though Sarah was a shield. His eyes had gone wild and Kori prayed the gun didn't go off, that the knife at Sarah's throat didn't cut deeper. "I never meant for you to get hurt."

Jared stepped in front of Kori, blocking her out and proving that even though he wasn't a member of McKay-Taggart, he was definitely in the brotherhood. "How did you think killing women I liked didn't hurt me?"

"They weren't right for you," Squirrel argued. "They wanted your money, your fame."

"The girl I had a crush on in high school wanted my fame? You killed her, didn't you? Her body is still missing, but you're the one who took her away."

"She was my first and I didn't mean to kill her," he admitted. "I only meant to scare her, but it felt so good. It was like a drug. I'd put animals down before, but it was nothing like taking her life. For once, I was the powerful one. For once in my fucking, useless, pitiful life, I was the one she looked at like a god. I didn't do it for a long time after that. I didn't have to because I could remember her. But it got real bad after the TV show took off. It was like no one ever saw me. No one sees me except them and only when I'm forcing them to."

"You're sick, Squirrel." Jared had paled.

"I'm not sick," Squirrel shouted. "They're the sick ones. They want to take and take from you and give nothing back. Can't you see I'm your soul mate? Why does it have to be about sex? Why can't it just be the two of us?"

Jared nodded. "It can. Let Sarah go and you can take me instead."

"I'm going to kill myself. I'm not going to jail. I can't stop now Jared. I need it more and more. It's a fucking drug. I can't go to jail."

"I know." Jared's voice was so calm. "So let Sarah go and we can discuss it. You remember what you've always said? You said it to me that night I realized I had to leave the house because I couldn't fuck for money anymore. I was scared and I felt so fucking alone and you said something to me."

The knife eased off a little. "I said you're not alone because where you go, I go."

Jared nodded, his eyes red. "Yeah. You were the only one who stood by me, the only one who gave a shit after Mom died. Where you go, I go."

Oh, god, he couldn't mean that. It had to be a ruse. He couldn't mean that he would go with him, allow Squirrel to take him out.

"Really?" Squirrel asked, his hand moving away from Sarah's throat.

"What would I do without you?" Jared's voice was a hushed plea.

Kori reached out, grabbing Sarah's hand as Squirrel's arm released her. Time seemed to speed up, the world flashing around her in rapid fire. She pulled Sarah out of the way and covered Sarah's body as best she could. There was a crack as the door came open and Kori watched as Kai kicked his way in. The gun went off, skimming by Kori's head, but Kai was already in motion. He tackled Squirrel and the gun went flying.

Kori sat up, tears streaming down her eyes as she started to move the both of them back. The sirens were right outside now.

"Kai!" she cried out as Squirrel got the knife in his hand again.

Kai kicked out, but that knife descended toward him.

The whole house seemed rocked by the sound of a gun going off. Jared stood over his former best friend, the man he'd spent half his life with, and stared down at the hole in the back of his skull.

Kai rolled Squirrel's body off him and looked up at his brother. "Are you all right?"

Before he could answer, the cops swarmed in. Jared dropped the gun and got to his knees, hands in the air. Kai did the same. Kori held on to Sarah as the world seemed flooded with pain.

* * * *

He fucking hated police stations. He was getting damn tired of interrogation rooms, too. Unlike the last time, he'd been separated from his brother. After the cops had talked to Sarah and Kori, he and Jared had been given the dignity of walking to the patrol cars sans handcuffs. The women had been taken to the hospital, and he hadn't seen Kori since. He hadn't had the chance to hold her, to tell her how terrified he'd been when he realized she was alone with a serial killer. He hadn't been able to ask for her forgiveness.

The door opened and Special Agent Rush walked in along with Big Tag.

"Your girl needs a spanking," Big Tag said flatly. "If you don't give her a doozy of one, I'm going to come up with some punishment that fits the crime. I told her specifically not to leave Erin's house without an escort, and if she tries to tell me subby Sarah is a proper escort, I'll spank her myself."

The words came out flat and angry, a sure sign that what Ian was really feeling was fear and guilt.

"I'll take care of her. Do you know if she's been released from the hospital yet?" His even words belied the knot in his gut. The two most important relationships in his life were in complete turmoil, and he wasn't sure what he could do about them. Jared had stared blankly ahead on the way to the station. He'd answered Kai's questions in a hollow voice. No charm. No emotion. It was utterly unlike his brother.

How would he handle it? The only person who'd ever stuck by him had been a rabid dog, infecting his life with tragedy. He'd been able to hear what Jared said to Squirrel, and for a moment he thought his brother meant it, meant he would rather end it all here instead of moving forward after such a betrayal.

Kai was part of that cycle. Kai had betrayed him as surely as Squirrel had, though in a more honest way.

And Kori felt betrayed.

What a fucking mess.

Ian sent Rush a frown that could have frozen fire. "Don't you have something to say?"

Rush's eyes rolled slightly, but he held a hand out. "I'm truly sorry for suspecting your brother and ask your forgiveness. Your brother is an amazing actor and a very good thrower of alien darts."

Big Tag grinned a little. "He has to wear a *Dart* T-shirt to work for a week, too."

"You made a bet on whether my brother was a killer?"

Ian waved that off. "I knew Jared wasn't a killer. I made a bet to put an asshole in his place. Rush is a smart guy, a useful guy, but he can be very single focused. He didn't like Jared because his wife left him for a younger man and so he took the evidence and decided it fit the man he liked least."

A light stain flushed Rush's cheeks. "I might have allowed personal feelings to complicate this case. But Tag's the real asshole here. And I am sorry to have gotten it wrong, but I was right about the killer. He was close to Jared. We couldn't have caught him without your help. I won't apologize for that. Jared's talking to the police. He thinks there are some cold cases he can help solve back in Seattle."

That might give his brother some closure. Or it might reopen wounds he hadn't known he had. Kai was worried about him. Jared had counted on that kid for decades and was going to blame himself for not seeing what was going on. Maybe Kai could work this out with him over the course of the filming. It would be good for him to help his brother deal with this.

Of course, helping his brothers had kind of been his thing lately. He stared up at Rush. "So you're going to honor your deal with McKay-Taggart?"

Rush nodded. "I always was going to honor it. I've already sent over everything we have."

"Which is next to nothing," Big Tag replied shortly.

"I got you an excellent lead on the base in Argentina," Rush shot back.

"The base that was completely empty by the time my man got there." Tag sat down across from Kai, running a hand over his hair. It was obvious he hadn't slept much. "I want you to give me everything you have on those three medical companies I sent you. I don't care how you have to do it. If you have to call in favors from Interpol, I want that information."

"I don't have connections at Interpol," Rush admitted.

Big Tag was having none of that. "Then start blowing some Euros because you owe me. I put my club at risk and all those subs under my protection in harm's way. I didn't do it for some shitty, out-of-date intel."

Rush glanced to the doorway. "I'll get in touch with my CIA contact and see what I can do. I won't forget this, Mr. Ferguson. You've saved a lot of women."

Now he had to see if he could save just one more from her own demons. "See that you help us bring back our man if you can."

The door closed quietly behind Rush.

"I talked to Harrison and he's already preparing a statement to the press. Your brother is being fully exonerated and all charges will be dropped within the hour. We'll make sure every newspaper and television station gets a copy," Tag explained.

"Hopefully that saves his job." There was more Kai could do on that front. "I've already explained how he saved me. Jared killed his oldest friend to save my life. I barely managed to save Sarah. I'm out of practice."

He wasn't sure it had been such a close thing, but if it helped Jared, he would call himself a weakling and give his brother all the glory.

"Sure you are." Tag sat back, regarding him seriously. "Serena's already gotten several calls about Jared and the movie. She made a statement that she didn't think the movie should continue without him. The TV show is standing by him. I think he'll get all his jobs back and come out of this more popular than ever."

"Yes, but what did it cost him?"

Big Tag looked at him from across the table. "I know what it cost you. Don't think I'm ignoring that. I know how much you've sacrificed, Kai. I think you should tell Kori why you did it. I won't have you lose her over this. There's been too much loss as it is. Simply ask her to be quiet about it."

He wasn't sure she could. He wasn't entirely sure she wouldn't think Erin deserved to know. It wasn't a question of Erin's competence or her place in the order of those who loved Theo. It was about protecting her. "I can't. If she decided Erin needed to know, she would tell her."

Tag groaned and shook his head. "I think that's a bad idea. Erin is starting to come out of it. Not entirely and she never will, but she smiled this morning. She told me she's already named the baby. If she knows, she'll want to be a part of the team that brings him back. I'm not a monster, Kai. I knew she needed revenge. It's why I let her and Nick take out McDonald. She's smart and one of the best operatives I have, but she's also basically my sister-in-law. Maybe they weren't married, but I think they would have eventually. I know it's what Theo wanted and I have to honor my brother by protecting his family."

"I can't tell Kori." Tag's words did nothing but make it even clearer. Kai had to get her back and he couldn't use the only tool that would work. "I have to hope she'll miss me."

Tag's eyes narrowed. "Seriously? Are you going to meditate on that?"

He flipped off his friend. "I'm going to keep trying to talk to her."

"Or you could make her listen. I thought you were the big bad sadist. Shouldn't the big bad sadist go hard after his girl?"

According to his brother when Kori discovered her old Master's issues, she left and he allowed it to happen. Was Kai playing into her fears? He'd been trying to take it slow, trying not to give into his instincts. He wanted to tie her up in ropes and contracts and legal bindings. He wanted to possess her, to own a piece of her soul and give her part of his. He'd seen her fear of commitment, but maybe it came from a fear that she wasn't good enough to pursue, wasn't worth the chase.

He could give her a chase. "Tag, I'm going to need you to make sure Sanctum's ready for me tonight. And I'll need to know when Kori's coming home from the hospital. Sarah won't want to be alone."

"I think Mia is planning on staying with her," Tag replied, pulling his cell out.

"Mia's staying?" He'd expected her to flee town at the earliest possible time.

"I'm hedging my bets. If Rush can't get me what I need, then maybe Drew Lawless can. I'm meeting him for lunch somewhere quiet. When you get a chance, I'd like your take on him. And his sister is hanging around for a while. She says it's about trying to save her friendships."

But it was likely all about Case. The question was would Case have anything to do with her now that the op was over.

None of that mattered as much as getting his girl back. "I need to teach my sub that she won't be allowed to walk away without a fight. The good news is, I think she'll like how I fight."

He intended to win.

Chapter Eighteen

Kori looked out of the car window and frowned. "This isn't home, Case. Are you taking me to work? Because I kind of thought the office would be closed for the day."

It wasn't day anymore. They'd spent the entire morning and afternoon at the hospital, getting looked over and then talking to police. Sarah had required two stitches on her neck, but mostly she'd been a terribly lucky girl. She was all right with the singular exception of her heart. Kori was afraid that was broken. Jared had sent her a text apologizing and asking her not to contact him again.

That was when Sarah finally cried.

"I was told to bring you to Sanctum, Kori," Case said. "And you know I always do as I'm told."

Why was she here? Well, deep down she knew why she was here. Kai wanted to talk to her and apparently they were doing it on neutral ground. She knew she needed to talk to him, knew it had to happen soon, but she'd promised her friend. "I need to pack a bag for Sarah and get to the hotel. We're all staying with Mia tonight."

Somehow after everything they'd been through it was easy to forgive Mia.

It was easy to forgive Kai, too. She just wasn't sure it was going to be easy to be honest with him about what she wanted.

She wanted him and only him for the rest of her life. She wanted to throw away all her inhibitions and love him and let herself be. She'd fought for so long to not be the girl she'd been with Morgan that she had to ask herself who she'd become. Becoming anti-Morgan was only another form of denying herself. What did she want?

Kori wanted Kai and she wanted to write. She was simply afraid to reach out and grasp them.

"I'll pack for Sarah and take it over," Case explained. "I want to talk to her anyway. I don't know that she'll feel safe in her house again. I've talked to some of her friends and they're willing to put her up until she's ready to make a decision. We're all here for her."

She might not have had a knife to her throat, but she'd still been a little traumatized. "You know I was there, too."

"Ah, but your Master will handle you, sweet thing," Case said with a wink. "Go on now. You don't want to piss that one off more than you already have. I think you'll find Sanctum is closed for the night, so you'll have the place all to yourself."

She stared at the building she knew so well. "I thought I was safe here."

"You were. You are. You're as safe as you can be, but Kori, nothing's truly safe. That's an illusion. I tell myself that every day. When I get pissed and angry because Theo died on an op, I tell myself he could have died while driving. He could have died when it didn't matter. Instead he died trying to help take down something horrible. It was a good death. Nothing is guaranteed, Kori. I know that now."

Kai could die tomorrow. He could have died earlier today. Jared had taken a step back and put a wall between himself and what he wanted. Shouldn't she be brave if Kai was?

She placed her purse on her shoulder and slid out of the cab of the truck, her heart starting to beat. What was waiting for her in there? Would Kai have rethought everything after what happened earlier today? "Maybe you should take me home and let me get my own car. I'll come back. I swear."

Case reached across the cab and pulled the door shut. He drove off with a squeal of his tires.

"Well, you could have just said no." Kori turned back to the doors that led to the lobby.

Luckily Case had given her his key card. He was a giver. She strode to the door because she wasn't going to be the coward who ran away again. There was a note taped there.

Welcome, Kori. I'm waiting for you in the conference room. Please join me.

So they were going to be civil. Her heart sank a little. It was all right. It was better this way. They could talk and figure out how this was going to work from now on because she knew one thing. She wasn't leaving again. She was going to help Serena with her script and she was going to find her place here. She wasn't leaving this crazy family now that she'd found it. She pulled the note off the door and slid her key card across the reader.

There was the sound of a click as the door opened. Kori walked inside, the door closing behind her.

It was so quiet. She never came to Sanctum by herself. Even when the music wasn't going, there was always the sound of people laughing and the bar being restocked or one of the dungeon monitors checking the equipment.

Not today. Today it was utterly silent. And a little dark.

She took a deep breath, telling herself everything was fine. Kai was here somewhere. "Hello?"

She took another step inside, turning toward the hall that led to the conference room. It was used for staff meetings and sometimes the MT crew met here. She'd never been inside before.

"Kai? What's up with the silent treatment?" She was starting to get nervous.

Which was probably exactly what the bastard wanted.

Mind games. He was playing mind games with her. She strode to the conference room and opened it. Nothing. It was completely dark and there was no sign anyone had been there at all.

"You know I was almost brutally murdered today, you massive ass," she said as the door closed. "So what's with the horror movie treatment?"

She was beginning to have a suspicion.

"You know I am a sadist, my love." His deep voice made her

From Sanctum with Love

shriek. It seemed to come from behind, but when she turned he wasn't there.

That was when she felt it. She felt something drop overhead and then her whole body constricted as the rope was pulled tight.

He'd lassoed her? She stumbled back as he tugged on the rope and before she knew it, she was being turned to face him.

Kai was staring her way like he was going to eat her alive. "I wasn't really trying to scare you. I thought if you saw me with a lasso in hand you might have run. It's been a while since I roped a sub. I wanted to make sure I did it right."

"Are you treating me like a cow?" She didn't think so, but she wanted to push him a little, too.

He tugged on the rope, drawing her closer. "No, you're a pretty filly I want to ride. And now I've roped you and you're mine. I have to make sure you're ready for that first ride. I think you'll like that. Won't you, baby? By the time I'm done roping and wrangling you, you'll spread those pretty legs for your Master and beg for a cock."

"What the hell is going on, Kai?" She struggled a bit as she realized things weren't going according to plan.

"You ran from me," he said, his tone a harsh growl. He wound the rope around her torso, tying her tight. "I'm going to make certain that doesn't happen again. You can spew any filth you want out of that pretty mouth of yours. I mean it, Kori. You can call me every name in the book and receive no punishment at all, but you can't run. We have to work this out."

"Normal people talk, Kai." Talking was exactly what she planned to do with him. They needed to work things out before they even thought about getting physical again. It was the only logical thing to do.

Her body didn't seem to care about logic. Her body was already heating up, already loving the feel of rope wrapped around her.

"We're not normal. We're us and this is how we work it out. This is how we show each other how important the other one is. Because you are, baby. You're the most important person in the world to me." He tied off a knot and pulled something out of his pocket. Naturally Kai had more rope. He seemed to have an endless supply hidden on his body. Kai tied this rope around the loops holding her torso. He fashioned a little leash for her. "Come on. I want to show you something. Something I made for you."

"Kai, this is ridiculous."

Kai moved in, his gorgeous face all she could see for the moment. "Is it? This is how I show you I love you. I know it's perverse and likely no one else would understand. The rest of the world can look at me and call me a freak. I only need you. You're the only one who can hurt me with words, with judgment because you're the only one whose judgment ever mattered. This is the language of our love. Can't it simply be? Do we have to question it? Do we have to change it so it fits some mold we didn't make?"

Her whole body softened because he was getting to her. Would it be rational to sit down and have a conversation? Yes. But that wouldn't be intimate. He was asking her for intimacy and she couldn't turn him down. No matter what he'd done. "No. This is our language."

This was their love and no one else got to control it.

Yes. She was in control. She'd learned that here in Sanctum. What she gave or kept for herself was her choice, but sometimes it was all right to give it up. Kai wasn't Morgan. Not even close and the Kori she'd become wasn't going to turn back into that needy girl who'd given up so much of herself that she'd had to flee to find it again.

This Kori stayed and fought and this Kori was going to find her faith. Erin had told her that if she could easily leave then Kai wasn't the one.

She couldn't leave because Kai seemed intent on tying her up. He was definitely the one for her.

Kori let him lead her up the stairs.

Up ahead she saw that Kai had rigged a play space for what looked like some serious suspension play. They didn't screw around at Sanctum. There were hard points in the ceiling along with suspension rings that could handle the full weight of even the biggest subs. Whatever Kai was about to do would likely be memorable.

Underneath the rig was a cushy mat, set there to ensure even if something went wrong, she wouldn't be hurt. The mat covered a lot of space and there was a sheet over a portion of it. She could guess that was where Kai had placed his toys. Ah, the mind fuck. She wouldn't know what was happening, couldn't tell how he would hurt her before it happened. Yes, that got her motor running.

Kai stopped in the center of the scene space, his eyes on her. "You ran this morning. You ran last night. I think you intended to quit today and not see me again. Come here. I'll get you out of that. I was only trying to make a point, but it seems you would rather talk."

She forced back the denial that sprang to her lips. She wanted his ropes around her, but she remained still as he quickly got her out of the bindings. "I wouldn't have run away. I needed time last night. Do you want to explain what you were doing?"

"I was tagging Mia's phone for Case," he said, his voice short. He laid the rope down. "He needed to look into her background and it was what he and the crew decided to do. They wanted to be able to listen in on her conversations with her brother. Now we've discovered it wasn't necessary at all and Big Tag is dealing with her brother directly."

That didn't run counter to anything she'd heard. "All right. Did you or did you not ask me to come out with you last night for the sole purpose of using me to get Mia's phone."

"I did. I would never have wanted to go to a nightclub with you. I would have greatly preferred going home and watching TV and spending time with you in bed."

"Did you manipulate me into bringing Sarah out even knowing that she would likely get hurt?"

His jaw tightened. "Yes."

"Did you sleep with me so I could be your cover?"

"Absolutely not. I slept with you because I finally got to. I finally had you in a place where you let me into your bed, where you allowed me to play with you. The two have nothing to do with one another except timing."

"I have a hard time understanding why you wouldn't come to me and ask me, Kai. I would have helped you. Even though she was my friend, I would have helped you do anything you needed."

"I was asked not to talk about it."

That simply didn't make sense to her. "By Case?"

"By Big Tag."

"So your loyalty to Big Tag is more important than our

relationship?" She wasn't sure she wanted to know the answer to that question.

Kai groaned in obvious frustration. "I don't understand why that's your conclusion. He's my friend. I didn't think for a second you would get hurt. Why can't I do a job for a friend and leave you out of it?"

"You didn't leave me out of it, Kai. You dragged me into the middle of it. From what I can tell, you and the Taggarts dragged everyone into it. Tell me you didn't know your brother was under investigation."

"I can't," he admitted. "I did know."

None of this made sense to her. "You let a potential serial killer into this club. Big Tag let it happen. How am I supposed to feel safe here again? He killed women like me and Sarah."

His eyes were tight as he continued to stare straight at her. "Yes. But I knew it wasn't Jared and I stayed close to you. I never meant to hurt you. I wouldn't do that."

And neither would the Taggarts. It was so confusing. Only this morning she'd gotten a hearty lecture on how she and Sarah were supposed to stay safe at Erin's house until everything got sorted out. These men were protective. So why the hell would they put everyone at risk?

"I can see all the questions you want to ask," he said quietly. "I can't tell you."

"Because you promised Ian Taggart you wouldn't."

"Yes. I love you, Kori, but I can't stop being me. Ian told me earlier today that I could tell you if it would make a difference between keeping you and losing you. I'm standing in front of you. I'm offering you everything I have. Will answering that one question make you love me again?"

She shook her head. "No. It won't."

His face fell. "All right then."

"Kai, I never stopped loving you. Not once. I got worried and anxious and about a million old fears hit me at once." She had made her decision and it was so much easier than she'd thought it would be. It was logic and faith. Kai wouldn't hurt her. Therefore if Kai had done something to put her in harm's way, it had to be for the greater good. There had to be meaning. What that meaning was didn't matter. A sense of peace came over her because she let that fear fly away. She didn't need it anymore. "I don't want to know. There's only one question that matters. Do you love me?"

"I love you more than you can imagine."

She either believed him or she didn't. He couldn't open his soul and let her read what was written there. She stared at him for a moment because maybe she could. A little. Before the last week she'd never looked past how beautiful he was, how stunning his eyes were to stare into. Kori took a step up. Kai remained still as she brought her fingertips up and brushed along his jawline. He hadn't slept. She would bet on it. He hadn't shaved either. He'd likely gone straight from the police station to here. There was weariness in those green eyes of his, but there was something else, too. She was there, reflected in them. She'd spent the first part of her life defining herself by how other people saw her. And then she'd rejected it utterly. She'd pulled into herself and the pendulum had swung so no one really mattered. She could say she loved her friends and it was true, but she didn't love herself until the moment she realized not only was Kai the one...she was his one, too. She was the one who could pull him out of his shell, who could tease and torture him with pranks and affection. If she walked away from Kai, he would be alone. She would be alone.

She didn't have to be alone. She could choose, and choosing him didn't mean leaving herself behind. It meant being a new Kori, a Kori who risked and loved. Who leapt and embraced the ride.

Kori took a step back, and she saw the moment his face fell. He thought she would leave. She'd spent so much time worried about Kai breaking her heart that she hadn't thought for a single moment she could break his.

She had to prove that he was safe with her, too. In their language.

She sank to her knees in front of him, the position once so familiar lit with new meaning now. It meant she was his. It meant she was vulnerable to him and only him. It meant she trusted him to love and cherish her.

His hand came out, covering her bent head. That hand cupped her, sending almost palpable emotion flowing from him to her. One gesture was all it took for him to say that he was hers. That he was vulnerable only to her and he would protect and cherish her gift.

One gesture turned them from separate to together.

"This is forever, Kori. I won't accept anything less."

Forever was all she could ask for. Forever with this man. "I think you'll have to find me a very nice collar, and that might not be the only jewelry I want from you."

The words were easy now because she understood him. He'd hesitated to talk about commitment for her sake, not his. Her walls had been thick, but she didn't need them anymore. Not with him.

His hand came down, lifting her chin up so she could look at him. "Don't tease me. I would marry you tomorrow."

No. She was only going to do this once and that meant doing it right. Her Master wasn't getting away with a quickie Vegas wedding. "I'll need six months to plan."

"Then I'll take six months of filthy sex with my fiancée." His face went hard, the Dom coming out in an instant. "Take the clothes off quickly or I'll rip them off you."

Though she'd spent way, way too much time in these particular clothes, she didn't want to parade around in whatever she might find here. It would make the trip home far too interesting, and she'd seen enough of the DPD to last a lifetime. She hurried to get out of those confining clothes, tossing them off because he hadn't told her to be careful.

"Those are beautiful marks, baby," he said when she turned to him. He stared at her breasts and brushed his fingers over the marks from the sadisticks. The little matchsticks were barely pink now, but he could see them. He ran his fingers down to her nipples and rolled one between his thumb and forefinger. Over and over. Very gentle.

Sadistic bastard.

"I've had a very rough day, baby. I need some play."

In this they were perfectly matched. "Yes, Sir. I need some play."

"Tell me what you want from me." His fingers were so gentle. It was frustrating and exhilarating because she knew something nasty was coming. "Do you want a sweet lover?"

"No, Sir."

"Do you want me to worship you with kisses and gentle caresses?"

"No, Kai. I don't want that."

"What do you want, sub?"

"I want you to hurt me." She said it without shame. There was no shame between them. There was only connection and acceptance. The world, she'd discovered, was so much bigger when she'd dropped all her shame and accepted who she was, when she forgave herself for her mistakes and accepted that she deserved all the love this man could give her. And the pleasure. For her there was such deep pleasure in pain.

His fingers tightened and twisted viciously, making her whole body tense and the breath flee her lungs. "That I can do. Turn around right fucking now."

She turned, giving him her back. Her body hummed, her skin heating nicely. What other delights would her Master gift her with tonight?

"We're going to talk about a few things, baby." He dangled the rope in front of her and she felt a tug deep in her pelvis. "Hands behind your back."

She folded her hands together behind her, leaving her breasts upthrust and exposed. She sighed with pleasure as he went to work, binding her.

He was rough with her, letting her feel the rope as he wound it around her. "The first thing is that you're not leaving work. I need you."

"I never said I was going to leave work. Did you think I expected to be a kept woman now that we're together?" That was a funny vision. She wasn't the kept kind of girl. She needed to work and she loved working with him. What Kai did was important.

"Oh, I'm going to keep you in every way possible, but you're going to feel free to use any time you need to write whatever you want. I don't give a shit if it's a shopping list as long as you write something creative every day."

Doms. They never stopped. Luckily, she'd already made that decision herself. "I'm glad because I'm helping Serena with her script tomorrow. She's coming in and we'll use the ladies' lounge to work."

He tugged on her wrists, tying off a section of rope. "Two, you have to fix up the men's room. The patients have started to complain. I think it's perfectly fine. It's a toilet. It doesn't have to be anything but clean, but no, once the guys started hearing about how nice the ladies' was they want their own freaking spa."

She would love to put in a nice, masculine space. The office was soothing but plain. Guys needed a little glam, too. "I can do that."

He wound the rope around her breasts, the material scratching against her skin. He pulled it just tight enough. "And you have to help me with my brother because I don't know how to reach him. I don't even know if he wants me to reach him."

Her heart softened. "Give him time. Let him know you're here. That's all we can do."

He tied off the last section and she was already feeling safe and secure. The bindings made her whole body feel warm and happy. Even when her Master tweaked her nipples again. Hard. She gasped but managed not to move. This was all a part of the game. "You're beautiful like this. You're always beautiful, but when I close my eyes, I see you like this, bound and trusting and needing me as much as I need you."

His mouth came down on hers briefly before he moved back to his work. She went silent as he bound her, preparing her for suspension with a chest harness and ensuring that she would be secure. He ran another length of rope down her spine and she felt it caress the cheeks of her ass before he shifted again, bringing it between her legs and back up her belly. He tied it securely to the lovely design he'd made that showed off her breasts.

The rope slid over her clit and against her soft pink parts, the roughness making her squirm. Kai stood and looked down at her. "I think that will do."

She loved ropes, but that suspension rig sent a delicious shiver of fear down her spine.

A happy peace came over her as she allowed Kai to move her into position. He tugged on the ropes, pulling her roughly to him and then positioning her right where he wanted her. The feel of the ropes around her was overwhelming, taking her out of herself.

"Relax and trust me," Kai whispered.

This was what she'd missed before. She'd played and fooled around, but none of it had been serious. This was serious. They prepared each other and took care before pleasure, as though their love was sacred and required rituals.

She closed her eyes and let the sensation sweep over her. She heard the sound of metal clinking. The carabiners. Kai was attaching them, getting ready for...she gasped and she was suddenly swept up and into the air.

Her whole body was cradled roughly three feet off the ground. She could feel the sway as she settled in, her legs splayed and her body completely open and vulnerable to him. This was flying. She wasn't sure why he'd settled her so low. She'd gone much higher, but she wasn't about to complain. Already she was feeling soft and warm and strong all at the same time.

Kai stood between her legs. "I don't want you to hesitate to use your safe word if you need to."

It was right on the tip of her tongue to call him a Nervous Nellie, but she was trying to be a good sub. Hell, she'd just gotten engaged. She should give her inner brat a night off. Kori gave him her sweetest smile. "Yes, Master."

Kai frowned. "Now that makes me nervous. But this is placed perfectly."

Now she understood why she wasn't higher. He'd put her in the perfect position to fuck her hard. "You're right. It is exactly where I need to be. I was going to complain it wasn't higher. The other suspension scenes I've done have been higher."

He frowned down at her. "I don't want to hear about other riggers. Especially not the Cajun guy. You played with him a lot."

"Don't get jealous. I only played with him." Remy had been fun and there'd been nothing sexual between them. Deep down, she'd always longed for Kai. Maybe even before she'd met him.

"I'll always be jealous of anyone you played with, but like I said, this is perfect." He moved between her legs, showing her that his cock was perfectly aligned. He held her hips and ground himself against her, the rope sliding between his pants and her skin. "Tell me how it feels. I like to know what I'm doing to you."

"It hurts. It's biting into me, but I like it. Oh, just a little more." How could she already be so close? He'd barely touched her, but being bound by his ropes had acted as foreplay. She didn't need much more than that. Her pussy was soft and ready, her clitoris ripe for orgasm.

Kai stepped back. "Not yet. Not until I say so. This is where I'm in control. And I control everything here, baby. You're mine here. Every. Single. Inch."

He tugged on the rope that ran across her pussy and then let it go. It hit her hard and made her body shake. She swung, her heart swelling as she felt like she was flying.

"Asshole."

He smiled. "Well, I did tell you to call me anything you liked. Enjoy that today. If you're going to curse me, I should give you something to curse about. Don't go anywhere."

Like she could go anywhere. Like she would go anywhere. She was primed for him.

And already a little subspacey. The feeling of being utterly helpless was starting to make her head float. She sank into the rope. It wasn't simply rope. It was his rope. Every loop and knot had been tied by him, a loving caress of her Dom. He held her there off the ground, his will and desire feeding her own. She let her head rest back, giving over to whatever her Master had planned for her.

She smelled that ozone scent before she heard the crackling that signaled he'd turned on the violet wand.

Oh shit. Oh shit. Oh shit. Her brain frazzled, her body tensing and waiting for the first feel of fire on her flesh. And she giggled because damn this was going to be fun.

"Did you think at all when you ran away this morning?" His voice had gone deep.

When she looked up at him, he'd taken off his shirt and boots and was standing there looking so fucking sexy with his hair still pulled back and his glasses on. Even when he was intellectual Kai, the Dom simmered underneath. He held the violet wand in one hand, the apparatus so seemingly innocent.

He'd fastened the flathead to the wand and when he flicked the switch, the glass addition glowed with a lovely purple light. And it made the evilest sound.

"I wasn't running away. I was going home. I'd had a long night. Erin talks in her sleep." And apparently had some hot dreams. Dreams that ended with her calling out Theo's name. But when they'd woken up, Erin had been calm and collected again. She'd thanked Kori and Sarah for cooking breakfast because her house had become op central once Andrew Lawless had shown up.

It had been surprisingly easy to slip away. Of course, it had likely been easy because the Doms thought she was smart enough not to run. She'd totally proven them wrong.

"I believe you were told not to go anywhere without an escort," Kai said forbiddingly.

"I had Sarah."

"Ah, yes. Big Tag told me you would likely make that argument." The violet wand cracked and he touched it to the sole of her foot.

He wasn't playing around. She screamed out, her body tensing as the electricity fucked with her system. Violet wands had settings. The pain could go anywhere from a pleasant whisper along her skin to the feeling of a knife cutting through her. Kai was way closer to the knife than the butterfly.

Tears pierced her eyes as Kai pulled the wand away.

"Sarah is not a proper escort unless she's some kind of super secret spy. Is Sarah an undercover spy? Has she had years of training I don't know about? Can she defend you from a killer?"

Sarah was hell on heels when it came to taking care of sick patients, putting arrogant docs in their places, and being super bratty to Doms. And the woman could do Disneyland in four-inch heels, a classic vintage dress, full pinup makeup, and never sweat or complain once on Dapper Days, but she wasn't so great with killers. Still, she felt the need to defend her bestie. "Hey, she managed to not die today."

He growled, a low sexy sound that was immediately drowned out by her howl as he tortured her other foot. He stared down at her, watching her every expression so she gave it all to him. She squirmed and pleaded and watched his dick get super hard. It was tenting the slacks he wore admirably.

He flicked the wand off and moved to her right side. "That is not a proper response and she's only alive because Jared and I figured out what was happening. You were told by a Dom I trust to stay put. Don't you fucking argue with me. You knew damn well Sarah wasn't an escort. This was about punishing me."

This time he lit up her nipple and for a second she couldn't breathe. Her body shook as the electricity flared through her. The burn felt so fucking good. It was a thing to be endured, a sensation that somehow filtered through her body as agony and thrilling pleasure. When he pulled the wand away she wanted to tell him she could take more. She could handle more. But she held back because what she wanted right now was him. There would be time to push all her boundaries. They had forever after all.

And he was right. Those tears that normally stuck in her eyes flowed down her cheeks. They wouldn't stop. She could cry for him, cry with him. It all slammed into her, the last few weeks, all the lonely days before, the time with Morgan, and more. Her childhood, so precious and perilous. Her career, everything she'd wanted and still empty because she'd never been brave enough to truly claim it. Her fears that Kai couldn't love her, that somehow she wasn't worth it. They all slammed through her system, so much more piercing than the pain.

He was right. She'd tried to punish him, but mostly she'd spent years and years punishing herself for the mistakes of a child. Of a girl who didn't know better. There, hung in a swing of ropes, she could finally let the past go. Finally forgive the girl she'd been and become the woman she could be. Tied up and bound, she could finally fly.

"That's what I want." Kai, the other half of her soul, seemed to know what she needed. He didn't stop, didn't throw down the instruments of his torture and ask if he'd done something wrong. He hit her again, keeping up the stimulation she needed to let loose. "I want you to let it all out. Give it all to me, baby. You're safe with me."

Over and over, he touched her with his light, scouring her flesh and setting her free. The tears seemed endless. There was so much pain stuck inside and it flowed like a volcano. So much heartache and anger that had taken up all the space in her soul. She released it, allowed it out because she needed that space for something more now.

It took a moment to realize Kai had stopped and put the violet wand away. She was still crying as he leaned over, his lips brushing the spots he'd hurt. His mouth moved over her, more tender than sexual. This was his promise to her, she realized.

It was safe to be open with him. It was safe to cry. He would do whatever it took to give her what she needed and then he would soothe her. He would ease her burdens. He would be there.

"I love you, Kai."

"I love you, baby." He worked her over with kisses, brushing her lips with his until he'd made his way around her body and down to the soles of her feet where he'd begun his torture. He kissed her there, too. Slowly he shoved his slacks off and freed himself. "Only you for the rest of my life."

"Only you," she said as he moved between her legs. There was something so sexy about being spread and open for him.

He touched the rope between her legs, pressing it down so she felt it scratch against her. Kori's body, tired from the emotion, came back to life. He pressed again. "Tell me you want me."

Because he was a man who needed to know he was pretty. Maybe not pretty, but it was sometimes so easy to forget that even beautiful men could need praise, too. Her Master needed more than her submission. He needed all of her. She finally got that. Kai Ferguson didn't simply need a sub. He needed a smart and creative and stubborn brat who would love him with all her heart and soul.

He needed her.

"I want you more than I've wanted anything in my life." More than her career. That should have scared her, but she'd finally figured out the right man wouldn't cage her in. The right man wouldn't allow her to sink into fear and doubt. The right man would set her free. Her Dom wouldn't hold her back. He would fly with her.

"I want you. I want you every minute of every day, and don't think I'll be easy on you. You're mine now. You're mine to torture and tease and torment and love. Mine."

It was easy to nod because being his meant he was hers. Hers to torture and tease and love. "Yours. I swear though if you don't take what's yours very soon I'm going to scream."

His hand slapped down onto the rope and she did exactly that. "Brat. I'll make you scream. I live to make you scream. And don't think because you're getting what you want this is over. We've got this place for the rest of the night, and I intend to see how far we can go."

He sheathed his dick in a condom and shoved the rope aside. It bit into her, but she loved it. That bite of pain made her so much more aware of him. His hands gripped her, spreading her wide. His cock shoved at her pussy.

She couldn't fight to get his cock, couldn't move. She was helpless and all that remained was to let Kai have his way. His cock teased her, rubbing her clit and making her moan. The ropes scratched along her skin, lighting her up everywhere. She could still feel the burn from the wand in places, as though her Master could touch every inch of her skin, surround her with his touch.

His cock invaded as he thrust hard inside her. "We're going to do this a lot. I'm installing a hard point at the office and when you're a bad girl, I'll put you in suspension and fuck you over and over and over again. You won't ever run from me again. You'll just sit there while I work and when I'm ready to fuck you again, I'll step up and take my sub like I want. Any way I want."

His cock pounded inside her. The ropes held her tight, but her whole body moved as he manipulated her. It was like getting fucked on a wave or on the wind. She was light and fluid and Kai tethered her, giving her pleasure and stability.

She watched as he fucked his way deep inside her, easing her up. He held the rope away from his cock as he thrust in and out, dragging her back every time. He angled up and brought his thumb down on her clit and she went sailing.

Vaguely she heard Kai call out her name as he held himself hard against her body, but her own pleasure seemed to never end. He kept up the pressure and she could feel herself clamping down, the vibrations sending her deeper.

Finally she relaxed back, completely spent.

Kai stayed inside her, a crazy sexy smile on his face. "Stay here. I'll be right back. Like I said, I'm not even close to being done. You have no idea what I have in store for you."

He stepped away, kicking his slacks off and easing the condom from his cock. She watched as that beautiful backside moved back to the prep area.

Where did he think she would go? She was caught and by way more than his rope.

When he turned with a flogger in his hand, she couldn't do

anything but smile.

"Let's have some fun, baby," Kai said.

She could use some of that. Kori floated in his rope and let her Master take her where only he could.

Chapter Nineteen

Six months later

Kai held his wife's hand as they walked down the hall toward the hospital room that was their destination. Their fingers threaded together and he could feel the ring he'd placed on her finger only three weeks before. To his surprise his wife had demanded and gotten her white wedding, complete with a church full of flowers and their hobbled together family around them.

The only thing she hadn't gotten was Jared to attend. The day after Squirrel was killed, Jared had dropped out of the movie and left for Canada. He'd spoken to Kai briefly only to say he needed time and space and he'd call when he was ready.

Kai was back to watching his brother's life play out in magazines and on television. At least Jared was still working on his TV show. He had that stability, but Kai knew his brother also had new demons to face.

"Hey, you two," a familiar voice said. Case Taggart was walking out of Erin's room, stretching his big body. "I thought you were coming up here later."

Kori stopped. "Erin texted and asked me to bring her something for TJ to wear home. She's getting out of here tonight I heard."

"Yeah, Doc said the delivery went well. It sounded brutal to me." Case went a little pale. "I don't understand how she can scream and curse my brother's name one minute and then be crying with joy the next. I'm so happy I'm a dude. Not that I'm ever planning on procreating, but at least we only have to do the fun part."

"Wait until you've changed a couple of diapers," Kori said. She went up on her toes and brushed a kiss across Kai's lips. "I'm going to play with a baby. Pretty soon my writing partner will have a new one. It's awesome because I don't have to have one of my own. Winning."

She flashed him a thumbs-up sign as she disappeared into the room with her stash of baby clothes and diapers.

"So now Serena's her writing partner?" Case yawned behind his hand.

"They're doing the screenplay for the next movie. *Love After Death* did shockingly well at the box office. Who knew so many women want to see that kind of stuff on screen. I have to admit, it was pretty fun." And hot. It helped that it wasn't his brother's ass on display. That made it much easier to take, but the whole while he watched the film he couldn't help but think Jared's version of Big Tag had been better. "So *Ship of Passion* is going into production. I wonder if Damon's going to be more self-aware than Tag."

Kori and Serena were forming their own production company. They were taking it easy while Serena was pregnant, but they had plans for bringing their favorite romance novels to the big and small screen. His wife had dreams and he was going to love watching her fly.

Case shook his head. "Yeah, my brother's smarter than that. I don't buy his act one bit. He just doesn't want anyone to know that he loves watching himself on screen. Even when he's played by another dude. I swear after the film he talked about how anyone who played Pierce Craig should be bigger than that actor, more muscular. He was practically preening. I wanted to punch him. All I could think about the whole time was how much Theo would have loved that shit. He would have gotten a kick out of it."

Kai looked around to make sure the door was closed. "Any

news on that front?"

He was out of the action loop now that he'd done his job. He was back in the role he preferred, prepping to help heal. He'd spent the last six months studying the effects of memory loss and Stockholm syndrome. He wanted to be ready if Theo came home. He'd also spent time studying their new partners. The Lawless clan was fucked up, but they seemed to fit with Big Tag. The brothers had been working with a select group of McKay-Taggart operatives, but it seemed like Mia was out of the picture. While Drew, Riley, and Bran had shown up from time to time, Mia hadn't been seen since she left about a week after that terrible day.

And Case never mentioned her again.

"Drew has a meeting scheduled. His connection has been cagey, but we think this time we might get something moving. I have to hope so because the last lead we got from the feds went nowhere. I'm almost at the end of my rope, Kai. I have to think if he was out there, he would find a way to let us know. Anything. I don't know. I have to think that Theo's gone."

"The type of mind conditioning Hope McDonald is known for involves the complete suppression of the victim's identity. Theo could be alive, but if he's had enough of the drug she's been developing, he might not know he's Theo," Kai explained.

"So we could get him back and he would still be gone?"

"I think with time and the right therapy, he could come back." It was what he was prepping for. "But we don't know a lot about the drug she's using. It's not something I can look up and find out the side effects."

Case shook his head, seeming infinitely weary. "I don't feel him anymore. I don't know what to do. I have a nephew to think about now. I have to think about Erin, too. It's what Theo would want. We've got a schedule to help her through the first couple of weeks, but eventually everyone has to go back to their own lives. I'm thinking of moving closer so I can be there."

For months Case had done nothing but work. He'd even stopped going to Sanctum. And he never dated now.

"Have you thought of calling her?"

Case frowned. "I wouldn't have to call her if I lived closer."

"I was talking about Mia."

From Sanctum with Love

A shadow slid over his face. "Why would I do that? Like I said, maybe it's time to concentrate on the future. I'm going home to grab a nap and a shower. Tell Erin I'll see her at the house later. Li and Avery are coming to pick her up. They're staying at her place for a few days to help her get in a groove. I'm bringing dinner by if you want to come."

"We'll stay with her until they get here." Erin would likely get far too much help and kick everyone out after a day or two. Once she'd made the decision to keep her baby, she'd calmed. Erin still had a rapier wit and used sarcasm as a form of affection, but some of her darkness had fled as though she'd known her child would need her light.

Would she have had that calm if she knew Theo might still be alive? Watching Erin grow into her role as a mother had made Kai believe Big Tag had made the right call. She'd needed some peace in order to do what she had to.

Case had no peace. It was there in the slump of his shoulders as he walked away. He was still haunted. He might not feel his brother anymore, but it was obvious he was still lost.

Kai walked through the door and found his reason to smile. Kori was cradling a baby wrapped like a burrito and Erin was looking through the clothes, holding up the tiny McKay-Taggart onesie Kori had specially made.

"Oh, thank god," Erin said with a smile. "We can put him to work right away. He's going to be so good undercover."

Kori smiled down at baby TJ, who seemed to definitely be a Taggart since the kid had clocked in right at ten pounds and had a cap of sandy hair. "You can poop on the bad guys. That's right."

The way his wife was cooing at that baby it might not be too long before he had to deal with the baby bug that seemed to be going around. Serena was due in a few weeks and Phoebe had recently announced her pregnancy. Everyone was having babies. Everyone was looking to the future.

Kori and Erin began talking baby clothes and Kai took a seat, happy to listen in.

His future was already here.

* * * *

Case turned off the shower and grabbed a towel, running it over his hair to dry it. The hot water had done wonders for his aching muscles, but nothing for the weariness he felt.

The joy of holding his nephew for the first time was utterly drowned out by the misery that he hadn't been able to bring TJ's father home. Theo had missed the birth of his child and it was all because Case couldn't find him. Theo had always been the smarter one. Once more he wished he could change places with his brother.

He stared at himself in the mirror, not quite recognizing the man who looked back at him. He could smile all he liked. He could go into work and pretend that he was the old Case, the Case who laughed and joked, but that piece of him was gone. When he was alone and there was no one to pretend with, he saw the hollow shell that had been left behind.

Theo had been shot, but he wasn't the only dead man in the family.

A vision of a blonde with the sweetest smile ever crossed his mind.

He ruthlessly shoved it out of his head. Mia Lawless was nothing but a scheming brat who'd used him to further her own agenda. Mia Danvers. Her legal name was Danvers. Damn. That girl had more aliases than a super villain. Another reason to stay away from her. He wasn't thinking about her. She didn't get to fuck up his life a second time. She was the reason he'd stayed out of his brother's schemes with Drew Lawless. They were currently trying to use Drew's position as CEO of a billion dollar corporation to infiltrate The Collective and find information on Hope McDonald. Once that happened, Case would be called on.

He was nothing but muscle after all. Theo had gotten all the brains, all the charm.

Now Theo's kid had been left with the lesser brother as his father figure.

Case sighed and moved into his utilitarian bedroom. Sometimes he missed the efficiency of Naval life. When he'd been in the Navy he hadn't had to worry about babies or meddling family members. He'd woken up, done his job, gone to sleep with the knowledge that he'd been useful.

He was so useless now. A gun without a bullet.

He had to get dressed and go over to Erin's where he would put on his mask and pretend to be alive. His brothers would be there. He loved them, but he wasn't truly one of them. Ian and Sean had a language of their own. They'd grown up together, survived together, understood each other like no one else.

He'd only really ever had Theo.

Now he only had revenge. That was what got him up in the morning. The idea of putting his hands around Hope McDonald's throat and squeezing had become his reason to live.

But briefly, just briefly, he'd thought he had another. He'd met a girl at Sanctum and for a few days, he'd thought of something other than killing. He'd felt like a dumbass kid the minute Mia had smiled his way. He'd thought about asking her out.

He'd wanted so badly to talk to his brother because Theo had always been better with girls than him.

And then he'd found out she was a fucking spy. Oh, they'd all turned out to be on the same team, but she'd lied her way into his life.

It was better to be alone.

The doorbell chimed and he sighed. It was likely Sean. Ian was on his way to Erin's to meet them all for dinner. They would all meet up at the house Theo had bought shortly before his death. Case could still remember ribbing him about the three-bedroom ranch in the suburbs.

Sean always rang the bell and then used his key to come in anyway, so Case sat on the bed, trying to put off the inevitable moment when the mask had to slide back into place.

He couldn't help thinking about the conversation he'd had with Kai earlier. He'd meant it. He couldn't feel Theo anymore. Maybe it had always been his imagination, but since they were kids, he'd had a connection to his twin. He'd known that night that Theo was in trouble. He'd been sitting having a drink with Ian and Sean and he'd felt his stomach turn and he'd known.

The bell rang again and he cursed under his breath. He schooled himself, standing and taking a deep breath so he could face his brother with a smile.

Clothes would have to wait a minute because Sean could be

impatient. And apparently forgetful since he wasn't using his key.

He was halfway to the door when he heard it. It was nothing more than a little scratching sound, the kind metal made when it came against more metal. The living room was dark, night having just fallen. His blinds were drawn so he couldn't see out. He could get his computer and check the security camera, but by then whoever was there would either get in or go away.

Case went still and then moved very quietly to get his SIG. It was never far away, a constant companion.

His body calmed, his whole being slipping to a place he'd trained for his entire adult life. Most people would feel their heart rate speed up at the thought of confronting someone trying to break into their home, but Case's slowed. His movements became methodical and silent, his every sense focused on one thing.

Taking down whoever was trying to get him.

Yes, he could use this. He hoped whoever it was didn't go down without a fight.

He very quietly moved to the wall so he would be hidden when the door came open. There was a snick and then his front door swung in an arc.

Before his intruder could fully walk into the room, Case moved in. He slammed the door and had the intruder against it. He shoved the muzzle of his SIG against the intruder's head and then he let himself process.

His intruder was face first to the door, having been turned around during the brief struggle. Shorter by at least a half foot, his thief had blonde hair, and that was when the smell hit him.

Citrus. Grapefruit. It was sweet but with a bite. Like the woman herself.

"What the fuck are you doing here, Mia?"

"I thought I was being clever. I…god, Case will you please put the gun down?" Her voice was breathless. "And the other…you know…I can feel it against my back. Unless that's another gun."

Nope. It was his dick. Damn thing only worked around her anymore, and he kind of resented her for it. "I think I'll wait until the police get here," he lied, wanting her to panic. Six months had gone by and this was how she renewed their acquaintance? Had she been trying to show him what a dumb fuck country boy he was?

How much smarter she was? "You stay right where you are."

"Case, I came here for you. I came straight to you because you know they'll both leave us out. We can do all the work, but big brothers will leave us behind when it comes time. We have to stick together," she said.

He could feel how soft she was. The round curve of her ass rubbed against him as she squirmed in his arms. His left hand was right under those nicely shaped breasts of hers. All it would take was an inch upward and he could cup one. He could haul her back to his bedroom. She'd been the one to break in. She'd poked the bear, and the bear could give it to her hard and then maybe, maybe he could stop dreaming about her at night. Maybe he could work up the will to find another woman, a woman who really made sense for him.

He took a step back because she was already fucking with his head. Two minutes of Mia and he was thinking like a caveman, tossing out all reason. He couldn't handle her. He flipped on the light because the dark was far too intimate for this discussion. "If this is something about the op my brother is running with yours, then talk to Ian. I don't have anything to do with that."

She was obviously flustered when she turned around. Her cheeks were flushed, her hair mussed as though she'd just gotten out of bed. Or been manhandled for intruding. Her eyes went straight to his towel. "Really? You walk around like that?"

Naturally he had a hard-on. There was zero chance he was letting her know it was for her. "Darlin', I just got off the phone with my girlfriend. She's good at getting me revved up, so to speak."

Her eyes flared briefly, but that stubborn look he'd come to know so well settled over her features. "I didn't come here to talk about your love life. I came here because we need to work together."

"So you decided to break in?"

"I didn't know when you would be back. And I kind of thought it would prove to you that I can be a good partner. I have skills, too. I thought if I was waiting here for you when you got back from whatever you were doing, maybe you would take me seriously for once."

She had no idea how he took her. He took her in his dreams about once a night. Took her hard and woke up sweating. "Oh, I take you seriously. You seriously annoy me and now you can leave."

She stood her ground. He would give her that. She had a set of balls on her like no one he knew. "I'm not going until you've listened to me. Drew told me to stay out of this and I have for the most part, but I never stopped looking. I never stopped trying to find him."

Case went still again, his every instinct on high alert as Mia pulled a folder out of her massive bag. "Who?"

"Theo." Mia handed him a grainy printout. "I found Theo and we're going to get him back together."

Case stared down at the photo. It showed two men, both holding AK-47s. One still had a mask over his face, but the other had slid it up so his features could be seen. His brother was looking up at a security camera.

What had he told Kai only hours before? His brother would find a way. His brother would let them know he was out there.

This was Theo's way of saying it's time. *Come get me, brother.*

"Where?" He couldn't seem to form whole sentences.

Mia seemed to understand. "It's from a bank heist in Colombia."

Then that was where he would start.

Case, Mia, and the entire McKay-Taggart crew will return in *Dominance Never Dies.*

Author's Note

I'm often asked by generous readers how they can help get the word out about a book they enjoyed. There are so many ways to help an author you like. Leave a review. If your e-reader allows you to lend a book to a friend, please share it. Go to Goodreads and connect with others. Recommend the books you love because stories are meant to be shared. Thank you so much for reading this book and for supporting all the authors you love!

Sign up for Lexi Blake's newsletter
and be entered to win a $25 gift certificate
to the bookseller of your choice.

Join us for news, fun, and exclusive content
including free short stories.

There's a new contest every month!

Go to www.LexiBlake.net/newsletter to subscribe.

Dominance Never Dies
Masters and Mercenaries, Book 11
By Lexi Blake
Now Available

A loss he can't forget

Since losing his twin brother, Theo, in the line of duty, Case Taggart has felt dead inside. The former Navy SEAL has dedicated himself to his family and their business but he can't help but feel stuck as he watches everyone else move on with their lives. Only meeting the beautiful Mia brings Case out of his misery, until he discovered she was just a reporter looking for a story. Betrayed, he turned his back on her and never looked back.

An attraction she can't deny

Mia Danvers can't get Case Taggart out of her head. Though they hadn't been lovers, she'd felt more for him than for any man she'd ever met. Growing up in the shadow of her over-protective, older brothers, she felt free when she was with Case and she longs to feel that way again. She knows that if she can find any trace of Theo Taggart, Case will be forced to let her back into his life. Months of searching have finally paid off and she knows this is her second chance.

A desperate search

Case and Mia follow the clues they hope will lead them to Theo and the villainous Hope McDonald, but the search becomes increasingly dangerous. From Dallas to South America and beyond, dark forces work against them and threaten their lives. With each step forward, Case and Mia are pulled closer together and forced to confront their mutual attraction. But when the truth about Theo is revealed, Case may have to make a choice between his brother and the only woman he's ever loved.

Devoted
A Masters and Mercenaries Novella
By Lexi Blake
Now Available

A woman's work

Amy Slaten has devoted her life to Slaten Industries. After ousting her corrupt father and taking over the CEO role, she thought she could relax and enjoy taking her company to the next level. But an old business rivalry rears its ugly head. The only thing that can possibly take her mind off business is the training class at Sanctum…and her training partner, the gorgeous and funny Flynn Adler. If she can just manage to best her mysterious business rival, life might be perfect.

A man's commitment

Flynn Adler never thought he would fall for the enemy. Business is war, or so his father always claimed. He was raised to be ruthless when it came to the family company, and now he's raising his brother to one day work with him. The first order of business? The hostile takeover of Slaten Industries. It's a stressful job so when his brother offers him a spot in Sanctum's training program, Flynn jumps at the chance.

A lifetime of devotion…

When Flynn realizes the woman he's falling for is none other than the CEO of the firm he needs to take down, he has to make a choice. Does he take care of the woman he's falling in love with or the business he's worked a lifetime to build? And when Amy finally understands the man she's come to trust is none other than the enemy, will she walk away from him or fight for the love she's come to depend on?

Ruthless
A Lawless Novel
By Lexi Blake
Now Available

The first in a sexy contemporary romance series featuring the Lawless siblings...

The Lawless siblings are bound by vengeance. Riley, Drew, Brandon, and Mia believe the CEO of StratCast orchestrated their parents' murder twenty years ago to steal their father's software program. And there's only one way Riley can find some solid evidence...

Heir to the StratCast legacy, Ellie Stratton hires a new attorney to handle a delicate business matter—and she's shocked by her attraction to him. Over the course of a few weeks, Riley becomes her lover, her friend, her everything. But when her life is threatened, Ellie discovers that Riley is more obsessed with settling an old score than in the love she thought they were building. And Riley must choose between a revenge he's prepared for all his life and the woman he's sure he can't live without...

About Lexi Blake

Lexi Blake lives in North Texas with her husband, three kids, and the laziest rescue dog in the world. She began writing at a young age, concentrating on plays and journalism. It wasn't until she started writing romance that she found success. She likes to find humor in the strangest places. Lexi believes in happy endings no matter how odd the couple, threesome or foursome may seem. She also writes contemporary Western ménage as Sophie Oak.

Connect with Lexi online:

Facebook: authorLexiBlake
Twitter: https://twitter.com/authorlexiblake
Website: www.LexiBlake.net

Sign up for Lexi's newsletter at www.LexiBlake.net/newsletter.

Made in the USA
Coppell, TX
17 June 2023